CW01211928

VAMP

THE NOVELIZATION

CHRISTIAN FRANCIS

BASED ON THE SCREENPLAY BY

RICHARD WENK

AND THE STORY BY

DONALD P. BORCHERS & RICHARD WENK

ENCYCLOPOCALYPSE PUBLICATIONS

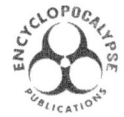

Copyright © 2022 Donald P. Borchers. All Rights Reserved.

The characters and events in this book are fictitious. Any similarity to real persons, living, dead or undead is coincidental and not intended by the author.

No part of this book may be reproduced in any form or by any electronic or mechanical means, including information storage and retrieval systems, without permission in writing from the publisher, except by a reviewer who may quote brief passages in a review.

To see more great titles, please visit www.encyclopocalypse.com.

Always for you Vicky
CF xxx

CONTENTS

Also by Christian Francis	vii
Foreword	xi
By Richard Wenk	

VAMP - THE NOVELIZATION

1. The Ceremony	3
2. Bargaining	19
3. The Journey	38
4. Arrival For Sin	49
5. Opening Time	69
6. Katrina	87
7. Mr. Dynamite	108
8. The Streets	126
9. Hotel/Motel	142
10. Stalking Danger	157
11. Heartbreak and Violence	179
12. Revelations	190
13. Disco Inferno	212
14. Ash and Blood	234
15. Rooftops and Sewers	257
16. Escape	282

MEMORIES OF VAMP

17. Donald P. Borchers	293
18. Dedee Pfeiffer	299
19. Alan Roderick-Jones	303
20. Gedde Watanabe	306
Photo Gallery	307
The Original Screenplay	319

ALSO BY CHRISTIAN FRANCIS

EVERYDAY MONSTERS: THE ANIMUS CHRONICLES BOOK 1

(Ebook / Trade Paperback / Hardcover / Audiobook)

"It will take a reader with a strong stomach to traverse the trail of gore and death, but *Everyday Monsters* is a captivating read that excels in unpredictable twists, strong characterization, and a plot that reveals real monsters in this world."

D. DONOVAN (MIDWEST BOOK REVIEW)

"It starts with a letter, a severed head and a book—and only gets weirder from there! Deliciously dark, with humour as black as sin and evocative descriptions of all the outlandish grotesques on display. In short, this romp was huge amounts of fun to read."

PAUL KANE (BEST-SELLING AUTHOR OF *BEFORE*, *ARCANA* AND *MONSTERS*.)

INCUBUS - THE DESCENT: THE ANIMUS CHRONICLES BOOK 2

(Ebook / Trade Paperback / Hardcover / Audiobook)

"Horrifying and hysterical. I love this batshit book!"

MARK MILLER (*HELLRAISER : THE TOLL* &
NEXT TESTAMENT)

"Readers not put off by graphic descriptions of violence and brutality, who look for the solid feel of horror paired with a complex dance between forces that vie for control, will find this both a powerful series addition and a readily accessible stand-alone read. Fans of literary horror will find *Incubus: The Descent* a worthy, involving read."

D. DONOVAN (MIDWEST BOOK REVIEW)

THE SACRIFICE OF ANTON STACEY (NOVELLA)

(Ebook / Trade Paperback / Hardcover / Audiobook)

"With this tale of a soul in jeopardy against a backdrop of apocalyptic terror, Christian Francis distills enough plot for a 500 page novel into a tight fable-like novella, poignant and horrifying in equal measure."

PETER ATKINS (*MORNINGSTAR,*
HELLBOUND: HELLRAISER II &
WISHMASTER)

WISHMASTER - THE NOVELIZATION

(Ebook / Trade Paperback / Mass Market Paperback / Hardcover / Audiobook)

> "This book was absolutely fantastic…. I'm calling this my favorite horror story for 2021. I highly recommend this book."
>
> TAMMY BULCAO (*SISTERS SPOTLIGHT*)

TITAN FIND - THE NOVELIZATION

(Ebook / Trade Paperback / Mass Market Paperback / Hardcover)

E AND THE NIGHT BEFORE CHRISTMAS (SHORT STORY)

(Ebook)

FOREWORD
BY RICHARD WENK

In 1985 Donald Borchers, who I had met through a mutual friend, and was a successful producer at New World Pictures, presented me with the opportunity to write and direct my first feature film. The caveat? It already had a title and Poster - *VAMP* - and it must include strippers, college kids and Vampires. The rest was up to me. If I could write a compelling movie involving each of those items, Don would let me direct it.

Nothing I had done to date prepped me for that task! I studied film at NYU. Was a PA on some After School Specials and the movie *Annie*, then made a short musical parody short called *Dracula Bites the Big Apple* that HBO bought. I had never written a feature script and I was not particularly a horror fan. But hey, Francis Coppola and Martin Scorsese started their careers making B movies. It seemed like a right of passage into the world of big time movie making. And Don Borchers was offering me a chance.

I took the plunge. It took a while to figure out a story that made sense to me. A story and characters I could have fun with. When I hit upon the idea for it to take place in one

BY RICHARD WENK

night, I became inspired. Three long days and nights later I had a first draft of *VAMP*. Don gave it his stamp of approval.

And here's where the real story of *VAMP* took off. Don set about casting and crewing the movie with incredibly talented people. I wanted Chris Makepeace for the lead character of Keith. Don persuaded him to come aboard. My eclectic Ideas for the other characters were met, not with skepticism, or what-do you-know it's your first time directing… but with support and excitement. Rusler, Watanabe and Sandy Baron. Not your typical horror film casting. The effervescent Dedee Pfeiffer became the glue. Add the great Billy Drago and you're suddenly on a different level.

All that was left was to find the heartbeat of the movie: Katrina. And to Don's everlasting credit it was his idea to approach Grace Jones. It was inspired and out-of-the-box thinking. And it set the film further apart from the standard fare of the time. But most importantly, Grace came aboard with her artistic team (Andy Warhol and Keith Haring) working on her look.

The shooting of the movie in 28 days was a blur. But Don had surrounded me with such accomplished people I never felt intimidated by the impossible schedule. Alan Roderick-Jones designing the sets. The great Elliot Davis creating the green and magenta look. Greg Cannon doing the special make-up. The legendary Dar Robinson choreographing and doing stunts. Marc Grossman's editing. And the music by Jonathan Elias was breathtaking.

Now 35 years later the movie is still has fans and web sites (vampafterdark.com) and multiple DVD reissues. Now come a novelization! Pretty cool…

So thank you to Christian Francis for capturing the crazy essence of the movie. My love and respect to all my partners and compadres on the film: Chris, Robert, Gedde, Dedee, Sandy, Brad Logan, Lisa Lyon, Paunita Nichols, Tricia Brown (who guided me through the real After dark Clubs), Dar and last but not least Don Borchers. Who first believed in me then gave me the support to chase my crazy vision.

We went to war together. We had each other's backs. And all these years later we're still friends. And that maybe *VAMP's* greatest success.

Enjoy the read!

Richard Wenk
February 2022

THE NOVELIZATION

CHAPTER 1
THE CEREMONY

It was a night of darkness that seemed never-ending. A night that suffocated with imposing, claustrophobic shadows in each and every corner—the next more impenetrable, somehow blacker, than the last. It seemed to grow thicker and faster with a predator's confidence, as if it believed it was winning a battle against the daylight, as if the sun would never return to illuminate the earth, and extinguish its inky presence.

This time of night, where the shadows hung the heaviest, was what came to be known as 'the witching hour'.

The more primitive and supernaturally-minded saw this 'hour' as the time when the veil between every world would fade into the background. Where bargains and sacrifices with gods and devils could be made with the greatest of ease. Where the dead could communicate with the living, and the living could lose their souls in the blink of an eye.

This was the kind of night that pushed the normally rational and moralistic of people into committing vile acts, all in the name of a sacrificial payment.

Some of these payments were in the name of their benevolent deity.

Some were in the name of their own murderous inner demons.

Some even in the belief that they were doing a greater good.

Most, though, committed such acts in the narcissism of their own value over others, normally using the religions of the world as excuses for their selfish deeds. These kinds of people merely believed that the oil-thick night was theirs to do with as they pleased, any beings they may pretend to praise were simply an affectation of their own devising.

Before the night had arrived, a violent storm approached the hamlet of Barker's Folly from within its weakly-lit sky. The clouds multiplied and darkened as the Sun bid its nightly farewell, and torrents of rain began to fall down onto this township.

As a bell rang high in the church's steeple, its tolling momentarily echoed over the slumbering buildings, until the cacophony of the intrusive storm rapidly consumed it, leaving only the thudding of rain and the rumbling of thunder in its wake.

With most of the townsfolk lost within their dreamland, seven hooded figures who shunned the call of sleep now marched in a single file procession. A procession toward their work within 'the witching hour'.

Their path led across the cobbled square that sprawled out in front of the large church. At the head of the procession, the figure wore an opulent, blood-red robe. Around its neck hung a large ornate golden medallion that depicted the moon and the sun. Behind them, the trailing figures' robes were much the same, though theirs were made of a much simpler, white hessian.

As more thunder reverberated and echoed high above them, the darkness was quickly split into two, as several pale white streaks of lightning raced across the skies, sending out a silent strobing light.

Despite this storm, the figures marched on, ignoring the rain that soaked them, ignoring the violence of mother nature high above them. They continued on, with more important things at hand, across the cobbles and into a large old building at the far end of the square. The doors of which lay open in expectation of their arrival. The glowing light from within, beckoned them inside.

Within the building—deep within the bowels of its expansive basement—the seven figures marched down a long corridor, toward a small room lit with orange candlelight. Their hoods still up, masking their identities.

An eighth figure waited within—they too dressed in a white robe, though without the protection of a hood.

His name was William. An apprentice to this order, still in training to become one of them, hoping that one day he too would be part of the procession as a fully fledged brother.

William's wealthy family had sent him here to learn the ways of the world. To bask in the intellect of academia. To prepare himself for a successful life. Instead, he had shirked the calls of education and instead chose to be indoctrinated into the arms of the order, whose sole aim was more base and debauched than could be found in any text book. This was a group who wanted nothing but ways to fuel their own desires. A group that although William did not personally like, he knew it was his best and only option. He knew that in order to succeed in this little world, a weak person needed to align with the strong in order to avoid becoming trampled by them. A lesson that no text would teach him, but one that he innately knew. The weak only succeeded on the shoulders of the strong. And William *was* weak. Very weak. Physically, at least. Yet, despite this, the order had taken pity on him, and enlisted him to train within their ranks.

William was barely a step into adulthood. His fresh face still lacked any ability to grow hair, and his body seemed that of someone many years younger. His slight, diminutive stature could easily be mistaken for that of a prepubescent child.

As the red-robed figure leading the processional approached, they held out their hand toward William, who in turn passed them a large, lit ivory candle. The candle's yellowing-orange flame danced high into the darkness of the stone lined room they stood in.

"Be strong," the red-robed figure quietly said as they took the candle from William, noticing a trace of worry on the youths face. "What we do now may seem extreme, but the dark ones command us, and they reward us for our obedience in abundance." This male voice sounded almost regal, with a pronounced and over-enunciated English accent.

William replied with a nod and a thin appreciative smile, as he then continued to hand out the rest of the lit candles to the other figures. When he finished, he hurried over to a large oak door at the far side of the room. Grabbing its large metal handle, he pulled hard, opening it wide, then standing aside to allow the procession to enter.

Within, a dark room awaited.

The robed figure's candles soon consumed the surrounding shadows in their comfortably warm hue, illuminating all it touched.

Everything within this dungeon-like chamber had been draped with old white sheets. All except for the long table that lay at the far side of the room and the two nearly naked men standing bound and blindfolded beside it.

The top of this table was littered with empty chalices,

burnt-out candles, open ancient books, loose pages and scrolls. All evidence of past conjurings and sacrifices.

From somewhere that sounded far away, a low chanting began. A monotone hum of male voices emanating softly around the stone walls.

Each of the hooded figures took their places about the room and faced the bound captives at the end of the table; These two men, with hands tied behind their backs, had been placed atop small wooden stools. With hoods over their heads, they could not see the nooses that dangled in front of them, affixed to the wooden beams high above them.

Beside these unwitting prisoners, three pale male bodies dangled motionless in the air, hanged by their own nooses. Each had been similarly stripped of most of their clothing, and were far from living. Even the warm candlelight did not hide the deathly blue hue of their lifeless skin.

The red-robed figure turned and nodded to one of his white-robed brethren, who—without a pause—stepped forward to the two bound men, now silently awaiting their fate.

"Remove their hoods," the red-robed figure ordered with a stern determination. The hum of the chanting seemed to grow louder around them as the figure spoke. "These paupers deserve to witness their own mortality, not in the comfort of darkness, but in the light of our infernal majesty."

As this command was obeyed, the captive's hoods were removed, yet did not reveal any expected fearful faces. It did not reveal any expressions appealing for clemency. It merely presented two young men. Both with cocky smiles adorning their faces.

"You are about to make the ultimate sacrifice," the red-robed figure continued as he motioned to the hanged men dangling beside the captives. "Many have trod this path before you, yet only very few have survived."

The captive's expressions remained unfazed by any of the

words uttered, or by the fate that had befallen the hanged men beside them.

The red-robed figure continued. "Nevertheless, glory awaits those who survive this supreme test of immortality... the trial of the demon rope."

The robed figure who stood at their side, dropped their removed hoods onto the table, then proceeded to place the empty nooses over each of their heads. As this was done, both captive men still continued to smile, not even displaying a solitary ounce of fear.

"Welcome...," the red-robed figure said, "to what may be your own worst nightmare, or your path to our world of our demonic glory." With this, he lifted his hood enough to display a hideous rope burn around the circumference of his neck.

"Now!" he bellowed, signaling his captive's demise. "Cast them—"

Before he could finish, his words were cut off as the sound of the rising chanting chorus began to stutter and repeat. Over and over.

"What the?" The red-robed figure said in confusion as he turned to William, who now raced with a panicked expression on his face across to the other side of the room. There, hidden in the shadows, sat a record player, who's needle now skipped on a vinyl album of Gregorian chants.

William grabbed the needle and skipped it forward with a large, audible scratch that spilled out through hidden speakers around the room.

The condemned men glanced at each other, both trying not to laugh.

As the next part of the song played, the red-robed figure tried to regain his stride. He continued, unsure. "The... Supreme sacrifice and... uh... the ultimate test… will—"

"Oh fuckin' hang me now," one captive exclaimed in a strong Brooklyn accent. This was AJ, rolling his eyes, shooting a glance to his fellow captive. "I'd rather die than hear this shit again. Wouldn't you?"

As AJ leapt from the stool to the floor, the rope around his neck slid harmlessly down from the beam above, and he removed his hands from the loose rope bindings behind his back.

"We haven't got time for this kinda shit," he said, amused.

The other captive, Keith, shot AJ a wide-eyed grin as he too jumped off the stool and onto the floor. He then removed his hands from the loose rope behind him, and stepped besides his friend.

The robed figures watched them motionless..

William, still standing next to the record player, stared around at his brothers, shocked.

"This ain't no Frat House," AJ loudly stated, addressing the whole room. "It's a half-way house for total morons." He raised his hand, motioning to all of their robes, "Spooky Halloween costumes?" He then glanced at the hanged bodies beside him, now easily discernible as badly made props. "And these cheap phony hangings?"

"And don't forget the music..." Keith added with a sarcastic tone.

AJ nodded. "Yeah, that music? Who's supposed to be singing it, anyway? No-one's here except us. Are we supposed to fear these hidden spooky singers? Gimme a break, guys." He exhaled loudly before continuing, "I'm gonna file this whole experience as 'must try a lot fuckin' harder...', sound fair?"

The red-robed figure erupted angrily, "Silence pledge! The Emma Dipsa Phi initiation has *only* just begun."

AJ took a moment then chuckled to himself. A laugh that Keith only knew too well. One that AJ did when he knew full well that he had the upper hand.

"Yeah, I get it, guys." AJ said softly as he turned and grabbed a bunch of balled up clothes from behind his stool.

"Lemme take a wild and random guess... This initiation is to do more cheesy shit, in order to bore us to death?"

Separating the clothes, AJ tossed some to Keith, then looked down in his hands at a crumpled designer shirt. He shot a glance of annoyance to the robed figures. "I told you to be *careful* with my clothes," he held up the creased shirt toward them, shaking it angrily. "Who wrinkled my shit? Morons!"

Intimidated, the white-robed figures slowly removed their hoods, exposing their youthful, confused faces. Shrugging their shoulders, they glanced at each other, like children caught with their hands in a cookie jar - all except for one; The red-robed figure, who did not look guilty at all. He slowly removed his hood, exposing a boyish, yet chiseled alpha-jock face. He glared angrily at Keith and AJ, then spoke sternly in his English accent, "It looks like we've misjudged you two. You're obviously not Dispa Phi material—"

"Oh drop the accent, sparky." AJ retorted with a snorting laughter.

"*You've ruined this whole goddamn night, you butthole!*" the Frat leader shouted at them. His regal English accent now dropped to reveal its California origins.

"Look," AJ said in appeasement tinged with sarcasm. "I'm really sorry to have put a kibosh on your little off-off-off Broadway theater show. I *really* am. We didn't come here meaning to screw this... whatever the hell you're intending here. But myself and my fellow initiate, Keith here..." he motioned to his friend, who busily buttoned up his shirt. "Well, we think *we* were mistaken. Am I right, Keith?"

Keith looked up and shared a telltale glance with his friend. Due to their longstanding friendship, Keith and AJ shared an unspoken shorthand, each always inherently knowing what the other's intentions were. Because of this, Keith nodded at AJ with a smile, despite not really paying attention to what anyone had said, "Yup. Fooled us completely."

Without skipping a beat, AJ continued toward the Fraternity. "*Fooled* us! Exactly! You see, we were under the impression that this was *the* house on campus. But you seem to be the kind of organization that takes in any adoring dickhole that'll leap from a stool with a noose around their neck."

Before the Frat leader could reply, AJ held his hand up to silence him a moment longer.

"Obviously," AJ's tone turned softer before continuing. "Obviously, you guys don't recognize the *true* advantage of your position here. The power you really have."

The fraternity stared back in a blank unison, unsure of what the cocky initiate meant.

AJ glanced at Keith with a mock-confused look. "Is it just us who get this?"

Keith shrugged, "Maybe they just don't understand?" Though in reality, Keith didn't know where AJ was going with any of this either.

Both of them gathered up the remainder of their belongings as they finished dressing.

"Should have gone to Kappa Lamda, Keith," AJ said, intentionally louder for the fraternity to overhear.

"Okay. Fine. I'll bite," the leader said, annoyed yet confused. "What *advantages* don't we recognize, then?"

"Gottcha ya dumbass." AJ muttered under his breath. He looked at Keith and winked. "Right into my trap."

"What are you gonna do?" Keith whispered, unsure of what this trap was exactly.

AJ quickly spun around and flashed his killer smile toward the fraternity. A smile that had helped him and Keith out of many sticky situations, many, many times. Whether it was trouble from the cops, or from bullies, or even the opposite sex, it was a smile that could win *anyone* over.

"Well, gentlemen," AJ began. "And I can see that you *are* indeed gentlemen." Pausing, he took a breath. A quick moment to look at each of the frat boys, one by one, ending on the leader. "Let us start with the basic situation in front of us, shall we? You have something I and my good friend Keith here want: plush accommodations, cable TV, alcohol, better food than the slop in other houses—"

"So?" the leader interrupted.

With a flash of disdain across his face, AJ solely addressed the leader. "Now instead of making us go through these stupid, immature... uh," he turned to Keith. "What's the word I'm looking for?"

"Asinine?" Keith proffered.

AJ continued with a nod of thanks to his friend."...*Asinine* tests which, by the way, we find incredibly boring, if you didn't get that message by now."

Behind him, Keith mocked an illustrative yawn.

"Wouldn't it be smarter, and better for you all," AJ continued. "If you used this situation to your best *advantage*?"

The leader couldn't help but look intrigued, even if still confused. A confusion that AJ enjoyed immensely.

"What potential benefit do you get with this sideshow dime-store bullshit? We can make this a much more lucrative partnership. Look, you're having a big party tonight, right?" AJ's demeanor turned more assured, as he saw his plan falling into place. "Now you gotta need something for it, right? So what is it? Beer, music, entertainment? Keith and I can provide that for you - It's our speciality. You name it, *anything* you want - and we're gonna get it for you. All in exchange for our membership into your fine establishment. Simple, right? Better than this hocus pocus bullshit, ain't it?"

The fraternity turned to each other, conferring about AJ's proposition in overly hushed tones.

Keith reached out and pulled AJ to one side. "Two things," he whispered.

AJ smiled. "Sure... What's the first thing?"

"You get that we could have just shut our mouths and jumped off these stools, right? Then we would have been right there in the fraternity. Instead you're making this whole initiation *that much* more annoying by making us do *more* shit for them?"

"You know me, my good friend," AJ replied. "Have you ever known me to take the road less-travelled?"

"You mean, have I ever known you to make my life easier?"

"You love me, you know it," AJ laughed as he spoke. "Now what's the second thing on your oh so inquisitive mind?"

"Why the hell did you say *anything*? Couldn't you have said *one* thing instead? Or *some*thing? Why *any*? You had to offer them *any*thing?"

"Relax, will ya?" AJ patted Keith on his shoulder. "These guys are operating' on empty here, not really bright sparks, are they?"

Keith spoke his words deliberately and slowly. "We just had to jump. That's all."

"Relax." AJ then turned his attention toward the fraternity, addressing them, "Whatta ya say, guys? We got ourselves a deal?"

"You did say *anything*, right?" the leader asked with glee.

Keith closed his eyes then shook his head. "Goddamn it, AJ." he muttered loud enough for AJ to hear.

The leader stared hard at them for a few moments

"*Anything*." AJ reassured them. "Anything at all."

At ten years old, Keith Emerson was smaller than most his age. This was not a disadvantage to him, though, as it may have been to others. Where anyone else may have believed they were weak and underdeveloped, young Keith knew that the true strength was both in his mind and in his heart. He did not see any value in how much he could lift or how hard he could punch.

At Valemore Elementary, the traditional bully system existed. One that was mostly ignored by the parents and teachers, as it was in most schools. Indeed, Valemore was a standard educational establishment in this respect, where insecure larger children beat on the smaller, more intelligent ones. Whether this bullying was out of a subconscious jealousy, or a hidden love or just plain sadism, anyone looking weak or vulnerable meant easy pickings to the bullies. Those unfortunate to be slight were destined to lose their money or limp home with a black eye and sore ribs.

Keith fit into all the usual categories for being preyed upon by the dumbest bully of all - Waylon McCafferty. A behemoth of a lug head, molded in the image of his lug-headed moron of a father, who had no issues beating on anyone smaller or different than him. All except one; Keith. Waylon would not beat on Keith under *any* circumstances. Not anymore.

It had all changed on the fateful day where Keith had simply had enough of Waylon. The day he had had enough of being chased down, punched to the ground, and having his lunch money stolen. This was the day when Keith took the words of Travis Bickle and used them for his own purpose.

In the summer of '76, *Taxi Driver* had hit the local flea-pit theatre down the street from Valemore. With his cousin working there, young Keith could sneak into all the adult rated films he wanted to see. No other kids his age did that— Especially not for a film like *Taxi Driver*. If his friends had wanted to sneak into the theatre and risk getting into trouble for their efforts, it was gonna be for a film like *The Texas Chain Saw Massacre*, *Alien* or *The Exorcist*. But for *Taxi Driver*—

which his classmates saw as being too boring—no chance. It was something Keith took full advantage of on *that* day.

And when Keith, then nine years old, turned the tables on Waylon during one of his many beatdowns, things changed.

"Someday a real rain will come and wash all this scum off the streets." Keith snarled, as he turned to Waylon with an intense stare. Though the ferocious demeanor on his face looked real, it was merely a mask. He was terrified, channeling his best Bickle at the bully, trying to ignore the very real chance that this plan may not work.

But it *did* work.

Taken aback, Waylon suddenly halted his beating.

"What d'ya say, squirt?"

"You talkin' to me?" Keith retorted, suddenly getting to his feet and adopting the same stance that De Niro did up on the theatre screen.

Waylon had no time to process anything, before the usually mild-mannered Keith continued.

"You talkin' to me?"

Waylon had no answer. He just stared wide-eyed..

Keith's impression got louder and louder with each word he uttered. "Then who the hell else are you talking' to? You talkin' to me? Well, I'm the only one here."

"I'm gonna..." Waylon started to say, trying to keep his bullying tone, but failing miserably as Keith deftly interrupted.

"Who the fuck d'ya think you're talking to?" he yelled. Before Waylon could react, Keith's volume lowered, "I got some bad ideas in my head, Waylon."

"What?" was all that Waylon could reply before Keith continued.

"Listen, you fucker… you screwhead. Here is a boy who would not take it anymore. A boy who stood up against the *scum*, the *cunts*, the *dogs*, the *filth*, the *shit*. Here is a boy who stood up."

Waylon's nine-year-old brain could not comprehend that this little object of his cruelty—the boy who normally was a compliant punching bag—would say these things to him. Say these terrifying words. Even Waylon wouldn't swear like that in fear that his dad would somehow hear him and beat his ass. But it was the next line that Keith adapted from the film that sealed the deal. That made Waylon vow to himself to cease any further bullying of Keith.

"My Dad has a .44 Magnum pistol, Waylon." Keith said suddenly calmly as he took a step forward. "I'm gonna kill *her* with that gun, Waylon. If you ever even speak to me again."

Now Keith did not know who the 'her' in this empty threat was, but Waylon must have assumed it was someone close to him. As without another second passing, the bully turned and ran—tail tucked firmly between his legs.

From the moment he summoned his inner Bickle, this was the new dynamic. Keith then enjoyed a peaceful existence in his school. Anyone with a keen eye could see that this was strange and exceptional. Physically, he should have looked as brow beaten and scared as the rest of the classmates his size were.

"You and I are gonna be buddies."

Those were the words that made Keith stop daydreaming, and jolt with fear as he walked in the corridor, as a strange boy's arm clasped over his shoulder.

Thinking his non-bully streak was finally over, Keith winced as he glanced to his side—to the boy that spoke and grabbed him—fully expecting to see Waylon. Instead, he was shocked to see that it was the new kid at Valemore. The kid from New York who had just arrived that week.

"W-what?" Keith asked, as this new boy walked with him

toward the playground, his arm still wrapped confidently around Keith's shoulder.

"After a few days at this dump, I can see that *you're* the man to know," the boy spoke confidently. "The man I need to be friends with."

Keith did not know if this was a good thing or a bad thing. It was too surreal. This new kid was way cooler than anyone at Valemore. He had a cool Brooklyn-Italian accent. He dressed in cool designer clothes. He talked about cool stuff. He just was... *Cool*. Keith had no other way to describe this kid.

"I've been watching everyone here, and it seems even the assholes treat you with some respect. And I like that. I like that a lot. I like anyone who can stand out." The kid stopped in his tracks, then turned to Keith with a smile. "So, like I said, you and I are gonna be good pals. You okay with that?"

Without the nerve of Travis Bickle, all Keith could do was smile and reply weakly, "Sure."

The new kid thrust his hand toward Keith. "The name's Anthony Joseph Romano. You can call me AJ."

Shake hands? Keith thought to himself as he took AJ's hand. *Even that was cool.*

"You're kidding me?" Keith exclaimed rhetorically as he trailed after his friend; The now confidently striding AJ.

As the front doors to the building flew open, AJ sauntered out with a look of triumph plastered on his face.

"A stripper? Really?" Keith shouted, as he grabbed AJ by the arm, then spun him around to face his interrogator. "You promised them a stripper? By *tonight*? Have you lost your mind?"

Without his smile faltering, AJ just glanced down at Keith

happily, then quietly replied, "And the problem with that is? You don't think we can do it? This ain't the backwoods of Kansas anymore, Toto. This is California. Land of dreams…. and strippers."

"You could have just jumped off that *damn* stool. Then that would've been it. We-"

"It?" AJ interrupted. "They weren't gonna let us in, Keith."

"W-What? Who?" Keith countered. "What do you mean?"

"You see 'em? Jocks and assholes, every last one." He placed a hand on Keith's shoulder. "Of which, I'm sure you are fully aware, we are neither! They would have found a reason to cut us. I wouldn't just promise shit unless I *had* to. Do you really think we could have just jumped, then be welcomed with open arms?"

Keith paused. *Damnit*, he thought, *AJ's right*.

"So why bother?" Keith's eyes reflected his confusion. "Not like we *need* these jock assholes."

"Hey, we talked about this." AJ's smile began to falter. "They got the best digs. Right? You saying you don't want all that now? Our big plan?"

Keith took a breath in. He knew AJ was correct. He just didn't like it one bit. "Yeah, okay," he said deflated. "I guess."

AJ wrapped his arm around Keith's shoulder—just as he did when they first met—then led him away across the rain-slicked courtyard toward their dorm, the storm having now cleared and left the night sky clear and fresh. The witching hour now absconded until tomorrow.

"After all these years, my friend?" AJ said. "You just gotta learn to trust me."

CHAPTER 2
BARGAINING

"Just one number," AJ pleaded into the telephone, exuding all of the charm that he could possibly muster. "That's all I need. Not much, right? You can help me out can't you? Pretty please?"

Standing next to him, Keith glanced up and down the dormitory corridor nervously, hoping to all that was holy that no one could overhear AJ trying to solicit a stripper. Though he had nothing to worry about. The throng of students lining the corridors were too involved in their own boisterous drunken behavior to give any attention to anyone's phone call.

AJ rested his elbow on the top of the payphone and looked as if he was leaning into the very call itself. His whole body looked as though he were flirting with a woman at a bar. Leaning nearer, to narrow the distance between them, talking softer and softer so that only she could hear.

"Now, I know you're a dancer," AJ spoke in an enticing tone, ignoring the hollers and wails of the drunken students around him. "I *know* you're professionally trained and all, but..." He paused for a moment, biting his lip coyly before continuing, "I was thinking how *interesting,* and artful it would be if you *did* do this, you know..."

Keith felt an embarrassed sinking feeling at the inevitable next words to come out of his friend's mouth.

AJ repeated for effect, "How *interesting* and *artful* it would be... to do exactly that same arty interesting dance... but without clothes on."

The person at the other end of the call hung up. AJ simply nodded in understanding, then removed his elbow from the top of the phone. "Good for her," he said to himself. "Right decision"

From his pocket he drew out a pen and a small scrap of paper with nearly a dozen names and numbers scrawled across it—the first half of them already crossed off. Taking the pen, AJ crossed off the next name and number on his list.

"Head's up!" slurred a drunken reveler.

Ducking, Keith narrowly avoided a flying slice of pizza. It came hurtling through the air, then landed with a splat on the wall between him and AJ.

AJ glared toward the reveler, who was now busily onto his next round of stupidity. One which included a fire extinguisher.

"I hate this place, Keith." AJ said, almost to himself, as he looked disapprovingly at the drunken chaos all around them. "Sincerely, I truly and honestly can say. I really, *really* hate it here."

"They're all drunken assholes," Keith said, stating the obvious. "But what can you do?"

Shaking his head, AJ turned back to the phone as he shoved the handwritten list and pen back into his shirt pocket. Then, with both hands on either side of the payphone's narrow frame, he lifted it off its wall hooks, and motioned to Keith to open the door opposite them—the door that led to their shared dorm room.

Without questioning, Keith did as he was asked. He took

out a key from his pocket, unlocked their door, then opened it wide for AJ to walk through holding the payphone. Its cable coiled out from a hole in the corridor's wall, and stretched comfortably all the way into their room, and onto AJ's bed. This was obviously not the first time the phone had been brought here.

Keith closed the door, conscious not to catch it upon the phone cable, and successfully shut out the drunken revelry. Turning, he clearly recognized the tinge of sadness in AJ's expression, and couldn't help but feel bad for him. Keith knew his friend's past, and knew that seeing inebriated people, even having innocent fun, was a trigger for some bad, bad memories. He knew better than to mention any of it. The best thing to do was just to carry on as if nothing was wrong.

After placing the telephone onto his bed, AJ performed the little ritual that he did each time he entered the room; He kissed his finger, then touched it to an old black and white framed photo of his mother—the one person directly linked to the bad, bad memories. Memories of unforgivable drunken behavior.

With that ritual completed, and without any other mention, AJ sat on his bed then grabbed the handwritten list of numbers from his shirt pocket.

Keith, meanwhile, busied himself besides his own set of drawers and picked up his pride and joy from its cradle; his Darton Mark I, high-energy compound bow. Thanks to his mother's need for him to participate in some kind of sport when he was young, Keith had eventually chosen archery, and now it was the one and only thing that he felt he was better than everyone else at. So, when his Dad sent him some money for food and school books, he immediately bought a professional sports bow instead - something he could never afford if he were still at home.

Buying this bow was probably the most rebellious thing he had ever done in his life, and if he hadn't known AJ, Keith would have probably never had the nerve to part with that large amount of money. But AJ knew that this bow was a non-negotiable purchase.

"Sometimes what you need runs deeper than what's sensible," AJ had said convincingly. Because of this, Keith's food and school books for that term would have to be acquired by other means. And for the first six months of being in this dorm, they indeed were. This situation was not to be for very long, as soon enough, another check came in from Keith's Dad and non-vending machine sustenance could be purchased once again.

Pulling the string on the bow, Keith smiled and looked at AJ, who studied the list in his hand while shaking his head, annoyed.

"You'd think someone would jump at this chance," AJ muttered under his breath as he glanced upward in exasperation, catching a reflection of himself in his mirrored ceiling.

AJ had decorated his half of the dorm room in what he referred to as 'motel-chic', and it always impressed Keith. That mirrored ceiling, the red velvet sheets, a wine and food cooler used as a bed stand - they all screamed class to Keith. As opposed to his own side of the room, which was a mess of clothes, old archery trophies and borrowed books. Placed on the wall opposite his bed was an archery target with a lone hole that was dead center.

The partying outside of their room now intensified in volume, causing AJ to speak louder. "I'm tellin' ya Keith, we gotta get out of here soon. This place is a goddamn zoo." He then picked up the telephone's handset and punched in the next number on his list.

Keith listened once again to AJ's charming pitch, as it tried to persuade a hapless contact to strip for money.

"I'm serious, Sandi." AJ spoke with a chuckle in his voice. Maneuvering the handset into his other hand, he leant down over his bedside cooler, then opened the door with his free hand. "It's only *one* dance," he said, as he grabbed an apple from the cooler's top shelf. "How bad could it be, really? Just a bunch of asshole frat boys. Not like you have to even do it that well."

AJ barely had time to place the apple on top of the cooler, when an arrow pierced through the air and cut the apple clean in half, embedding itself into a book placed against the wall. The book had over a dozen arrow holes already in it. With zero reaction from AJ—he pulled it out of the book, then tossed it back, onto Keith's bed.

Keith, meanwhile, smiled widely as he stood with the bow down by his side. He *always* smiled when he fired his bow. It was one of the few things that made him proud.

Without so much as a stutter in his telephone conversation, AJ grabbed one half of the split apple and tossed it over to Keith who—with the same wide-eyed smile on his face—caught it, and quickly took a bite.

"Hey..." AJ said on his call, his voice now with a note of dejection. "I'd do it for *you*, Sandi. I really would. If you ever need me to—"

The line went dead.

Furrowing his brow, AJ glanced annoyed at the handset, then replaced it onto the receiver box beside him. After a beat, his eyes quickly widened. He had an idea.

Noticing this, Keith's smile fell away, as he knew that AJ's ideas were normally impossible, or trouble waiting to happen, or both.

"Eureka!" AJ exclaimed.

Oh no.

"I got it!"

This is gonna be bad.

"Field trip!"

Field trip?

AJ couldn't contain the excitement in his voice. "We'll hire ourselves a pro! Direct from the source!"

Oh, God no...

"It's a goddamn spectacular idea, right?"

Keith grimaced. "Let me know about it when you get back."

Ignoring him, AJ continued, "How much money you got on ya?"

"Are you not hearing me?" Keith protested.

"I'm ignoring all your negativity. Now, how much ya got?"

Putting the bow back onto its holder atop the set of drawers, Keith replied without facing AJ. "They're not worth it. The frat guys. They just aren't."

"They? I couldn't care less about those guys. It's their house we need. What a place to operate from! You see those rooms? Really dude, I can't honestly stay here much longer without killing all those drunk asses outside." He paused for a moment and looked sincere. "You wouldn't want me to kill anyone would you?"

Keith knew that any argument he posited would be futile, yet he couldn't help himself. "C'mon... This is all giving me a headache. We're two hundred damn miles from civilization, with zero money and zero way of getting anywhere. You're really telling me that Dipsa Phi house is worth this kind of aggravation."

Standing up from his bed, AJ silently walked over to the door, opened it, then stared blankly back at Keith.

The drunken noise poured in from the party in the corridor. A student staggered by, bent down in front of their door, and vomited all over the floor.

With this foul presentation complete, AJ calmly shut the door and shrugged. "Have I made my point?"

"I got eighty-two bucks in change," Keith stated, defeated. Yes, AJ's idea may have been dumb. But Keith finally admitted to himself that this place was far, far dumber.

Reaching into his pants pocket, AJ brought out a loose bundle of bills. "You got 82? So with mine, we got a total of $148. That and a little charm should get us a stripper, right? I mean, how much can strip clubs be?"

"Will it be enough?" Keith asked. He knew despite the bluster, AJ did not have a clue about the going rates for strippers, though he *did* normally have the charm to get what he wanted.

"Now, all we need are some wheels," AJ said, as much a question as a statement.

Quickly, both of their faces dropped as they realized that this was a huge issue. How the hell would they get anywhere without a car?

Suddenly, the sound of a THWACK and a cheer emanated from the room above them.

They both smiled as they glanced upwards, coming to the same realization.

"Duncan!" they agreed, in a happy unison.

"Anthony... You're no fuckin' son of mine, you're just a worthless little leech!" Sal Romano, deep in his alcohol-fueled rage, spat the words toward his son. Before any protest could be made, Sal staggered toward the nine-year-old and punched him hard in his stomach. "You're just a preenin' little faggot!" he slurred as he watched young Anthony crumple down onto the floor in pain.

"You spent *my* money on a *goddamn* queer shirt?" Sal's voice rose to a booming roar. "Caca cazzo!" he screamed. The sweat dripped in streams from off of his forehead and onto the floor. It was not only a reflection of the humidity in this

Brooklyn slum but also of the sheer amount of alcohol he had imbibed all day.

Anthony could not reply. He was in too much pain, and winded on the floor. He wanted to say it was *his* birthday money, given to him by his mother. She had told him that he could spend it on *whatever* he wanted. And he wanted *that shirt*. That exceptional paisley shirt. The same one Tony Curtis bought a week before—Or so the salesmen had said. But it wasn't just *who* had bought it; it was that the shirt would *fit* him, and not be another ill-fitting hand-me-down from the local church that donated clothes to the poorer neighborhood kids.

Not to mention *that* pattern. That glorious pattern.

"Your bitch of a mother, stealing my *goddamn* money and giving to *you*?" Sal growled, just before he rammed the toe of his dirty work-boot into Anthony's exposed side.

This was violent abuse.

It was sick.

It was cruel.

It was brutal.

But it was not an unusual occurrence.

None of Sal's behavior ever was.

It was exactly what Anthony expected after his father drank.

Whenever Salvatore Romano lost money from his drunken gambling, or was turned away at some dive-bar watering hole for running out of a way to buy his alcohol, he would invariably stagger home. In a violent stupor, he would normally take his anger out on anyone he could find. He invented things to be angry about, then loosed his mouth and fists—and in this case, his foot—onto either young Anthony or his mother.

Over the past few nights, Bridget Romano had worked extra shifts in order to get forty bucks more to give to her son on his birthday. She knew that Anthony wanted the shirt from Macy's, so she would do all that she could do to make her son happy. After all, he was her little angel. The only light in her life.

Unfortunately, Sal had seen his wife hiding money in the coffee jar earlier that week.

So, when he had come home needing money for more booze and gambling, having predictably missed his son's birthday. He had expected to find the coffee jar stash waiting for him. Money that he had already decided was *his*, and no one else's. He did not expect that Anthony would have been given every last cent, nor that he would have spent it on clothes.

Discovering this, Sal snapped.

Just like he always snapped.

But this time. *This time*, that snap would not be forgiven by an apologetic promise that he would never do such a bad thing ever again.

As young Anthony lost consciousness from the latest and most violent beating his father had ever doled out, all he could think about was his mother. He needed to know that she was ok. All he knew was that he had heard her scream, then the quick succession of sickening thuds that soon followed.

Little did young Anthony know that his mother—his best friend and confidant—had lost her life from Sal's latest fury. Having been strangled by his gorilla-like grip, she had then been thrown down the stairs, her neck snapping upon the impact of the first step. Mercifully, she was free of pain and breath before she had hit the last step. Her torment was brief.

Anthony surely would have suffered this same fate if it had not been for the police soon breaking down their apartment door.

. . .

When Anthony had woken up in the hospital, he had expected to see his mother sitting by his bedside, but instead he saw his Grandmother. His Mother's Mother, looking at him with an expression of deep and debilitating sorrow.

How long was I out for? Anthony pondered confused, knowing his Gramma lived over a five hour flight away.

"Gramma?" He spoke, with a woozy lilt in his voice.

"It's ok, baby boy... You're safe now," she reassured, "You just had a bit of a sleep, that's all. I'm here for you now."

"Where's mom?" The only question he had had in his mind.

The Grandmother slowly and carefully explained what had happened to the best of her ability. She told him the things no child should ever hear. She told him that his mother had *'gone with the Angels, to sit at God's right-hand.'*

Anthony's world soon fell away. A sinking feeling emerged that ripped his stomach downwards, like a roller coaster on an infernal ride.

With a terrified, trembling tone, Anthony asked, "What about... Dad?"

His Grandmother could not help but smile bitterly as she replied, "Your father... Well, he can't hurt you, nor no-one else, no more. No more, *at all.* Can't hurt a soul from the fires of Hell."

Anthony had, up until now, expected his father to walk into the hospital to beat him more, even with the knowledge of his Mother's passing. But his Grandmother's words quickly dispelled this notion.

"May the baby Jesus pardon my French, but thank God that evil bastard is gone."

A neighbor had called the police after hearing Bridget Romano's scream. Soon after, the police had broken down their apartment door. Salvatore Romano had apparently resisted arrest. He had attempted to attack the police officers who advanced on him, and even attempted to grab one of their guns. Anthony could not have been happier to hear that the police protected themselves successfully. And as Anthony lay unconscious on the kitchen floor, the police gunned down Salvatore Romano until death.

"My baby boy. Your sweet mother... We'll bury her back in Kansas, where she came from. Do... Do you wanna come live with me there?"

She continued to speak about how lovely her hometown was, and how great the schools were, how nice the people were, but it was all unnecessary. Anthony had already decided that he wanted to get away from New York. Away from the ghosts that he knew would haunt him, should he decide to stay.

"What about Dad?" Anthony asked with trepidation. The same question as before, but now with a different meaning. He didn't want his Father to come to Kansas as well, even in death. He didn't want that man anywhere near him and his mother.

"Well, I'm not gonna bury him that's for sure. The city can do that here. In an unmarked grave for all I care. That man can rot for what he did to you and my sweet girl."

Anthony could not help but burst out crying. Not just from the incredible sadness at his loss, but also from sheer relief. Relief that it was all finally over. The tirade he had known his whole life was, at last, done and dusted.

"I see you're awake?" came a soft voice from behind the curtain, as a female hand gently opened it, and a junior nurse walked in wearing a friendly smile. "No, I can't call you Mr Romano can I? That's an old person's name. So what do you prefer? Ant? Anthony? Tony? AJ? Tone?"

Anthony looked at the nurse, confused for a second, before replying absently. "AJ..."

"Then AJ it is." The nurse's smile grew wider.

In his mind, Anthony was the name of the weak child that got easily beaten. Anthony was the name of the kid that lost his mother tragically at the hands of a sadistic drunk. AJ, however, was someone new. Someone stronger. Someone who had the confidence to be who he wanted to be without fear of a parental beatdown. Someone who would live *for* his mother's memory, not just with it.

Turning to his Grandmother, he asked with a stutter, "Is-Is that alright? Can I be AJ now?"

"You can be whatever you want to be, my sweet boy. You could even ask to be a hot dog, and I'd do my best to make that happen!"

Before he could cry again, the nurse turned from checking AJ's monitor and said to the grandmother, "We'd like him to stay overnight for observation, if you don't mind. But he can go home first thing tomorrow. Anytime after eight a.m.. That is, if you're picking him up?"

"Eight a.m.? That's no problem at all. I'm only staying in a motel just a mile away." She reached out and gently put her hand upon AJ's. "You need anything before I go, Anth—" she quickly corrected herself, "—I meant, AJ."

"He'll need some more clothes, that's for sure," the Nurse cut in, as she glanced apologetically to AJ. "I'm afraid the ones you came in with, well, we had to cut them off from you. They had a bit of blood on them."

"My shirt!" AJ cried aloud. "Not my shirt! Mom gave me that—"

"It's ok," the Grandmother interrupted. "We'll buy you another one. *As many* as you want! She would want that, wouldn't she?"

Standing in the dorm corridor, outside of Duncan's room, AJ straightened the cuff of his shirt in a proud fashion. He then noticed Keith's slightly confused expression.

"You ok?" AJ asked.

Keith glanced up at the CCTV camera affixed to the corridor wall, then to the porch light above that same door, then to the private mailbox sat next to it. Shrugging, he said, "This guy's a bit insane, you know that, right?"

"That he is, my friend. That he is." AJ smiled. "Nice enough though, probably."

"We've never really spoken to him before. What the hell are you gonna say? You think he'll just hand us over car keys and say bon voyage?"

"Relax Keith, we can handle this." AJ said with his standard level of self-belief. He then pressed the ornate doorbell. "It'll be no problem at all."

As the bell chime sounded its quick upbeat tune, Keith couldn't help but notice that these fixings were beyond ridiculous to be placed in this corridor. The walls in this dorm were cheaply plastered with stained, peeling wallpaper. Yet this rich kid, Duncan, had an antique doorbell, lights, and a postbox put there. Why? What was he proving, and to who? So, he was rich? Not like he was popular and could command any actual respect. Quite the opposite. He seemed to never be involved in any of the dorm's activities, nor did he ever appear to leave his room at all. He just existed there and everyone knew that. *Come to think of it*, Keith thought, *dunno if I could even pick the guy out of a line-up.*

As the chime echoed away, the door was soon answered by a skinny looking seventeen-year-old. A kid with a paler than pale complexion, wearing a t-shirt that read *My other shirt's Linux*, with an expression that read of utter boredom.

"Hey," AJ said with a friendly, loud confidence in his voice, "Duncan, my good friend!"

"*I'm* not Duncan," came a contemptuous reply.

"Nice start," Keith said with a wry smile, as he nudged AJ.

Opening the door further, the kid motioned behind him, "That's Duncan with the golf club."

Walking into the room, both AJ and Keith jaw's quickly fell open in awe. As this room sat directly above theirs, they had expected Duncan's to be one that was of the same size and shape. But, this room was over four times the size of any other dorm room they had ever seen. It even had a walk-in kitchen, wet bar—not to mention the latest AV tech, in the form of an almost futuristic looking audio system that stood as high as AJ did, resembling a chrome monolith that housed a vertical turntable in its center. It was the absolute height of ostentatious designer tech.

He must have paid for all the rooms on this side of the building, then converted them all. AJ mused. *How rich is this guy, exactly?*

Across the room, four students worked diligently at a bank of computer terminals. Each of them busily typing away, deep in their respective concentrations, yet each of them wore the same resigned look of consummate boredom as the other.

Facing away from AJ and Keith, stood the man that could only be the mysterious Duncan. This diminutive man stood on a patch of astroturf in the middle of the living room, dressed in brightly colored pants, shirt, with a matching golf cap—as if he had just walked out of a PGA tour. He gripped a 9-iron in his hand, and was driving golf balls into a giant net erected on the opposite side of the room.

Next to Duncan, another student stood holding his golf bag while talking into a *Mr. Microphone.* He was commentating on the events at hand through this electric device. His voice came out of the speaker in a loud, tinny tone. Around his neck, hung a mobile tape recorder.

Duncan coiled and whacked a golf ball, sending it speeding across the room and into the net.

"Duncan Spriggs unleashes a monstrous drive, right down the center of the fairway," the student announced into the *Mr. Microphone*. His voice, monotone and bored, as he stifled a yawn, "It's a beauty," he continued.

Then, he pressed the play button on the tape recorder

around his neck, then rolled his eyes as the loud sound of a roaring crowd filled the room for a few seconds.

Duncan turned with a gigantic smile on his face, and gave a thumbs-up to the obviously miserable students that toiled about his dorm room. The announcer student stopped the tape recorder, abruptly cutting off the pre-recorded cheers.

Noticing AJ and Keith, Duncan's smile quickly faded from view, only to be replaced by one of panic.

"Whatever I did, I'm sorry," he said in a hurried, nervous voice. "I wasn't thinking. You gotta believe me."

Though puzzled, AJ sidestepped this statement and cut to the chase. "Duncan, you've got a car, right?"

Dropping his golf club to the floor, Duncan stepped forward apologetically, speaking at the speech of a machine gun, "I'll pay for whatever damages. I shouldn't have had it parked there, I know that... What car was it, anyway? Toyota, right? Volvo?"

AJ and Keith looked in bemusement at each other.

"I'm lost," AJ said to Keith, as if Duncan was not even there. "What is he talking about?"

Keith glanced back toward Duncan and offered a polite smile. "I think you're mistaking us for someone else."

"Oh, I am?"

"You see, *we* need a car," AJ chimed in. "We gotta make a *liiiiittle biiittty* trip. So..." AJ paused for dramatic effect, before continuing. "In summation. We'd like to work out a deal for... some transportation. Capeesh?"

A loud buzzer sounded throughout the room, followed by a collective sigh of relief from the silent students working around the room.

Without another beat passing, each student stopped what they were doing. The students at the computers stood up in unison. The student holding the golf bag put it down, then placed the tape recorder and microphone onto a nearby table.

There were no nods of acknowledgement nor any

goodbyes uttered, as every student proceeded to walk toward the door, each with a look of relief plastered over their previously tired expressions.

Their work day had now ended, and they had no intention of staying a second longer than necessary.

Almost in a panic, Duncan followed them with his arms outstretched pleadingly, "Hey buddies, where ya goin'? I was gonna order some pizza." His voice grew more frantic as he continued, "Stick around, fellas... C'mon, I'm buying. Please? We can get any pizza! Or burgers?"

One student broke off from the pack, then began walking back toward Duncan, whose eyes lit up in happiness at this glorious return.

"So what toppings ya want?" Duncan asked as the student approached. "We can get what you want. Wanna play some video games as well? We can go to the theatre if you'd prefer."

Duncan went on, oblivious to the student now reaching into his bag and producing some papers.

"Hey," Duncan said excitedly, "we could even go to a bar?"

Ignoring the offer, the student held the papers up. "You're Russian Lit."

A flash of realization crossed Duncan's eyes as his smile fell. He took the paper solemnly. "Oh," was all he replied.

"That's fifty bucks then," the student continued.

Without another word, Duncan sadly reached into his pocket and took out his wallet. Sliding out a fifty-dollar bill, he handed it to the student with a half smile.

As the student moved to leave, Duncan snapped himself out of his temporary maudlin state. "Leave your number on the service, okay?" Duncan asked, "I could use you during midterms."

The student left the room without another word, and Duncan turned to his two new guests. His two guests who were willingly standing here, and not being paid for the privilege. He greeted them with a big grin.

"A car you say? A little trip you say?" Duncan spoke, as he put his arms on his much taller visitors' shoulders. "It'll be a pleasure to help you guys out - can I call you *guys*?" He didn't wait for an answer before continuing. "Great. Ya know, I mostly get your basic dorks hangin' around here. They just seem to gravitate toward me. I don't know why!" As he laughed at his own joke, he snorted and turned toward his now empty room, gesticulating at it. "This place is usually swingin'. You ought to pop by some time. Bring some honeys with ya!"

Keith and AJ could only smile. Neither knew what they were supposed to say now. They wanted to leave, but they also needed that car.

What are we getting into? Keith and AJ both thought to themselves simultaneously.

"So, this little trip?" Duncan said, as he hurried over to a row of key hooks along the far wall. "Need a hot rod, huh?" All the hooks were empty except for one, which hung a single key from off a large golden fob. Staring at it for a second, he paused in thought, then took it from the hook. "You're in luck," he beamed. "One left, and it's a doozy too!"

Spinning the keyring around his finger he turned back toward AJ and Keith. "Now, normally I'd charge your average schmo, oh I dunno, about—"

AJ interrupted, instinctively knowing which tack to take. "C'mon... Duncan, we're not talking about money here, are we?"

Nervously, Duncan's confidence dropped as he stuttered, "N-no... You're right. S-sorry.... Of course not." He then paused for a beat, lost in this conversation. "Wait... what *are* we talking about then?"

Before AJ could promise something he shouldn't, Keith stepped in. "We were thinking of something along the lines of a favor. One to be returned, of course. We would owe you. Cos we're friends."

"I see," Duncan said, as he beamed a bigger smile. "Hey, that's a *great* idea!" He laughed as he nudged Keith playfully. "One hand washes the other, right friend?"

"Right!" AJ jumped in. "And if there's anything we can ever do—"

"*Something*," Keith corrected, silencing AJ immediately. "If there's *something* we can do. Then just let us know. Okay?"

Holding the car keys out to them, Duncan's smile grew even wider as he said happily, "Hey guys, I already know what you can do for me in return!"

Keith swallowed hard, as he took the keys hesitantly. He knew what was coming.

AJ, on the other hand, had not solved the riddle, and stood there, ignorantly thinking that his plan was falling into place without a hitch.

"Be my best friends for the rest of the year," Duncan said ecstatically. "*And* take me with you tonight."

Keith handed the keys back out to Duncan. "No way. Can't do."

"Okay, okay," Duncan conceded as he ignored the offered keys. "Take me with you and be my friends for a week?"

"We should go," Keith said, as he glanced at AJ, who just stood confused at what was unfolding.

The happiness in Duncan's voice almost turned distraught. "P-please? Just friends for this one night then?"

AJ reached over and took the keys from Keith's hand. Duncan's smile returned as AJ said, "C'mon, Keith. What's the worst that could happen? Don't be such a sour puss."

"This... is... *fantastic*!" Duncan exclaimed loudly as he ran into the next room. Before Keith could make any protests, Duncan then came running back out, tucking in a bright Hawaiian shirt underneath a bright blue yachting jacket.

AJ could only look helplessly at this fashion disaster approaching him.

"How did you change clothes that fast?" Keith asked, half to himself.

"Hey, pals!" Duncan shouted, "I'm psyched! Let's P.A.R.T.Y! Why? Cos we gotta!"

Keith turned to AJ with some urgency. "This is a bad, bad idea."

AJ motioned to Duncan, who was busy adjusting his clothing in a long mirror, oblivious to what was being said. "Look at that poor guy… Paying for friends? C'mon, this is a good deed, right?... Like charity work... We gotta let him come along... It's the right thing to do."

Keith did not interrupt, he just listened then shrugged, begrudgingly accepting. He knew AJ could not help but be a nice guy to an underdog. Just as he had been when they had first met. It was simply who AJ was at heart. No matter how many women fawned over his charms, AJ always looked out for people like Duncan. No matter how annoying they were.

"Where are we going then?" Duncan asked innocently as he continued to adjust his ill-fitting clothing.

AJ said."How d'ya feel about strippers?"

CHAPTER 3
THE JOURNEY

The beating throng of traffic reflected upon AJ's mirrored sunglasses as he drove down the freeway.

Instead of a cool, laid back expression that he would usually don during a road trip like this, he quietly gritted his teeth, trying to stop his annoyance from consuming him.

Riding shotgun, Keith glanced over his shoulder to speak to Duncan, who had been relegated to being scrunched into the tiny back seat. "Can't this thing go any faster?" he asked.

Duncan shrugged, with a twinge of embarrassment lining his ever exuberant smile.

The clanging of valves, the squeaking of rubber upon metal and the chattering of the transmission emanated from the struggling bowels of the 1973 Cadillac Sedan DeVille. Its howls of mechanical pain were almost lost amongst the cacophony of car horns, as cars overtook the Cadillac, venting their frustration as they passed..

From the outside, you couldn't tell that this car would struggle on its journey. Its paintwork—though a grotesque shade of yellow—was nearly immaculate. As was the metal trim lining its chassis. The Cadillac's interiors were also in pristine condition. All the leatherwork shined unscuffed. Even the panelling was as shiny as the day it had come off the factory line. It was only the mechanical guts that were ancient and in disrepair.

"Duncan?" AJ said with a forced calm, as he glanced in the dashboard mirror. "When's the last time you had this boat tuned?"

"Huh?" Duncan replied in confusion. "Tuned? Tuned to what?"

AJ rolled his eyes behind his mirrored shades. "Goddamnit... Tuned! Serviced. Looked at by a professional. Oil changed. Sparks changed—"

"Oh!" Duncan exclaimed, now understanding the question. "Serviced! I don't know. I guess when I bought it. Not like I drive 'em anyway."

"Did you even look under the hood when you bought it?" AJ asked, knowing what the answer would be.

Duncan just shrugged. He didn't check the car when he bought it. He saw it in the lot and took it on sight. Why shouldn't he? He trusted the salesman. Hell, he trusted everyone he met.

"Just had to help the unfortunate, didn't ya?" Keith muttered under his breath, feeling smug that he was right about not wanting to accept Duncan's offer, yet annoyed he had not stayed in the dorm.

AJ shot a disapproving glance toward Keith. "Fuck you," he said deadpan. With a sudden smile he returned his gaze ahead. "Could always be worse. So much worse."

"I don't have a license, you see? I don't know about cars." Duncan said from the back seat. "But don't worry. The stripper whores'll dig it. You just wait and see."

"Stripper whores?" Keith repeated in amused shock.

"Wow," AJ said. "You better keep that phrase to yourself my friend."

"What?" Duncan replied, genuinely confused.

Keith chuckled to himself. "We're not gonna get out of the city alive, are we?"

"Ti Spriggs?" The immigration official asked, holding a Korean passport in her hand, looking at the photo inside.

Standing in the first class arrivals desk at LAX airport, the official stared down at the diminutive man. "That's your *real* name?" she asked.

Dressed in his pristine business suit, he nodded nervously and replied in broken English, "I change it to be more American." He attempted a smile, but it was just met with a dour expression from the official.

Exhaling loudly, she read the rest of his passport pages. Clearly not impressed with him, or his reply.

Ti Spriggs could easily sense the bubbling undercurrent of contemptuous racism this woman had for people like him. Not just for foreigners, but for people rich enough to buy whatever they wanted. People who could move to any country on a single whim. People who could change their name, and start a new life if the mood took them. But who was *she* to judge *him*?

Ti Spriggs was done with being Park Tae-Hyun.

The same Park Tae-Hyun who had been the owner of a growing printing company, up until the American investors had purchased it from him.

From that single sale, Park Tae-Hyun went from being the stressed yet successful owner of a company that ran out of his own garage a decade prior—one which had earned him little in terms of disposable income, to being a multi-millionaire, almost overnight.

This sale could not have come at a better time either. With a huge influx of money, he could easily move his wife to the

West, to get her the medical treatment she so sorely needed. He could afford to buy his way into any of the American medical trials. Anything that had a chance to cure her breast cancer. But with his own country offering in the way of hope, they had no option but to set their eyes on the land of Uncle Sam.

Within a month of him becoming disgracefully rich, Park Tae-Hyun, his wife Si-Woo and their five-year-old son, Kwan-Boo, had their immigration paperwork paid for, approved, and ready to go. Their bags were almost fully packed. Their house was now mostly full of boxes, days away from being picked up by the movers, ready to ship them across the globe to a delightful house in Los Angeles. One that had been rented especially, waiting for their arrival.

Then—as it so often does at times like these—tragedy struck.

A week before they were to fly to their new life, the cancer stole Si-Woo away without even a warning shot.

This left Park Tae-Hyun and Kwan-Boo alone. Yet despite this setback, nothing would stop his plan to emigrate to the West to start a new life. Si-Woo had loved America—after all, it was her idea for them to move there in the first place. As soon as the sale had gone through, *she* had been the rudder that guided their path.

She had not only chosen the house where they were to live, she also chose their new names; He would be Ti Spriggs. She would be Helen Spriggs. Their son would be Duncan Spriggs.

And Ti Spriggs would stop at nothing to see this dream through, all in memory of his beloved.

After the immigration official reluctantly stamped their passports, Ti with his son Duncan made their way out of the airport, and into the waiting limo.

Over the years, Ti had invested some of the vast fortune into shares of startup tech companies, and because of that, his fortune soon blossomed into limitless and obscene wealth. One that a single person could not spend in two lifetimes.

This money would buy everything they would ever want. Ti wanted their new life to be one of ease, just as Si-Woo had wished for. Whatever his son asked for, he would get. This money would buy them happiness at *any* cost.

"It says corner of Holden and Shelly," Duncan said from the back seat, as he read aloud an advert printed in the classified section of a local newspaper. "'Guaranteed to get you off', or so it says."

Holding up an unfolded city street map, Keith squinted to read the street names. "Would be helpful if they building numbers on here. The streets are so damn long I dunno which end of the street any of these places are on?"

"What was that one called, again?" AJ asked, keeping his eyes ahead. "The one with the guarantee?"

Duncan replied joyfully, "The Dirty Hole!"

"Nope... Next!," AJ replied point blank.

"What's wrong with it?" Duncan asked.

"Aside from sounding like it's got no class. It probably comes with a free side of gonorrhea."

"Can't find it on this thing, anyway." Keith muttered.

"Okay... Uhhh. We got..." Duncan continued reading from the classifieds. "Tallywhackers?"

"Next," AJ answered, almost cutting him off.

"The G Spot?"

"Next," AJ said again, almost as immediately.

"Boob-O-Rama?"

"Next."

"The Meat Locker?"

"Next," AJ and Keith said in unison.

"Give it here," AJ said as he held his hand back toward Duncan.

Reluctantly, Duncan closed the pages and placed it in AJ's expectant hand.

Spinning the newspaper around, AJ flicked to the back pages. Peering over his sunglasses he alternately scanned the classifieds, while still keeping an eye on his driving.

Within a few seconds, his eyes settled on an advert. With a smile, he passed the paper over to Keith, then tapped his finger on an all-black advert that was adorned with bright white lettering. "This one. This is the one."

Keith glanced away from the map, and looked at the ad. "You sure?" he asked.

AJ s nodded as he kept his gaze on his driving. "Yeah...I can feel it."

Craning his neck between the seats, Duncan peered over Keith's shoulder to see.

"The After Dark Club," Keith read aloud. "Hottest Acts Anywhere! 1627 Linconfirm Parkway." Keith stopped as he read the address again, "Linconfirm? Who made that name up?"

"Sounds classy, right?" AJ said. "Like Abraham Lincoln. But firmer?"

Keith smirked. "So classy, I'm sure we'll need reservations."

"No problem, guys. We don't need reservations with this." Duncan thrust his open wallet proudly between them. The designer snakeskin leather in his hands was fit to burst with credit cards as well as many hundred-dollar bills. "I'm ready!" he said excitedly.

Grabbing the wallet from out of Duncan's hand, AJ

examined it quickly, then handed it back. "Not a bright idea to bring *that* much out with you." AJ said, shaking his head.

"Why not?" Duncan's expression turned to innocent confusion as he caught AJ's gaze in the rearview.

AJ looked over his mirrored shades toward Duncan as he spoke slowly. "You're in a car with two guys you hardly know, going somewhere you've never been. So—and this is a life lesson for ya—taking that much money with ya makes you a mark. Easy pickin's for the assholes of the world. You get it, right?"

Without really understanding the gravity of AJ's words, Duncan just smiled again. "Hey, you're my bestest buddies! I don't have to worry about anything with you."

Keith turned in his seat to stare at Duncan quizzically.

"Sorry, I mean you're my buddies for the night," Duncan stuttered nervously. "*Just* the night. Buddies for the night. That was the deal. And it's a great deal. After you'll wanna loan *me* a car to be *my* buddy."

"Look, Duncan," Keith said. "We just don't want you walking around looking like a meal ticket. So hide that money, okay?"

As AJ drove on, he removed his sunglasses and hooked them into his open shirt. "Some people find it hard to resist taking advantage of people like you," he said.

"People like me?"

"Yeah," Keith replied. "Rich people."

"Case in point," AJ said as he held up a credit card in his hand. He then fanned the card out, revealing three others hidden behind it. Each of them bore the name *Duncan Spriggs*. "It's that easy to take advantage of you."

"That's neat," Duncan said, as he leaned between the seats and took his credit cards back. "How did you get them? Can you do it again?"

Keith shook his head and turned back to face the street

ahead. "Lost cause, I'm tellin' ya," he muttered under his breath. "Total lost cause."

"Ain't we all, my friend." AJ smiled resignedly. "Ain't we all."

An hour later, the Cadillac turned off an exit ramp and into the heart of the city's downtown district.

As they puttered across the intersection, they hit the main drag.

Here, the early evening hustle and bustle was in full swing. As they stopped at some traffic lights, AJ glanced out his window to the Hotel DuVeer—a less-than-budget accommodation that pretended it wasn't—he smirked as he saw the hotel's new arrivals, deboarding from a decrepit minibus. These were obviously tourists, fresh off the plane, whom no doubt expected a higher-class place to stay. Instead they stood outside of a building, fifty years past its sell by date. The looks plastered on their faces said it all as they stared up at the hotel's crumbling brick and grime-stained windows. Then like a funeral procession, they shuffled inside mournfully.

With the light now turned green, the Cadillac spluttered as it moved on, down the street and past a row of department stores. Each was now ending their day's trading, as fleets of taxis zig-zagged through the regular traffic to pick up the customers leaving their shopping sprees for the day..

This was a typical American city.

It was just a bit more out of date than most.

Struggling with the map, Keith glanced at the passing street signs as he tried to locate any of them on the map that now sprawled across his lap. His efforts though, were to no avail.

He grunted in annoyance as he closed his eyes.

"What's up?" AJ asked.

Keith tossed the map into the footwell in front of him. "We're goddamn lost, that's what's up!"

AJ shrugged then turned to look out at the passing streets. He noticed that the 'look' of downtown had started to change as they ventured into a more derelict and forgotten part of town. Gone were the boutique stores, hotels and eateries. Now in their place were liquor stores, hour-rate motels and pawn shops. This was the wrong part of town, where there were very few people walking the streets, and the shops that *were* brave enough to be there, were now closing. The store owners didn't dawdle as they pulled down the heavy iron gates in front of their meager display windows.

As Keith's gaze followed AJ's to the streets outside, they both noticed a bag lady screaming at the traffic.

"Some swingin' place this is?" Keith said, motioning to her.

"Patience." AJ grinned. "When the sun goes down, this place'll be crawling with life."

"The worst kind of life, I'm guessing."

As they pulled up to another red light. Duncan suddenly yelped joyfully as a figure approached their car. "Hello there!" he said happily from the back seat.

Before AJ could react, a pock-marked arm leaned into the driver's open window. The heavily made-up face of an aged prostitute offered a junkie-toothed smile to each of them.

"Getting dark, boys," she drooled, as she took a sloppy drag off her cigarette. "Don't 'spose any of ya wanna go *bump* in the night? If ya get my drift?"

AJ smiled, tight lipped. "No thank you," he said politely, as he urged the traffic light to change to green with only the power of his mind.

"I can take one at a time or all at once," she leered as she thrust her pelvis at them. "Only five-bucks a pop, and any hole's a goal."

Keith ignored this woman, and instead focused on the brick wall behind her. It entranced him as he stared wide-eyed at the multitude of missing persons' posters. There were posters plastered over each inch of the brickwork. If he were to guess, he would estimate that there were over fifty different people up there. All ages, colors, and creeds. All missing.

"No," AJ replied to yet another sexual offer. The light mercifully then switched from red to green. "Sorry ma'am, maybe another time."

He quickly pressed on the gas, moving them forward, leaving the offer of very cheap and very infectious sex in their wake.

"Wait!" Duncan exclaimed, "Maybe I was interested, she seemed nice!"

AJ shook his head as he drove the car deeper into the underbelly of the city.

Outside, the streets were now shrouded in deep shadows as the evening set in to become night. A time where the only people brave enough to be out on these streets seemed to be winos, prostitutes and junkies.

After fifteen minutes of looking at the map again, and *still* getting nowhere, Keith sighed, "I don't get it. How am I supposed to know where the hell we are when there aren't any street signs, and the ones I *do* find, aren't on the map?"

"C'mon, be fair," AJ said with a mischievous smile. "You've never been any good at reading those things!"

Keith nodded in defeat. "I guess we could ask someone?" he proffered.

"Look out!" Duncan shouted from the back seat.

Reeling around to look down the street, AJ suddenly slammed on the brakes. One part of the car that worked flawlessly. As their car was forced to a screeching halt, a homeless man threw himself across the Cadillac's windscreen, pressing his face onto the glass, meeting their shocked gazes with his.

"They got 'im!" the homeless man screamed in a drunken slur.

"Fuck me," AJ muttered.

"They got my frieeeeeennnnd!" the man screamed again as his words became choked by tears. "Please," he whimpered. "They got my friend."

"Floor it!" Keith screamed.

AJ pressed his foot onto the accelerator, causing the car to bolt forward. The homeless man reeled off of the windscreen and fell away, landing onto the asphalt with a thud.

Quickly checking the rearview, AJ breathed a sigh of relief as he saw the man get to his feet, then stagger away, with no obvious injuries.

"What the hell was that?" Keith said in shock.

"Some poor bastard," AJ replied.

Duncan then thrust his finger in front of Keith's face, pointing dead ahead. "Linconfirm Parkway!" he shouted. "We found it!"

CHAPTER 4
ARRIVAL FOR SIN

S tanding in front of the Cadillac, AJ, Keith and Duncan stared up at the windowless red-brick building that loomed ahead of them. A single neon sign blinked away above a pair of black double doors. The words *After Dark* lit up in bright yellow as the third word *Club* remained unlit and broken.

From the desolation of the surrounding streets to this half-lit club sign, the whole area of the city carried with it a sense of discomfort and foreboding, as if the apocalypse had come and gone, leaving a dangerous ghost town in its wake.

"Is it even open?" Duncan asked, with a disappointed look on his face.

No one replied.

After a few more moments, Keith, feeling a pang of trepidation, leaned into AJ and uttered under his breath, "What d'you think? Should we just go to another one? I'm not sure about this place"

AJ—feeling no such discomfort —replied, "I think we may be years too late for this place. Sure it seems a bit... neglected." He shrugged as he continued, "Let's check it out, anyway. It may be a diamond in the rough."

"I don't think this is the place for us, AJ," Keith said.

"Maybe…" AJ nodded then casually strolled over to the Club's front door and knocked on it loudly. "Beggars can't be choosers my friend," he said loudly, glancing back over his shoulder.

Before Keith could reply, an eye level slat in the door shot open with a loud screech. Behind it, from the darkness, stood a figure wearing a pair of mirrored sunglasses that glared out at them.

"What ya want?" the voice snarled.

"Uhh," AJ scrambled to turn on his charm, "Don't suppose you're open to a few ne'er do wells, on their journeypath to watch some fair maidens in a state of undress?"

No reply.

The sunglasses just stared out.

AJ's humor had fallen flat.

He took another tack, "I mean… You open yet?"

After another uncomfortable pause, the voice replied sternly, "No."

AJ glanced back to Keith quizzically, then returned his gaze to the slat. "So… When ya gonna open?"

"When ya think?" the voice grunted, "After dark!" The slat slammed shut with another screech.

Slowly and with a shrug of his shoulders, AJ turned and walked back over to Keith and Duncan. "Guess we wait then."

"Guys?" Duncan smiled meekly, "Can we go somewhere else til then? I gotta drain the main vein, if ya get what I mean?"

"Main vein?" AJ asked rhetorically as he shook his head in disbelief. "Just say ya need to piss. No need to be so poetic about it."

"You're one to talk." Keith laughed as he clapped his hand

on AJ's shoulder. "Journeypath to watch some fair maidens? What the hell was that?"

AJ laughed. "I dunno what I was talking about. Seems my charisma failed me for once."

"Journeypath, AJ." Keith reiterated, unable to stop himself from mocking his friend. "You said *Journeypath*. What the fuck is a journeypath?"

"What can I say?" AJ replied as he began walking back to the car. "I guess my nerves turned me into a real prick!"

As Duncan lifted the driver's seat to get into the back seat of the Cadillac, AJ glanced at his watch.

"Best-case scenario," he said. "We come back in an hour or so, find a stripper, and get to the party at ten or eleven? Sound good?"

"You really think it'll be that easy?" Keith asked with a chuckle.

"Oh, fuck no." AJ replied, affecting a mock arrogance. "But that, my good friend, is the way of the journeypath."

Keith burst out laughing again.

"At least when we fail, we will know that we tried. And that's something, right?"

"I remember it as clearly as today, Padre. As do you!" Hayim Kominowski said, agitated and frustrated at this priest for being so dismissive of the situation at hand. "How d'ya just forget what we saw?" He paused for a moment as he thought to himself. "Is it a gentile thing? That's it isn't it? Stopped you from seeing them take Davis, *right in front of us*."

Father Jonathan Dyer chuckled to himself. Aged in his sixties and dressed in a smart pinstripe suit, he looked more like a tax man than a man of the cloth. Hayim, on the other hand—despite being the same age—was significantly more haggard. He looked more like a low-life elderly crook, dressed in an oversized grubby suit, than the business owner of the local coffee shop.

"What's so funny, huh?" Hayim protested. In the 40 years he had known Father Dyer, from well before he entered the priesthood, Hayim had known his friend to be a straightforward and logical man. Someone who would never deny facts, even if it proved his religious teachings wrong. He was a modern liberal priest who believed that science and religion should work hand in hand to develop the real truths, not work against each other. But strangely, with this particular situation, with what they had witnessed, it should have proved some parts of the priests' faith as an undeniable truth. Yet here the Father was, making excuses for what they had witnessed only a week ago. What they had both seen happen on the street, very close to the *After Dark Club*.

"It's not that I'm saying you're wrong, Hayim. I'm not. Far from it.." Father Dyer said, before taking a sip from his glass of beer. "It's just that it does no-one any good to jump to conclusions. I know you want to make sense of it the best way you can, but I still think it was most likely some junkies hopped up on smack. Not... not what *you* think it was. Not... *Demons*." Changing tack, he picked up his glass and held it up toward Hayim, "Anyway... To Davis... May God treasure his soul."

Hayim begrudgingly held his glass up in salute. "To Davis. And fuck God."

"Fuck God?" the priest asked, amused. "That a Jewish thing?"

"Probably... But that bastard took our friend, so fuck him," Hayim replied. "Though, I gotta admit, it was a nice service, don't ya think?"

Father Dyer nodded in agreement. "It was. It really, really was. Dave would have hated it, though. All that singing, all those tears."

Hayim sighed as he glanced around the dive bar they were now sitting in. He knew that any more conversation between them on this topic would just lead them both down that familiar spiral of anger and sadness. Their friend was gone. Forever. And as Hayim saw it, that was it. The priest would not accept that it was because of any supernatural cause. He had it in his mind it was anything but. Junkies.

After a few moments. Hayim took a deep breath in. He began to actually notice every decaying bit of furniture here. Every peeling bit of wallpaper on each of the bar's yellowing walls. This coupled with a constant stench of piss and booze in the air. A stench that almost colored the very oxygen they breathed. He had not noticed any of this up until this point. He knew it was not a high-class joint, but he suddenly felt a bit dirty just sitting in here.

"What happened to this place?" Hayim mumbled as he turned back to Father Dyer. "I know it's been a while since we last came here... But it used to be nice, right? I swear it did."

"It's been over a decade," the priest smirked. "And trust me, I remember it very well. It's *always* been a shit hole. Just like the rest of this town. A shit hole filled with shit people wanting to steal shit that isn't theirs. Only difference is that there's just more drugs and guns nowadays, that's all." He gestured around the room with his hand, "And this place? The only change here is that time hasn't been kind. Same thing happened to us. We ain't wallflowers anymore either. We're crumbling too."

"You tell your congregation all this upbeat shit?" Hayim joked. "Their home's always been filled with shit and with shit people?"

Father Dyer shrugged. "My congregation? All three of them?" He smiled as he shook his head. "They're probably too drunk to notice."

Hayim laughed heartily. Though he knew this was Father Dyer's self depreciation, it was also sadly too close to the truth. Underneath their joviality both had a mutual well of sadness concerning the state of their city. A city that was slowly decaying physically and morally. They didn't only know it, they *felt* it, more and more with each passing day; waiting for and constantly expecting that moment when it would all finally crumble into itself, leaving nothing but rubble and blood.

"Seriously," Hayim said, as his smile faltered. "This place hasn't got much left on its clock. I gotta keep a gun under the counter at the shop now. Just in case. 'Cause aside from those *After Dark* pricks. I gotta be worried about garden variety gun totin' weirdos that seem to have multiplied here… Junkie scum the lot of 'em."

"I told you before, I'll tell you again," Dyer replied, taking the last swig of his drink. "You gotta get out of here. Or you're gonna end up shooting someone or getting shot, or end up like Davis."

"And do what?" Hayim said. "Go where? With who? I got nothing to go to."

After a pause, the Priest acquiesced. "I don't know. I'm just saying what I would do. Beyond that, I'm afraid I don't have much." Without waiting for a reply, the priest then stood up. "Well, that's me. I gotta sleep or I'll pass out. You gonna be okay?"

"Aren't I always?" Hayim murmured as he also stood up. Motioning to Father Dyer's non-holy pinstripe suit, he then looked worried. "You're not gonna walk home dressed in that getup, are ya? You should get a taxi."

"What's wrong with this?" the priest glanced down at his suit.

"Aw, don't play dumb." Hayim replied, annoyed. "You might not wanna admit the shit we saw, or how fucked up this place *really* is with all the monsters, but you're safer walkin' in your God-getup. Not just from what got Davis, but from the gangs, too. No one fucks with a holy man. *No one.* You really should call a taxi, okay? Be safe, not stupid."

"You're being paranoid, Hayim!"

The next morning, on the *one* day Hayim decided to open the Coffee Shop later than usual, a loud banging at the door stirred him from his hungover slumber.

Staggering out of bed, he opened the door in a groggy state, and was soon faced with the mournful expressions upon two police officers.

They were there to inform him that his friend—Father Jonathan Dyer—had been found dead in the early hours of that morning. They knew both he and the Priest had been drinking that night, and wanted to know if anything had happened that could be considered out of the ordinary.

"I can assure you, Mr Kominowski, you're not a suspect." One of the officers had spoken softly. "This was clearly an unfortunate animal attack, we just need to have a clear picture of his journey.

They believed a stray dog or some other wild beast had happened upon the priest as he walked home in the dark.

But, Hayim *knew* they were wrong. He *knew* what had happened. Every fibre of his being screamed quietly that the monsters got him. The police would not want to hear his opinion though. There was *nothing* he could do about it.

The police then requested that Hayim formally identify the body, as he was the closest to next of kin that they could find.

It was the last thing he wanted to do. But he knew he had to.

When he arrived at the morgue, though, there was very little for him to recognize. Father Dyer's body had been ripped into pieces. There was nothing but tiny shreds of gore, all held within in an expensive pinstripe suit.

AJ sat at a table in the coffee shop, looking out of the window, up at the night sky stretching high above the buildings.

"I mean," he said, mid-conversation, "it's dark *now*, right? Or am I taking this all too literally?"

"No idea... It's dark, but is it *after* dark?" Keith posited sarcastically. "How long is dark to be around before it has passed? Then again, isn't after dark actually morning? Sunrise?"

"I guess?" AJ replied, ignoring Keith's tone. "But it's definitely dark now, that's for sure."

"But it could have *just* turned dark." Keith said, the sarcasm still front and centre. "And that guy clearly said *after* dark, so…"

AJ smiled, though he felt some frustration. "How are we supposed to know the exact moment it's dark? If we knew that, then we could just wait for a few seconds, then *bam-presto* it'd be *after* dark."

"First journeypath, now bam-presto?" Keith snickered, "You becoming a Vegas magician?"

AJ didn't reply, he just sipped from his cup his coffee and continued to look outside.

"Seriously though," Keith continued as he dropped his jocular tone. "Why the hell are we even bothering? No way we can make it back in time now. Let's just cut our losses and get back to campus. Not like it's our fault. The strip joint doesn't help matters by not having actual opening times."

AJ sighed. "We came this far, Keith. We shouldn't give up now. Even if it's just for the experience of going in and getting rejected, we gotta see it through."

From the other side of the shop, Hayim Kominowski stared anxiously at his customers. It was *that* time of night again, the time of night he didn't like one single bit.

Hayim gulped and turned to the clock on the wall. It read 7:34pm. "Hurry it up over there," he shouted over to AJ and Keith, "Closing time was four minutes ago!"

AJ nodded to the old man, then turned his glance to the door marked *Toilets*. "Duncan," he loudly called out. "Finish shakin' it and get out here. They wanna close up."

From the other side of the toilet door, Duncan shouted back, "I'm going as fast as I can! You can't rush a masterpiece!"

Not wanting to wait around for them to finish, Hayim buttoned up the top of his shirt as he rushed over to the coat-stand by the door. Grabbing his coat from a hook, he threw it on hastily. From the coat pocket he produced a costume clerical priest's collar, then attached it around his neck.

As he watched his customers still sipping their coffees, he pulled out a large golden crucifix on a thick chain from the coat-stand, and quickly slipped over his head.

For the last five years—ever since his only friend's murders—Hayim performed this same exit ritual every single night he had to lock up. In the summertime, it was easy, as closing time was in bright daylight, but when fall turned to winter, he knew he had to make sure he was locked up safely before the streets became a much more dangerous place. There was at least an hour of the sky turning dark where he could get home safely, as the bad elements in this town usually waited a while before they emerged to wreak havoc.

Tonight, though, the clock was ticking fast. Hayim had foolishly put a few extra dollars ahead of his own safety, and let these late customers into the shop when he really should have called it a night and hurried home.

As he regarded the encroaching shadows out of the window, his nerves got the better of him and he felt sweat break out over his face. Almost in a panic, he flipped the door's sign over to read *closed*, but, before he could feel any sense of progress, the door was suddenly thrown open toward him—pushing him backwards against the wall.

A black leather biker boot stepped in from the evening.

"Please," Hayim squeaked, "We're closed. We gotta close."

"You just opened again," snarled the imposing figure who now stood before him. This figure, dressed in a long black trench coat, stared with the coldest eyes. His long, straight, white hair framed a pale, angular and kind of otherworldly face. Hayim knew this man by the name Snow.

Behind Snow, two women followed, both dressed in matching leather jackets. Emblazoned on the backs of each, was a single word: *DRAGONS*.

"Snow, please," Hayim said, as he looked more and more anxious. "I gotta get home. You get why."

Hayim knew the *Dragons* well. They were the gang that ruled the streets in the daytime, and it was Snow who was their leader. They frequented his coffee shop often, and Hayim had enjoyed a mutual co-existence with them, yet he also knew that nothing was equal here. If they wanted him gone, he *would* be gone. So, he had no choice but to play nice and kowtow to all their wishes.

"Every night, we see you, *Coffee man*," Snow snarled with a smirk, his voice low and mean. "We see you dressed like a man of that Abrahamic God, scurrying back to your bed like a scared child."

"Y-you know. I have to..." Hayim stuttered.

"Besides, aren't you Jewish?" Maven—the more vicious of the two women—asked with a wicked grin.

Hayim gulped. He knew better than to contradict or argue with these people.

Maven continued with a chuckle, "I thought so."

From the other side of the coffee shop, Keith stared silently, toward Maven in particular. He was entranced by her beauty. Her complexion was a polar opposite to the leader;

Her hair and skin were onyx black. Her eyes, hypnotically dark.

"Coffee man," Snow hissed, "I'll do you this favor. We won't stay long, so you can run on back to your bed soon. Okay?"

Hayim felt a pang of relief. "Thank you… What can I get you?"

"Coffee." Snow ordered. "Six… To go…"

Glancing around the shop, Maven caught sight of Keith's gaze and smiled a closed lipped smile toward him. He, in turn, couldn't help but return the gesture, blushing as he did so.

Noticing them, AJ hurriedly whispered, "Don't be stupid, Keith. Mind your own business."

Maven winked to Keith playfully, her dark eyed stare not leaving him.

Ignoring AJ's words, Keith winked in reply. Then, playfully, winked with his other eye.

"I'm not fucking kidding here," AJ uttered, his voice getting slightly louder. "You're just asking for trouble if you engage with them."

Seductively, Maven pulled a stick of lip gloss from her pocket, then coated her pouting red lips with it, not once breaking her stare with Keith.

The other woman in the Dragon jacket, Dolly—with her blond hair tied back in a tight ponytail— noticed Maven's flirtation with Keith, but quickly dismissed it. Her only interest was getting a coffee, not caring if Maven toyed with a man. Turning back to Hayim, she leaned across the counter. "Hurry!" She said sternly, as he fumbled with a stack of disposable coffee cups. Her overly made-up face could not mask the look of agitation she felt here. Agitation as she *needed* that coffee. She was a junkie for the caffeine, and didn't care that she was. "Faster, old man," she commanded Hayim.

Snow raised his hand to calm Dolly's obvious rising irritation at waiting for her dark liquid fix.

Acquiescing obediently, Dolly did not question or comment about Snow's silent command. She knew better. She would wait silently, and keep her mouth shut.

Keith, meanwhile, grinned more and more toward Maven. He could not believe that this *beautiful* woman was paying him any attention at all—let alone flirting with him that much. He took a sip of his coffee then raised his hand to nervously wave at her.

AJ felt ignored as he could only witness his friends actions. He shook his head in disbelief. He knew the dangerous waters Keith was swimming in all too well. It was a place he had found himself in before.

Maven's smile gradually spread wider, showing her teeth… Or lack thereof. As toothless as a smile could be, she only three remaining pegs sat within her gummy maw.

Stunned, Keith spat his coffee out onto the table in front of him, narrowly avoiding AJ.

"Damnit,!" AJ reacted loudly, as he frantically wiped the coffee spots from dripping off the table in front of him, ensuring they didn't get onto his clothes.

As Keith broke off all eye contact with Maven, he turned at AJ wide-eyed and in shock. "I fucked up didn't I," he whispered.

"You think so?" AJ rolled his eyes. "You should have listened to me."

Maven, visibly angered by Keith's reaction, turned to her leader. "Snow," she said in a fury. "That boy mocked me!"

Keith swallowed hard. He had heard Maven address the pale man, then watched helplessly from the corner of his eyes as they walked slowly across the shop toward him. "AJ," He pleaded to AJ. "Save me."

"You're on your own, kid," AJ replied as he wiped the last

spots of coffee from off of the table. "I warned ya, now you can make your own way out of it."

Snow took his time walking over to their table. He found it amusing to watch the man who offended Maven look more and more uncomfortable the closer he got.

"See somethin' funny?" Snow snarled as he leaned down over the table, glaring icily at Keith.

"AJ," Keith whimpered to his friend. "Please?"

AJ just sat quietly opposite, intentionally ignoring what was happening, staring out of the window and into the night sky.

Keith's expression switched from worry to annoyance as he muttered under his breath, "If I live through this... I'm gonna be really pissed at you."

Before more could be said, Snow produced a switchblade from out of his pocket, snapped the blade open, then grabbed Keith by the chin, turning it slowly toward him to meet his gaze.

"It's rude to not answer a question, or even look at the person addressing you" Snow said, with an overtly threatening tone in his voice, "Your momma not teach you right, boy?"

As Keith went to reply, Snow's grip on his chin tightened, silencing him immediately.

"I should let young Maven here…" Snow said as his smile grew wider, "...cut off your balls"

On cue, Maven produced her very own switchblade, then stepped closer to the table. Her smile now long gone as her toothless mouth held only a grimace for Keith.

AJ tried his best to remain looking outside. Hoping Keith would just apologize to them and learn from his mistake.

Dolly, still standing at the counter, shook her head as she reluctantly pulled out her own switchblade. She was visibly annoyed at what was happening. She wanted her coffee. She glanced back toward Hayim, and noticed that he was staring at them too, instead of making their drinks. She waved her knife in front of Hayim's gaze, then pointed to the coffee cups.

Hayim prayed for this to end as he rushed back to make the order. If they didn't go very soon, he would have no other choice than to sleep on the stockroom floor again. Something he hated to do. But he could not walk these streets in the dead of night. The streets with a strong emphasis on *dead*.

As if on cue, the door to the toilet swung open and Duncan strutted in, totally oblivious to what was happening within the shop.

Duncan's mind raced as he halted suddenly, surveying the scene; the strange man holding a knife to Keith. The two women in matching jackets. The petrified owner looking almost in a tearful panic. The annoyed looking AJ.

Glancing over his shoulder, catching Duncan's wide eyed-gaze, Snow snarled at him like a wolf.

"Uhhh...." Duncan scrambled for words before turning to Hayim. "Hey... Uhhh... Louie... It looks like I'll be another hour or so on these toilets." He nervously chuckled. "Those pipes are *tough*. So... If you'll excuse me..." he turned and strode back through the swinging toilet door "I'll get back to work," he called out as he retreated.

Snow stopped growling and turned his gaze to Hayim, breaking character for a second "He thinks your name's *Louie?*"

Hayim just shook his head, not wanting any part of this. He just finished pouring the last cup of coffee as fast as he could, then placed it up on the countertop next to the five other plastic cups.

From inside the toilet, Duncan's voice began talking loudly, badly acting out a scenario. "I wish you S.W.A.T guys wouldn't clean your automatic weapons in the bathroom! I'm trying to work here, damnit."

AJ slowly turned his stare from the outside, across the table, past Snow and Keith toward the closed toilet.

"Tell me the truth, Keith," AJ said, still staring at the toilet.. "Was it his yacht jacket, or the fact he said a S.W.A.T. team was in there, that gave the game away?"

Keith shrugged as much as he could within Snow's grasp.

Another creak of the door caused everyone to turn back toward the toilet again. They clearly saw Duncan peer out through the crack, before disappearing back again, checking to see if his ridiculous ruse worked.

"Snow.. .Let me have him," Maven said, pointing to Keith, not letting Duncan's interruption change the situation. "He is mine."

Nodding, Snow released Keith's chin, stood back, folded his switchblade away, and stepped aside for Maven. She walked by cockily, then slid down into the seat next to Keith, forcing him to move closer to the window.

AJ turned to look at Keith, shrugged, then turned back to stare out of the window—much to Keith's dismay.

"You're not gonna help at all?" Keith blurted in surprise at AJ's lack of assistance. "Please, can you—"

Maven moved her switchblade up Keith's shirt, blade first, causing him to quickly cease his protest.

With a low chuckle, Snow watched as Maven cut Keith's top shirt button off, forcing his chest to become a fraction more exposed. Much to her obvious delight.

"Okay, fine," AJ sighed, still focusing out of the window. "I'll help you. But only because I'm such a nice guy."

Maven turned her attention to AJ, unamused at him talking when this time was hers.

Snow looked at Dolly, who was still at the counter drinking her coffee. He glared, unimpressed at her for not standing with them.

"Keith," AJ continued. "My friend you are threatening so

beautifully... Well he, he is on what I loving refer to as a journeypath."

Keith's eyes did not move from Maven's blade, that still hovered threateningly in front of his chest. "Journeypath? Really? Now?" he whimpered to AJ.

"Yeah... And now... It's definitely after dark *now*..." AJ then turned back to face the gang, smiling up at its leader. "Snow, is it?" he asked. But before any answer could come, he carried on regardless, "Snow, my good man. C'mon. Really, buddy?" he gestured to Keith "All this... and for what?" He turned his gesture now at Maven. "All this for three lousy teeth?"

"Who spoke to you?" Snow suddenly erupted into a terrifying rage as he slapped AJ's half full coffee cup out of his hand, spilling everywhere.

"Uh oh..." Keith said softly as he saw where the coffee had hit—All over AJ's designer shirt. These were not harmless drops either. None of the spill could be mopped up with ease. The cup of brown liquid had covered his front, soaking in deep through the expensive fabric.

AJ, keeping his cool, slowly turned his gaze up to Snow and he gave *that* smile. The charming smile Keith knew, but in *this* situation, it meant something completely different. This was not charm.

Within a split second, AJ grabbed Duncan's abandoned coffee and threw it into Maven's face.

In a flash, Snow's switchblade was out again. He lunged at AJ's chest—blade first—headed straight for his heart. But the blade's seemingly inevitable path stopped to a grinding halt a few inches from its target, as AJ's hand reached out and grasped Snow's crotch in a sudden vice-like grip.

Snow's eyes immediately widened in pain as he gritted his teeth, struggling to hold his focus. The knife in his hand shook as he tried to overcome this intense torture.

Maven, without even wiping the coffee from her face, grabbed Keith and held her knife up to his throat.

"Drop the blade, Snowflake," AJ spoke calmly as he nodded his head toward Maven. "Her too..." Without even waiting for a reply, he gripped harder. Snow groaned louder in agony.

Dolly, still standing at the counter, was still sipping her coffee, staring at this situation quite bored.

"C'mon, man," AJ said in his most jovial tone. "Or you'll be picking up your junk from off of the floor."

Snow dropped his switchblade onto the table obediently. Maven begrudgingly followed with hers, then wiped the rest of the coffee from her face.

Standing up with hand still squeezing Snow's crotch, AJ slowly moved the gang leader back to the counter on the far side of the shop, beside Dolly and the coffee cups.

Keith quickly grabbed the switchblades from off the table and turned to Maven. "I'm sorry, I didn't mean to..." he muttered meekly as he shrugged. "I really am. I hope you can forgive me."

She stared blankly back at him with boiling hatred in her eyes, as she reluctantly stood up and let him out from the table.

"Duncan?" AJ shouted toward the toilets, not breaking eye contact with Snow. "If you're finished with that S.W.A.T. team, it's time to go!"

Immediately, the toilet door began to slowly open, with Duncan peeking out cautiously. Assessing this new situation, his slow movement suddenly turned into a confident strut into the middle of the shop. "Luckily they didn't try to come into the bathroom." He said loudly and cockily, "I was ready in there... I was holding back, cos I didn't wanna hurt anyone. The things I would've done to them... My martial arts training would have left them in a *mess*... Just thinking about what I would have done…" He faked a mock shudder in self-response.

Before he could speak any more, Keith grabbed him by the shoulder and pulled him out toward the door, into the awaiting street.

AJ, smiling once again, pulled out a five-dollar bill from his pocket with his free hand. Placing it onto the counter—while not letting his grip on Snow weaken—he nodded to Hayim. "Thank you, kind sir, you have a wonderful establishment." He then nodded in Snow's direction. "Apologies for any inconvenience."

With one final hard squeeze, AJ sent Snow falling to the floor in agony, letting his grip go as he did.

When one would expect a sensible person to run away, AJ did not. Instead, he casually walked over to the napkins, took one out, then dabbed it into the jug of water from on the counter. Dolly regarded him, amused at his confidence. He smiled flirtatiously at her as he dabbed the damp napkin onto his coffee stained shirt. Dolly couldn't help but return the smile, then took a sip of her coffee, her switchblade still absent-mindedly in her other hand.

Turning, AJ then walked calmly out of the shop, speaking loudly as he left, "Good thing I brought a spare shirt, or I'd have never let you go."

As the door shut, Maven ran over to Snow worried. He was still in a heap on the floor, wheezing as he gasped for air.

"Why didn't you step up?" Maven snarled at Dolly.

Dolly just smiled innocently back, "Wasn't me he offended." She sipped her coffee again.

Hayim, meanwhile, took off the priest's collar and crucifix, then placed them on the preparation counter next to him. *Sleeping in the stock room it is*, he thought to himself, as he sighed deflated.

· · ·

Further down the street, as Keith hurriedly threw the two confiscated switchblades down an open storm drain, Duncan grinned happily to himself. "That was frickin' *great*," he said.

Keith noticed AJ catching up with them in a semi-sprint, still dabbing the napkin onto his coffee-stained shirt.

"I'm sorry," Keith called out sincerely, looking sheepishly at AJ.

"Hey, it's ok," AJ replied. "Not your fault. Wait no… It *is* your fault. But…" He motioned around them. "This is a big city, where ya get much bigger assholes than we are used to. Next time, don't engage. Ever."

"Can't believe they messed with *my buddies*." Duncan said, as he ran up to walk by AJ's side. "*Wham!*" he shouted as he held his balled fist in front of them. "Right in the tchotchkes! You really are the best friend to have!"

With a slightly exasperated expression, AJ turned his gaze at Keith and shook his head. No words needed to be said. They were both tired of Duncan constantly… being Duncan.

As they reached the Cadillac, as AJ unlocked the doors, for the first time that night he actually *wanted* to drive straight home to their dorm. Yet he also knew that he would never forgive himself if he didn't continue on with this mission, even though it was doomed to fail from the outset.

Even if they *did* get a stripper to agree to perform for the fraternity, they would still never get them back in time for the party itself.

AJ, though, was not a man to readily admit defeat, even in the face of adversity and improbability. He knew that even if he got a stripper to the frat house by late the next morning, while the frat brothers were all hungover, they would *still* love it. And they would *still* welcome him and Keith into their brotherhood.

"One guy? Two girls? Little bitty knives?" Duncan continued in his *Duncan*-ness. "Who are they anyway?

Nobody that's who. Thinking they can take on the three of us? *US.*"

As he watched Keith get into the passenger side, before getting in the car, he turned to AJ, "Hey, why are we even leaving *now*? It should have been them running off with their tails tucked between their legs! Not us! We should go back there!"

AJ took a breath, and replied calmly as he put a hand on Duncan's shoulder "Dunc... They ordered *six* coffees, not three. You get what that means, right? They are not alone…"

Keith looked out of the window at Duncan and smiled as he witnessed the boy's bravado suddenly dissipate. As the realization of what AJ just hinted at was over him like a tsunami.

CHAPTER 5
OPENING TIME

The neon sign of the After Dark Club flickered in the distance as AJ stood in front of the now open Cadillac trunk. Putting on a grey blazer, he also had put on a fresh designer shirt—The coffee-stained one now sitting damply in the trunk.

Keith and Duncan meanwhile, were by the hood of the car, looking down the darkened street toward the club. The sense of foreboding in this dark street was palpable. One that Keith felt all too keenly. Duncan on the other hand just smiled at what awaited them.

The street lights between them and the club seemed to either be broken, or incessantly flickering—A sure sign that the city officials had given up on repairing anything in this part of town. Not to mention the multiple cracks and potholes along the streets' aging asphalt, and the state of dilapidation the buildings found themselves in. Each reaching up high above them like forgotten tombs.

AJ slammed the trunk shut, then walked around to the front of the car and without any hesitation, toward the club. He motioned Keith and Duncan to follow him as he passed by.

With a hint of anxiety, Keith glanced around at the various shadows lining the street as they slowly drew nearer to the club. Though he would never say it to anyone, that meeting with Snow and Maven shook him to his core. He was certain that the switchblade was going to end up in his neck, causing all of his blood to spill out across that cheap plastic table. That cheap plastic table in that cheap plastic coffee shop. Helpless to stop his demise in a place so desperate.

AJ strode toward the club with a look of determination. He did not spare a second thought for Snow nor his cronies. Why should he? *They were bullies*, he thought. *And bullies got what was coming to them.* Though—of course—Keith provoked them. But he could never blame his friend officially. Only to his face. If anyone else ever asked, they started it. They initiated the provocation.

"I'm in the mood for loooovve," Duncan sang loudly, as he danced around besides AJ and Keith. *"Simply because you're nakeeed."* He stared at the club's entrance with continual wide-eyed enchantment.

"Rein it in," AJ interrupted not even turning to Duncan. "You wanna play hard to get, not just hand them your wallet and get your dick out at the front door."

Without listening to the advice, Duncan turned with an ecstatic grin and replied "Guys, I'm gonna be a *legend* tonight. You watch me, I attract women like flies!"

With AJ not reacting, and not even acknowledging what was said, Duncan turned to Keith, trying to attain some approval.

Keith, though, *did* react. He nodded with a fake grin to Duncan, and followed that up by giving him an enthusiastic thumbs-up. A sarcastic thumbs-up that Duncan read as sincere.

"Don't encourage him," AJ said to Keith, not caring if Duncan heard. "He's a walking liability."

Realizing this could be a mistake, AJ stopped in his tracks, causing the others to do so as well. He turned and tossed Keith the car keys. "I'll be quick," he said.

Catching them with one hand, Keith nodded in thanks, understanding instinctively what the plan had changed to become.

Confidently, AJ continued his stride down toward the glow of the club's open door. He didn't look back as Keith grabbed Duncan by the arm, stopping him from following.

"Whoa, what are you doing?" Duncan said in surprise.

"AJ's got this," Keith said as he patted Duncan on the shoulder. "We gotta wait in the car, he won't be long. Trust him, okay? It's for the best."

"Wait a minute, my friend," Duncan protested politely. "That's not fair." He looked back in the club's direction as he continued to speak. "We came all this way in *my* car, and what? I don't even get to *watch*?" He looked back toward Keith. "I think I should have a say in the selection at least!"

"I doubt we'll even find anyone to come with us," Keith tried to console. "But if we *do*, by some miracle, get a woman to agree… You can interview her in the car all you want for the whole ride home. That'd be good, right?"

"Uh huh, that's not what's going to happen here, buddy." Duncan broke free of Keith's hand and hurried after AJ, leaving Keith grimacing. "One for all and all inside!" Duncan exclaimed as he walked away, exuding his standard delusional confidence.

"Please don't go in!" Keith pleaded after him.

Without slowing down, Duncan glanced back over his shoulder and said loudly with a cocky grin, "They ordered *Six* coffees, remember? You wanna stay out here waiting to see who the other three are?"

Keith's expression then fell flat. He had briefly forgotten about Snow et al. So now, there was nothing anyone could do to make him wait out in the car on his own. Not tonight. Not on these streets.

. . .

Walking down the narrow, velvet lined corridor, AJ led their way deeper into the club's bowels.

"I'm sorry," Keith called out to AJ from the rear. "I tried to stop him!"

"It's cool," AJ called back as he slowed and turned on the spot, halting Duncan's overexcitable march behind him, Keith closely behind. "Hey, Duncan. If you go in, you *gotta* promise me one thing, okay?"

Duncan, slightly distracted by the sights and smells of where they were, took a few seconds before looking at AJ, then said in confusion, "Huh?"

"Buddy, you gotta play it cool in here. Capeesh?" AJ spoke as kindly as he could.

"Buddy? *You* called *me* buddy," Duncan smiled. "Of course. Buddy, whatever you say! Cool as a cucumber! Cool as a Cadillac!"

AJ nodded, though barely convinced. He then turned back to continue leading their journey inward, but as he did, he found his path blocked by a large figure.

The imposing bulk that stood in their way, was that of an obese, pale man dressed in a crumpled, stained white suit. On each of his fingers he wore large golden sovereign rings. Around his open-shirted neck hung a large gold medallion of Saint Jude.

He ran a large sweaty hand over his balding pasty pate. His remaining hair, white and slicked backward, was thinning so much that his liver spotted head could clearly be seen beneath. He did not look like a well man.

"Boys," the man said in a gruff, low voice. "Good evening, and welcome to the After Dark Club."

AJ and Duncan smiled politely in return, but Keith was too busy staring at the many beads of sweat that dripped down this man's blotchy skin, and soaked into the stained collar of his suit jacket.

"I am the Maître D of this fine establishment," the man continued, "You can call me Vic."

"Pleasure to meet you, Vic," AJ said with a polite nod. "Could we-"

Enthusiastically, Duncan interrupted, "My name's Duncan, and I *looooove* women!"

Vic smiled at this almost child-like outburst. "Of course you do, but before I let you in, I really gotta see some IDs. You're all over twenty-one I take it? I mean we run a classy establishment here. Gotta obey the law, after all, don't we?"

Out of all of them, Keith was the one who had the most unconvincing poker face. He just looked shocked at the Maître D, whereas Duncan and AJ both smiled, unfazed by the request.

"You see-" AJ started to explain before being interrupted yet again by Duncan, who quickly produced his wallet and fumbled with its contents.

"Twenty-one?" Duncan cut in with his overly confident smirk, "Of course. I have my ID right here."

Before he could produce the no doubt overpriced yet still badly made fake ID, Vic spotted the wealth of credit cards and cash crammed in Duncan's wallet.

Grabbing the wallet, Vic took a closer look at its contents, then quickly took out a hundred dollar bill. Sliding it casually into his jacket pocket, he handed the wallet back to Duncan. "Perfect, gentlemen. Your IDs check out just fine."

He turned and led their way, further down the corridor, up to an opening between two large red velvet curtains. Standing in this opening, blocking their way, was a tall bouncer dressed in a black suit. His long thin face like granite.

"This dour looking gentlemen you see before you is Vlad," Vic said as he motioned to the the bouncer, "he's here to make sure you're all safe, and that no one does anything stupid. But don't be fooled, he could pull your arms off without breaking a sweat if he wanted to."

Vlad grunted as he stood aside, clearing their path into the neon lit *After Dark Club.*

"We'll get only the classiest acts!" Victor Manciamo decreed as he ecstatically shook hands with Mark 'Squeak' Coombs.

"Frankie, Sammy and Deano all the way, baby," Squeak exclaimed in return.

Both men, barely over twenty years of age, now stood proudly as business owners in front of the old wool mill on Linconfirm Parkway. Dressed in matching stylish white suits, they also wore matching sovereign rings with matching golden crucifixes around their necks. They may have been peas in a pod in style, but they were obviously from different fields in terms of looks and stature. Vic was over six feet tall, well built, with perfect eyesight and a chiseled jaw-line—a perfect quarterback. Whereas Squeak was none of these things. Over eight inches shorter, he was more skinny than lean, with large black horn-rimmed glasses and would be too bookish-looking to be considered sporty.

"We did it, my good friend." Vic said as he thrust his arm around Squeak and dragged him into a brotherly embrace. "I *told* you we'd do it. You and me!"

"It's happening." Squeak squeaked with joy, "It's really, really happening!"

With one arm still around his friend's shoulder, Vic pointed down the street ahead and grinned wildly. "This whole place is gonna boom soon. There's gonna be classy restaurants, classy art galleries, a picture house or two. It's gonna be..."

"Classy?" Squeak proffered.

Vic nodded enthusiastically. "Yeah. 1954 baby, it's the year that puts Manciamo and Coombs on the map, and it'll also change the city—*our* city—to be on its way to being better than Vegas."

"But we *are* still going to Vegas, right?" Squeak asked, sounding unsure.

Running his hand over his thick, black, slicked-back hair, Vic looked at Squeak, smiled and then winked. "It's all the plan, baby."

"Aw, thank the baby Jesus," Squeak said as he quickly lifted the gold crucifix from around his neck and kissed it, "thought you changed your mind for a minute."

"It's *all* as we planned, nothin's gonna stop us," Vic said. "54, open the doors. 55, the club thrives. 56-"

"Drown in chicks!" Squeak interrupted.

Vic smiled as he continued, "57, open our second club in heaven."

"Vegas baaaby" Squeak chimed in.

"58, we'll be heavyweights! 59…" Vic then paused, "Uhhh." He shrugged with a smile, "I ain't planned *that* far."

Squeak joked, "59, Open an airline?"

"Who knows, my friend?" Vic looked back to the old wool mill building. "Who indeed knows?"

With matching glassy, dream filled eyes, they both looked up at the abandoned building which they were now the proud owners of. They stared, both excited for their futures together.

"So, you sure you're happy with the name, the After Dark Club?" Vic asked, knowing what Squeak's answer would be.

"Damn skippy, Vic. It's so..." Squeak searched for the right word, then smiled even more than he had been.

"Classy?" Vic prompted.

"Yeah." Squeak was almost close to tears with happiness. "Classy!"

He and Vic had *made* it.

They had *finally* got their club.

"Frankie, Sammy and Deano, all the way, baby," Vic reiterated their mantra.

"Frankie, Sammy and Deano, all the way, baby" Squeak repeated.

As they stared in awe at their brick building, both Vic and Squeak pictured how it would look when finished. Large neon lights. An enormous billboard on top, adorned with the faces of the stars that would play there.

Neither of them noticed when the black limo pulled up on the street behind him. It was only when the door to that limo opened wide that they turned around, alerted by the voice inside.

"Gentlemen," a man said as he spoke from the darkness of the limo's back seat. "I have a proposition for you."

With the power of hindsight, Vic would have turned and walked away, dragging Squeak along with him. He would never have gotten into that limo. He would never have made a deal that neither of them could escape. He would have saved his soul if he had known what awaited them.

Over the years since 1954, Linconfirm Parkway did indeed change as Vic predicted, but instead of bringing in the cool and the wealthy—as young Vic had once hoped—it brought the desperate and the violent. Many people tried, as Vic and Squeak had, to gentrify this part of town, each attempting to alter the spiral of moral and physical decay this city was on; Over the years, new shops occasionally sprouted up amidst the dirt—trying to change the inevitable tide—But they disappeared just as fast. Of Vic and Squeaks dreams, only a few survived. A pawn shop that sold goods stolen by junkies. A coffee shop that served the waifs, strays, and violent alike. Of course, the church continued to preach its redemption to any who listened—but that was nothing but words of comfort. Even the After Dark Club, a place of intended classy joy, remained throughout the years. But that club was not at all what Vic and Squeak had hoped it would be.

The decor of the club was a decayed 1950s fever dream. Red velvet and gold metal littered the view in almost shocking quantities. The many tables surrounding the runway of the stage were each made of glass with gold metal edging. These may have been high class once—but now, with their metal tarnished and their dulled and cracked, they just looked perpetually cheap. The carpet fared no better; From the years of badly cleaned up spillages, it was perpetually sticky underfoot, no matter how hard anyone would try to clean it. The walls too, a mix of dusty velvet curtains that masked featureless damp walls behind, as well as large framed pictures of big band celebrities and actors from yesteryear, ones that patrons presumed once came here, though none of them ever did.

At the left of the entrance, a long curved bar snaked its way down to the end of the large room. Two female barmaids stood behind its long glass and golden metal bulk, as they busily prepared various drink orders for the dozens of men who were sat around the club—each and every one of them waiting impatiently for the next show. Waiting for their next titillation.

All of the staff were female, and each wore a uniform that consisted of hot pants and a crop top. This uniform appeared quite conservative compared to the performers that also stalked the club's main room, each wore a variety of revealing costumes, teasing their customers as they passed with a show of flesh and a wandering hand.

On the stage itself, one performance had just finished. A

young, fresh faced woman in her late teens was dressed in a bikini. She busied herself as she scooped up her discarded clothes, as well as the single dollar bills that lay strewn on the floor—tips from the hungry hoard that gawked at her show. She quickly slipped back on a pair of shorts and a halter top over the bikini then gave a happy smile to her lascivious audience, who did not seem that interested in her anymore. Not since her titillating stopped.

"Give it up for our newest bit of sweetness, Amaretto!" said the leering voice of a DJ over the speaker system. His voice cutting in over the fading music. "And don't worry, next time, we will make sure she shows a lot more skin! Now stay around for more hot action from our many other buxom beauties. Each here for you. To make you feel hot under the collar, not to mention hard in the pants."

At the other side of the stage, a row of heavily shadowed booths lined the wall. From within each of them, dull table lamps glowed, revealing little of the moving bodies within.

On the far side, at the farthest area from the stage, two tattered pool tables added the finishing touches to the layout of the club.

"Bar, table or booth?" Vic asked with his cheshire cat grin, motioning with his arm around the club in front of them.

AJ smiled and walked over to the bar as Keith replied. "Table… Please-"

"A ringside one!" Duncan interrupted in his usual enthusiastic fashion, as he held up a ten-dollar bill to Vic.

Taking this money with a nod, Vic led the way toward a vacant table at the side of the stage's runway. Duncan pushed excitedly past Keith to be first to their seats.

As he followed, Keith looked to the bar, and whistled a short, sharp whistle to AJ.

Immediately recognizing it as his friend calling, AJ turned and saw Keith shrugging, then motioning toward Duncan racing to the table. AJ winced comedically, dreading what their new friend would do if a stripper danced too close to him. What trouble he might get them into.

Walking off the stage from her performance, Amaretto spotted Keith. Her eyes lit up as soon as she spotted him. A genuine and happy smile crept over her face, but soon dropped as she felt a sweaty hand grab her ass, then thrust a dollar bill into her waistband.

Glancing down, she nodded in false appreciation to the perverse old man, who leered back at her like she was a cooked steak, all while rubbing his crotch at her suggestively.

Now at their table, Keith mulled over what to do. He knew he should look after Duncan—who was obviously in danger of bankrupting himself in a place like this—but he just wanted to leave and get home soon. He always disliked the thought of these places, and now that he had come to his first strip club, he disliked them even more. The place made him feel like he needed a shower as soon as he entered its neon-lit doors.

Turning back to the bar again, Keith's view of AJ was suddenly blocked by Amaretto. She stood a few tables away, semi-waving in his direction. Her friendly gesture soon dissolved as Keith looked back toward the stage, wanting to avoid engaging with anyone.

Don't look, he thought to himself. *Just don't look, they just want your cash. They don't like you. They don't know you. They just want to fool you.*

Picking up a bar tray in her hand, Amaretto moved closer as she stared at Keith, her smile waning.

"Please welcome to the stage!" The DJ's voice cut in over the music, his voice laced with a tinge of perversion. "Hard Hatted Hannah!"

On cue, the lights sprang to life as the music blared out. A dark-skinned woman dressed in a hard hat, wearing a tool belt and not much else, strode out onto the stage to perform. This was less of a strip show and more of a display of her body—inside and out— one that the audience watching greatly appreciated. This show was in stark contrast to Amaretto's dance, one which had finished with her still wearing a bikini bra and panties.

Vic sidled back up to Keith and Duncan's table. As he placed a napkin each in front of them, he smiled. "There's a basic six drink minimum and fifteen dollar entertainment charge... Per person."

Duncan nodded, fit to burst with excitement as he glared happily at the performance. Keith, though, just smiled weakly at Vic.

"Tipping is more than just a courtesy here," the large man continued. "It's expected." He then leaned in between them, speaking in a mock whisper, "Our ladies get *very* enthusiastic about tippers, *very* grateful. If you get what I mean?"

Duncan—whose smile should have been hurting him by now—stared up at Hannah's near-naked performance. As he did, she caught his stare then seductively winked and turned her gyrations toward him for a moment. He couldn't believe the attention he was getting, and blew her a kiss, blindly taking out a wad of cash from his wallet—much to Keith's dismay.

"This boy's got the idea!" Vic said as patted Duncan on the shoulder. "Have a glorious night boys, your waitress will be with you shortly." He then turned and walked to the bar, leaving Keith and Duncan to their own devices.

Keith tried his best to become invisible, as Duncan threw money and wolf whistled to Hard Hatted Hannah, who continued her seduction from the stage. As she licked her fingers and ran them down her navel—all while looking intently at Duncan—Keith could only look away. But as he did, his eyes immediately caught sight of Amaretto again, who was now walking straight toward him.

Suddenly feeling his stomach drop, Keith tried to turn his gaze anywhere else, but shot right back to her as a short man from a table of rowdy businessmen accosted her. As she had walked past, the man's hand shot out and cupped her groin on top of her shorts.

Before Amaretto could say anything, the short man grinned grotesquely, "It's a bet, see?" he slurred. "My friend here says you could only fit three fingers. But I know a full fist when I see it."

Amaretto rolled her eyes and pushed his hand off of her.

"So?" the short drunken man continued. "Whatta ya say. Let's go to a booth and give it a go, huh?"

"How about... Instead I just walk away, before I have no choice but to stomp on your junk?" Amaretto retorted. "Besides, you're not my type. I like guys with much, much bigger... Hands."

Her comment was met with a sudden explosion of loud, derisive laughter.

Keith was transfixed, staring at this situation unfolding, unable to look away, even as it ended and Amaretto turned to notice him. With her smile back on her face, she walked away from the short man's table, and stepped happily over to Keith. Bar tray locked firmly in her hand.

"You don't remember me, do you?" she chirped cheerfully.

Keith did not expect those words to come out of her. *This cute—damn cute—woman... Stripper... No wait, can you call them strippers? Dancers? Oh God, I'm sweating aren't I?* His thoughts raced as he felt more panicked.

Duncan though, his time with Hard Hatted Hannah now gone, stared up at Amaretto. "You don't remember me? Now that's a great first line, that. I gotta remember it," he said.

Keith, meanwhile, had no words that he could speak.

"I know it's been a *long* time," Amaretto continued, "but I sure as hellfire remember *you*."

Quickly putting down her bar tray onto their table, she produced a pair of glasses from out of the pocket of her shorts.

"Maybe these will jog your memory?" she said as she modeled the pink horn-rimmed glasses for him.

Before Keith could reply, though, the short drunk man appeared behind Amaretto. With a drink spilling about in his free hand, he yanked at the knot at the back of her halter top, undoing it instantly. In a flash, he has also undone the string of her bikini top. With these quick drunken movements, her clothing slipped down, exposing her breasts beneath.

In an instinctual, knee-jerk reaction, Keith whipped off his jacket, stood up and tossed it over Amaretto's nudity. But as soon as he did that, he immediately wondered why. *She wouldn't be embarrassed, would she*? He thought. *She's a stripper, right? A dancer? Oh God.... What do I call her?*

Without a breath being caught, Amaretto spun toward the short man, raised her fist to strike him square in the nose, but before her punch could land, Vlad the doorman had appeared, seemingly from out of nowhere.

Vlad caught Amaretto's fist with his huge hand, then pushed her backwards into Keith, pushing him back into his chair, pulling her down with him, onto his lap.

Vlad then grabbed the short man, who turned and threw his drink all over him. With a growl, the gargantuan doorman hoisted the little man high into the air, as if to throw him.

"Yeah, Frankenstein!" Duncan leapt to his feet, cheering on, "Go on, rip him apart! Pulverize him!"

Vlad, an obvious person of few words, paused for one-second. Holding the short man in mid-air, he turned to Duncan, the weight of his victim seemingly effortless to hold. Saying nothing, the doorman just stared blankly at his new cheerleader.

Duncan quickly found himself able to restrain the usual verbal diarrhea that flooded from his lips, as he slowly sat back down on his seat, He smiled apologetically, sensing that he just did the wrong thing.

Vlad then turned away, carrying the short man back to his own table.

Amaretto, still holding Keith's jacket to her exposed chest, smiled graciously to him as she stood up from his lap. "You always were the gallant type," she said, winking at him. With ease, she then managed to re-tie her bikini and halter-top one-handed, all with Keith's jacket still covering her

"Miss, I think you got the wrong guy here." Keith didn't want to say that, but he felt he had no choice but to be honest. "I'm not whoever-"

"What the hell d'ya think this is? Madison Square Garden?" Vic bellowed as he stormed across the club, his voice so loud, it stole them away from their exchange.

The Maître D stopped by the short man at his table. He and his friends looked furiously at Amaretto. The short man, in particular, was fit to burst with indignance.

"It's her first night," Vic said with an apologetic smile, as he motioned to Amaretto with his thumb. "Haven't broken her in yet, you understand? Next round's on me, okay? And we got loads more flesh to go on show. How's that?"

The short man's angry expression immediately dropped, as did those of his friends. They all cheered, willingly trading their drunken fury for more alcohol and more nudity.

"And let's throw in a couple of complimentary dances, eh?" Vic offered, as the drunk men at the table now looked like Christmas had come early.

Vic then turned his gaze toward Amaretto, his fake smile gone.

She handed the jacket back to Keith and picked up her tray from the table.

"You," Vic pointed at a cigar wedged between his large fingers at her. "Ya want your first night to be your last?"

Amaretto just smiled submissively.

"That's Rule number three, *never* compete with the stage show. It's hard enough up there." Vic railed. "And Rule six, no visible violence! We want them to come back here."

Amaretto meekly nodded.

"You hurt?" Vic asked, almost sarcastically. "Something broken?"

Amaretto shook her head, and only barely uttered the word "no" before Vic cut sternly in.

"No? Then why aren't you moving? Showin' skin? Getting' some green for that pink!"

"Wait a *goddamn* minute," Keith blurted out, unable to contain his disdain any longer. "That guy attacked *her*! Not the other way around! *He* should be screamed at! Not offered free goddamn drinks! What kind of establishment is this anyway?"

Nearby, the angry short man heard Keith's accusation, and began to look perturbed once again.

With a smarmy grin returning, Vic draped his arm over Keith's shoulder, steering him back to his seat. Ast he spoke quietly, his cigar hand gesticulated with each word. "By *that guy*, ya mean my paying customer, right? The kind of person that will pay enough to make any request he has reasonable. Someone who will spend a lot more money that you? Wanna know the reason we can stay open? Guy's like that?"

Keith attempted to reply, but Vic was on a roll. "And by *her*, you mean that helpless, *innocent* maiden in the skimpy outfit who just showed her skin for a few bucks, right? *They* took advantage of *her*? Don't you know women have all the power here? Not the other way around."

"I—" was all Keith could get out before Vic sat him down, Duncan could only look on in silent awe.

"Now sit, cool off, or I'll get Vlad to explain it to you

outside, gottit?" Vic motioned to the bouncer, who stood only a few feet away, waiting for his next command.

"So, my good friends, drink. Buy some fun. And stop any shit." He smiled as he shoved his back cigar into his mouth. "We'll have no more of this nonsense, okay?"

Glancing at Amaretto, he motioned to the drinks tray in her hand. "You got that thing. Make some use of it. Get these boys some drinks."

As Vic left without another word, Keith and Duncan both noticed that the short man still stared at them hatefully.

"I'm Amaretto," she said as she walked between the short man's stare and their table. She looked at both Duncan and Keith in turn with a smile.

"Amaretto?" Keith said under his breath. "I've never heard that name before Are you sure you know me?."

She shook her head playfully and whispered, "It's not *really* my name, silly." Then she spoke louder, for the benefit of her boss, who seemed to have supersonic hearing. "I'll be your waitress for this evening. Now what can I get for you fine gentlemen."

Her halter top slipped off her shoulder for a moment, to the wide-eyed silence of Keith, but she managed to pull it back up without missing a beat.

"My dear," Duncan said with a twinkle in his eye, and a confidence that bordered on delusion, "I would *love* a slow, comfortable screw."

Keith shot him a stern look. He did not know why, but he felt protective of Amaretto. Not that he would even admit it to himself.

Duncan, noticing Keith's disdain, quickly spluttered out, "Beer! I meant a beer! And please, one for my good friend here too!"

This time as her halter top slipped again, Amaretto noticed Keith's staring at her as she pushed it back up. "I know," she said with a mischievous glance. "I've gotta get a new one. It always does that. Drives me crazy!"

Then with a smile, she turned and headed toward the bar.

"Drives her *crazy*..." Duncan leaned over the table and whispered, "How d'you not remember *that*? I'm gonna remember *that* til the day I die!"

Keith did not know the answer to his question, and found that he could only shrug in reply.

Duncan looked back to Amaretto, who was now at the bar, then to every other woman in the club, "I'm gonna remember each and every one of these beauties forever!"

A smattering of applause and wolf whistles broke out, as the onstage performance concluded, as Hard Hatted Hannah performed a pas de deux with her prop hammer. With her tool belt now lying on the floor; her hard hat was her only clothing.

"There you have it, my friends," a voice said over the speakers. But instead of the DJ, it was now Vic addressing the crowd. "Hard Hatted Hannah, the builder of *major erections* worldwide, thanks you graciously for all your tips."

CHAPTER 6
KATRINA

"Gentlemen..." The sound of Vic's voice slimed out from the club's speakers and into the ears of the waiting audience. His tone was almost vulgar in the way it spoke that otherwise innocent word.

The background music began to fade to total silence, as it did, so did everyone else in the room.

The lights then dimmed to almost total darkness.

Vic continued with each word dripping with perversion. Each syllable was spoken slowly yet deliberately. "Wait... Just wait..."

The anticipation in the now blackened club began to swell.

"Are you ready to become her victims?" Vic almost whispered.

Duncan glanced around the stage, excited by the possibilities of this next show. Whereas, Keith couldn't care less. Instead of staring where everyone else was, Keith tried to get a glimpse of AJ at the bar, but the light was too low to see anyone's face. This was all taking too long for Keith's comfort. How long did it take to get a stripper, anyway? All he could see were silhouettes of a throng of lecherous men staring at the stage hungrily, waiting for the next slice of flesh to expose itself under the glaring spotlight.

Vic's voice continued to ooze out from the speakers with an increasingly aggressive and lustful tone. "Are you ready to give yourselves over to the ultimate in agony and ecstasy?"

From the bar, Amaretto, now with a full tray of drinks in her hands, navigated her way through the dark room. Winding her way around the tables until she sidled up to where Keith and Duncan sat. With a smile on her face, she casually plopped an open beer bottle in front of Duncan, then lovingly placed an empty glass in front of Keith. As her shadowed smile turned to him, her gaze stayed with his eyes as she proceeded to slowly fill his glass with beer. An obviously better brand of beer than she had given Duncan. "You figure it out yet?" she said. "C'mon... You gotta remember me."

Duncan stared in joyful awe as he witnessed the flirtatious display between Amaretto and Keith. Leaning across the table he asked, "You got any friends that want to remember *me*?" Before waiting for a reply he followed it with, "Just kidding. *I* wouldn't even remember me."

Meanwhile, the confusion on Keith's face was evident, and Amaretto clearly enjoyed his confusion. With great pleasure, she laid the now empty bottle on her tray then gave it a spin. As she did, she looked coy, as if to say *'get it?'*

Vic's continued his sales pitch to the perverse. "She will drain you dry..." his voice boomed.

Keith broke into a big grin as the penny dropped. "Are you Tina Ryan's little sister?" Keith asked. "The girl who used to sell lemonade on the street outside my house?"

Amaretto's expression fell.

Keith's grin fell. It was not the right penny at all.

"Who?" Amaretto asked, offended. "You don't remember? You pig! Is that all that meant to you?" She then turned and marched away angrily, grabbing her tray under her arm as she went.

Keith stared after her.

"Pig?" Duncan repeated, just as confused as Keith.

"This is one of the strangest nights I have ever had." Keith muttered, still watching Amaretto as she strode away. "I have no idea who she is. None at all."

Suddenly the lights dimmed to total and utter blackness. Even the neon strip lights behind the bar.

"For your viewing pleasure," Vic spoke with sickly glee, as he paused for a beat. Then, proudly purred, "The one the only... *The Queen of Damnation... Katrina*!

At the bar, AJ had been in mid-conversation with a barmaid, but as lights fell and Katrina's name was announced, the waitress stopped any interaction, as if in a sudden trance.

AJ turned his head to follow the barmaid's gaze to where the stage sat in the dark.

In the lightless room, everyone - staff and clientele alike - paid close attention to the direction of the stage, waiting for this Katrina.

Suddenly, a bright red spotlight burst into being, illuminating the center of the stage in a bloody hue. Katrina was simply *there*, seemingly coming into being from within the very darkness itself.

Sat on a wooden chair, she had her bare back facing the audience, as the eerie strains of *Welcome to my Nightmare* burst out over the speakers.

This was clearly the main event. *She* was obviously the headliner in this club. No other performer had this fanfare.

Slowly she stood. Her movements were certain and slow, and somehow dreamlike.

Wearing a long white satin nightgown, the darkness of her

skin shone out like brilliant onyx, contrasting against the platinum wig she wore that was cut to a shoulder length bob.

Even from this view, her strength could be felt. It was palpable. Her power flowed off of her, just like the material did on her body.

Her slow swaying to the tempo changed with the music. Her whole body contorted into a fiercer series of movements with each passing beat. As Alice Cooper sang *'I hope I didn't scare you'*, Katrina—still with her back to the audience—grabbed her hair in one hand, her virginal dress in the other. With a sudden, swift movement, both were removed on the downbeat. As they were ripped away, the red spotlight switched to a brilliant, blinding, bright white.

As she removed her platinum wig, a shock of blood-red, waist-length hair billowed down her back.

Her white gown dropped to the floor, exposing a mix of black lace and leather that hugged her flesh. Tossing her white wig to one side, she grabbed the chair with one hand and spun it around.

On the next beat, she turned to her enthralled audience, giving them a clear view of her face; Surreal in its beauty, it seemed almost too perfect to be real. Her sharp angular cheekbones sat below dark, hypnotic eyes that darted around the room with each slow, sensual thrust of her pelvis. She knew she had control, and she would not let go.

On her cheeks, she had painted precise angular shapes in Day-Glo inks. Resembling a sort of disco warpaint. This detailed feature was repeated down her arms, and around her full breasts. In all it transformed her body into a surreal art piece, with the paint acting as her clothing.

Her plump lips smirked as she held the audience's attention in the palm of her well-manicured hands. Not one person in this room looked away - not even Keith. Even *he* stared, utterly hypnotized by her performance.

Suddenly, forcefully, she thrust herself down and

straddled the chair, letting out a loud sexual moan as her head tilted upwards. Timed perfectly with the line *'We sweat and laugh and scream here'*. Her back then arched as if she was deep in the throes of the world's most intense orgasm.

The audience was enchanted.

She was seducing every single person.

This was Katrina. *The Queen of Damnation.*

As the music ended and the lights came up, AJ stood in awe. The performance he'd just witnessed felt like it could have lasted a few minutes, or even an hour. He had no idea. One thing was very clear, though: he *needed* Katrina for the party. She *was* the x-factor he'd been looking for.

At their table, Keith and Duncan turned to each other with jaws agape. Both of them were at a loss for words. They then both turned to look at the club in unison, wanting to see if everyone else felt the same. Which they did.

The patrons were showing their appreciation in a myriad of ways. Some showered the stage with money, paying their tributes to Katrina's performance as she turned and walked off. Some screamed and applauded rapturously, and some sat like Keith and Duncan. Silent and amazed.

A small girl, no older than twelve, ran onto the stage after Katrina left and began to collect all of the offered dollars, picking up the bills and putting them into a leather satchel she had strapped over her shoulder.

Keith and Duncan then caught sight of AJ as he walked away from the bar toward the stage. They saw him make his way, turn to them, then wink assuredly.

. . .

At the bar, Hard Hatted Hannah stood without her hard hat and dressed in the standard waitress uniform of hot pants and a crop top. She watched AJ, too, as he tried to catch the attention of the child-like girl collecting the money from the stage floor`.

Another waitress sidled up to Hannah and followed her gaze toward the stage. Upon noticing AJ, she smiled and whispered, "I'd like *that* one."

"Wouldn't we all?" Hannah replied with a smile.

"Hey, kid!" AJ shouted, calling to the girl cleaning up on the stage. "Hey!" he called again.

The girl looked up at him, wide-eyed.

"Yeah, you! Thank you!" AJ said. "Can I talk to you?"

The girl glanced around the room, trying to find someone from the staff to help her.

At the bar, Hannah whispered under her breath, "Hey Seko... Over here."

The child—Seko—immediately turned to the bar. She had heard Hannah's whispers from clear across the busy noisy room. A sinking feeling hit her stomach, as she knew what was about to happen.

"All alone?" Hannah said, keeping her gaze fixed intently on Seko.

"All alone?" the girl asked, her face devoid of any emotion.

AJ shifted his eyes from the girl to his friends - Duncan giving him a thumbs up; Keith rolling his eyes - and then back again to the girl.

"Yeah," he replied. "I'm all alone, why?"

· · ·

"You from around here?" Hannah whispered, still watching from the bar.

AJ smiled at Seko. Her tone was so strange and stilted. He presumed she may be playing with him, but proceeded with his plan nevertheless. "Nope. I'm from Brooklyn," he half-lied.

Hannah took a sip of her drink.

Seko stared dumbly at AJ, who found the long pause very uncomfortable.

Putting her drink back down, Hannah whispered, "Married? Got kids?"

AJ, though relieved that Seko had finally spoken, was feeling creeped out that this child was asking these questions. He laughed nervously. "Me? Nah. Young, free, and single all the way."

"You looking for some company," Hanna said. "Do you want-"

"Look, Kid," AJ cut into the question. "I wanna speak to Katrina. You know if she does private bookings? I got a party that I need her for. I can pay what she wants."

. . .

Hannah smirked. "Oh come on, big boy. Why don't we go somewhere more private? You can show me how much of a man you really are."

AJ looked sickened. "Kid, really. Stop. You're just a child. Please. I'm not like that. I just wanna talk to Katrina."

"Fine. Be like that. Ruin my fun." Hannah laughed. "Follow me then."

AJ felt a wave of relief, as Seko motioned him up the stairs to the side of the stage.

"She's this way" Hannah whispered, as she watched Seko repeat her words, then lead AJ backstage.
Before he disappeared, AJ turned back to his table, and gave his friends a sly smile.

"Yay!" Duncan exclaimed watching AJ leave, punching the air. "He scores!"
Keith turned, sarcastically matching Duncan's enthusiasm. "Yay! That was a kid, you sick bastard!"
Duncan pulled his fist out of the air and said at a machine gun pace, "No, no, no, no, no, no, no, no, no, no. I didn't mean that— I meant... I... Oh God." He threw his head into his hands in embarrassment.
"Relax," Keith laughed. "I'm just playin' with ya."

· · ·

"Are you sure you don't want me?" Seko asked as she led AJ down a backstage corridor. "Most men would kill for a chance to fuck me."

"Kid, I don't mean to be rude, but can you stop? Like right now. That's sick." AJ said. He was beginning to regret following her back here.

"Oh stop your whining," Seko laughed. "I'm joking with you. If you had said yes, I'd have had my friends rip you into itty bitty pieces."

AJ let out a nervous laugh. Unsure of what the hell was going on. A laugh that halted in its tracks as Seko spun on the spot toward him.

"Seriously though. If you want to fuck me, I'd let you..." she said with soulless, dead eyes and a slack expression.

AJ started to take a step backwards. "This was a mistake. I'm just gonna go."

Seko's demeanor suddenly changed. She looked as if she had woken from a dream.

AJ began to turn back, to return to the main room, "Can you just tell Katrina I'd like to book her?"

"Katrina?" Seko said, her voice somehow different from before, with a strong Asian accent. Thinking on the spot, and remembering all that Hannah had done with her manipulative puppeteering, she continued, "She is this way. I'll show you."

AJ glanced back as Seko walked to the end of the corridor hurriedly and opened a door. "This way," she said, still very nervous.

AJ knew better than to follow. He knew he should just go back and call it a night. But then he thought of Katrina. *Something* made him still follow the little girl. Despite *everything* in his bones telling him not to.

As he walked into the dressing room, following Seko, he saw the backs of some of the performers, applying their makeup and changing costumes.

"Loved the shows, ladies!" he said politely.

Inside this dressing room, it was small, cramped, and messy. Clothes racks, make-up cases, and more were strewn over the tables. Down the center was a row of make-up tables. Only there were no mirrors in the middle of their bulbed frames. Instead, there was nothing but empty space.

AJ looked at them puzzled.

One of the dancers sat across the table from another dancer, each of them applying makeup to each other through the empty frames, using themselves as the mirrors.

Seko walked across this room, up to another door that led to a upward staircase.

AJ followed cautiously, and as he did, he noticed how these dancers—up close—looked different. *Very* different. The make-up they wore had been caked on extra thick. The patches of skin beneath their paint seemed sunken and blotchy. Their eyeliner and lipstick looked... *off*. Misaligned. Like old makeup on a cadaver.

The illusion of the stage had provided them a disguising sheen of perfection that was no longer evident here in this room.

"This way..." Seko said softly.

"Great lighting in here, ladies." AJ joked, then regretted it straight away as they stared at him unimpressed.

After the flight of stairs, and a few more corridors, AJ found himself being ushered into a plush dressing room. This was nothing like the one he had just been in. This one was pristine and opulent, instead of cramped and messy. Every bit of metal design here shimmered, every bit of material on the furnishings looked as new as the day that they were installed. Though AJ noticed, like the other room, there were no mirrors here either.

"Katrina will be with you shortly," Seko said as she left, and closed the door behind her.

AJ, now alone, turned and looked around the room. "I'm

guessing this was a big mistake, bubba..." he muttered under his breath. "This is somehow gonna be a damn *big* mistake."

"Frankie, Sammy and Deano," Vic called out as he walked down the rickety wooden steps that led into the After Dark Club's basement.

The darkness here was like oil; thick and impenetrable. Even when Vic flicked on the light switch at the bottom of the basement steps—which caused a string of lights that ran down the long room to burst into life—their glow barely pushed the shadows far enough aside for even the stock on the shelves to be clearly seen.

This was no matter though as Vic never had much of a problem seeing in the dark, despite the fact he always switched on the lights down here. It was more out of habit and a courtesy for others. More specifically, the *other* that was down here all the time. The *other* that could not leave.

"Frankie, Sammy and Deano?" He called out again, waiting for any kind of confirmation.

But there was nothing offered in return.

Shrugging, Vic moved down the long room and over to one of the large metal stock shelves. Grabbing a crate of orange juice bottles, his calm expression changed to one of concern.

He stopped in his tracks.

He could feel *something*.

Something not right.

Something slightly off.

He took a look around the barely lit room, listening quietly.

But there was only silence. Nothing but silence. *Too* much silence. "Squeak?" He called out.

Nothing.

"Squeak, stop fuckin' around and answer."

Nothing.

Putting the crate back onto the shelf, he strode over to the other side of the room, where in the darkness, a large door stood shut. Made of solid steel, it looked like a door from a prison, complete with a viewing hatch leveled at eye height.

Sliding open the hatch, Vic peered inside. "Frankie, Sammy and Deano, Squeak?" he said. "Frankie, Sammy and Deano?"

Nothing.

"Goddamn it." Vic snarled, as he unlocked the door with a large metal key that always rested in its lock. It clanked loudly as the bolt slid open. "Squeak, you better not be fucking around in there."

Opening the door, he peered inside. Though the darkness here was too impenetrable for even him to see clearly.

"Say something, Squeak." Vic said, as he squinted into the shadows. "If ya don't say anything, I'll have to turn on the light."

Nothing.

"Frankie, Sammy and Deano?" he asked yet again, almost pleading. But, as before, nothing came. No reply.

Leaning back out of the door, Vic grabbed a pair of large protective goggles hanging from a nail on the wall. Putting them on, he shook his head. "Squeak, sorry for this, but you gave me no choice."

Running his hand along the wall, he found a large red button. Pushing it down sent an electric signal to a large bank of UV lights that ran across the ceiling. They sprang to life, flooding the room with bright incandescence.

As the UV light poured into the room's every corner, Vic winced and retreated into the shadows of the corridor, while still trying to focus his sight inside the room.

Suddenly a wail painfully echoed from within. Sounding like an animal being skinned alive.

Frantically trying to focus his eyes into the floodlit cell, Vic finally saw what he was looking for. Leading up the wall from the floor was a trail of blood, and in the opening of the vent at the top of the room, a large mass of exposed flesh and bone quivered in pain as the light touched it, causing its flesh to smoke and bubble.

"There you are, you *asshole*!" Vic exclaimed as he slammed the button again, causing the UV lights to turn off instantly.

Storming across the cell, Vic reached up and grabbed a bone that protruded out from the mass of flesh, then pulled at it. From out of the vent, came more broken meat and bone. It all tumbled to the floor with a wet thud, narrowly missing Vic's feet.

"Where are you?" Vic muttered as he grabbed the pile of flesh and rooted around it, turning it over, until he saw what he'd been looking for. "There you are, you sonofabitch, you worried me!"

In the middle of the ripped sinew, seeping blood, torn flesh, and broken bone, Vic stared down at part of a head that comprised some of this carrion. An eye and a mouth; the remnants of Mark 'Squeak' Coombs.

Squeak looked as if he had been fed through a combine harvester, and left as nothing more than a heap of mangled remains - and impossibly still alive. His head had been split into many pieces. His eye, lidless, was still intact but now rested within this pitiful mound of flesh. Below this eye, a patch of skin framed his moaning mouth.

"You know better than to do shit like that," Vic snarled as he reached into his pocket and brought out a hip flask. Opening it, he poured the contents onto Squeak's mouth. The red soupy liquid fell from the metal container and splashed over his mouth, which quickly began to move. His lacerated tongue shot out and began licking around his mouth, messily sopping up all of the flask's liquid. Squeak's eye then darted around the room, reinvigorated.

After a few moments, Vic took the flask and put the lid on it. He looked at the blood trail that led up the wall ,up to the vent, then back down to the living meat pile. "Excatly how the fuck d'you do that?" he asked with a smirk. "I'm pissed, sure... But I'm also impressed. You learning to move like a slug now?"

Putting the flask back into his pocket, Vic stood up and walked to the door. "I'll send someone down to bolt that shut. Don't want ya getting any ideas again do we?"

After walking out and closing the cell door, Vic took one more look through the viewing hatch, and gazed upon the remains of his old friend.

"Frankie, Sammy and Deano?" Vic asked again, his tone more maudlin.

After a moment of hearing the slurps from the quivering flesh that was Mark 'Squeak' Coombs, Vic finally heard the words he wanted to hear.

"Aaaaaa dduuuuuhh aaaaaaay, baaaaaayy-beeeeee" came the grotesque voice.

"Yeah. All the way, baby," Vic whispered back, repeating the words with a smile.

Vic then closed the hatch to the cell, grabbed the orange juice from off the stock shelf then walked back up the steps to the club.

Before he turned the lights off, he called back in a loud voice, "One day, Squeak. One day... Frankie, Sammy and Deano, all the way, baby. Somehow... Somewhere... somewhen... Just keep on holdin' on."

A mirror ball descended over the stage, as the spotlights pulsed in multiple colors, signaling a new performer to the stage of the After Dark Club.

On roller-skates, this performer wore a catsuit and pigtails, she danced and spun on the spot. Lifting her leg up to the sky as she twirled, exposing the hole in her costume, displaying her sex to all and sundry.

"She melts in your mouth *and* in your hand..." The DJ said over the speakers. "Give it up, for Candi!"

The strains of *Disco Inferno* blared loudly as Candi began her routine.

Keith was transfixed, not by the performance, but by Amaretto, who flitted about the room serving drinks.

He studied her face, *still* trying to place her. A couple of times she caught his glance from the other side of the club, but she feigned indignation, and carried on collecting orders and delivering drinks.

Keith turned to Duncan, who was busily staring open-mouthed at the stage—at Candi, who was now removing parts of her catsuit, exposing more and more of her porcelain-like skin.

As Amaretto disappeared behind the bar, and out of sight, Keith checked his watch. *Well, that's it,* he thought. *No strippers for the frat boys.* Part of him was very relieved for this turn of events. Most of him, in fact.

"I'm gonna hit the head before we leave." Keith said to Duncan. But his friend was in a world of his own. Noticing that he wasn't listening, Keith joked "I'm also gonna punch a baby, wanna join me?"

Candi, though, was clearly more important. Duncan's priority. So, standing up, Keith said now more, and walked across the club floor, slipping past the tightly packed tables, toward the men's room.

As he passed one of the booths, he noticed Hard Hatted Hannah's hard-hat on the table, and from within the booth's thick shadows, he could see a vague undulation of limbs in the darkness.

Gross, he thought, as he walked on. He could not think of anything worse than making out in this place.

Within the small bathroom, Keith moved his way up to one of the far urinals and unzipped his fly.

Sighing, he pondered the events of the night as he shook his head. He knew you were supposed to be carefree in your youth, you were supposed to do stupid things, but instead, Keith longed for some normalcy. Ever since coming to the University with AJ, everything had felt like a gameshow, complete with bright flashy lights, and blurs of sparkly colors, yet there were no prizes of worth to be won. He just wanted the ride to stop.

The sound of a running faucet jolted Keith's attention away from his maudlin daydream. He glanced over his shoulder to find the humongous bouncer, Vlad, standing by the sink. With his shirt removed and his torso exposed, this man washed a red stain from his shirt collar.

It was Vlad's body though, that had caught Keith's eye. Across his expanse of skin, dozens upon dozens of tiny holes littered every inch of him. Irritated looking puncture wounds that were red and seemed excessively sore. He looked like a human pincushion, sans the pins.

It was only after a few moments that Keith realized that he was being stared back at, as he caught the bouncer's eerie grin in the mirror. At the pale wide eyes staring right back at him.

Keith jolted back to the business at hand as he tried to force the rest of the liquid out from his bladder.

Just as the last drops were being pushed out, Keith made a quick finish and zipped his fly back up.

He couldn't get out of there fast enough.

"I'm tryin' to run a respectable joint here." Vic exclaimed in annoyance, as he grabbed a man in a suit from the booth where Hard Hatted Hannah had been. The man came out like a rag doll. Eyes closed. Body limp. "Anybody wanna claim this lush?" Vic called out to the surrounding club, but no-one was listening or paying the slightest bit of attention, despite it being between performances and there currently being no flesh on display.

At the bar, a barmaid smirked as she watched. This was something she had seen many times before. And every time it happened, Vic asked the same thing to the crowd, said the same exact words, and that gave her a chuckle. Mainly as she knew what was really going on.

Keith hurriedly exited the bathroom, still creeped out by the sight of the bouncer's hole-filled body. As he walked, he regained some of his composure, then caught sight of Vic and the suited rag doll man.

He noticed it was the same booth he had passed, but unlike before, there was not a hard hat to be seen. She must have plied her trade and left, he thought, as the only ones there were the Maître D and the man who looked dead to the world.

Vic continued to speak aloud as the throng of customers around him totally ignored what he said, "Once... Twice... Going... Going... Gone..."

With that, Vic turned to Keith and bellowed toward him, "Hey, clean this mess up."

Keith stood frozen. Why should he clean anything up? This wasn't his—

Suddenly the hulking figure of Vlad barged in from the bathroom behind him, and marched up to the booth.

As the bouncer scooped up the limp body like it was light as a feather, Keith couldn't help but be amused at his own confusion.

Shrugging, he made a beeline for Duncan, who was still sitting at their stage-side table ogling every waitress that passed by.

Sitting down, Keith looked at his watch again and sighed. "Guess you haven't seen AJ yet?" he asked.

———◦✕◦———

Wandering around the plush dressing room, AJ was still waiting patiently for Katrina.

This room was sparsely decorated with only a few functional antiques; a lamp, a chaise longue, and a table. In the middle of the room ran a long water tank, filled with brightly colored tropical fish. This tank seemed very out of place for the club, yet it did have a calming effect upon him.

Next to this tank was a long, golden clothes rack on which hung half a dozen black plastic garment bags.

From everything here, AJ could tell that Katrina was more than just a dancer here. She was *the* dancer. *The* money maker. *Maybe she owned this place?* He mused as he regarded the fish tank, checking out his own reflection in the glass, then fixing his hair.

He sighed as he looked at himself in the tank. He had had enough of waiting. This was not worth it.

He then turned to exit—only to jump backwards, startled at the sudden appearance of Katrina behind him.

Wearing a thin dressing gown, a black shoulder-length wig, and nothing on her feet, she stared at AJ.

"Katrina," he gasped. "Uhhh... Pleased to meet you."

She did not reply. She just stared at him blankly, then slowly took a few steps backward, to lay down on the chaise longue, her eyes never leaving AJ once.

His surprise gave way to discomfort as he uttered, "Katrina. Nice name..." He swallowed hard. He could not understand why he was so nervous around her. He was never nervous around women. "I.... I'm AJ. My name... It's AJ." He smiled weakly, praying to drag his composure—and his usual cool—back into the equation.

Her eyes did not leave him once. She didn't even seem to blink. And even in her silence, she sensually commanded him with ease.

"Caught your act out there. Some show, huh?" he continued. "But then again..." He paused as he gathered his nerve. "Then again, this audience seemed very easy to please."

He thought she may look offended by his words, yet still, she just stared intently. Studying his every move.

"I wonder if you'd be interested in an encore performance, later tonight. Or tomorrow if you'd prefer."

She continued to stare.

Then, a strange smile spread over her face. Moving her legs off the chaise longue, she stood again.

AJ could hear her breathing getting heavier.

Slowly, she stepped toward him, then began to circle him.

AJ could only stand in place. He had no idea what she was doing. "I'm willing to pay top dollar," he blurted out. "'Cause I think you're worth it. I like you—"

Before he could say another word, she grabbed him by the arm, then swung him around toward her, maneuvering him back toward the chaise longue.

Swiftly, she managed to remove his jacket before pushing him down onto his back.

He smiled nervously as he lay on the chair's fabric. "I guess you like me too, huh?"

Quickly straddling him, she removed her dress. Her nudity took AJ by complete surprise. As she slowly unbuttoned his shirt, Katrina craned her neck over his chest and began to lick his skin hungrily as each button was released.

This wasn't his first rodeo, and there was no reason he should be anything but confident, but with this woman it seemed different. With this *divine* woman...

As she moved her way up him, licking his chest. She traced her tongue over his nipples, then up to his neck.

Slowly, her knee came upward, and she pushed it caressingly into his crotch.

AJ could not restrain his manhood at all, as it swelled beneath his pants.

Her knee caressed it in a rhythm as she grabbed both of his hands by the wrists, and pinned them behind his head.

He was all too willing to let this happen.

Her knee rubbed against him faster.

She growled softly by his ear, nibbling at his neck.

A small bead of sweat dripped down from her face and onto him, she exhaled heavily, and moaned.

Unseen by him, the veins on her head started to pulse, as her skin became slightly more translucent, revealing a hint of the bone, crisscrossing veins and arteries below.

AJ was now close to bursting, as Katrina's knee moved out of the way. She reached down, tore open the buttons of his trousers with ease and thrust her hand inside, grabbing him in her bare hands.

Barely missing a beat, she began pumping.

He tried to free one of his hands, so he could touch her too, but the grip that held his wrists seemed impossibly strong. So strong in fact, that he could not move in the slightest.

But, before he could protest, he felt his climax fast approaching.

Katrina raised her head up.

Now gone was her beauty.

In its place, a ferocious animal. Her very skull had seemingly changed shape. Now it was far more angular. Bat-like, even.

She stared into his eyes, gleefully basking in his sudden terror, as her hand sped up its rhythm. Despite the horror of her monstrous visage, AJ could not stop the inevitable.

Her mouth opened and distorted, revealing a set of razor sharp fangs that protruded out from in front of her human teeth.

AJ tried to scream, to stop this surreal nightmare, but was fast caught between terror and ecstasy.

With animalistic ferocity, Katrina wailed, and drove her teeth deep into his neck. Her fangs ripped into his jugular like a hot knife in warm butter, as she gouged out a large hole.

He attempted to scream for help, but all he could do was emit a whimpering gurgle as his throat drowned in blood.

Katrina growled in ecstasy as she then felt his warm seed release over her cold, scaly talons — all while his lifeblood sprayed into her serrated maw.

As his body lay in draining shock, she brought her claw up to her mouth, and lapped at the semen that had commingled with his blood, and watched him, as the last of his life left his twitching, anguished body.

CHAPTER 7
MR. DYNAMITE

Keith stood next to the large curtained door, situated by the stage-side DJ booth that led out to the backstage section of the building. Glancing coyly past its red velvet lining, he had hoped to catch a glimpse of AJ. Wanting to urge his friend to hurry the hell up, but all he could see were some stage props leaning against a pile of empty drink crates.

'Don't worry about it', Duncan had tried to assure him earlier. *'He'll be out when he's out. Enjoy the show. Enjoy the ladies! There's nothing to worry about.'*

Keith could not, though, enjoy any of what was on show. He hated waiting for people, coupled with having to stand in an establishment which made him feel distinctly uncomfortable. Both factors together, it sent his anxiety skyrocketing.

Just a few feet away, Keith noticed Vic striding over to the DJ booth, grab a microphone from the top of a mixing desk, then speak into it, addressing his audience.

The DJ stood by, obediently. Allowing Vic to take control.

Between his words Vic took a small handful of black

licorice-like lumps from a glass mint bowl on the table next to the booth.

"She's not much upstairs, but *what* a staircase," Vic laughed as he announced the next act. "The glorious, the voluptuous, the pliable, the supremely sexy, Dominique!"

As he placed the microphone back on the booth, the DJ hit play on the music.

Wake Me Up Before You Go Go erupted loudly over the speakers as the song jumped straight into the chorus, much like Dominique's show. She cartwheeled onto the stage. Naked aside from wearing clip-on pigtails, sports socks, and the two pom-poms in either hand.

The crowd cheered in their appreciation of this display. Applauding the no-nonsense approach to what they craved.

Vic, headed back to the bar, smiling at the impressionable and predictable audience. As he walked, not one of the customers even glanced at him. They were more or less hypnotised by their own lust, and that fact never failed to amuse Vic.

He caught a passing waitress by the arm, a full tray of drinks in each of her hands.

"Hey," he said. Then turning to reach over the bar, grabbing a few cocktail umbrellas with his hand. One by one he opened each umbrella, then placed them into the glasses resting on the waitresses' trays. When he was done, he glared at her intently. "Class!" His voice was pointed, and irritated. As he had told them time and time again. "Claaaaaaassssss, get it? Every drink. *Every* single drink. Even the beers!"

Nervously, she nodded, then scuttled away to deliver her drinks.

Keith, still standing by the DJ booth, was growing more and more flustered by the second. Unconsciously, he reached into the mint bowl beside the podium and popped a piece of what he thought was licorice, into his mouth.

Only it was most definitely *not* licorice.

His mouth seized as tiny sharp legs struggled against his closed lips.

Spitting the lump out onto the floor, he watched - horrified - as he saw a cockroach scuttle away. Glancing back to the bowl, he saw it spilling over with dozens of those grotesque insects.

Looking away, he couldn't control his retching. "That's it," he spluttered to himself, "that's fucking *it*." As he spat onto the floor again, he could swear he saw a severed cockroach leg resting in his spittle. "Fuck this place. Fuck these people."

Feeling on the precipice of vomiting, Keith then rushed over to the bar and grabbed a napkin. He wiped his mouth and tongue, using all of his willpower to hold down the contents of his stomach. Not that there was much to come up, as they hadn't eaten anything since lunchtime.

Just then, Keith spotted the child—Seko—strolling by nonchalantly. He reached out and tapped on her shoulder.

"Excuse...me, miss?" he called. But his words barely came out as he continued to feel his stomach contracting with disgust.

Stopping, Seko turned to him with an innocent smile. "Yes?"

"Hi… Uhh…" Keith tried his best to maintain his composure, despite his mind trying to convince him that there were more cockroaches in his mouth. "Could you tell my friend that I'm waiting for him. We… gotta leave now."

Seko looked confused, then glanced around the bar before turning back to Keith and smiling politely. "Friend? I see no friend. You have friend here?"

Keith smiled. *Of course*, he thought. *Vague as ever, Keith.* "Yeah, that guy you took backstage, remember?" he explained. "Tall guy, nice shirt, black hair?"

The smile slowly fell from Seko's face, to be replaced by fear.

"No one," she spluttered. "I took no one back." She quickly glanced around the bar, looking for Hannah—the one that was responsible for this situation.

Before Keith could question her further, Amaretto cut in between them, a full tray in her hands. "Aren't we fickle," she said playfully to Keith, oblivious to the preceding conversation. Her halter top strap fell from her shoulder, but with both her hands occupied, she couldn't do anything about it.

Keith, his mind temporarily forgetting the matter at hand, reached over and slid the strap back onto her shoulder.

Seko used the distraction to her advantage, disappearing through the backstage curtain before anyone could stop her.

"How's your evening going?" Amaretto said, her smile more flirtatious by the second.

It was then Keith noticed that Seko had gone. He sighed. "Ever have one of those nights?"

The sun's glare was too much for Keith's twelve-year-old eyes, as he held the bow string taught in his fingers.

His grip on this archery bow had started to weaken, and he felt himself falter.

"Hold it, Emerson!" the seventy-year-old Mr. Miller shouted from behind him. "You wanna be the best, you better train like the best."

"But it hurts," Keith whined.

"Pain's nuttin' but a feelin'," Mr. Miller shouted back. "Now you hold that full draw till I say otherwise. You gotta hold on for at least another three minutes!"

Keith's mother had sent him to the Miller farm every

Sunday for the past three years. After discovering that the old man used to be a state champion archer, she paid him to teach her son. Keith presumed it was to teach him a sport. To give him some discipline, whereas in reality it was to get him out of the house. Not being an active child with many friends, he spent most days at home, giving his parents little time to themselves.

Keith had never even thought of archery before. He never even knew that bows and arrows existed outside of fairgrounds, and films about Cowboys and Indians. But, as he had never been a big child, nor a tough child, his mother had pushed him to try and learn something outside of books, something active, something outside—away from the house. But only something without the danger of other children attacking him, like in football.

Though resentful at first, Keith had felt a near-immediate kinship with the sport. Despite Old Man Miller (a pet name of AJ's) being a harsh taskmaster, Keith still felt a kind of focus with the bow that he lacked with anything else.

Right now, though, all he could feel was the pain shooting through his fingers, and the ache in his wrist as he tried to hold the bow steady.

"Hey, asshole!" came a familiar voice, followed by "Sorry, Mr. Miller. I meant *that* asshole with the bow."

Keith heard Old Man Miller laugh until he began to cough. This did nothing to help his concentration.

"Hello, young AJ" Keith heard the old man say. He dared not move from his position though, less he be made to start it all over again. So instead, he just focussed on the hay-made target laying in front of him, as he held his stance as still and steady as he could.

"You guys gonna be done soon?" AJ asked.

Before Keith could answer, Old Man Miller replied, "Fine… He can finish early… Well only if he can hold…for three…"

Thank god...
"...Two..."
Hurry, please.
"Fire!"

With that, Keith released the bow string, launching the arrow out of the bow, forcing it sailing through the air toward the target.

Jetting at incredible speed, the arrow then skirted past the target and landed in the grass behind it.

With a sigh, Keith turned to face AJ and the old man, disappointed in himself more than anything else.

Old Man Miller smirked as he took a corn pipe from out of his pocket. "You're gonna keep doing that same thing every Sunday, til you can hit the bull's eye, every time. Then after you do that hold and release perfectly three times in a row, we can move on."

"How many bullseyes has he hit so far?" AJ asked.

"You wanna field that one, bucko?" The Old Man chuckled as he lit his pipe.

Keith shrugged.

"AJ," The Old Man said. "You changed your mind yet? Ready to learn the ways of the arrow?"

"Rather punch myself in the dick, sir."

The Old Man guffawed.

AJ turned to Keith. "You comin' then, Robin Hood?"

Keith nodded, picked up the ground quiver with his free hand, walked over to the Old Man and returned it along with the bow.

"After you master this, we'll work on speed shots, okay?" the Old Man said, "That's the fun stuff."

Keith nodded with a polite smile.

With the lesson concluded, AJ and Keith now walked over the fields toward their town. As they shuffled through the rows of high corn, they could still hear Old Man Miller talking to himself behind them.

"Why d'ya still do that stuff?" AJ asked, turning to Keith. "Looks like torture."

Keith shrugged. He had no answer. He just knew he loved it. Even if he wasn't that good at it, yet. But for those times where he felt any doubt, he just remembered Old Man Miller's first lesson; "It'll hurt. It'll piss you off. It'll take you years to get good at. But it'll make you one tough sonofabitch when ya get there."

"Who we meeting in town?" Keith asked, changing the subject.

"The usual suspects." AJ smiled.

Keith knew that meant the girls that fawned over his friend. The ones that referred to AJ as *Mr. Dynamite*. A nickname neither of them fully understood. Keith though, was more than happy to tag along, even if he never got such attention from the opposite sex.

Mr. Dynamite was just another in the long litany of nicknames people gave AJ.

Brooklyn. Slick Rick. Shades. Corleone.

Keith, on the other hand, got called only one name… Keith.

The click clack of hurried, hard-heeled shoes echoed down the backstage corridor. It was Seko, running in a panic.

Getting to the foot of the staircase, she scrambled upward, her small legs struggling to climb as fast as she needed them to. Her breathing becoming more stilted and pained the more she ran.

As she turned a corner onto the second floor corridor, the decor changed from the peeling magnolia wallpaper that covered the walls downstairs. Now the walls were immaculately painted a deep shade of red.

Seko's clattering footsteps became muted as the exposed floorboards gave way to a lush black carpet.

Along this lengthy corridor, gold-gilded upward-facing light fixtures glowed an orange hue, lights that seemed unable to really brighten up the dark corridor, they instead lent an air of warmth to the surroundings.

Seko approached a large black oak door, grabbed its golden handle, then opened it.

She stood in the now open doorway, out of breath, filled with an equal mix of shame and fear.

On the floor in front of her, naked and cross legged, Kristina lapped at her bloodied hands with her tongue, tasting every last drop she could from them. Her face was still monstrous; her movements seemingly more animal than human.

At the other end of the room, Vlad was busily wrapping AJ's lifeless body into one of the black plastic garment bags that had hung from the clothes rail.

Neither Vlad nor Katrina looked up as Seko entered. They paid her no mind until she spoke.

"There is a problem." The little girl's voice trembled with her thick accent. "He was not alone..." Her words trailed off to a whisper as she continued. "But, he *said* he was..."

Katrina's head snapped toward her with a growl.

"...That's it." Keith shrugged, after explaining everything to Amaretto, both still stood at the bar. "We needed a stripper to get into a stupid Frat house."

"You mean *performer*," Amaretto corrected.

"Yeah, Sorry. Performer." Keith replied quickly. "Except now, I don't really care. I don't think I ever did. I'm not even sure AJ *really* does."

Amaretto's attentive expression then fell. "Wait. AJ? You're looking for *AJ*?"

"You know AJ?" Keith asked, surprised, but suspecting that this was all still some kind of ruse. A performance as she never knew either of them, and was playing with him for some reason.

"Do I know Mr. Dynamite? Well only what you told me about him. You guys still hangin' out, huh?"

Keith could only nod. *What he told her? When?* There was no other way she would know *that* nickname. One he hadn't heard in years. She *had* to be telling the truth.

"Who are you?" he managed to ask.

"Wait, why didn't you ask *me* to perform at the frat house?" she asked with a coy smile. Then she was back on the move, heading toward the curtains that led backstage. "I bet *AJ* remembers me, and would love me to do it for you guys."

"You would do that?" Keith called out after her.

Without answering, she smiled, then disappeared backstage—through the gap in the velvet curtains. Keith quickly shot a look toward Duncan, who was still sitting rooted at their table, throwing dollar bills at the semi-clad performer who was now finishing her dance on the stage.

He'll be fine, Keith thought to himself, as he then turned back and followed Amaretto through to the backstage.

"Welcome to the world behind the curtain!" Amaretto said with a chuckle. "No glamour here, by the way,"

Keith looked shocked at what he saw, not knowing where he could look. The backstage was abuzz. Half-naked bodies hurried around the corridors, zipping in and out of their dressing rooms. Flesh on display with no qualms. More than he had ever seen in one place.

The lighting was so bright here it glowed unforgivingly upon the skin of the women as they rushed on by. Under this light, their makeup was obviously thickly caked over gaunt and sickly looking skin—Just as AJ had noticed.

On stage each one of them looked almost perfect, here they looked... *diseased*. It was the only word Keith could think of to describe their pocked and blotchy skin. But still. The nudity. He gulped hard.

"Hey!" Amaretto called out to a group of dancers at the side of the corridor. All of whom were busily tying up each other's corsets for a group show. "You see a guy back here? Tall, good looking, young?"

All the dancers remained focused and didn't turn to Amaretto. Instead, they just shook their heads dismissively, then carried on.

There was an uncomfortable pause as Amaretto waited for more from them. When she realized there were no more coming, she walked on. Keith followed as she strode over to one of the dressing rooms and peered in—to ask the same question. But there was nothing in there except empty chairs, vacant mirrorless stations, and the strong smell of sweat and groin.

"Hmm." Amaretto turned, confused, to Keith. "You sure he didn't just leave?"

"He definitely came back here," Keith insisted. "I saw him. He was *brought* back here." From the corner of his eye, he spotted Seko again, this time walking down the stairs. "By her! That kid there!"

Before Amaretto could say more, Seko walked up to Keith, guilt plastered across her face.

"Very sorry. I remember your friend now. I was very confused."

Keith smiled. *Finally, some answers!*

"Your friend went to see Katrina," Seko continued in her broken english. "I tried to say. No one can see Katrina. No one."

Leaning to Keith, Amaretto whispered, "He didn't have much of a chance with her. *Trust me*." Before he could ask why, she explained, "She owns this whole place, sweetheart, and everyone here works for *her*."

"Ah," Keith said. Of *course* AJ went after her. Of *course* he went after the most powerful, untenable person in the whole club.

Seko continued, "After that..." she shrugged, then looked at the floor, muttering. "I don't know where he went."

Exasperated, Keith sighed. "A guy doesn't just disappear—"

"Wait a moment!" Amaretto interrupted in a *Eureka* moment. "Where's Candi?"

"Half-shift." Seko replied. "She gone tonight."

Smiling, Amaretto gesticulated toward the girl, "And *there* we have it!"

"We do?" Keith asked, having not followed the same train of thought as her.

Grabbing his sleeve, Amaretto tugged. "Yeah. It's obvious. Mr. Dynamite is holding auditions!"

"Mr. Dynamite?" Seko asked in confusion.

"He wouldn't just leave," Keith protested. He *knew* AJ. He *knew* he wouldn't do that.

"Are you saying he wouldn't leave you, even with a girl that'll 'melt in your mouth *and* in your hands?'" Amaretto persuaded.

"No, I—" Keith then fell silent, as his confusion turned to anger. "I'm gonna kill that sonofabitch."

Keith knew full well that AJ would *never* abandon his friends.

Never.

Unless there was a beautiful girl in the equation. Then all bets were almost certainly off. He was stupid to presume otherwise.

Amaretto beamed. "But *what* a coincidence!" She linked her arm into his, then walked him back toward the club.

Quietly Seko slinked away again, and neither Keith nor Amaretto noticed.

"Coincidence? How d'ya mean?" he asked, wondering where Amaretto was going with this. He did not know whether she was still messing with him, if this was some elaborate joke, one that AJ was in on as well. He knew nothing.

"Coincidence because it's time for my break and I gotta pick up some more clothes at the hotel. You see some of us new girls stay there until they earn a room in this place. *Including* Candi. I bet we'll catch AJ if we hurry there!" Amaretto stopped and faced him. "Meet me outside the side entrance in two minutes, okay?"

If this was a joke, if she was lying about everything. It was one hell of a long con.

Seko remembered the reeds.

She *always* remembered the reeds.

No matter the day, or the situation that she found herself in, when she closed her eyes, she could not escape being confronted by the image of her mother's blood flowing out from a gaping wound in her neck. It spilled all over the reeds. The reeds in which Seko had been hiding.

In front of her, the large black creature roared, still holding her dying mother by the hair. It then reared down again and feasted on her quickly exposed intestines. All the while, it stared through the reeds, directly at a trembling Seko, who—crying and terrified—had crouched only a few feet away. The little girl watched in anguish, unable to run, knowing that this beast would come for her as soon as it finished with the last of her mother's blood.

Then as her mother's body slumped to the ground, lifeless

and decapitated, the beast slurped the remnants of her innards into its mouth, then it started toward Seko.

The girl now noticed that the beast was in fact female, and aside from its claws and fanged face, it seemed very much… human.

The stormy skies above had masked the moon's glow from her village, hiding the finer details of this obsidian entity, until it approached her. Seko then saw it all: claws fully extended; mouth dripping with blood of her mother, with dark eyes now fixated on *her*.

Seko closed her eyes tightly, wishing this beast away. She wanted to remain alive. She wanted to see another sunrise. She wanted to be spared the same fate as the rest of her family and the entire village.

Only one of these would come true.

The beast did not go away.

The beast did not allow her to survive.

And she would never see another sunrise.

The beast, however, did show Seko a perverted kind mercy. It brought her back from the comfort of death, then placed her within the world between. The world where the beast and others of her kind held a violent and parasitic dominion.

When Seko returned from her first death—as her eyes re-opened into a new reality—she felt herself breathing, yet could not sense anything feeding her lungs. She felt no beating of her heart that had pounded blood through her veins. She also felt no discomfort or pain. And, most curiously, when she thought of her slain family, she had felt absolutely *nothing*. No love for them. No hate for their murderer. No guilt that she couldn't stop it. Nothing. A nothing which sat like a lead weight in the pit of her stomach. She knew she should cry. She knew she should scream. But all

VAMP

she felt was an insurmountable confusion over her own apathy.

The first new truth she had learned was that her breathing was merely a reflex; an echo of her humanity that would stay without reason. As if her body was needlessly mocking her undeath.

Later that night, Seko felt something else; an incredible thirst that came from her new condition—a debilitating focal point that would shape her new half-existence. This was a thirst that she would find the truth about, soon enough.

But she was not free to try and quench this thirst that gnawed at her from within. Far from it. She was shackled to her maker, forever, just like the rest of those made by *her*. Seko existed at the whim of this beast. Only able to feed on the scraps thrown at her feet.

She counted herself lucky, though.

At least she was given this life as one of the monster's own kind, as opposed to one of the others that were forced to serve her; the familiars. These ones were poisoned by just enough of the beast's blood to force them into obedience, yet not enough to change them fully or allow them to live for an eternity. Their blood remained tainted but not fully converted. They existed to serve—all at the beck and call of their master's whim and sometimes hunger. It wasn't this condition that Seko was happy to have avoided though. It was their punishment. A punishment she had witnessed several times. A punishment that her master reveled in the cruelty of repeating.

She had heard it referred to the Devil's Torment. A damnation for any familiar that disobeyed. The master would begin to turn their familiar into one of her kind, yet stop before the point of full transformation. Then this familiar's body would be decimated into a pulp—ripped apart—with the heart and brain remaining untouched. Then, when this mass of gore would return from the human death, they would find themselves unable to reform their body from such an extreme condition. Their half-transformation, now cursed against them. These damned ones would be trapped in a butchered state, doomed to their own existence. It was a torment that could only be ended by a vampiric death. Death only their master would allow. But all masters were incapable of mercy. So it was almost always an eternal sentence.

Seko had followed her master and murderer throughout many different guises, over many, many years. Followed over every corner of the earth. She had witnessed cruelty and horrors by the claws of her maker. Violence of such depravity, that the Devil's Torment was just a small footnote amongst an expansive tableau of savagery.

Despite her own vampiric state, coupled with her absence of any humanity, she often felt something deep inside of her when she witnessed such horrors. It was something she could not place a finger on. An emptiness inside. In her human form she would have known this for a mixed feeling of revulsion and fear, but as a monster herself, she could only presume it was hunger.

After all, there was never any option but to serve the master. Never any option but to feed on the blood of the living. This child, forever trapped in her girlhood, had been bound by tainted blood. And now her existence was *all* a blur of blood, darkness and torment.

Vampires, though, were not without their own punishment. Even her master was not above the ancient laws of the elders who presided far above her; Those that were her makers. And when her master's feeding and cruelty got so high profile that humanity began to notice. When the term *vampyre* became a known word, she and her coven were sentenced to a punishment that was to last a century.

A punishment that cast them away from the frightened gaze of the human masses. Trapped in the fringes of the world, where they could only feed on the dregs. Sentenced to exist in a dying city, in the filth of what was called, the After Dark Club.

"I'll stay here. You can come get me when you find him," Duncan said to Keith dismissively, waving him away while keeping his gaze on the gyrating flesh onstage.

Turning, Keith headed toward the club's exit. He made his way through the closely placed tables, each full of baying men with their hungry eyes on the performance.

As he approached the door, Keith started to notice a change in the atmosphere.

He felt his stomach sink as he slowed his pace.

Glancing over his shoulder, he caught a glance of Katrina sitting in a candlelit booth, her pupils seemingly glowing in the light of a flickering flame. He began to realize then, that he was surrounded. It was not only her, but the waitresses, barmaids, dancers and all the other staff, too. They seemed to be eyeing him. All watching him intently with every step he took toward the exit.

By the curtained doors, at the host booth, Vic was on a phone call. He had seen Keith approaching.

"So, you amenable to the offer?" Vic said on the call, nodding as he heard the answer he wanted.

Keith sidled up slowly to the podium. Without needing to wait till the end of the call, Vic lowered the handset, then smiled at Keith.

"I- I gotta run out for a minute." Keith stuttered. "Do I need my hand stamped... or anything, for getting back in?"

"Not necessary." Vic shook his head. "Have a lovely night."

As Keith left through the curtains, Vic raised the handset again and continued his call. "Yeah, he's on his way now. Just left."

When he heard the reply, his face twisted, though his voice remained restrained. "Sure, whatever you want, as long as it's an accident. And I *mean* an accident with a capital *A*. Now those are the orders, so don't screw up.... And wait 'til he's far away from here…. Yeah we got our own people out there too. So if you don't get him first, you get nothing. Gottit?"

He then hung up the handset onto the receiver, moved his hand away, then flipped the telephone the bird.

"Fucking street rats," he mumbled.

He then walked away from the entrance, over to the booth where Katrina sat. She glared intently at him as he arrived.

"I told 'em like you said. So, everything should be copacetic. Okay?" Vic said reassuringly.

Katrina then extended her hand past the darkness of the booth, motioning to the booth next to them.

Turning, Vic saw what was being shown to him. Without a word, but with a loud sigh, he smiled and nodded. "It never fucking stops, does it?" he muttered to himself.

Walking the few steps over to the next booth, Vic noticed Hard Hat Hannah was sitting there, her costume was covered in blood. "Jesus, girl. I gotta clean your mess up again?" he said as he quickly removed his jacket and threw it over her, covering up the red splotches over her. "You eat like a slob, you know that, right?"

Exposing a row of ferocious fangs, Hannah glared threateningly at the Maître D. "You shouldn't talk to me like—"

VAMP

"Take the jacket on and go clean up. Okay sweetheart? We can't have you being noticed by the customer." Vic interrupted, speaking in a kind though stern tone, as if schooling his own child.

Without another word, but with a snarl, Hannah nodded, then wrapped Vic's jacket over her shoulders, then headed backstage.

Reaching into the darkest shadows of that booth, Vic grabbed hold of the body that lay hidden inside. Just like the last one he removed from the booth earlier, this one was limp like a rag doll.

His next words were the same very rehearsed ones, the ones he always said in these situations.

"Hey, I'm tryin' to run a respectable joint here!" He said loudly. Loud enough for nearby customers to hear. All so they would believe that he was dealing with a drunk, not a corpse.

Vic, though, was exhausted. He was tired of cleaning up after these dancers. They never listened to the rules, and he felt like his life was like a glorified janitor.

How could they be so stupid? Rule number one - *Never* feed *in* the club. It was too dangerous. And tonight he had to clean up after them. *Twice*!

Then again, not even Katrina obeyed the rules. Vic knew, though, that no matter what was ordered, there was nothing *he* could do to stop them. They just fed when they wanted, and it was up to him to clean it up. Something he had been doing for over three decades. And, he didn't know how much longer he could do this for. But, he had a role to play right now, and he would play it with gusto.

"Anyone wanna claim this lush?" He called out loudly as he picked up the limp, lifeless body. "Once... Twice... Going... Going... Gone..."

CHAPTER 8
THE STREETS

Snow stepped out the phonebooth, the stript light inside cutting out as the door fully opened.

Outside, waiting impatiently on the street were Maven and Dolly, who stared curiously at their pale leader.

"C'mon, what'd they say?" Dolly asked.

Snow shrugged, slightly confused. "Seems they got someone they want taken care of… If ya know what I mean. And… I guess they offered us a payday if we find 'em first." Without any reply from Dolly or Maven, he continued. "And I'm thinkin' we got a vested interest in this…" He turned to Maven, "Looks like we didn't manage to chase off your new man after all."

Maven scowled. "That asshole is still here?"

"Yeah. Seems they didn't get the message. Well, its someone matching his description anyway.." Snow said.

"Aw shit, we're not gonna help those fucktards, are we, Snow?" Dolly protested. "They're *monsters*!"

Snow smiled. "Rule number three, Doll. Always. Rule number three."

"Good," Dolly smiled. "Thought for a moment we were actually gonna do their dirty work for 'em."

"If we find him. We'll scare him off. Tell the club he's dead. Get paid."

Maven silently stewed in her anger.

"Hey," Snow put his arm around her. "I get it. He was an asshole to ya."

"A fucking asshole," Maven corrected.

"A big fucking shiny asshole." Dolly added.

"Sure," Snow smiled. "And so was his friend... Who I presume didn't make it, as they didn't mention him. Nor the little one. But no one, *no one* deserves what he's into. Besides... Was just a description I got. May not be him after all. Could be any skinny, innocent-looking teenager with brown hair, a sports jacket and checkered shirt."

"Hundreds of people like that round this city tonight," Dolly chimed in, laughing.

Maven kept her mouth shut. She knew better than to vent her anger. She knew the rules, but she wanted that boy to atone for his insult to her, and was surprised Snow didn't want revenge on the one that grabbed his balls.

"We better hurry though, they got their own out here looking for him as well." Snow said. "Guess they are hedging their bets by asking us into the mix."

Unlike Snow, Maven believed that feeding all three of them to those *After Dark'ers* would be just desserts for their insult.

At fifteen years old, Maven had been on the streets significantly longer than any child or adult ever should have. The streets were all she had known. Her mother had been homeless–until she OD'd. Her father... Well, she had no idea about him, but she had survived on her own just fine even as a child.

Up until that night.

That night when she found herself in a motel room, covered in a fat pervert's blood.

Prostitution had been the only real way she could get enough money to survive day to day here, and with her being so young in this desperate part of town, there was a never-ending stream of despicable people willing to pay her for sex.

And that money paid for food, shelter and most importantly, drugs.

There were also no pimps to deal with, not on these streets. Pimps existed to sell sex to out-of-towners or people from higher classes wanting something forbidden. Here, though, the only clientele were the people who dwelled here . The ones who didn't always have a few bucks to spare, but may pay in booze or crack or anything else tradable in order for a cheap, dirty release.

That night, though, it had *all* gone wrong. The fat man had gone too far. He had tried to put things inside of her. *Bad* things. He had not been into sex of any normal kind. This disgusting man only wanted to give pain.

Screaming, after an hour of the worst torture anyone could stand, Maven finally managed to fight him off as he violated her yet again. In the struggle he had smashed he ended up tumbling backward and smashing his head off of the bedside table. Cracking open his skull upon impact. His lifeblood sprayed in an arterial arc all over the motel walls, and all over her.

The motel owner, upon hearing the commotion, burst through the door carrying his large 12-gauge shotgun. He was more than ready to defend his establishment and get rid of any bad elements. Yet, here he only found a bloodied and terrified, young girl. Crying in a corner. Her mouth bleeding profusely as her smashed out teeth littered the floor. Blood also pooled onto the carpet from her crotch.

Expecting her freedom to be taken away and her life

damned to a dark prison cell, it surprised her when it was not the police that the motel owner called. Instead of a uniform arriving, the person that arrived was a young man in his early twenties. Pale as winter, with hair to match. He wore a long black trench coat that touched the floor, and though she could not see them, she could hear that he wore cowboy boots as they clipped the concrete path outside of the room.

"The Dragons can do more for her than the cops can," the motel owner said to this pale man. "I can get rid of the body, if you can take her?"

Smiling, the pale man knelt down to her. "What's your name, little one?" he asked. "My name's Snow, and I'm gonna take care of ya."

"Rule one?" Snow asked Maven as she sat on the couch in the Dragons' hideout.

Now cleaned up and dressed in a leather jacket emblazoned with the gang's logo on the back, she sat timidly. She had been in their care for 6 months. Her gums and groin had mostly healed, and for the first time she had food on her plate and a place to sleep, without having to give up more of her innocence. That healing process had also allowed her to kick the need for drugs. She owed them. She owed Snow.

Around the room sat a few other people in similar attire. All young, all looking at her expectantly.

"C'mon Maven," Snow persisted, "Rule one?"

"Protect with extreme prejudice."

"Good," Snow smiled as he motioned to the rest of the gang.

In unison they said, "We keep the innocent out of hell."

"Rule number two?" Snow continued to ask.

Maven swallowed hard. "I..."

"C'mon, you *know* this," a gang member of the same age, named Dolly said.

"Never show a kind face." Maven quietly said.

Almost immediately, the rest of the gang again replied to this in unison, "Always be feared. Never show weakness."

"And last but by no means least?" Snow spoke with a smile. "Rule… Three?"

Maven looked up at him. "Fuck the vampires?" she said.

"Fuck the vampires," the gang repeated out loud.

Vampires. Something Maven initially scoffed at. But Snow had shown her the truth. The monsters that stalked the streets may hide and be protected by their human helpers, but if one knew what to look for, one could see them clearly. Whether it was their helpers disposing of bodies out of the club for them, bitten and drained of blood. Or seeing the creatures hunting in the shadows—the truth when it was shown, was irrefutable.

Maven, though, had heard of the Dragons before they saved her. She presumed they were terrifying. *Everyone* was scared of them. From bums to business owners, they were seen as a scourge of this city. Now she saw behind the curtain and realized that this could not be further from the truth. They were the only thing standing between this place and total chaos. Any deaths that occurred, in the eyes of those who didn't see the whole picture, believed they were the fault of the Dragons. Rumors that Snow would not discourage, but actively encourage.

The gang had a singular mission; To keep the streets of this decrepit part of town bloodless. Maven did not know why, though. She had heard from one of the gang that Snow's family had broken down on the way through to the west coast. The parents had called into the After Dark Club to ask to call a tow truck—leaving little Snow and his brother in the car as they did. But the parents never returned, and Snow made it his mission to stop anyone else suffering the same fate, so he and his brother formed the Dragons.

Another gang member told her that Snow was a vampire himself, and had found God, so was fighting the good fight.

Dolly, though, told a different story. She believed Snow was just a good person who found his calling. He knew he was a scary presence. He used it to his advantage. He would see strangers in town after dark and would rob them, threaten them, not for any other reason than to scare them off and force them never to return. Anyone who lived on these streets would see that violent masquerade, and would also fear him. This was all done so he could keep them in safety, for very few knew the truth of what dwelled within that club. Even those who had been here decades had no idea. It was just too unbelievable to be told casually. A person had to experience it, and most that did, didn't live long enough to dwell on the facts of their discovery.

The police were no help either. If they had been, Snow would not be able to do what he did. Maybe they avoided this part of town because they knew the truth and were too scared. Maybe they were in cahoots with the monsters. Maybe they just protected those better off, those in nicer neighborhoods. Therefore, if Snow bullied a shop owner as the sun went down, it was for the sole reason for that shop owner to be too scared to open when anything could pose him real harm.

To everyone else, Snow was a scary and violent person. To them he was their savior. Snow only ever showed his human side to the Dragons.

Whatever the truth of his reasoning, Maven owed Snow her life. She would become a Dragon. She would protect the streets with him, through the use of violence and fear.

"Why don't you just kill them all?" Maven had asked.

Snow smirked. "They're just one small shitty strip club. There's many more aside from that. So if we attack them, if we kill all those in that building we'd be wiped out overnight by others. You see they are everywhere. And not just them. Other things too."

"So, why don't they just do that anyway?" Maven countered innocently. "You scare their food off every night."

"They don't know what we do. They think we're just thugs." Snow shrugged. "Besides, we can't stop all the people going there. We gotta remain hidden just as much as the club does, for our own safety. We can only help those we find. Not like we're a huge gang. Can't protect everyone after all."

"And they never try to feed on you?"

"If we cross paths, sure... But we fight back. We're not helpless or stupid like the ones they usually get. The streets in the day are ours, they *know* that. And in return we let the club stand. It was that way for years, when they tended to stay put, but now, feels like we're fighting a losing battle. They spread out more each night. Get more and more people to cover for them. Now there's more and more attacks, further and further out. We can only do what we can, we're not an army. So deal is, if one of them feeds out on our streets, and we find em? We kill 'em. If we can stop *anyone* coming here, we do. On the flip side... If one of us steps foot into that club? Then that's us sealing our own fate."

In the alley beside the club, Keith stood under a light by the back door. The shadows around him dripped off the walls and covered almost everything. Within the darkness opposite he could see the outlines of trash cans and boxes. At least he thought that's what they were. *Hell, there could be monsters there*, he thought nervously, *all lying in wait to attack me.*

More than the shadows, the worst part of this alleyway was the sound, or lack there of it. An extremely oppressive silence seemed to blanket the place. Almost deafening, and pressing down on him like a lead weight.

Before he could get any more impatient, the back door of the club swung wide open with a sudden creak of the hinges. As it opened out toward him, Keith—for no discernible reason—backed away from the light on the wall and into the protective dark shadows. Moving as if his sixth sense knew that it would not be Amaretto standing there.

Indeed, it was not.

From out of the club, came a rolling trash can. Its wheels squealed loudly as it was pushed, the weight inside pushing down its plastic. It came out closely followed by the bouncer, Vlad.

This bin's lid sat half open, exposing the large black plastic bag overflowing from within it.

Toward the other end of the alleyway, leading onto the street at the back of the club, Keith continued to watch from the darkness. He witnessed Vlad wheeling that bin toward a small parked dumpster truck sitting at the far end of the alley. A truck Keith had not seen there before.

As the bouncer approached, the truck door opened, illuminating its interior cab, and the driver got out.

Gasping, Keith worried that the driver *must* have seen him waiting there before Vlad came out. *He must have.* He had to have seen him hide from the bouncer. Yet despite the worry, nothing seemed to come of it. Vlad handed the truck driver what he thought looked like several wallets, in addition to passing him the bin.

The driver looked at the wallets, nodded to Vlad, then took the bin to the back of the truck. Vlad then walked around the outside to the front of the club, out of Keith's sight.

Keith had no idea what he had just seen, nor what it meant, but he felt that something was not right. Not right at all.

Moving out of the shadows, he gently stepped toward the truck, as the driver was busily emptying the bin into the back; lifting the large heavy plastic bag over the metal side with a maximum effort.

"Keith!" came the voice of Amaretto from behind him, stealing him away from his spying.

Reeling, Keith saw her standing in the brightly lit doorway with a huge grin on her face.

"Aren't *we* jumpy tonight?" she laughed as he tried to retain his cool.

On Hewitt Street, the night had settled in hard. The whole street was now deserted, without a parked car in sight. Every building seemed lifeless and empty, with all but two street lamps left working. These, along with a solitary pair of traffic signals, provided the only break in the darkness. Not even the moon allowed much of its illumination to spill through the thick clouds from above.

The silence in the dead street was quickly broken by the heels of Amaretto's shoes. The clack-clack they made echoed down the seemingly endless streets.

With a look of unease at the surroundings, Keith walked beside the ever-smiling Amaretto.

"What's going on 'round here?" He asked rhetorically. "It feels so... I dunno... Apocalyptic."

"I know what you mean..." She replied. "It's weird. Like a disaster happened or something. I only moved here last week, and it's... all a bit weird."

Keith nodded in agreement.

Smiling, she linked arms with him happily and pulled herself closer. "And *this*," she said, motioning to them with her free hand. "This is like a reunion."

"I just wish I knew who it was with."

Amaretto, feeling playful, said, "I'll tell you when the

time's right, I promise, I'll tell you. But I'm quite hurt that you don't remember."

As they turned a corner, Keith glanced up and saw a street sign to the street they entered. Lindley Avenue. He smirked to himself. AJ had lived on Lindley Avenue back in Kansas. He didn't know why that was funny to him, it just was. Until it reminded him that he still needed to find his best friend. That was the point of this excursion. Why he was with Amaretto. That's when he stopped smiling.

A break in the darkness lay ahead as Keith and Amaretto approached a dilapidated housing project. A six story block that had seen better days many decades ago. A block that now, even in this darkness, could clearly be seen as a horrible place to live. The brickwork had been stained with what looked like a horrible rising black mold. The glass windows, those that were not broken, were all caked with so much dirt, that Keith doubted they would even need curtains to block out the sun.

Outside on the stoop, a small figure sat alone. A small girl of five, thin and exhausted. She held a home-made doll in her tiny hands, and stared blankly at Keith and Amaretto as they walked near; they were unwelcome visitors walking past her house.

"That's so sad," Amaretto said as she noticed the girl. She unlinked her arm from Keith and walked nearer to the child. "Hey dear," she said kindly. "Where's your mommy? Your daddy?"

The girl, not breaking eye contact, nor changing her blank expression, got to her feet. Dropping the doll onto the stoop without any care, she began to step backward, keeping her gaze locked on Amaretto. Her movements were almost unnatural as she took very small steps back, one after the other, through the open doorway and into the pitch black of the building block. Her steps were fluid, as if walking backwards were as natural as walking forwards to her.

After that, Keith and Amaretto silently walked on, intentionally not talking about the girl. It was all too depressing to consider the life she may lead, and too freaky to discuss the way she moved or how she made her exit with such ease.

A few streets away, after walking in silence for a while longer, Amaretto was busily lost in thought as Keith looked at her warmly. Sure, he did not know who she was, nor did he think it mattered. He was just happy to be in her company. She was nice. Not at all the kind of person he thought might be in the employ of a strip club.

Catching his stare, she smiled back at him. "You're dying to ask me..."

"I am?" Keith asked, unsure.

"Why I strip there?"

"No. No, I—"

"Yes, you are, and that's okay. I understand."

Despite his denial, *of course* Keith had thought that. In his mind, only a certain type of woman would work there, well that was what he thought before he went through the doors of the After Dark Club. After-all, that was the first strip club he had ever been to. He could not help the prejudice he unwittingly believed, that all strippers were junkies and glorified prostitutes. Not that he had ever met a junkie or a prostitute before either.

"I'm really not *dying* to ask," Keith continued to lie, both to her and partly to himself.

"Why not?"

"It's really none of my business." Keith didn't know why he was lying here. What harm would it be to tell her that she seemed too nice to work in a place like that, in this part of town. Sure she was weird, but he felt happy around her.

"It's nothing to be ashamed of. It's natural curiosity," she said. "The club's not a permanent stop or anything, if that's what you think? I only just started there. Just trying it out. I've been trying out new things all over. This just happened to be my next destination."

Keith had no chance to reply.

"I mean, the job was easy to get. They liked my body. They said if I stay long enough I can get free accommodation above the club like most of the girls, but I don't wanna do that. They're a bit of a weird clique sometimes. But it'll do for now. You see, I do what I want and I get to *express* myself. And that's important. Because I'm still looking for my purpose in life. *God knows* I've looked. I mean, I tried the acting thing for a while. Was on the Dating Game. I got picked, too—"

"Okay," Keith finally cut in. "I *do* have a question."

"Shoot. Ask me anything."

"Why here?" he asked.

She looked at him, confused at the question. "I don't follow."

"You're too good to be in this city. Why not Vegas or somewhere high class?"

Amaretto could read between the lines. *Too good*? He meant *too attractive*. She *loved* that.

And too attractive was exactly what he had meant, yet after he spoke those words, he immediately regretted it.

Vic, face flustered, with his hands balled into fists, paced Katrina's dressing room.

Katrina, dressed in a long red silk robe, lay on the chaise longue staring at the ceiling blankly.

A timid knock on the door stole her and Vic's attention to it.

"About Goddamn time," Vic grumbled as he walked over to, then opened the door wide.

Standing in the doorway, looking nervous, stood the child, Seko. Her face, still pale and still very much worried.

She stepped inside, slowly past Vic.

As the door closed behind her, he leaned in over her shoulder.

"You screwed up," he sneered. "You screwed up *bad*."

Katrina moved her long legs from off of the chaise longue, and sat facing the child. Her face was as blank as ever, with wide and unblinking eyes. Impossible to read, but mercifully more human at present.

Seko tensed.

Like a child waiting to be scolded after stealing from the cookie jar. She expected to be screamed at, beaten, berated.

But, Katrina just did nothing.

Vic just smiled behind Seko, sensing her nerves.

"H-He was so beautiful. I was sure you would like him." Seko tried to explain. "It was not me, though—It was Hannah. She made me…"

"You know the rules," Vic muttered from behind.

Katrina did not speak or move a muscle.

"They bullied—" Seko tried to explain before Vic interrupted her again.

"Only the untraceable. The transients, the loners, the strays. You opened your Queen up to *danger*. And we can't afford that."

Seko pleaded, keeping her attention only to Katrina, "Hannah ask him. We always ask. He said he was alone. He said he was passing through. And he fit profile. But it was not me…"

As she spoke, Vic wondered to himself, how come after so many years in this country, this girl still spoke in broken English with a Japanese accent. Was it intentional?

The child now would have been close to tears, if her dead body could produce them. She continued to plead. "But I thought you would like too. He was a gift to you, my beautiful Mistress."

"So, it Hannah but it was also *your* gift?!" Vic guffawed sarcastically. "*Nice* goddamn gift!"

Seko quickly fell silent, panicked. Knowing her reasons were seen as feeble excuses.

Vic said to Katrina. "We'll have to get rid of the others with him."

Katrina broke her staring at Seko, looking up and glaring at Vic with some disdain.

Realizing that he spoke out of turn, he demurred as he tried to course correct. "I'm sorry. I just mean, I could stop things like this happening. Protect you. If I just had a bit more control. I—"

With just an icy glance, Katrina cut into Vic's flow with ease. Raising a hand she waved him away.

Though he should know better than to protest, he couldn't help the complaint that fell out of his mouth next. "You're not going to punish her? Nothing? If it was me, I'd—"

A loud hiss sprang from Katrina's mouth as her eyes turned crueler.

Vic knew better than to stay and dig deeper. He knew that being the lowest on the ladder, a mere familiar, meant he was —by nature—expendable. Yet he also knew that he had made himself as indispensable as possible. He ran this whole joint. He kept the girls protected and fed. He covered up their mistakes. He also knew when it was time to exit.

"I'm going. I'm going..." he said apologetically.

Before the door could close behind him, Vic muttered, "This wouldn't have happened if we were in Vegas."

As he walked away down the corridor, his mind wandered to the neon lit city of Las Vegas. To The clubs that existed there. The vampire clubs. High class and governmentally protected.

. . .

Back in her dressing room, Katrina patted the seat beside her, beckoning Seko to sit down, which the child quickly did, obedient yet still nervous.

Katrina smiled kindly as she stroked Seko's long black hair.

"Thank you," the child said. "I am loyal. I always have been. Hannah made me. They always do that. Use me like a toy. But I don't fight back. He looked so nice though. Tasty. He—"

"I love you, my Child," Katrina interrupted, "You are my very favorite." Her voice was filled with warmth like a mother to her child. It filled Seko with something she could previously only barely remember, a feeling of love and happiness.

Finally.

This was what Seko *prayed* would happen in this room. She had only longed to please. But in reality the child had only managed to say the words *'thank you'*, before Katrina wailed an angry cry then plunged her talon-like hand into Seko's chest, piercing her heart with her claws in an instant.

Within seconds, Seko felt the approach of death. Then her skin began to burn from within, as her body disintegrated into ash.

Seko had witnessed this beast, this monster, Katrina decimate her family. She had been victim to Katrina's spreading of the vampiric curse, condemning her to exist as an eternal child. Forgetting her humanity and dedicating her life to this queen, Seko had become a monster herself. She had spent decade after decade doing every minute thing that was asked of her. She had thought Katrina loved her above all the others within this coven. Seko was *always* by her side. *Always* tending to her needs. But all of that was extinguished in the blink of an eye.

And, in the brief moment before her second death, Seko could swear she heard Katrina laugh.

At the end of the corridor, Vic grinned. He had heard Katrina's angry wail, and knew full well what that had meant. At least he didn't have much to clean up this time. No usual blood and guts. Ash and bone was always easily removed with a vacuum cleaner and a garbage bag.

CHAPTER 9
HOTEL/MOTEL

A mist slowly crept through the streets of the now humid city. Like a living creature, it mercilessly rolled its way through the streets.

A yellow and red glow of the tall Trilby Motel sign blinked brightly in the night, casting its illumination into the encroaching mist, lending it an eerie glow. This sign was a beacon within the desolation surrounding it. An inland lighthouse, but instead of steering ships away, it beckoned people toward it.

On the street leading to it, Keith listened happily as Amaretto continued her story.

"...So for a while I was a limo driver but I kept getting tickets. After that, I did the receptionist thing; 'Hello, may I help you'... 'Hello, may I help you'... really boring, menial work." She barely stopped for breath as she talked about her life.

Up ahead, a car was parked outside of the hotel. It's passenger side door swung open. From the pavement, a woman in a short mini skirt accepted the invitation from the driver, sidled up, and got in with a smile.

Silently, Keith watched this from out of the corner of his

eye, and witnessed the transaction of money in the car's front seat. He thought of Amaretto and couldn't help but wonder if this was something that *she* had done before.

"I don't know what it is," she continued, oblivious to the car ahead or Keith's questioning stare. "But I just can't seem to stay interested in anything for that long. How about you?"

"I'm in school still," Keith replied. The first word he had said for two blocks, but before he could continue, Amaretto took command of the conversation yet again.

"So am I! In a way. Actually it's a correspondence course. Called *Training Seeing Eye Dogs*. Isn't that a great thing to study?"

Keith had no idea how to react.

"See, I was watching the news," she began to explain. "And there's a demand for trainers, you know? I mean, have you ever met someone who trained seeing-eye dogs? It's kinda cool, right? Not like a normal job that's dull and boring. This would not only help people, but it would be actually spending all your time with cute doggies! Win, win all around!"

Keith really, really liked Amaretto, but had found that adjusting to her energy was quite exhausting.

He could only reply wearily, "Uhh... No... I haven't heard of that."

In an instant, that conversation strand was dropped like all the others she had started. Dropped in favor of the latest distraction.

She pointed up at the Trinity Hotel sign. "Here we are," she exclaimed joyfully. "Home sweet flea-pit of a home!"

Closer to the sign, Keith smirked as he noticed that it had been altered. The *H* in Hotel was a newer addition to the other letters. Underneath the glowing light of the letter, he could clearly see the letter *M*. Someone, for some reason had originally decided on *Motel* then changed it to *Hotel*, presumably when they realized what the difference between the two words were.

Getting closer to the building itself, he wondered why anyone would spend money on even changing that sign, yet not changing anything about the building itself. It had obviously been in quite bad disrepair for a long, long time. Each of its six stories resembled the many other abandoned buildings they had walked by, on their journey here. Like the others, this hotel's brickwork had crumbled in various places. The dirty windows all over it seemed to be held in rotten wooden frames. The only difference between this hotel and those buildings was that this one had lights on, on the inside of it.

The lobby of the Trilby Hotel/Motel was as seedy as they come, with vomit-green paint lining the cracked walls. The furniture looked as if it was also infectious due to the mildew that clearly covered it.

The air hung thick with the smell of stale body odor and stale cigars.

Amaretto skipped up to the reception desk, fronted by thick protective glass. Behind it, sitting below a handwritten sign that stated *I have a big gun. Don't fuck with me,* sat the desk clerk. A plump woman in her 70s, she had wild, bright hair that sat atop of her wrinkled, unamused face. In her hands she held a pulp magazine, emblazoned with the title *'Police Stories: True Crimes from the Scum of the Earth'*.

Without looking up from her reading, the desk clerk spoke, her voice carried over the small metal speakers placed either side of the protective glass. She reeled off a tariff for what felt to her, was for the gazillionth time. "Twenty bucks a half hour. Towels a buck. Condoms are five each. Lube—"

"No thanks," Amaretto cut in.

Keith thought that maybe she would have been

embarrassed by him hearing the kind of hotel it was. But she was not. At all.

Suddenly, he felt a pang of guilt that this thought meant that *he* thought less of this place, or at least that she would think less of him if she knew he thought that.

"I'm from the After Dark Club," she continued speaking to the desk clerk merrily. "Checked in last week? I'd like the key to my room... 1401?"

Looking up from her magazine, recognition spread over the desk clerk's face as she saw Amaretto.

Keith watched silently as the clerk grabbed a room key from a large rack of matching keys, then put one into a metal slot below the glass. Amaretto took the key and smiled politely.

"When you moving to the club?" The desk clerk asked, in a very bored and tired tone. "We got more girls coming soon. We need the beds."

"Probably never." Amaretto shrugged.

The clerk looked deadpan at her response. Keith found her demeanor curious as she looked angrily at Amaretto. Maybe she just didn't like her?

Changing the subject, Amaretto asked, "Could you please ring up to Candi? The redhead. I can't remember the room. It's on the top floor, I think."

Without even a smile, the desk clerk turned to the small switchboard in front of her. She picked up the phone, and pushed some buttons.

"It's busy," she croaked as she replaced the handset, then turned back to pick up her magazine. "But you can go on up." She spoke, no longer looking up at either of them. "Room 6019."

Without another word spoken, Keith and Amaretto headed for the elevator.

As they walked away, the clerk slyly glanced up from her magazine, watching Keith be led through the elevators opening doors by Amaretto. The clerk suppressed a cruel grin.

Standing in the elevator, a strange and very gnarled old man greeted them with a simple nod. He was the elevator operator. Dressed in a weathered and stained red bellhop suit, obviously from when this hotel had seen much better days. He was thin as a rail, with hollow eyes and drawn cheeks. He just stood silent, and stared forward blankly. Atop his head sat a jet black toupee, crookedly resting on his obviously otherwise bald pate.

As they shuffled their way into the small confines of this elevator, Keith and Amaretto shared an amused grin at the man's appearance.

"Floor five, please," she said, trying hard to not allow the laugh to escape her throat.

Without another word, the operator pressed a button on the panel in front of him. Buttons that over the years had now lost any trace of their original markings. The once presumably shiny golden panel was now stained and darkened with thick grime. The old man, though, innately knew each and every button without even having to look at them.

Without warning, the car jerked to life as it then started its ascent. It's very slow ascent.

As the elevator passed the first floor, the corresponding number above the door lit up, and sent out a weak bell chime.

Soon as it passed the second floor, the car suddenly bumped, shaking them momentarily; even shifting the operator's toupee around on his head.

Both Amaretto and Keith noticed this, then both found each other locking eyes. Keith struggled to maintain his composure, as he watched the toupee start to slowly move again, beginning to slip off the old man's head.

Amaretto still tried her best to contain her laughter. But it was simply futile.

She uncontrollably guffawed, which caused Keith to also

release his laughter. He snorted loudly as he tried to catch his breath.

The elevator operator did not move, nor show any reaction to either of them, or their sudden joviality.

On the next floor, the door chimed, then opened.

Keith couldn't regain his composure, and quickly exited the cab, snickering.

Feeling something was amiss, Amaretto caught sight of the number above the elevator door. It stated clearly with its orange light; '4'.

"Wait," She called urgently out to Keith, her voice still tinged with laughter. "It's the wrong floor!"

Surprised, Keith reeled back toward the open cab. But he was unable to get back in before the door slammed shut in front of him, leaving him on the 4th floor alone.

Even though he only saw back inside for a moment, he was able to very quickly discern two things: One: Amaretto found this *very* funny—he could hear her laughter from the other side of the door; Two: the old man—he now had a smile on his face, though it was not a nice smile. It was a smile that clearly stated, *'Fuck you, asshole'*.

"I deserve that." Keith muttered to himself. With another chuckle, he pressed the elevator call button, hoping it would force the doors to open again.

His smile soon faded as he realized that the button was not going to do a thing.

He then pushed it a few more times out of annoyance.

Just my luck, he thought as he sighed aloud.

He had to find another way.

Looking left, then right, he discerned nothing but rows of doorways. Each direction he turned seemed identical to each other.

With his finger, he alternately pointed one way down the corridor, then to the other, and back again. "Eenie. Meanie.

Minie. Mo," he said in a whisper. "Makes. No. Difference. Which way. I. Go."

Giving up, he turned and walked down the left hand corridor.

As he walked he glanced at each door that he passed. At each identical one with gold numbers embossed upon them.

Then turning his attention to his feet, he noticed the state of the carpet. It was stained, frayed, and very, very old. He could not fathom why anyone would willingly sleep here. It seemed unsanitary. A place where contagions are born and bred. Much like the club.

It was now he had to admit to himself that he was a snob. A snob with no money, yet still a snob.

As he approached a door marked 'Fire Exit', he came to a stop.

He pushed the door open with his elbow, conscious that he did not want his skin touching any part of the grime here. He then peered inside the stairwell beyond.

It was dark, so much so that Keith couldn't even make out the stairs inside.

Glancing back into the light, he looked down the corridor toward the elevator, then back into the foreboding stairwell.

Every ounce of his own self-preservation screamed at him to stay out of here.

Ignoring his better judgement, he took a tentative step inside. But, just as quickly stopped with a fright.

Had he just heard breathing inside?

After pausing silently, all he could hear now was his own heartbeat speeding up. Beating quicker and quicker the more he focused on what lay inside.

"Not today, Satan," he said as he stepped back into the brightness of the hotel corridor.

· · ·

VAMP

Unknown to Keith, but from within the darkness of the stairwell, the breathing continued. A shard of light from under the fire exit door illuminated a set of fangs within. A set which fanned out into a wide, vicious smile.

The ping of the elevator chimed loudly, as Keith still stood facing the fire exit door.

He quickly found himself racing down the corridor, racing toward the open elevator.

When he arrived at the now open doors, he found the cab inside, empty.

No sign of Amaretto.

No wigged old man.

Just the panel with worn down buttons, and the emergency glass box below it that housed a fire extinguisher.

The hairs on Keith's arms began to stand on end. Some part of him urged caution even here. His senses screamed at him loudly.

Tentatively stepping inside, the elevator door then slammed closed at speed—on him, pinning him to the door jamb in a split second.

Stuck half-in/half-out, this door crushed his shoulder, causing pain to shoot up his arm.

He tried, but could not yank himself free.

Using his outside hand, he tried to push the large metal door open, but it would not budge. From within the door itself, he could clearly hear the mechanism as it whirred and clanked trying to crush him.

With his arm still inside the elevator, he reached as far as he could toward the buttons on the panel, hoping he would be able to find the right one to re-open the door.

He strained.. Nearer and nearer his fingers got to the grimy buttons. Then, finally, his fingers made contact. Greasy to the touch, as if covered in a thick layer of petroleum jelly,

149

he smashed and poked at as many of the greasy buttons as he could blindly find. He just prayed to hear the sound of the door chime, signaling some sort of victory. But each button he depressed seemed to do nothing at all.

Suddenly, the elevator itself started to move.

It was going down, and it was trying to take him with it—even with the door still open.

Keith's mind flashed with images of being torn in two by this machine.

His hand continued to wildly stab at the buttons on the panel inside, but as the elevator moved down, the buttons moved out of reach.

Then, he remembered something.

The emergency box! He recalled. *The fire extinguisher!*

Balling his fist, he quickly—albeit still blindly—punched into the rising glass panel below the buttons.

The encasement for the extinguisher smashed with ease and fell in shards onto the floor.

Using all his strength, Keith reached for the extinguisher.

With the ceiling now almost upon him, the slow elevator continued to move.

Keith painfully managed to slide his body downward, forcing most of him back into the corridor, leaving the top of his chest, head and arm still pinned.

The gap between him and death was fast closing.

The elevator door squealed as it tried its best to keep him caught in place.

Without a second to spare, with the metal of the cab looming upon his skull, Keith managed to pull the fire extinguisher nearer and placed it next to his head. Between the rising floor and the ceiling.

As the top metal beam slammed into the extinguisher, it jolted the whole cab into stopping, inches from crushing Keith's skull.

With all his might, he finally squeezed himself out into the corridor. First his chest. Then an arm. And finally, his head and shoulders.

At this last second, Keith's shoulder hit the fire extinguisher, knocking it off balance. The elevator jolted, pushing the extinguisher back into its cab.

Scurrying away on all fours, Keith was free as the elevator door slammed viciously shut and the cab continued on its journey down to the lobby.

"What the hell..." was all Keith could manage to say. Shaken and trying to catch his breath, he quickly scrambled to his feet, cradling his shoulder as it pulsed painfully.

He tried to think of a different way out of here. He knew he had to escape. As crazy as it sounded, he felt that this place was against him. He should have listened to his paranoia and waited outside.

He then saw a window at the other end of the corridor.

He ran toward it, his mind flooding with all the other ways the building may try to hurt him. He pictured doors swinging open into his face, or floorboards giving way. But as he arrived at the window unharmed, he looked outside.

AN EXTERIOR FIRE ESCAPE!

A smile of relief broke across his face as he opened the window with ease, then hurriedly climbed out onto the metal escape.

He had momentarily convinced himself that the window would have been painted shut, or just bricked up. Yet, as he stood on the rusted and rickety escape, he breathed happily that he was out of that hotel. Though he knew that he was not quite out of the woods yet.

Steadying himself, he gripped onto the rusty bannister and descended the ladder. Each step he took creaked as the old, weak metal strained under his weight.

The whole platform shuddered with each movement he made.

Keith gritted his teeth, as he tried not to disrupt the stability of the escape any more than it needed to be.

But as he got to the last ladder, the one that should lead to the ground, he found that it was missing. All that was there was a large hole in the grated floor. A hole that stood twenty feet above the solid concrete below.

He calmly turned around.

As luck would have it, the window next to him was slightly ajar.

Don't do it, Keith, his mind screamed at him as he found himself opening the window anyway. He squeezed himself through, yet again ignoring his better judgement, but having no other option to take.

As he stood in the half light of an apartment's bedroom, Keith tried not to cough. But the strong stench of garlic had hit him so hard that he found himself almost unable to breath.

As he steadied himself, a confusion washed over him when he noticed that the room was littered in crucifixes and mirrors. Every inch of the walls. Covered in hundreds of them. The garlic stench was coming from large wreaths covered in cloves as they hung from the ceiling above the ornate bed.

In the next room, he could hear a television blaring away. The theme from *Green Acres* uncomfortably spilled in.

Slowly tip-toeing across the bedroom, Keith slowly opened the door leading into a darkened corridor.

Before he could even take a step onto the mustard carpet, Keith suddenly felt a gnarled hand wrap around his neck, as another reached across his face. His eyes bulged as he felt himself slammed back into the door.

Through the fingers that gripped him, Keith saw another

figure rushing through the darkness toward him—with their arm raised high, a pointed weapon in their grasp

"Get him, Eva! Now!" came an old male voice with a heavy Hungarian accent.

Managing to break himself free of the hands, Keith pushed himself away, and stumbled forwards… into the living room.

As he entered, he tripped over a coffee table, and tumbled onto the old shag pile carpet.

"Quickly, Oscar, don't let him bite us," an old female voice cried out.

"Nosfuratu!" the voice of the old man, Oscar, then shouted.

Keith clambered to his feet, then turned to face his attackers.

From the dark of the corridor, the two figures emerged into the light.

Keith saw that it was a couple. A *very* old couple. The man, Oscar, held up a large wooden crucifix in one hand, brandishing it toward Keith, and a sharpened wooden stake in the other. The old woman, Eva, screamed as tears streamed down her face. They both looked terrified but insistent to attack.

"Nosfuratu!" Oscar continued to bellow. "Back to hell!"

A splash of liquid hit Keith in the face as he noticed Eva spraying a bottle at him. She screeched loudly, "Ego te Absolvo in nomine Patris, et Filii, et Spiritus Sancti... Ego te Absolvo in nomine Patris, et Filii, et Spiritus Sancti..."

Spotting a second doorway in the living room, Keith darted toward and through it. The old couple followed in pursuit, as fast as their old limbs allowed.

As Keith finally found himself at the apartment's front door, he flung it open, then sped out into the outside corridor.

After a few meters of running away from this apartment, Keith glanced back in a panic. Standing by their door Oscar and Eva watched, not taking a single step outside of their apartment.

Keith wanted to say something to calm them, to assuage their hateful yet terrified stares. But he could not find the nerve.

Oscar then held up the crucifix and shouted after Keith. "Go to Christ, Prince of Darkness! Die! You undead bastard, you mockery of all that is holy!"

Eva spat on the corridor carpet, something that was clearly the ultimate insult in her mind.

Keith could only stare back, wide-eyed, as he pushed the door to the stairwell open, then went inside.

As the door closed in front of him, he turned and began his dark descent. He wondered how long the old couple would continue to stand at their threshold, staring hatefully in his general direction.

He did not know that he was lucky that he did not enter the stairwell a floor above, or he would have met what he had heard breaking from the fourth floor.

Keith now walked out into the night air, out of the hotel, wanting to kiss the ground.

Before he could get his bearings, he quickly spotted Amaretto far down the street, walking back in the direction of the club alone. She was now dressed in jeans and a jumper, carrying a plastic bag full of clothes.

Running after her, he failed to notice a large tow truck that was busily hooking a car to its cable. The same car that he had seen a woman get into just a short time before. A car that now had an inside windscreen that was slicked with blood.

"Hey!" Keith shouted, short of breath from the events that he had just endured.

Turning, Amaretto looked genuinely surprised as he

approached. "What the hell happened?" she asked. "They told me you left."

"D'you find him? AJ?" Keith asked, ignoring her question, and just wanting this night to be over.

He wanted to go home before he left the club, how he *needed* to go home. Just for his sanity. He liked Amaretto, a lot, but there was only so much he was willing to endure for his attraction to her.

"No, I didn't," Amaretto replied, then changed tack, "God, you look awful. What hap—"

"The girl. Candi," Keith interrupted. "What did she say?"

Amaretto turned then walked on, quietly annoyed at being interrupted.

Keith hurried up to walk beside her.

"It's so weird." She said, her tone softening. "I went to her room and there wasn't anything in it. Empty. Like no one ever stayed there..."

"That's just great ... just fucking great." Keith began, pointedly. "Today I was nearly hanged, then I got into a fight with a psychotic albino, met a human pincushion, ate a cockroach, my best friend disappeared, I was almost assassinated by a runaway goddamn elevator and now this really hot girl keeps saying she knows me, and I'm afraid I'm gonna die before she tells me how."

Amaretto slowed, then stared at Keith confused. Though concerned at the sudden outburst, she was also simultaneously flattered by what he said about her.

She took a breath. "I appreciate the compliment, but I hope you're not blaming me here. Because by your tone it sure sounds like you *might* be. Are you?"

Keith's expression fell. He felt bad for making her think he blamed her, but he felt worse that he'd said that she was hot. He hadn't meant to say that part out loud.

"Look," he spoke apologetically, "I... I just want to find AJ then get back home. Is that too much to ask? I don't blame you at all. I'm really thankful for your help. But we *have* to hurry."

"This hot girl doesn't see what the big rush is. He'll—"

"Please," Keith said. "I didn't... I mean you are... But.... Oh God... Where else do you think a girl like Candi would take him." He instantly regretted his choice of words.

"A girl like Candi?" Amaretto asked. "You mean a girl like *me*, don't you? Why don't you just say it? Stripper. Hooker. Whore. Slut."

Without giving him a chance to reply or atone, she then stormed off at a fast pace, screaming over her shoulder as she strode. "I was only trying to help. I thought we might spend some time together... *Maybe*... Apparently you find me hot, but you obviously think of me as dirt... So, that's fucking nice of you. Thank you. Asshole."

"C'mon" Keith called out after her.

"Fuck off, you prick!" She shouted, as she marched onto the other side of the street.

Staying on his side, Keith caught up and walked parallel to her. Ignoring the parked cars between them, and shouted over. "I didn't mean it like that. Please. I'm just really tired and—"

"If *you* knew me better..." She shouted angrily, marching forward.

"I don't know you at all," Keith replied. "Please, tell me!"

"And that's another thing—" She stopped then turned to him, glaring over the cars and street between them. "How come I remember you *so well* and you... obviously our moment together wasn't as important to you as it was to me."

"Look... I'm sorry!"

"Look *yourself*," she said, then stormed off again at speed.

Keith was left dumbfounded on his side of the street, watching her march off in a fury.

CHAPTER 10
STALKING DANGER

The club was still in full swing. The music blared even louder than before. The skin on display seemed sweatier. The men had also not stopped baying like wild animals as they howled at every performance that graced the stage. Dollar bills rained constantly from these men's hands, falling down at the performer's feet as well as being forced into the g-strings that clung around their oily, gyrating hips. These men continued to be willingly bled dry of their cash in exchange for the merest illusion of sex.

Duncan, though, in a now drunken stupor, had watched, one by one, noticing that the men who gave any amount money got equal attention as he did from the near-naked dancers. He wanted something more personal. Duncan wanted a one on one show.

With great effort, he clambered to his feet, then began to stagger around the room. As his leaden legs took him clodding across the club, he stared at every waitress that walked by him.

"I love you," he slurred to one redhead who walked by with a bottle of wine on a tray.

Then his attention shifted as he caught sight of a waitress. One with the physique of a body-builder. "No, I love *you*," he giggled. "Wanna bench press me?"

When he finally arrived at the bar, he sank his elbows down onto the glass, then placed his chin in his hands. He focused dizzily on the waitress across from him, who was busy drying some freshly cleaned glasses.

He looked adoringly at her. "Hey, can I get a dance with you, beautiful?" He smiled a toothy grin, hoping to charm her.

Shaking her head, she silently walked away to another part of the bar.

"She'll be back." Duncan slurred to himself. "They always come back." With that, he knocked over a glass, emptying its contents onto the counter.

"Hey, you spilled my drink, asshole!" cried a deep, indignant voice.

Duncan turned toward the spilled drink—then toward the voice—and found himself face-to-chest with a bearded, long-haired biker. Looking up, Duncan met the man's eyes with an unfazed smile.

"Such a beautiful beard!" Duncan said in a whisper, then turned back and went on his way, stumbling back into the crowd.

The telephone sat motionless on the large oak desk.

"I don't like it," Vic said, as he leaned back in his rickety office chair. His considerable bulk pressed against the chair's aging wood, causing it to creak loudly. "We should've heard something by now, right?"

In this tiny room off from the basement, Vic had tried to make it as homely as he could. The lightbulbs were warmer than in the club. The furniture, less aged and dirty. The shelves that lined the room had been decorated with mementos from Vic's past. Trinkets picked up from his youth; A signed baseball, a china figurine of Frank Sinatra, a ticket stub to the World's Fair.

Framed, autographed pictures of bygone celebrities such as Sandler & Young, Pat Cooper, Phil Harris, and Vic Damone adorned the walls. In the middle of them, one picture stood out—the only one that Vic ever dusted and kept clean—a picture of him as a young man, next to his old partner Mark 'Squeak' Coombs. In it, their faces were plastered with big, proud grins as they stood outside of their newly acquired business. The one that was to become the After Dark Club.

Vlad was on the other side of the desk, sitting in a chair that was far too small for him. He was cradling an ancient wooden etching in his hands. It was a piece of antiquity that seemed out of place here, where most other things were arguably cheap dime-store tat. With a cloth in one hand, Vlad caressed the wood lovingly, as if it were a child in his arms, cleaning it softly.

"We definitely shoulda heard by now," Vic continued. "And *if* it went wrong, The queen bitch upstairs'll chew my ass out, and not in a good way."

Vic's words fell on deaf ears as Vlad continued to gently polish the etching, his mind clearly lost in its detail.

Vic sighed. Vlad had arrived the day Katrina had forcefully took over - the day that he and Squeak had no choice but to accept the demands of the man from inside the limo. A man far more powerful than Katrina was. Vic shook his head in frustration. He was alone here, no matter who was around him. It was times like these that he wished Squeak had been sitting opposite him; someone who would be there every step of the way. Instead, he had a large, almost zombie-like associate, who struggled with forming coherent sentences.

"Vlad!"

Vic's call stole Vlad from his focus. He turned and looked up at Vic, with wide and vacant, doll-like eyes.

"Forget that thing, ya big lug," Vic said as he motioned to the etching in Vlad's grasp. "She don't dig ya anymore. You're not the wallflower ya once were, are ya?"

Vlad's wide eyes then narrowed.

Vic shrugged and stood up, making his way over to the door. "You're nothing but a quick fix for her now. Dunno why you fawn over her so much..."

A deep wolfen growl broke out from Vlad's gullet. His narrow eyes shot anger toward Vic.

Vic, though, paid this no mind. He was used to goading Vlad. For the last few decades it had been the same script on repeat. Vlad walked around like a lost puppy. Vic called him out on it. Vlad got angry. Vic walked away. Rinse and repeat.

As he left, closing the door to the office behind him, Vic grumbled, "Ah what the hell do I know. I'm less than nothin'."

As he slowly walked toward the stairs up to the club, Vic walked by the door to Squeak's cell. Each step he took seemed labored. Though, before he would trade the smell of the basement's dust and damp for the smell of lube and sweat, he called out to his old, condemned friend.

"Frankie, Sammy, and Deano...?"

A pause, then came the gurgled and grotesque reply, "Ahhhh uuuhhh aaayyy aaayybbbbeeee".

"All the way baby." Vic smiled bitterly as he ascended the stairs. "All the way."

Keith had not seen Amaretto for a few minutes now. She had stormed off at great speed away from him, despite his pleading for her to stay.

With each step along the empty tarmac, he racked his brain, searching each and every memory of who the hell she could be. Every recollection of school friends, or girls he met over the years. He would sort this out when he saw her again. He had to. If only for his own peace of mind.

"We've been lookin' for ya, pretty boy."

The snarling voice snapped Keith out of his musings. In the middle of the street, waiting for him, stood Snow. Behind him, a large black car.

Keith stopped in shock as he watched the doors to the car open, then four of Dragons step out; first, Dolly and Maven, then two more male members of the gang. Both bald. Both with moustaches. Identical to each other in every way, except for their necks; the skins of which were adorned with different tattoos. One read *Clay*, the other, *Dade*. Their names, Keith guessed.

"You should run, little buddy." Snow called out. "Run while you still got legs."

Keith couldn't help reply cockily. The uncontrollable reaction he seemed cursed with. "Great threat there, Snowball." He called out. "Really effective. Bravo." And once again, after speaking, Keith immediately regretted it.

Snow waved his hand to the car. The driver's door opened, and a huge man stepped out. Standing at least seven feet tall, the man had muscles that seemed like they wanted to break through his white t-shirt and white jeans. The man had a strong familial resemblance to Snow; same white hair, same cruel face, same deathly pallor.

"I'd like to introduce you to my brother, Ice." Snow said, grinning.

"Snow and Ice? Really?" Keith *still* couldn't stop himself. "You're parents really hated you didn't they?"

Ice roared at Keith like an animal, as the whole gang then began to move toward him.

"Oh shit."

Knowing he had overstayed his welcome, Keith spun on his heels, and bolted in the opposite direction.

"Take his shit," Snow commanded. "Cut him up. Whatever. Just make sure he *never* returns."

"We know, Snow." Dolly laughed, passing him. "Not our first rodeo."

Snow smiled, then motioned to Maven—whose face was a picture of bloodlust. "*You* know, sure... But make sure Maven does too."

As if in reply, Maven pulled a switchblade from her pocket and began running in Keith's direction.

Keith sprinted as fast as he could. As his heart pounded hard in his ears, he wheezed loudly gasping for breath. Right now, he wished he had taken track in school, anything physical instead of archery.

He could sense the Dragons closing in behind him. He couldn't see or hear them, but he felt like they were constantly about to catch up.

Darting around the corner, his lungs burned as came to a halt in the middle of a four street intersection. He looked around frantically—looking for some hint of the best direction to go in. Anything.

Before he could figure out which street to take, the mixed sounds of footsteps, yells, and car engines blended into one symphony, echoing all around him as the gang seemingly drew closer, and closer.

At the end of one of the alleys leading onto the intersection, Maven appeared. Dolly soon caught up behind her.

From across the street, Clay and Dade strode out from the shadows, holding matching crowbars in their hands.

Then, the black car transporting Snow and Ice rolled slowly from a third street into the crossroads of the intersection.

They all met in the middle.

The car slowed to a stop. Snow and Ice exited, confusion on their angry faces.

"Where the fuck did he go?" Snow said.

In the center of these meeting streets, underneath a manhole cover under where Snow and Ice had stopped their car, Keith was hanging onto an iron ladder that led down into the sewer system. A single shaft of light spilled in from a hole in the cover and illuminated Keith's nervous, sweating face. He closed his eyes and waited, hoping for everyone above to give up their chase.

After what felt like an eternity, he soon heard the Dragon's car start back up. When the sound of them driving away echoed down to him, Keith began to make his way back up the ladder.

He took each step slowly, gently, conscious that some of them may still be nearby. *Hell*, he thought, *They could know I'm down here, and be just toying with me.*

As he climbed closer to the iron cover, he held his breath, then positioned his eyes to look through the little holes in the cover's large metal body.

Above, Keith could only see the clear night sky.

He smiled, relieved.

"Gotcha!" came Snow's snide voice, as his face moved into view. He stared down at Keith through the hole, broke into a vicious cackle, and reached down to lift up the cover.

The sound of the metal sliding against the concrete reverberated all around Keith as he retreated back down the ladder, faster and faster, further and further; down into the dark sewers below.

The laughter above seemed to increase in volume the further Keith got from them, as Maven and other gang members soon joined in with Snow, creating a terrifying chorus.

With the cover now fully removed, the moonlight flooded down into the manhole. At speed, Keith jumped off the last few rungs of the ladder then landed into the inch of sewer water below. He tried frantically to get his bearings, but instead was overcome, and staggered as the stench of human waste hit his nostrils like a sledgehammer.

The laughter continued from above. Keith looked around anxiously to find an escape route. Across from him, a small pipe less than half a meter in diameter led to an unseen chamber.

"This can't be happening," he said weakly, as he rushed over to the pipe and blindly crawled through.

On the street above, Snow and his friends looked down into the sewer.

"Is it even worth it?" Dolly asked. "I mean... *I'm* not going down there."

"If we don't scare him off, he's a dead man, or worse, another one of *them*," Snow replied. "We may as well kill him ourselves, if we don't get him out of here.."

Maven grimaced. "Maybe we *should* kill him then."

The other side of the pipe was a chamber about twelve feet tall, and almost twenty feet wide. In the middle of it, a small current of brown water ran down a man made groove in the floor. From high above, moonlight spilled in from various sidewalk sewer grates.

Walking tentatively forward, Keith moved across this concrete room. Each step he took was slow and conscious, so as to not soak his shoes any more in the flowing waste.

As he stepped across the running stream of human

feculence, he noticed various lumps within its water—Hairy lumps. Stopping for a second, he tried to focus on what those lumps were. They seemed to be out of place. Then he realized that the lumps were dead rats, each in varying states of decomposition. Turning his gaze around the room, the shadows came into focus more. There were many dead rats here. *Too* many dead rats.

Moving quicker in his step, he then noticed that there were also live rats in the shadows too. He could not see them, but he could hear them scuttling.

He picked up the pace even more, wanting to get as far from here as possible.

"Go look for other ways in, okay?" Snow said. "If you see him. Make him *leave*." He turned to Maven pointedly. "*Don't* follow your anger."

He turned, knelt down to the manhole, and shouted downward into the darkness, "You're going to rot down there... So, run little piggie! Run, run, run, all the way home."

Duncan staggered through the club, on his way back from an uneventful trip to the toilets. He glanced around trying to remember where his table was located, but was failing miserably. The room spun like a Tilt-A-Whirl, and it was a ride he was very much enjoying being on.

As he walked by one of the scantily clad waitresses—one who was bent over a table, cleaning it with a cloth—he stopped in his tracks as if hit by an invisible wall.

Sniffing the air, Duncan said happily to her, "Excuse me. What is that *incredible* perfume you're wearing? It's so... sensual."

Standing up, the waitress rolled her eyes, then turned to walk away. "It's called sweat and annoyance, ya pig."

Duncan laughed. Though, before he could take another step on his quest to sit down, he heard a voice from behind him.

"So it looks like I have you all to myself," the velvet female voice said seductively.

Turning with a smile, Duncan grimaced when he saw it was indeed one of the performers talking, but that she was speaking to another drunken man. This woman grabbed the drunk man's hand then led him to the shadows of the private booth.

Duncan took a step closer. His grimace turned into a smile when he saw that the shadows inside the booth began to undulate with moving bodies.

"Oh, you lucky bastard," Duncan slurred.

Unsteady on his feet, he walked by the booth, trying to catch a better glimpse of what was happening inside. Though, through the darkness he could see only the woman nibbling on the man's neck.

Turning, he spotted an empty table opposite: a vantage place to watch from. He almost fell into the chair, giggling as he landed, ready for his private shadow booth show.

Hoping to see more from here, he stared ahead squinting. He could see them clearly, but only from the table downwards. The only place the light from the room hit.

For a second, the man's legs twitched, much to Duncan's joy.

"She is gooooood." he mumbled in his stupor.

The woman then moved one hand out of the shadows, to rest on the man's knee. Duncan didn't notice the red liquid that dripped from off of her fingers down the man's suit trousers. He also did not notice the red liquid dripping from her mouth as she stood up, then departed the booth. Leaving the man motionless inside.

In fact, Duncan's drunken revelry was so oblivious, that he did not even notice anything untoward when Vlad arrived, then carried the man's limp body away, as Vic gave his usual spiel. "Anybody wanna claim this lush? Once... Twice... Going... Going... Gone..."

The smell had almost numbed Keith's senses as he traversed the vast network of sewer tunnels spanning underneath the city.

He had no idea what direction he was going nor any idea if the gang were still in pursuit. But he did not concern himself too much about that. He was too preoccupied with Amaretto, about whether she had managed to avoid the gang and got back to the safety of the club. Not to mention AJ and *his* whereabouts. He had caused this whole debacle. Keith wanted to scream at his friend for disappearing in favor of chasing some woman.

Approaching a ladder built into the stone wall, Keith looked up and saw the glow of streetlights seeping into the darkness around him.

Taking a breath, he listened intently. He could hear *something* from up there, but could not tell what it was.

Quickly checking his watch to confirm the time, he saw it was 11:30pm. Everything *should* be silent except for the sound of the gang following him. Maybe it was them making these tapping sounds to lure him out? If that was the case, it was working, but he would take the stone ladder upwards as slowly and quietly as possible.

Approaching the sewer grate, Keith peered into the street outside.

His eyes widened as he saw the little girl from earlier, still holding the homemade doll in her hands. She was playing hopscotch along the asphalt. The tapping he heard, her tiny footsteps skipping.

"Psssst," Keith whispered, careful to not shout too loud. "Hey kid? Psssssst."

Suddenly, before the girl could answer, a huge heavy boot stepped down from off of the curb, and in front of the grating where Keith looked out from.

It was Ice.

Keith had *not* outrun the gang.

"Hey," Ice called out to the small girl, who quickly turned and glared back at the gang member, slightly afraid.

Ice was a Goliath of a man, who was terrifying in look, as well as having a mean voice to match. He knew this girl was probably scared of him, so he consciously tried to sound as nice as possible. He tried to break from his intimidating character to make sure this child was okay out here alone. "Where's your momma, little one?" he said as he crouched down in front of her.

The little girl, her skipping now stopped, swallowed hard, looking more and more afraid by the second.

"I won't hurt you," Ice said, trying to speak as softly as possible. "Please don't be afraid... I just want you to be safe."

"It's not *that*," The little girl replied weakly. "I know you won't hurt me." Before he could reply, the girl continued, all the while speaking in her same sweet tone, "You won't hurt me... But, I will hurt *you*."

Ice only had a few moments to register his confusion before the child bared a set of tiny pin-like fangs. Lunging forward, she bit hard into Ice's wrist, and clamped down on the bone.

With a yelp, Ice staggered to his feet and tried to shake her off. But it was futile. She clung on like a terrier. Her body flopped around like a rag doll as she bit harder and harder.

Then, she released her jaw and scampered up Ice's body, heading toward his meaty, exposed neck. In a flash, she reached her target, and bit down hard into his jugular. Ice screamed as she wrapped her legs around his shoulders and loosed a vicious growl. His blood sprayed out around them and jetted down her throat.

Keith watched horrified from behind the sewer grating as Ice staggered, with the girl still drinking from his neck, over the grate and onto the pavement above.

Now only able to hear this animalistic attack, Keith began to grow more queasy as the sickening squelches and cracks became impossibly louder.

After a few moments, there came a final gurgled scream, followed by a grotesque crunching sound.

Then nothing.

Silence filled the streets.

A slight breeze whistled through the night air, as if nothing had ever happened.

Keith stared out onto the street, trying to see anything, but there was nothing, save for the asphalt, and the girl's discarded doll that lay on the pavement.

Suddenly, from above him with a wet thud and squelch, Ice's decapitated head rolled into view—within inches of Keith's face.

Ice's dead-eyed stare glared back at Keith with his face frozen in terror.

Keith had to run.

He had to get out of here as fast as his legs would carry him.

But when he turned from off of the stone ladder—almost from out of nowhere—a hulking shadow loomed over him.

Stumbling backwards, Keith's legs buckled as he lost his balance, and fell against the wall behind him.

The large shadow shuffled forward and emitted a gleefully slurred giggle. As it drew closer, the light hit its dirt-caked face. Keith recognized it as the homeless man who had thrown himself against their car on the way to the club. The same man who screamed into their windscreen about his lost friend; a situation that Keith now felt he could relate to.

The homeless man peered curiously down at Keith, the grime on his face and his scraggly dark beard made the whites of his eyes pop brightly—almost glowing in this half light. The man then lifted up an object in his hand and raised it toward Keith.

The object came into view. This man was holding a large, squirming rat in his firm grip.

Keith straightened cautiously, getting to his feet as he nervously smiled, moving back against the wall — as far away as he could get.

"Cute little thing," Keith said with a tremor in his voice. "What's its name?"

The homeless man stared back widely, giggling.

Keith, struggling to maintain his composure, moved along the wall. He needed to get away from not only the man, but the murder scene above.

"Hey kid," the homeless man suddenly called out in a guttural slur, his laugh subsiding.

Keith didn't want to, and would soon wish he didn't, but he slowed his exit to peered over to the man.

"I found my friend, see?" the man shouted joyfully, holding up the trapped rat in his hand. "He was down here all along. So you can call off the search party."

Keith nodded unsure, but before he could utter any more nervous pleasantries, the homeless man bared a gleaming set of fangs from his darkened, dirt-crusted mouth.

With a roar, the man bit down into the rat's plump body, its insides breaking out all over his face and hands like yolk from a poached egg.

Gliding through the backstage curtain and into the club, Amaretto smiled confidently. She was dressed in bright hot pants and a sequined crop top. A top that rode so high it exposed the bottom of her braless breasts, the material stopping just short of her nipples.

Grabbing a tray, she walked with a new determination across the stage, silently mouthing the words to *Hit Me With Your Best Shot*, that now played over the speakers.

The lights span around the club, they too danced to the beat, matching the pace of Amaretto's steps. In her mind, this song and light show were *for her*.

Duncan, meanwhile, was now sitting at a booth, half in the shadows, speaking to someone whose face even he couldn't see.

"The problem with me is the *money*," he slurred to the unseen figure, just on the brink of being too inebriated to function. "I have too much of it. Always have. And I just wanna *belong*. But *nooooo*. You see, I got everything I wanted as a kid. I said 'Dad, I want a bike'. New bike was there... *that... day...*" He took a swig of the drink in his hand, then continued, "So I buy everything I want, *still*. Varsity letter. College place. Hell, I've bought sex plenty of times before as well! But you see, my friend..."

There was no reply or reaction from the figure.

"You see, my good, good buddy... None of it ever makes me *happy*. And what? I'm here again, knowing I'll be depressed soon after one of these fine lovely ladies takes my money, and let me—" he trailed off as he saw a familiar face approaching the booth. "Am-a-ret-to!" he exclaimed loudly toward her. "Wassappenin'? You seen my buds around? I can't find 'em."

Amaretto glanced into the shadowed figure in the booth, then nodded in apology.

She turned her gaze to Duncan, and noticed that his eyes were having trouble staying in one direction. He was giggling to himself at nothing in particular.

"You don't look too good," Amaretto said as she placed

her free hand on his arm, the other still holding her bar tray. "You ok?"

As soon as this question was asked, the veil dropped, a string of drool spilled out from the side of Duncan's mouth, and he felt a tsunami of nausea washing over him. One that took his smile away and replaced it with a grimace.

"Excuse me," he said, trying to stop the lump in his throat from escaping. Leaping, with renewed energy and focus, out of the booth, Duncan rushed across the club's floor, snaking his way through the perverted masses, and headed straight for the toilets.

With a smile, Amaretto turned back to the shadowed figure. Even though she could not see her face, Amaretto knew it was Katrina.

Smiling nervously, she said, "Sorry to interrupt... I know, I was told to never stop any booth activity, but I wanted to come over and say that I love working here, and thank you for the opportunity."

There was no reply from Katrina.

"It's my first night, see? My name's Amaretto," she continued. "We were supposed to meet later. So, I thought I'd say *hi* now. I'm sorry if I shouldn't have talked to that guy. You see, I know him... Kinda. Well, I know someone who knows him. So I just wanted to make sure he was okay."

Still no reply.

The pause grew uncomfortable.

Amaretto blurted out, "I'll see you later."

With a polite nod of her head—knowing she had overstepped—she walked away from the booth, leaving Katrina to the silent shadows.

"All this for a fucking fraternity," Keith muttered, as he climbed through a broken section of sewer tunnel.

For the first time since coming down here, he had noticed

that the ground under his damp trainers was now dry. He hoped this meant that his subterranean journey may come to an end soon.

Instead of having to rely on dim moonlight from passing grates in the ceiling, this new tunnel was lit along the walls by old yellowing bulbs.

But Keith had little time to consider anything, as his head swirled with a conflagration of horrific images. He couldn't help but replay in his mind the demise of Ice and the homeless man's rat murder...

and....

those...

teeth...

those...

Fangs?

They can't be fucking vampires, his mind kept repeating. *That's not even remotely possible.*

Then his mind darted to the old couple chasing him with crucifixes, calling him *Nosferatu*... It was all falling into place, but that was a place that *couldn't* exist. Could it?

Since escaping the homeless man, he could only come to one solid conclusion: he must be losing his mind. He *must* have imagined it all. The gang chasing him must have caused anxiety-induced hallucinations. *Are anxiety induced hallucinations even a thing*? If they weren't, should he call the police? What would they say? Would he have to lie?

From further down the tunnel, faint music drifted through the air toward him, stealing him away from his thoughts.

He carried on his pace cautiously, farther down into the well lit tunnel, his eyes darting from left to right. With each step he took, the soft music grew heavier and heavier.

As he stopped for a moment, he noticed a small billow of dust trickling from a crack in the ceiling, forced out by the bassy notes of the song.

Listening intently, Keith began to smile as he softly sang along, "Why don't you hit me with your best shot, fire away."

He *knew* where he was. By some miracle, he was beneath the After Dark Club itself. Back to the safety of strippers, booze, and pincushion bouncers...

...And Amaretto.

Or worst case scenario, a different club. Either way... there would be some help there.

Keith felt a need to hurry. He had a gang after him. He had a friend to find. He had a woman to make amends with. He had an abandoned... *colleague? Compatriot?* Keith couldn't decide what Duncan even was to him. Either way, he *had* to leave this tunnel, and this city—as soon as physically possible.

The quandary of calling or not calling the authorities would have to take a back seat, at least for now. Until he got back in the club, or back in his dorm.

His pace quickened as he ran farther down the tunnel, desperately hoping for an escape route, but as far as he could tell, there was no door from here that led directly into the club above.

The pulsing music overhead soon started to fade into the distance behind him. And in equal measure, his panic rose, knowing that he would have to exit at street level again.

Hopefully it would not be too far from the Club's entrance - more specifically: nowhere near the gang.

But then Keith's eyes caught sight of something beautiful; A manhole cover at the top of a ladder right in front of him.

Barely pausing for thought, he scaled its rungs, scampering upward joyfully.

Flicking the latches around its edge, he almost cheered for joy when he pushed the manhole cover open.

Now stood on the street, he took a breath in. But without having a moment to enjoy it, Keith heard a voice from somewhere further down the street.

"There he is! Kill him!"

It was Snow, shouting venomously.

How did they find me so fast?

"You thought you got away?" Snow screamed. "You think we didn't know where the tunnels went?"

Of course they did, Keith thought as he ran into an alley opposite. *This is their city.*

Dolly stood at Snow's side, and noticed the tears that streaked down his sharp cheekbones.

After they had discovered Ice's mutilated body, Snow became a different man—no longer in the scaring business; he was far more interested in revenge. Bloody murderous revenge.

He could not entertain the notion that the After Darker's could have been to blame. The red mist in his eyes blamed one person. Keith.

Dolly, though, thought otherwise. But her arguments fell on deaf grief-stricken ears.

"They know better than to fuck with us," he had screamed.

Dolly pointed out the bite marks around the edges of Ice's severed neck. But Snow would not listen to reason. He had it fixed in his head that the stranger *must* have killed Ice. His rage would not allow any room for any other explanation.

Snow could not be reasoned with in any way. No matter what Dolly and the rest of the gang tried to say. They had no choice but to follow his lead, or suffer his wrath.

Maven, of course, was quietly pleased by this turn of events.

Keith sped down the alley, trying to outrun the screaming mob behind him.

Sprinting out of the other side, across the street, then down another alley, he quickly hit a dead end.

As he glanced over his shoulder, he could barely catch his breath. He could not see a soul following, but knew that they were approaching; he could hear them.

He then turned and scanned his surroundings. It was familiar, but he had no time to think why.

Quickly he spotted a fire exit door on the adjacent building.

Running over to it, he grabbed its large metal handle.

DAMN.

The door wouldn't budge.

He ran back down the alley toward a large grey dumpster resting along its wall.

Getting nearer to it, he saw the words 'After Dark Club' spray-stenciled onto one of its metal sides. Realization flooded him in a millisecond; the building he just failed to enter *was* the club he was looking for. The back door he had met Amaretto at.

If he ran out into the street and tried to make it to the front of the club, he would—no-doubt—run into the clutches of the Dragons. Instead, he leapt over the dumpster's metal edge, and threw himself inside its metal body.

Landing in the trash, he buried himself as much as he could.

From the street opposite, the Dragons appeared. Snow leading their vengeful charge.

"I'll fucking kill you!" he screamed. "I'll feed you your own heart!"

From under the heap of soggy trash, tears began to well in Keith's eyes as heard the sounds of the gang drawing closer.

"Please," was the only word Keith managed to whisper, and for the first time in his life, he silently prayed to anything that would listen.

. . .

When he awoke, Keith couldn't tell if he'd been asleep for one minute or one hour.

Shortly after uttering his prayer, the screams and shouts of Snow and his entourage began to fade as he had lost consciousness from exhaustion.

Now though, he was in no rush to risk running into them again, so planned to stay in the dumpster a while longer.

Suddenly, the sound of a huge engine roared. A sound too overbearing to be that of a ca

Keith's suspicion that it may be a truck was instantly confirmed when the whole dumpster jerked violently and began to be slowly lifted off the ground. Caught in the grip of the dumpster truck's metal arm.

Garbage tumbled around Keith like clothes in a washing machine. Paper, cardboard, old food, broken glass and what he hoped weren't dirty diapers spun around him. Some bits were dry, some wet and stank of booze. All items gross and grosser all slammed indiscriminately into him.

As he tried to gain some balance, and climb out from under the churning trash, something large dislodged from the bottom of the dumpster and tumbled toward him.

It was not garbage.

It was not garbage at *all*.

In the split second before his face was smothered, Keith recognized that it was a human body. He had seen a flash of an arm tumbling, and some hair silhouetted in a crack of moonlight.

Then... Something wet hit Keith's face.

A suppurating wound on the dead body collided straight onto his face, making contact with his nose and mouth, covering them with their greasy, fetid gore. Keith immediately tasted the copper tinge of blood, mixed with the pungent aroma of spoiled meat as the corpse hit his lips.

Keith screamed, then pushed the body off of him with all of his might. That's when he saw that the wet wound that had covered his face was a huge gouge, where the skin had been ripped from the neck of this poor deceased soul.

As the garbage can jerked and rose toward the mouth of the dumpster truck, a chill suddenly hit Keith when recognition reared its terrifying head.

The shirt.

That shirt.

Keith pushed this body back so that the face was no longer turned away.

It was AJ.

His head lolled in Keith's direction, as the moonlight caught a deathly pallor.

Keith's world fell away from him.

CHAPTER 11
HEARTBREAK AND VIOLENCE

It was the summer that they had both turned fourteen, that Anthony Joseph Roman and Keith Emerson became friends for life.

Previously they had been *good* friends but that was it.

Ever since AJ latched onto him when they were ten years old, they had spent most of their free time together. This, though, was when they were merely childhood friends; ones who would normally drift apart when college beckoned. Ones who would be inseparable during the evenings and the summers during adolescence, yet when adulthood would call, they would invariably lose touch with one another. Childhood friends that would presumably reconnect only at school reunions and funerals for the rest of their lives.

The summer of their fourteenth year, however, changed their relationship.

Since the school let out for the summer vacation, AJ had been absent. His grandmother had to go back to New York to deal with the sale of his parents' apartment—and she had taken AJ with her. Though it had been years since they had left that city, it was finally time to deal with everything. AJ's old home had stood vacant all this time, untouched as the day the police closed their investigation. But now it was time to clean up and sell the place, even if the goats of the past hung heavy above them both.

Without AJ around during that summer, Keith had contented himself with playing on his own. Between mastering *Canyon Bomber* on the Atari, and diving headfirst into practicing the bow, he had little time to miss his friend, or the times they would have had.

It was only when AJ showed up in late August, looking crushed by the events of the previous weeks, that Keith realized how much he had really missed his best friend.

And a few days after AJ had returned, as he and Keith sat cross-legged in front of the flickering dots of computer tennis, AJ suddenly burst into uncontrollable floods of tears.

He had not cried while in his old apartment.

He had not cried as they sorted through all his parent's belongings.

He had not even cried when they had left the apartment one final time.

Here though, in the safety of Keith's room, he finally let himself go.

Keith was at a loss. One of the coolest of kids he knew was bawling his eyes out, hugging Keith as if his life depended on it.

Keith didn't know what to do or say. He had never seen a friend cry, not unless they had just been beaten up at school by Waylon. He had not even seen any adults cry. Now though, he just held his friend in a confused silence.

They didn't utter a word for a few hours. After he had finished with his tears, AJ turned as he wiped his nose, grabbed the Atari controller, and passed the other one to Keith. They then began to shoot starships and avoid falling rocks, neither mentioning what had just happened.

They continued to play all of the games Keith owned, escaping into the pixels for as long as they could.

When the evening finally drifted in, and the smell of a cooked dinner wafted up the stairs, AJ reached into his pocket, brought out a folded piece of paper, and meekly handed it to Keith.

"It's from my mom," he said, the words catching in his throat. "She never got to give it to me on my birthday."

"You want me to read it?" Keith asked, taking the paper.

AJ shrugged.

Keith knew AJ's mother had died, knew that AJ's father had caused it, but did not know much more than that. AJ did not talk about it, and who could blame him? But now, with the letter in his hand, Keith began to understand the pain AJ carried with him every day.

My dearest boy,

It's your ninth birthday today! WEEEEE! Congratulations, you fine young man, now walking into manhood with his head held high. I am sorry I could not spoil you as rotten as I wanted to. If I could, I would have got you everything your heart desired if I could.

So I am writing this letter to you now. This is your actual present, and one that is more precious than any money, any shirt, any toy. This letter is my love. This letter is my love, to you. My promise and dedication... to you.

Though I will not be able to protect you forever, I will always be right next to you. Every time you look at yourself in the mirror, know that I am there. I am with you to hold you when you are cold, and kiss you when you are sad.

You are my boy, you are my world. You are the reason I wake and the reason I sleep with a smile. And because of you I smile even though the world may seem like a sad place at times.

The past few years have been rough on us both, but I promise you, come hell or high water that it WILL end. That the sun WILL shine again. That you WILL become the man I know you can be. My beloved boy. My Anthony.

I love you more than the sun loves the moon,
Mom

They never talked about the letter after Keith handed it back to AJ. They did not need to. The moment had cemented them as brothers, forever.

A blood curdling scream jolted the truck driver from out of his daydream. A scream that came from the dumpster, his truck was now emptying.

He slammed the emergency kill-switch on his truck's dashboard.

Those assholes, he thought. *They left one alive again!*

Though he did not consider himself an evil man, the driver knew what he did for the After Dark Club was wrong. He knew… but he didn't much care. It was not his business what other folks got up to. And if they paid him to make midnight trips to incinerate what they wanted to dispose of, who was he to argue? And they paid him *very* well. So much so, he no longer had to struggle to put food on his family's plate. He knew that his work was good for *him*, even if it was bad for others.

And if it meant that, occasionally, there was still a live one, he figured that anyone in this part of town—at this time of night—well, they likely weren't on the straight and narrow anyway. Besides, this was not the first time he had been in this situation, and though he didn't much like it, he knew that if he didn't handle it, then someone else would handle *him*.

At the end of the day, the bodies he had to dispose of were dead already, even if they still screamed.

He was not a murderer in his mind.

He was just a cleaner earning a wage to feed his family..

As the dumpster shuddered to a stop, Keith scrambled to escape up its metal side. He leaped up, grabbed the edge, then levered himself upwards. Quickly, he swug one leg over its side, followed by the other.

Unbeknownst to him, at the bottom of the trash, there was another body; one of ash and tiny broken bones, all housed in a tiny black bag. All that remained of the small vampire child named Seko.

Keith presumed that he was only a few feet off the ground when he jumped over the edge of the dumpster. With his legs swinging in the air, he frantically looked for a place to stand, then panicked when he saw that the ground was over a dozen feet beneath him. The truck had lifted the dumpster as high as it could, ready to swing it over its hood and empty its contents into the collector.

"Hey! Help!" Keith screamed, trying to catch the driver's attention. "Heeeey!!!"

The dumpster hung precariously in mid-air as Keith looked around in a panic, trying to find another way down.

With a jolt, the winch of the truck slowly started to move the dumpster back down to the ground, though it was too little, too late. As Keith's grip slipped, he fell off the dumpster's edge, then crashed against the hood of the truck. Careening onto his side, he rolled and fell hard onto the pavement below, like a sack of bruised potatoes.

A few moments went by in a daze, as Keith wheezed in pain. He expected to hear the sound of the truck driver exiting his cab to see what had happened. But that sound never came.

Painfully, Keith rolled onto his back and looked upward. The last thing he expected to see was a wave of trash and human remains raining down upon him. But that's exactly what was falling from the now tipped dumpster high above.

In the midst of this torrent of cardboard and trash that landed on and around him, the twisted body of AJ suddenly slammed onto the street close by, his dead-eyed glare staring directly at Keith.

Keith had no time to register anything, as he met the gaze of the driver in his cab. Where he expected to be met with a look of shock, the driver instead gritted his teeth in a fury and reached for a lever.

Keith stared in disbelief as the dumpster tilted above, and the locks holding it, released.

Without a second to spare, he scurried out of the way, and the falling metal crashed loudly beside him.

His mind reeling, Keith turned again to look at the driver. Though he could not hear him over the engine, he could read his lips.

"I'll kill you!" this driver screamed.

The forks of the truck then moved downward.

The truck itself then bucked as this large machine was slammed into gear. The hulking vehicle began to wheeze as its accelerator pedal was pushed at full force. The wheels span, as the rubber smoked against the asphalt, trying to get a grip.

Lurching forward, the forks narrowly missed Keith as he ducked under them.

Scrambling to his feet, he sprinted out of the alley and onto the street, moving as fast as possible—absentmindedly running in the opposite direction of the club.

The truck quickly stopped, as the driver looked around in a panic, losing where his victim had run to. He slammed the steering wheel with both fists and a scream of fury.

But, before the driver could plan to solve this problem, he

noticed something. Outside his windshield, standing in the headlights, was Vlad. He carried two large body bags, one slung over each shoulder.

After a few moments of staring back at the driver, Vlad's gaze slowly turned to the trash and bodies lying around on the street.

The driver shifted in his seat nervously, unable to read the emotion on the large man's face, wondering if he was in trouble.

Keith had thought it too risky to consider calling the authorities before, but now he realized if he didn't, he may not find any other way out of this town.

He now *had* to call the police.

That gang *had* to pay for what they did.

AJ's death could not just be ignored.

Choking back the wealth of grief that consumed him, Keith raced to the center of the street, frantically searching for a phone-booth on either side.

He couldn't just run back to the club - not with that truck there.

He cursed himself for running in the wrong direction. Into the direction of the vengeful arms of the Dragons - the Dragons who were after his blood.

He did not even consider where Amaretto fit into this, nor even Duncan. All he thought about was his own life, and the murder of his best friend.

Getting to the next street, he spotted a lone phone booth glimmering in the night. It's outside light flickering at the end of the bulb's life.

The booth had been covered with so much graffiti that there was very little way to see inside, and Keith was so grateful for that.

Getting to the door, he stepped inside, almost

hyperventilating at the mix of every negative emotion known to man. He didn't realize it, but tears were streaming down his cheeks in torrents.

Closing the booth door behind him, the internal light flickered on.

He suddenly froze as he noticed the receiver box.

He felt sick.

The handset was missing; torn off at the cord.

That's when the sound of a revving engine roared out from the other end of the street. A familiar, ominous, sound.

The Dragons had returned to finish the job.

Sinking down in the confines of the booth, Keith opened the door with the top of his shoe, deactivating its internal lights, casting him into the darkness inside.

As the Dragon's car drew nearer, Keith closed his eyes tightly. Tears still seeped down his cheeks.

The sound of the engine crept by slowly, as Keith's heart beat wild and erratic.

He expected the car to stop.

He expected his luck to finally run out.

But against all odds, he heard the car pass by without even slowing down, then disappear down another street.

Only silence was left as the engine sound dissipated into the night air.

And in this silence, Keith blamed himself for everything.

This was all his fault.

If he hadn't reacted to that girl's teeth the gang would never have come over. Then AJ would never have made them so mad and they would never have hunted him down and...

In a velvet lined room adjacent to her dressing room, Vic paced nervously in front of Katrina. She, meanwhile, was sitting on an ornate wooden throne. Dressed in a black kimono, her wig was a shock of neon yellow, held up by two long hairpins that jutted out from either side of a rear bun.

Her eyes were hard and cold as she silently stared at Vic.

Behind and to the left of the throne, Vlad stood like a granite statue, staring forward unblinkingly.

"It's a goddamn shit show," Vic spoke as speed. "First we got some girls feeding in the streets, *despite* me ordering them otherwise. Then we got some new nests movin' in on our patch and feeding on whatever they want. Then we got goddamn hoodlums still tryin' to drive our custom away. Then we got that one guy, out there somewhere, cos of his friend you killed—"

Stopping himself, Vic then turned to Katrina.

As their eyes met, his stare widened as he realized the tone in his voice. Smiling apologetically, he held his hands up, palms up to her. "I mean, not your fault. No disrespect. It was all on Seko."

She did not react, nor reply.

After a moment, Vic began to pace again, and continued his tirade. "So we got that guy's friends, right? One's here and is fine for the moment. The other? He causing so much fuckin' trouble. Stirred up a loada crap at the girls' hotel. Fucked with our disposal guy. And is probably runnin' straight to the cops as we speak."

Vic abruptly stopped talking, then turned to face his Queen in shock, her face was a picture of fury, and Vic could hear her shouting, despite her not making an audible sound.

"You know, I'd do anything you say," Vic replied to her silent anger. His tone now turned weaker and pleading. "But not that... Please, not that."

Katrina's stare intensified; her dark eyes shone like endless pools of black. Eyes that beckoned Vic nearer as she silently commanded again.

He broke into a cold sweat, all of his bravado now gone.

His pale complexion somehow grew paler, as his breathing became more stilted.

"Look, I can take care of the police," he spoke quietly. "I'll explain it just like I always do, and they'll never follow up. I'll just slip 'em the usual green."

Katrina's fierce expression began to dissipate.

"As for the guy you killed, I think I know what we can do. You might not like it. But it would stop any issues we get, dead in their tracks."

She tilted her head curiously.

"See, that guy. He's dead... But... He doesn't have to be, right?"

Katrina, for the first time in months to him, showed a thin smile. She then turned to Vlad and nodded.

With that command, the bouncer quietly left the room.

Katrina then turned back to Vic, her smile now gone as quick as it came.

"Me? Now?" Vic replied to her voiceless command. "I... Uhhh... Yeah, it was about... Look, it's about something dear to me." Without waiting for her permission, he continued. "Could you see it in your good graces to release Squeak? I know it's only been decades, but I—"

Tuning on a dime, Katrina stood from her throne, back in her familiar fury.

"I'm sorry," Vic cowered, as she took a step forward, towering over him.

Her eyes bored into his. Her jaw bones twitched beneath her skin. Her words violently spit their way silently into Vic's mind.

"You're right. I'm sorry, I'm so sorry. I'll never ask again," he cried in anguish.

The psychic berating continued.

Vic nodded frantically as his voice trembled, "I'm sorry... I'll never ask again."

Katrina then took out one of the long pins from the back of her hair, then turned its point toward her wrist.

Gently she traced it to and fro over her skin. All the while not breaking her eye contact with Vic.

She licked her lips seductively, then jammed the pin through her skin, into her main artery.

Vic flinched, knowing what was to come, then pleaded, sniffing back his tears, "Please, not again… It's getting too much—"

She dug the pin harder into her wrist.

Vic winced like the pain was his.

Removing the pin, blood started to pour out from the wound and onto the floorboards below.

Unable to stop himself, unable to disobey, Vic did what any familiar *had* to do; exactly as their master commanded.

Dropping to his knees, he began to lick the blood from the old boards. Small shards of wood splintered into his tongue with each lick he was forced to make.

Even if he wanted to stop, he couldn't.

He would lick for as long as she wished him to.

He was *her* play thing.

He only wished that she would either take his mind—like she had Vlads—so he could no longer feel his human guilt, pain and anguish; turn him fully so he could *finally* have control. Or she could just end his torment for good.

Keith ran for his life.

Speeding in the opposite direction of the Dragon's car.

His lungs burned hot and felt ready to burst.

It was the last thing he wanted to do, but he *needed* to get back to the club.

CHAPTER 12
REVELATIONS

"Welcome to the stage," Vic announced over the strains of *Burning Down the House.* "The hottest firewoman on the planet. The firewoman who wants to slide down *your* pole... The one, the only... *Alina!*"

The lights flickered red as this latest performer graced the stage. Though unlike the previous dancers, this one was neither young nor beautiful. Her makeup masked nothing, even under these forgiving lights. Her blotchy, wrinkled and sagging skin was clear to all as she gyrated her way into the spotlight. Her movements were slower and more awkward.

At this time of night, the premium showgirls had done their duty. They were the ones that drew in the more sober clientele. Now, though, the quality didn't matter. Every customer was blinded by alcohol. So, any performer who may have disgusted the crowd a mere few hours earlier, was now seen as sexy as the rest.

None of the drunken, leering patrons here noticed nor cared about this geriatric nudity. They saw one thing and one thing alone, naked flesh on display for their viewing pleasures.

Vic, on the other hand, glared at Alina, grimacing to himself. Shaking his head he walked from the DJ booth, and over to the bar.

Hard Hatted Hannah, stared at him approaching. "You're a pig!" she snarled.

Taken aback, Vic replied, "What I do now?"

"I see how you looked at poor Alina."

"*And*?" He turned and gestured toward the dancer, who was still trying her best to be sexy, attempting to match the skills of people a lot younger and a lot more limber than her. "*Look* at the state of her?"

"You're no spring chicken, yourself!"

Vic laughed. "And if I was shaking *my* bare ass on stage, I'd expect some criticism too!"

Despite being his usual old self, inside he hid the pain he was in. His tongue throbbed. He had tried to remove all the splinters, as well as to stop the bleeding as best he could. But, he could still feel some shards in there, all mixing with the copper taste still pooling in his gullet. A taste of his own human blood and Katrina's foul tasting essence.

Hannah shook her head and walked away toward the stage. Cheering her friend's floorshow as she went.

Vic shrugged and eyed the whiskey bottle on the back of the bar. Before he could ask the barmaid for a glass of it—a glass he craved to wash the nasty taste from his mouth—he noticed Keith stagger in, past the entrance curtains and inside the club.

Bedraggled, sweating profusely and wearing stained clothes. Keith looked as if he had been dragged through hell and back.

"Whoa..." Vic called out loudly as he made a beeline for Keith, stopping him before he got in any nearer to the customers. "What's going on, kid? We can't have you coming in like this. It doesn't look good for the club."

Vic had handled dead bodies, but the smell coming off of

this boy was something else. A pungent aroma of death, sweat and shit, all mixed into one horrific bouquet.

"A phone," Keith spluttered in a panic. His voice broke, and his breath was labored. "I gotta call the police! My friend —" his voice trailed off, as his eyes filled with tears. "My friend," he managed to weakly repeat.

Putting one arm over his shoulder, Vic maneuvered Keith toward the bar. "Hey," he said soothingly, as he intentionally stood between the clientele and this emotional boy. "Of course. You can use this phone." He motioned to a bright pink telephone that rested on top of the bar. "But you gotta be quick. You're stinking up the joint here, okay?"

Vic picked up a sign next to the phone that read *Calls $1 a minute*, and placed it face down. "As this sounds like a real emergency, call is on the house... Anything we can do to help."

Keith nodded thankfully as he shakily picked up the handset and dialed 911.

Holding his other hand over his ear—blocking out the strangled vocals and pounding beat of the song—he listened intently as the ringing tone was picked up on the other end.

911. How may I transfer your —

"Police," Keith blurted out, cutting off the operator.

One moment, sir.

Keith felt his panic subside. *Finally* he would get help. He would get the answers that he needed.

More than anything, though, he had hoped that he was wrong about all of this. He had hoped that this was indeed all in his head. He welcomed the thought that he may be crazy or drugged. That was much more preferable to the horrific alternative. The alternative that he knew in his heart was actually the case. That AJ was dead. That a gang was after his blood and that there were vampires around, or at least things that seemed like vampires. *But what if they killed AJ? No. It had to have been the gang.*

He was confused but hadn't lost all hope yet.

You have reached the 911 emergency service. All lines are busy at this time...

The line then cut dead.

"It's busy," Keith said weakly. Feeling his stomach dip as he slowly placed down the handset. He then sat himself down on an adjacent stool.

Vic looked on, smiling his best fake smile, "Keep tryin'," he said. "If ya need me, I'll be just over here." he pointed to the other end of the bar as he walked away, keeping an eye on Keith as he left.

Keith watched the Maître D order a drink, down it as soon as it arrived, then order another, then another.

Turning and gazing about the room Keith struggled to sit up straight; a stark contrast to high energy in the club; He noticed Duncan at the stage, still throwing money like it was nothing, having a wail of a time. He saw a stain of vomit dripping down Duncan's jacket—he was obviously encountering his second wind now.

Keith then watched the dozens of customers cheering at the aged naked dancer, finishing her act by rubbing her bare crotch onto a customer's bald head.

The music blared.

The lights twirled.

Then the music faded.

The aged dancer slowly hobbled off, picking up the tips strewn at her feet as she went.

As the DJ introduced the next act, Keith managed a smile. He felt a pang of relief as he watched Amaretto prance onto the stage miming the words to *Bette Davis Eyes*, as it blasted loudly from the speakers.

During this, her third performance of the night, Amaretto had noticed Keith at the bar. Despite storming off before, she now made a few flirty winks and half-waves toward him, all while de-robing to her almost-invisible bikini underneath.

She had obviously forgiven him for earlier, at least enough to engage with him.

Keith then turned, picked up the phone and dialed again. His tears had stopped and he regained some composure.

911. How may I transfer your call?

"Police, please," Keith said. Less panicky than before.

One moment, Sir.

Keith held his breath waiting for the same busy message.

Emergency 108, a male voice answered. *What's your emergency?*

Springing to life, Keith's eyes widened with relief, as he spoke above the blaring music. "I'm at the After Dark Club. My friend's been murdered. By a gang I think... They were... I dunno.. Albino or something... One was missing teeth. He was in a dumpster. In a bag."

There was a pause.

Excuse me, sir? the male voice replied

"Please send someone," his voice pleaded. "Please... The After Dark Club."

We'll send someone right away. Can I take a name?

"Keith Emerson."

Please stay where you are, sir.

Keith exhaustively hung up the phone, then doubled over like he was going to be sick.

From the side of the stage, Amaretto spun on a stripper pole, noticing Keith get up and rush toward the bathroom.

Vic noticed this rushed exit too, and quickly motioned across the room—to Vlad—for him to follow.

The water in the bathroom sink felt like a sharp shock of reality, as Keith cupped a handful of the icy liquid and rubbed it over his face.

Repeating the process a couple more times, he stood up

and looked at himself in the mirror. Until now he had no idea that he was in such a battered state.

The water had washed away most of the blood and grime, but his clothes were still caked and stinking.

With water still dripping off his face and down onto the floor, he took off his jacket. Tentatively taking a sniff of the large brown stain on the back, he retched. The stench almost knocked him backward.

How did I not smell this on me before?

Taking out his wallet and transferring it into his trouser pocket, he threw the ruined jacket into the trash can next to the sink. Then, reaching for a paper towel from the dispenser to dry himself off, he sighed as he noticed that the dispenser was empty.

Turning he walked over to the last stall and walked inside. Closing the door behind him he sat on the closed toilet seat and shut his eyes. He took a moment to pause in the quiet and safety of this room. Grabbing a wad of toilet paper from the roll beside him, he began to slowly dry his face and hands.

Breaking the silence, the door to the club squeaked open.

The sound of the music drifted in for a moment until the door closed behind this person entering.

Heavy footsteps echoed throughout the porcelain and tile room.

Keith sighed.

He just wanted to be alone in here.

Bang.

The sound reverberated of the far stall door being thrown open loudly.

Bang.

The second stall door opened with force.

Keith was in the third. Lowering the now wet wad of toilet roll from his face, he started to tremble.

Underneath the door, a pair of large leather shoes came into view.

"It's occupied!" Keith called out weakly.

No reply.

The figure just stood right outside his stall, as if waiting for him to leave.

"It's occupied!" Keith reiterated. "You hear me?"

The door suddenly began to rattle as the silent figure grabbed the stall door's handle.

"What the fuck's your problem?" Keith shouted out, his upset starting to give way to anger. "Someone's in here, *Goddamn it*!"

The door began to be shaken harder.

Keith barely has time to look for a weapon, as the rattling got louder and louder and louder.

"*LEAVE ME ALONE!*" he screamed.

Without another second passing, the lock on the door broke inward.

As the door swung inward, Keith winced, expecting to see one of the Dragons, the truck driver, or *anyone* who would mean him harm.

Instead, standing there, with a huge shit-eating grin on his face, was no other than AJ himself. Alive.

Officer Jackson Jackson had suffered plenty of things in his life. Ridicule at his repetitive name. Sizeism at his wide girth. Racism at his dark skin color. Homophobia at his sexual preference. Yet, nothing was more mocked in this city, than the fact that he was a police officer.

Though despite all the mockery and insults he had experienced, he *still* loved his job, loved himself and loved his life. He was an extremely positive person. An annoyingly positive person. He also considered himself a good person, which he felt was key to being a good police officer.

Though, there was one thing he did not like in his life, and that was going to— what he called—the lost side of the city.

Being a church-going man, he very much believed in the existence and constant threat of true evil. And he felt there was a real evil thriving in the area between the train tracks and the old airport. With the After Dark Club being smack dab in the middle of it all.

Every time he had to go there, he felt his very soul was being tainted with… *something*.

Jackson's partner, Officer Sheila Lorenzo, had been on the force as long as he had. But unlike him, she *hated* everything about the job. Hated the people they had to help. Hated leaving the station. Hated the uniform. Hated the paperwork. She just wanted out, and thankfully, this month was her very last on the force. She had arranged an escape, and gotten a nice quiet security job at her brother's meat packing business.

Jackson, though, wanted her to stay his partner. He greatly enjoyed her nihilism. Besides, he knew he had a positive enough disposition for everyone. Lorenzo was his polar opposite. The ying to his yang, or as he loved to phrase it, *'The dick to my hole!'*

Lorenzo on the other hand, had had enough of all of the constant happiness that flowed out of Jackson's mouth. As she described to her husband, it was like *'working next to a rainbow puking unicorn on acid.'* Something she had no qualms in repeatedly calling Jackson to his face, and something he saw as a great complement.

'10-65 at the After Dark Club', the radio buzzed.

"Fuck!" Lorenzo exclaimed, reaching forward to grab the handset on the dashboard.

Driving the squad car, Jackson smiled as he stepped on the accelerator. "You love it really, my dear," he laughed.

Lorenzo shook her head. "Fuck you too!"

Her annoyance made Jackson laugh even more.

"Car 122, on route," she reluctantly muttered into the handset.

Jackson knew that his partner felt the same as him about that side of town, especially about the After Dark Club, but he also knew that the job was the job. It was the good *and* the bad. So even if he hated that patriot of town, he was happy to go there in case he could do some good and bring some light to someone.

"I fuckin' hate that place," she sneered.

Jackson's grin remained. "We could save an innocent life tonight, just keep reminding yourself of that."

"Fucking rainbow puking unicorn," she grumbled.

"On?" Jackson prompted.

Lorenzo grimaced even more, "on acid, Jackson. On a fuck-ton of acid."

"Hey, relax there buddy," AJ grinned. "It was just a joke, okay?"

Keith remained speechless, yet visibly angry as he stared at the disheveled AJ.

Stepping out from the stall, Keith walked up to his friend slowly, and prodded his chest, as if to make sure that he was really there and not just a figment of his possibly hallucinating mind.

"What happened to you?" Keith asked under his breath. Trying to regain his composure, and stop himself losing his temper

"I look *that* bad, huh? Yeah I may have taken it all a tad too far."

"What do you—" Keith fumbled over his words as he gritted his teeth. "I thought you were..." He suddenly grabbed AJ by both arms and shook him hard. "*You stupid fucking idiot*!" he shouted. "You scared the livin' shit out of me, you know that? Huh? This was not funny!"

"I got ya, though, right?" AJ burst out laughing. "I got ya real good! Now relax, will ya. Take a chill pill."

"Chill pill?" Keith screamed. "An hour ago, I saw you were dead in a dumpster. I thought that that Snow White asshole prick got ya, you total fucking—"

"It was all a *joke*!" AJ interrupted. "I set it all up! All makeup and acting."

Letting go, Keith shook his head. "Fuck you. We're leaving. *Right goddamn now*."

The door to the club opened wide, as Vic poked his head inside. "Hey you," he shouted to them.

Keith turned, saw the Maître D. "I found my friend!" he said, pointing to AJ.

"Yeah?" Vic looked annoyed. "Well, we got some uniformed people here to see you..."

"You called the police?" AJ turned to Keith, looking very impressed.

Vic shook his head in annoyance. "Backstage." He turned to leave, but quickly glanced back before the door fully closed on him. "And keep all this bullshit to yourself. I don't want my clientele getting nervous at cops being in the building!"

Sat in the mirrorless backstage dressing room, Officer Lorenzo and Officer Jackson looked frustrated at being here. Even Jackson's sunny disposition was rapidly retreating. Coming out to a crime here was bad enough. Being called out to one that was a false alarm was much worse.

Keith, looking sheepish, swallowed nervously. He perched on a makeup table feeling his hands getting sweatier by the second. Turning, he noticed AJ, who was sitting on the couch, paying the presence of the officers no mind. He seemed too preoccupied, focussing all his attention toward Hard Hatted Hannah who was sat next to him, happily playing footsie under the table.

"Well, your friend doesn't look dead to me, or am I missing something here?" Jackson said to Keith, as he motioned to AJ on the couch.

Lorenzo smirked, as she glanced at Duncan who was lying down on an opposite couch, giggling to himself in his state of extreme drunkenness. "And *this* one looks like he's not too far from being dead himself. Well I guess tomorrow, he'll feel like he is."

Duncan, noticing this attention from the officer, peered up to her with a smile. "Hi beautiful," he slurred as he fumbled a wad of cash from his pocket and held it out to her. "Can I get a dance, Miss sexy police woman?"

From the doorway, Vic looked in at them, still unimpressed.

"Well, I'm not lying. I *saw* him in the dumpster—" Keith began before trailing off.

Lorenzo ignored Keith's comment, as she kept her eyes on Duncan then addressed the room. "Your drunk friend here apparently likes to flash around his money. In this neighborhood that makes him a meal ticket. You know that right?"

"Hey, tell me about it!" Duncan giggled loudly as he threw the wad of cash in the air. The bills, raining down upon him as well as the floor. "I *am* a meal ticket, loud and proud. And I should know..."

AJ smiled, overhearing Duncan's ramblings, while continuing to look lustfully into Hannah's eyes.

"Look, officers," Keith began. "You—"

"No, *you* look..." Jackson's unicorn nature was far in the rearview. "My stomach's all upset now, thanks to you and your dead buddy over here. This is *not* a nice area and I don't like coming out to it. So before I lock you up, I want all three of you outta this city. Get the hell home, gottit?"

"I've been trying to do that for the past three—"

Lorenzo was the one to interrupt Keith this time. "Now, boy! Now!"

"I'll walk you guys out." Vic smiled, motioning the officers to follow him out of the dressing room. "I gotta cue up the music for the last act anyhow."

Duncan's eyes then lit up as he slowly sat up. "Hey guys... if you don't mind, I think I'll catch this last act before we split..."

AJ chuckled as he looked at Duncan, "Go ahead, buddy. We'll be out in a minute." He then turned at Jackson and Lorenzo before they walked out. "Officers, I promise, you'll never see us again."

Vic smiled as he closed the door behind the departing officers, closely followed by the staggering Duncan, who cheered as he went, "Boobs! Boobs! Boobs!"

The back door to the After Dark Club opened, as Jackson and Lorenzo stepped out into the cool, fresh night air.

"The end of the month can't come soon enough" Lorenzo sneered as she closed the door behind them.

"You'll miss it really," Jackson replied. "Especially me, your rainbow puking unicorn."

They continued out of the alley, toward their squad car, parked next to the large dented dumpster.

"I'm so fucking pissed at you," Keith shouted, still annoyed at AJ, who was now having his shoulders massaged by Hannah.

Keith stepped toward them, "I'm not kidding around here!" he continued.

The bright light in the room showed something Keith had not noticed about AJ. His skin. It was now almost grey in color. He also noticed the large dark bags under his eyes.

"Please." Keith implored. "Let's just *go now*."

"What's the rush?" AJ said, not looking back, instead staring next to him—into Hannah's eyes, "Anyway, I think I'm staying… I've found a home right here in the club."

Hannah briefly turned her attention to Keith, winked, then grinned. A grin that Keith did not like one bit.

"Hey Hannah," AJ said, as he stood up from the couch. "Why don't you clean up my friend here. He can't leave looking like that."

"I'm fine," Keith lied, uncomfortable in this whole situation. "I think we should get going… *NOW*," he implored once again.

But Hannah stood up anyway, and despite the protestations, stepped over to him. Grabbing a tissue from a box on the makeup table, she moved in front of Keith, and then started to wipe his face with it.

Her eyes, wide and hypnotic, bored into Keiths—Making him feel somehow weak, and not weak in any good way.

Moving behind Keith, Hannah then pressed her body against his as she dropped the tissue and ran her hand down his front. He could feel her body getting warmer and warmer against his back. More and more, until it felt unbearable. Like leaning against a boiling radiator.

Keith suddenly went to move, but was stopped by Hannah's powerful grip upon his arm. Her fingers squeezed like a vise, holding him firmly in place.

Keith let out a cry of pain and looked back at her. But instead of Hannah, he was met with something he did not expect. Her *other* face. The face she hid from the customers in the club. She had bared fangs. Her skin had become translucent. Her veins now popped as her eyes burned a deep red color—*at him*.

Before Keith could scream for help, she effortlessly threw him across the room, as if he weighed nothing. His body flew across the room and above the couch where Duncan had been lying. He hit the wall with a thud, then fell downward.

Quickly trying to regain his senses, Keith managed to scramble to his feet.

He noticed AJ by the couch. His grin had disappeared, and he looked torn and weak.

Then, grabbing a chair from next to him, Keith held it aloft toward the advancing Hannah, warding her off. She hissed angrily toward him.

Despite the makeshift weapon in his hands, she advanced.

He swung at her.

The legs of the chair collided with force across Hannah's head. The wood splintered into pieces as it broke apart, littering down onto the floor around her.

She seemed unfazed by this attack, and her hiss continued on as loudly as before. Her eyes traced up and down Keith's body, sizing up her prey.

"AJ, help me!" Keith pleaded, but AJ didn't react or move. His expression just grew more and more pained by the second.

Something inside AJ was hurting and he couldn't control it. It was the most pain he had ever felt. Even more painful than his demise.

Hannah's clawed hand then swung through the air, colliding with Keith's arm, cutting through the clothing as well as his skin. The force of which, sending his whole body careening to the floor.

She roared terrifyingly into the air, as Keith lay, grasping his new wound, dazed and moaning in pain.

As this monstrous creature commenced her final attack, she leaped through the air towards Keith. Without even thinking he reached out and grabbed the nearest thing to him.

The next moments were a blur, as he found himself laying on his back, the object he had grabbed still resting tightly within his grasp.

The vampiric Hannah, now sprawled on top of him, made

a weird, squealing noise. Her fangs, long and dangerous, hung mere inches above his neck.

But she didn't strike.

She didn't move much at all.

Instead, her eyes slowly filled with blood as her face contorted in extreme torment.

Around his hand, trapped between them, Keith then felt a liquid pooling over his skin. A warm sickly liquid.

In a panic, he pushed her squealing body off of him.

As she rolled to the floor, a weapon came into view, protruding from her chest. A spiked high heel; The object Keith had managed to grab in his panic.

As her body twitched, it then started to blister. He watched in awe as a fire emanated from within her body, taking her flesh and bone from the inside.

"I didn't think you had it in you." AJ said bitterly as he clenched his teeth. "Looks like you discovered the only way out of here."

Keith turned to his friend in shock, and looked into his soulless eyes. AJ's face contorted as if he was crying, but he no longer had the ability to produce any tears.

"You see, this is my new home. I got no choice about that." AJ said. "I *have* to obey. You see... I have these... thoughts. Thoughts that tell me stuff..."

AJ took a step toward him, but Keith backed away nervously.

"What the hell are you saying?" Keith asked, his voice brimming with dread.

AJ paused for a moment, then spoke in a maudlin, sober tone. His words came as if he was breaking the worst of the worst news that he possibly could. As if he were a policeman informing a mother of her child's untimely, tragic death—which in a way, he was.

"The club, Keith," AJ replied. His eyes getting wider,

darker, with a mix of alternating innocent yet evil expressions. "Everybody here. They're all vampires."

In his heart, Keith had partly known this news already. He had seen vampires tonight. He had seen one murder. But with it now being said aloud, it seemed even more ridiculous than he had previously thought.

A dismissive smile crept over his face as Keith shook his head. "No. That's imposs—"

Before his sentence could finish, AJ opened his mouth and a pair of large fangs snapped into place. His dark eyes adopted a more reddish hue, appearing to glow like a rabbit's in car headlights.

Struggling to speak through his conflicting emotions, AJ tried to explain as best he could, "You see... the thoughts... they tell me... they tell me that I can't let you leave. Like orders... No, not *like* orders... They *are* orders."

Keith's forced smile dropped as he backed away even more.

"All I wanna do is cry," AJ continued, taking a step forward for each one Keith took back. "But you know, I can't now. Vampires can't. Cos they're dead. *I'm* dead."

Momentarily bending down, Keith picked up a shard of broken chair that had been strewn upon the floor. He then held it outward. Pointing it at AJ.

"Stop this now," Keith commanded in disbelief. "Ha, ha. It's funny. Good. Let's go home."

AJ glanced at the pile of ash and bone on the floor—The remnants of Hard Hatted Hannah—then back to Keith. "You saw what you did to her, right? It's past denial now, it's only an inevitable end left to face. *Your* inevitable end. There's no use tryin' to tell yourself it's not real. You can't do that. Not when monsters are all around you."

"We'll find you a doctor or something." Keith said as his eyes darted around the room, looking frantically for another way out. "Let's just go. You and me. Hell, they can cure anything nowadays, right?"

With a sudden spasm, AJ's body jerked. He swallowed painfully as he raised his hands up in front of him, watching them tremble in front of his dead eyes. Like a crack addict getting their first withdrawals, AJ was both in agony and confusion, wincing as his stomach tied itself in knots. He gritted his vampire teeth together, as his neck strained and broke apart the thin veil of makeup that had masked his deep neck wound. The wound that Keith had seen in the dumpster, very, very close up.

"You don't get it, do you?" AJ strained through his agony. "Home's a million miles away from me now. Home's another planet." He yelped in a fresh torment, as he clutched his stomach tightly. The pain beating through him like a tornado.

"AJ" Keith worriedly called out, still holding up the splinter of the chair leg between them.

AJ, with blood now trickling out of his eyes, nose, mouth and ears, stared back. "I'm a fucking zombie now. Can't ya tell, buddy?"

Keith's eyes began to well with tears as he could only stare at the torture AJ was going through. He tried to figure out if there was anything left of his friend that could be rescued.

But with a sudden burst of energy, AJ broke free from his pain and lunged at Keith—his friend's living blood commanding him to consume it.

A chorus of ancient voices in his head commanded AJ's new animalistic needs. They told him his purpose. No matter if he wanted to hear them or not.

Narrowly avoiding AJ's new claws from connecting, Keith scrambled around the room, managing to get on the other side of the makeup tables.

"Watch out, man," AJ said as he grimaced a smile through his pain and blood lust. "Wanna know how bad things are?

You and my Grandma are *all* I care about in the world. Both of you. You're *all* there is... *I love you*..."

Keith wanted to hold his friend. He wanted to tell him it would be all right. But then AJ growled a terrifying wail into the air, then quickly turned his focus back to Keith.

"AJ—" Keith said. Beginning to beg his friend to stop.

"Despite all my love for you, all I see right now is food... you're carrying my next meal around in your veins. And I'm... *starving*! And if Grandma was here too? She'd be on my mind as well. You see they *got* me... They got me real *good*..."

"Please, don't!" Keith asked desperately, knowing it was in all likelihood a futile plea. "If you love me, we'll figure a way out of this. We've gotten out of jams before."

"Not like this, buddy. Nothing like this."

Almost instinctively, Keith held out his arm and with one finger from the other—still holding the splintered wood—he pulled his shirt sleeve up. He exposed his forearm towards his friend. "Here... take what you need for now," he said. "To get you through."

With a laugh and a jolting spasm, AJ bared all his fangs in a bittersweet grin. "You're too much, man. Of course you offered me that." His grin then fell to a mean grimace, "But no... Do I look like a fucking mosquito? I can't just take a *little*. I have to take it all."

Keith did not reply. He just dropped his arm silently back to his side.

"I'm a monster, Keith. Even a muzzle would do jack shit. I can't be trusted..." AJ spoke as he looked emotionally and physically torn. As his insides begged for food, his mind begged for some escape.

For a brief moment, AJ suddenly regained some of his personality, as he glanced down at his shirt and trousers, noticing the dirt and blood caked all over them. "Awwww, Goddamnit, will you look at my clothes? Ruined!" Then glancing at Keith, it was as if he was back at the dorm when he then asked. "How do I look? Do I look real bad? I do don't I?"

Keith didn't answer, he was too busy finding a way to get out and save his friend.

"You know it's just like the movies," AJ joked, suppressing his hunger for a moment. "There's no reflections. You can't see yourself. But I don't get it... I should be able to see my own clothes. Not like I'm wearing vampire clothes. *Right*?" Looking around the room, still trembling, yet trying to make sense of everything, AJ motioned to one of the mirrorless light frames. "Also, wouldn't their makeup show up in a mirror if there was one? And their fake eyelashes? And their fake boobs? None of this makes any logical sense at all."

With a sudden twisting spasm, AJ's mind was stolen back to the matter at hand as he pounced up onto the makeup table in front of him, resting on his haunches—a step closer to Keith. His bloodlust, suddenly much louder and much more persuasive than his fading humanity.

Keith moved fearfully across the room "You're really gonna do it, aren't you? You're gonna kill me? Or am I gonna come back like you?"

"Sorry pal," AJ's voice quickly became more and more detached from his emotions with each passing word uttered. "Only the women can do that..."

Keith sidestepped nearer to the door.

Now toying with his prey, AJ kept speaking as he slowly crept over the table. His words belying his ferocious expression. "See, it's the female blood. *They* have the gift. *They* have all the power. If you die then drink some of their juice, you're walkin' and talkin' forever. Us guys though can only feed... just blood... no turning anyone... and no booze if you can believe that." He chuckled, and through this laughter came a low growl.

"How do you know all this?" Keith whimpered, edging even closer to the door. "I saw you alive not that long ago."

AJ crawled off the table, his back now slightly hunched, his claws outward. He pointed to his head as he explained. "It's in here. In the blood I drank. It's not just a living death... It's actual knowledge. I can barely think, trying to listen to it all." His footsteps toward Keith were very slow and very deliberate. Threateningly so. "You see, it's like a beehive here. You have the queen. You have the soldiers like me, and you have the drones like the bouncer and Maître D... those poor schlubs."

Keith suddenly felt the wood of the door, as he had backed himself up as far as he could go. He dropped one hand to its doorknob.

"I wouldn't do that if I were you. It's locked," AJ said, still approaching at a snail's pace.

Despite the warning, Keith tried to open the door with his free hand.

No luck.

He *was* trapped.

AJ moved closer and closer until he stood mere inches in front of Keith. He placed a clawed hand on either side of the wall next to Keith's head. He smiled as he noticed the tears staining Keith's cheeks.

Unable to move. Unable to think. Keith could not control his desperation. He just started back into AJ's demonic eyes. "Please, AJ..." his words were quiet and quivering. "Please just do one thing for me, if you are gonna kill me."

With a sadistic grin, AJ replied in an equally quiet tone. "For old time's sake? Sure, buddy, anything. Anything at all."

Amongst the blood that dripped from his facial orifices, a string of hungry drool slipped over AJ's lips and landed on Keiths' shoes.

"Make sure they don't bring me back like you, okay? Don't try to get them to. Don't ask them to. Cos I know you would."

AJ's viscous expression turned offended. "Hey, you think I

like this? Or them?" He took a step back angrily and began a tirade. "They're boring creeps, the lot of 'em. I hear them all, constantly... I may have just been born, but I *know* them. You know they don't call 'em the walking dead for nothing! Just talking to one of them will make you wanna kill yourself!"

"I *am* talking to one of them," Keith interjected, as he half heartedly held up the broken chair leg defensively.

AJ, without any emotion, took a step closer, and pushed the spiked wood against his shirt, pressing hard into his breastplate.

"Go on then," AJ urged quietly.

Keith could not tell if this was sincerity or a threat. Either way he tried to make himself push the wood forward. Hard enough to pierce AJ's heart like he did to Hannah's. But he could not.

"Shit," Keith said as he lowered the stake. He could not do it. AJ, even as a monster that was about to kill him, was still his friend. His best friend. His only friend.

AJ quickly grabbed the lowered stake and raised it back to his own chest - the other end still in Keith's hand. "You know this works. Stakes through the heart can kill us. Fire and sunlight, too. I got given a list, see?" He tapped his head with his free hand, the other still held Keith's stake up. "It's all in my head somewhere." He then changed tack as he looked intently into Keith's eyes. "It's just like the movies, mostly. They're strong as bulls. And they can jump like... giant frogs..."

"Frogs?" Keith asked. He didn't know *why* he asked. He was barely able to focus. He was just breaking apart emotionally as he witnessed AJ's transformation.

"Yeah. But go figure it... they *can't* fly. No bats. No capes." Looking off into the space above Keith's head AJ smiled as he thought. "Consider the poor fuckers who wanted to become like this just to be able fly, then after they found out. Nada. Nope. Tough luck."

A sudden spasm hit AJ—harder than it had done before. A hunger that screamed at him.

"You're ready to die for me, aren't you?" AJ said through the pain. "You can't believe I'm not me anymore? That, maybe, there's something left, huh?"

Before Keith could reply, AJ growled the next words out of his terrifying maw, "Jesus... Maybe there is still something human in me."

With a sudden flinch, AJ loomed high over Keith, leaning in; his mouth opened, fangs ready to eviscerate flesh.

Closing his eyes tight, Keith awaited the inevitable.

Yet, instead of his own cries, he heard AJ's howl of pain, coupled with a ripping squelching noise.

Keith, opening his eyes, quickly realized what had happened. As AJ had hugged Keith hard, he had forced the stake into his own chest.

Keith struggled to hold onto his friend's body as AJ slumped to his knees, crying in pain like a wounded puppy.

"Get out of here," AJ said as blood gurgled in his throat. "Get lost! I don't want you to see me burn..."

Before he could run, AJ grabbed Keith by the collar. "Burn 'em or keep 'em from their coffins past sunrise... or..." He then smiled weakly as he glanced down to his own chest, to the splintered chair leg sticking out of him. "Well, you know the other—" As his body stiffened as he shouted, "It's coming. It burns so bad... RUN!"

Before Keith could process anything, or grab another weapon, the doorknob behind him started to rattle as the door was unlocked then opened.

Standing there was Amaretto. Shocked. Confused.

Then, as she saw the carnage, the whimpering and nearly re-dead AJ, she screamed.

CHAPTER 13
DISCO INFERNO

Famously, history had a way of being re-written by the victors, without the real truth ever becoming known to the populous. None moreso than that of Vladimir Alexandrovich. The Grand Duke of the House of Romanov during the reign of his nephew, Emperor Nicholas II.

Vladimir had made it his mission to vanquish an ancient scourge across his mother Russia. A scourge that the books of the occult named *Vampir*.

Folklore told of these night fiends, the children of the Devil's darkness. Those who stole babies away as families slumbered. Those who reduced whole villages to ash in one single night of bloodletting. According to many—as it remained to this day—these were only stories to scare the young. Parables and allegories to teach about the *real* dangers and ills of society in a colorful way.

For Vladimir Alexandrovich though, he knew the truth. He knew it was all very real and very present.

When any ruler comes to rule over a land, there were certain truths that must be told to them. Things that the population *cannot* know for their own safety. These were the secrets never to be told, but to be considered by the powerful.

Yet despite this, when Vladimir turned twelve, his father Emperor Alexander II broke the secret to him, as told his son the unbridled truth.

But, despite his father's sincerity, young Vladimir paid these truths no mind. Why should he? He spent his life in a palace surrounded by an army of soldiers. He was as safe as anyone could ever be.

This childhood dismissiveness also caused him to forget about the *Vampir*, up until he was in his thirty-fourth year when he was faced with the truth in a more brutal way.

That was the year that his father would die.

The history books now told of Alexander II being assassinated by an insurrectionist, as a bomb was thrown his feet. This story, though, was only that. A *story*. A *lie*.

The truth had been covered up. Emperor Alexander II had been murdered while vacationing at his winter palace, by one of the *Vampir* he had secretly told young Vladimir about. This *Vampir* in particular had been seen fleeing the palace after the Emperor was discovered, in a state of undress. Mutilated. His genitals having been gnawed off, leaving him to bleed to an undignified death.

The fleeing creature had been described by the guards as a dark, beautiful woman. It was this description that sent the Grand Duke on his quest for revenge. For he knew who and what this monster really was.

Known only as Queen Katarina, the Emperor had previously sent armies after her. For this *thing* had spent years tormenting the country. She had wiped whole families out of all history, not to mention damning some victims into being *like* her. Transforming them from holy to unholy. And with this, as the population lessened, her coven grew.

Over the years, the royal army had killed many creatures like her, yet they never managed to catch Katarina herself. She was elusive, and her followers were more than ready to lay their undead lives on the line in order to protect their Queen.

With this in mind, her attack on the Emperor *could* be viewed as self defense, but not so by the Grand Duke.

He viewed her as an ultimate evil, and now, with his father gone, that secret mission to eradicate her and her kind became his own.

In regards to history, it was not just the Emperor's fate that was changed to a more believable lie, but that also of the Grand Duke's.

For three decades, his life continued just as his father's did. He sent armies out after Katarina, with the blessing of the new Emperor. And as previously, there were some losses and some gains on both sides of this hidden war.

All until the night Vladimir disappeared.

The dynasty could not say what had really happened to the Grand Duke, that he was captive, either dead or undead, at the hands of what they saw as a devil. They had to lie. Rewrite the truth to save the people of the Russian Empire from seeing behind the curtain. From knowing that unholy creatures not only existed, but had free rein to massacre as they pleased.

For many years after he was taken, Vladimir remembered who he really was. He remembered his full name. His family. His home. But over centuries, time took its toll. The disease in Katarina's blood stole his identity away forever.

Unlike other familiars who aged normally, Vladimir was not permitted to. He was constantly held halfway between life and death, to be fed on forever, with a mind that could never disobey. He was not given the gift of becoming a *Vampir*. He was condemned to torment in payment for his and his father's crusade against Katarina's kind.

But, time being as it was, this torment soon also faded from his mind. His fate became accepted as the norm.

His fragmented psyche saw the constant feeding upon

him akin to how people would view love making. He loved Katarina. He did not know why. He did not know why *anything*. He only did as he was told, and existed in a state of nothingness. Happily submissive. A slave with a mind that only knew her, and only accepted her as his truth.

Vlad stood at the exit of the After Dark Club. He watched from the other side of the room as Vic stood with microphone in hand, talking to the DJ.

Vlad felt nothing as he watched. Thought nothing. He did not remember when he first began standing here. He just knew that he *was* here now. For that was all he *could* know. He loved his Queen, and he did what was commanded. Everything else leaked from his ruined mind in an instant, never to return.

Vic, meanwhile, nervously tapped his fingers as he avoided watching Alina end her second act of the night. He didn't need to see her finale, where she bent over and opened herself up with her fingers, much to the perverse delight of the baying crowd.

Instead, Vic finished his smalltalk with the DJ, then eyed the backstage curtain with some trepidation.

Across the other side of the room, Duncan now stood with an untouched drink cradled in his hands. He, too, stared toward the backstage curtain, waiting for his friends.

The velvet fabric soon parted, as Amaretto walked through into the club.

She tried her best to steel her emotions.

She had just witnessed the impossible.

Keith had grabbed her before she managed to run away, convinced her of the reality of the situation they were now in. If it had been anyone else trying to convince them about vampires, she probably wouldn't have believed them. But with Keith... It was different.

Hurriedly, while pushing all her fear deep inside of her, Amaretto sauntered over to the bar—trying her best to appear like her normal happy-go-lucky self—picked up a drinks tray then turned toward the tabled section with a smile.

As she walked around the pit of tabled gawking revelers, Amaretto could feel eyes *on* her. She knew she was being watched closely, but she dared to not look up, she dared not show a flicker of concern, she just carried on.

Passing Duncan, she gave him a nervous nod of greeting.

He just smiled back. His exuberance from before, now gone. The second wave of drunken joy evaporated and was replaced by an emptiness. He was just blank, trying to stay awake. Trying to not vomit again.

"Gentlemen!" Vic began to talk into the microphone, as the DJ faded the music into silence.

The stage then dimmed its lights.

"You've seen the hot, the needy, the beautiful and the grotesque."

The crowd applauded and cheered .

"But now..." Vic continued. "Welcome back... To close out our perverse night. The finale to end all finales. Please show your love for... Our Queen!"

Without any more to say, the opening riff of *Back in Black* blared loudly through the speakers. The stage's whitest lights flooded on, illuminating Katrina who now stood on the stage. Her whole body, painted with white stripes and patterns over every inch. She appeared like an art deco sculpture for the neon age.

As she began to gyrate to the music, with severely stuttered movement, she stared out at the baying crowd, at each and every person who screamed for her.

Avoiding the Queen's eye contact, Amaretto glided by the tables looking for anyone who needed a refill. Her expression clearly showed her tenseness, though she tried her best to appear normal. She just focussed on the clientele and avoided any interactions with the rest of the staff.

But Amaretto's avoidance was noticeable to Vic. His gaze followed her intently. As did Duncan's, though in a more sluggish and tired way. Both of these men stared at every move she made, but for very different reasons.

Duncan felt the nausea flooding his body, as he leaned his back against the wall. He tried his best to focus on anything to not pass out. He stared at Amaretto. "Oh jeez," he mumbled as the room spun faster, though not as enjoyable as the last time.

As Amaretto took an empty glass from one table, she turned to the next then picked up another. Soon, she was at the table of the short man with his cronies.

With a smirk, the short man flipped her the bird, then blew her a kiss from the tip of his middle finger.

Shaking her head, Amaretto walked by him, but before she got much further, she stopped and reeled around to face him and his whole table. "What the fuck did you call me, you little bastard?" she screamed.

Without waiting for an answer, she tipped her tray onto the short man's lap. The half-full glasses poured over him then smashed onto the floor.

Without missing a beat, she turned the tray in her hands, took a tight grip on it, then whacked the short man over the head.

Reeling backwards from the force, the man collapsed off his chair, sprawling onto the now glass covered floor. He was so drunk he was the easiest of targets.

The surrounding tables all turned to gawk at the commotion now being caused. Customers at the bar all watched on with a mix of fascination and grim interest.

On stage, though the music still blared, Katrina had

stopped all movement. Her eyes wide and furious at the attention being taken away from her. Away from her *glory*.

As the short man tried to get to his feet, Amaretto kicked him in the face, sending him back down with a thud.

Most of the surrounding men cheered on. Even some of the short man's friends.

Duncan staggered around the table area to the crowd now gathered near the bar. All of whom were cheering in raptured interest at the burgeoning violence. Duncan knew it was time to go home. He needed sleep, badly. He needed Advil, badly. The hangover had begun to approach early, and he could feel that it was going to be a doozy.

As Duncan got closer to the crowd surrounding the fight, a hand suddenly reached out, and pulled him back to the bar. Back behind the line of people, and out of sight of Vic and the other staff.

Turning, Duncan smiled as he saw the person that had grabbed him. None other than his paid-for-friend, Keith.

"Hey buddy," Duncan slurred, trying to ignore his sickness. "I need to go home now, please."

"Yeah. We're out of here," Keith replied in a hurry. "Now."

Meanwhile at the tables, Vic waded in and pushed Amaretto away from the short man, breaking up the fight.

"Nothin' to see here!" he shouted, as the gathered crowd all moaned in unison, then turned their attention back to watching the stage.

As their gazes drifted back onto her, Katrina continued her performance. Yet, unlike before, she now gritted her teeth with each and every sway, making every movement that followed more and more severe.

Vic checked the backstage curtain again, and not seeing anything, turned back to lift the short man up off the floor. Then placed him, bleeding and beaten, back into his seat.

Vic then turned to Amaretto, who just stood there, wide-eyed and scared.

At the bar, Duncan was being pulled along by Keith, dragged toward the exit.

Almost there, Keith thought as his panic began to abate. *No-one's guarding it, thank God!*

Katrina continued her angry dance, as Vic continued to check the back stage curtain.

With most of the customers now on their feet, still not settled back down at their tables, it was difficult to see anything in here.

At the exit, Keith dragged Duncan faster.

About to turn the corner through the curtained doorway, Vlad stepped into view. His massive bulk suddenly blocked their only route out.

From behind them; up stepped Vic in an instant. He angrily grabbed Keith by the shoulder and spun him around.

Duncan, still with his arm held by Keith, was busy trying not to lose any more of his stomach onto the floor.

As Vic and Keith's eyes bored into each other, Vic suddenly smiled and motioned Keith back into the club, back to where the performance was still blaring, and Katrina was still dancing.

"Gentlemen!" Vic spoke loudly over the music. "There seems to be a problem with your bill. If you don't mind, let us proceed backstage to straighten this unfortunate matter up."

Keith's eyes darted, searching for another escape route. But every exit he saw was blocked by either Vlad or performers, all of whom stared back at him intently. Hungrily.

Breaking away from the tight grip, Keith hurriedly dragged Duncan into the center of the room to where Amaretto stood, still looking afraid.

As Keith held his hand out to her, she took hold of it without hesitation. He then led both on a path through the tables.

Katrina continued dancing on stage, but her glare was now fixated on them.

Looking over his shoulder, Keith noticed all the staff walking through the crowd toward them. Each with the same wide-eyed blank expression in their eyes.

The customers noticed none of this, and only paid attention to the closing act. To Queen Katrina.

As the song began to fade, and her dance came to a stop, Katrina did not move. She did not leave the stage as she would normally have done. She stood still, arms outwards. Staring at Keith and the others.

The show was not over, only that song was.

"Hey, get outta the way!" A leering customer shouted to Keith, who was now stood in front of the stage with Duncan and Amaretto, blocking people's view.

"Down in front!" Shouted another.

Keith couldn't remain silent.

He couldn't protect these monsters at all. He *had* to let everyone know. They *all* had to escape.

"These people are *vampires*," Keith screamed over the fading music to all who all watched the stage. "I'm not kidding. *Real fucking Vampires*!

"Yeah, I saw my bill," a customer heckled. "They sucked my paycheck dry!"

Laughter erupted amongst them, followed by shouts of 'move' and 'fuck off' as Katrina still stood on stage, arms outstretched.

She then began to silently gyrate her hips. Stealing their attention away from Keith with her hypnotic, pendulum-like movement.

The crowd cheered as another song faded up, and Katrina timed her movements to the strains of *You Shook Me All Night Long*.

Meanwhile, the staff all closed in to Keith and his friends, working their way around the tables, toward the front of the stage where they stood, helpless.

Each of the staff now bared fangs. All except Vic and Vlad, who just stood by the entrance letting the vampires do their thing.

No customers paid this any mind. They had no idea what was going on around them, as they watched enraptured at Katrina's encore. Hypnotized by her.

The Queen's eyes remained on the three in front her. The three who then made a beeline toward the pool table at the back of the room.

As Duncan staggered forward, he tried to keep his focus and consciousness. He didn't even notice as Keith removed the wallet from his back pocket.

Three large inebriated bikers were in the middle of playing pool, not giving any attention to anything around the rest of the club. They were there to drink, not to watch a dance.

One took his final shot, aiming the black on a rebound to the top left pocket. As the cue ball struck this ball, it spun off the cushion and rolled with purpose and precision toward its intended pocket. Moments before it could sink, a hand reached down to the table and picked it up off the table..

With a furious glare, the biker stood up and stared at Keith, now holding his winning ball.

"I hear you cheat at pool," Keith grinned, with Amaretto and Duncan stood beside him. "Is that cuz you're a roided out asshole?"

The biker's race turned redder, as his two buddies—both as large and as mean as him—slid off their stools and surrounded these three interlopers.

"What... did... you... say...?" The bike growled at Keith.

Glancing around quickly, Keith noticed that all the vampires had stopped following him for a moment. Instead, they all watched. Wondering what he was doing.

With a smile, Keith rifled through Duncan's wallet, then brought out a wad of cash—Much to the confusion of the man and his cronies, who stood by wanting to punish Keith, but not following the train of events.

"I'm sorry, I was just trying to get your attention... I got $450 to your $10 that says you can't beat this guy at pool," Keith said aloud, as he motioned beside him to Duncan.

"What?" the biker asked as he stared down at Keith, over a head and shoulders taller.

"$450!" Keith reiterated, struggling with his fake expression of confidence, desperate for it to remain on his face.

Duncan suddenly caught up with what was happening, and said in a half-focussed slur, "Huh? I gotta beat that thing? He's a mountain!"

On the next beat, the biker grabbed Keith by the collar, then sneered into his face. Without breaking his glaring eye contact, he commanded his friends, "Rack 'em up boys! We got pussies to beat."

The vampires meanwhile, held their ground a few meters back. Kept at bay for the time being by a silent command that came from the stage.

Katrina, her performance still in full swing, did not take her stare off of Keith. No matter her movement, no matter the direction her body swayed, her eyes stayed almost impossibly fixed in one direction.

Leaning into Keith's ear, Amaretto spoke in confusion and fear. "What are you doing?"

"Buying time?" He shrugged. Not knowing what he was doing, feeling or saying. He had no idea how he was not still crying, or screaming for mercy at the feet of these monsters."

"Buying time for what?"

Keith didn't answer. He *couldn't* answer as he didn't know either.

Duncan, meanwhile, trembled as one of the bikers handed

him a pool cue. His advanced drunken state barely allowed him to hold it upright.

Keith put a hand on Duncan's shoulder and spoke in a hushed tone. "Just keep the game going, I'm sorry to ask. But just focus. If you take it slow and just don't think of anything else, you'll feel better. Trust me."

Duncan stared at the balls getting racked. "But..." was all he managed to reply before he felt his stomach retching.

Managing to keep his vomit down for once, Duncan was just about to run to the bathroom when a biker gestured that the pool table was now set up.

"Your break," this biker said.

"Great," Duncan muttered under his breath as he staggered over to the table. Grabbing the chalk from the edge, he began to rub it sloppily onto the tip of his cue. Striking it over the tip like a match on its lighting strip.

The bikers shot each other confused glances.

Of course, Keith worried that Duncan could be sick or pass out at any second—he had been drinking all night after all, and he was obviously now in a state of limbo between drunk and asleep. *Maybe though, maybe it'll all be okay,* he hoped, knowing what he was asking of Duncan was a lot.

With Keith barely finishing his thought, Duncan struck the cue ball, sending it clear off the table. Missing every other ball in its path, it just spiraled through the air and rolled onto the floor about ten feet away.

The sweat began to break out on Keith's forehead as he turned to Amaretto with a helpless stare.

She didn't notice though, as she was busy looking around her, looking at the waitresses and staff that were now all walking back to their positions. Teeth hidden. Business as usual. As if they were granted a stay of execution—which is exactly what they had been given.

Keith stepped over to the side of the table and leaned against the wall, trying to work out what his plan really was, what the point of getting Duncan to play pool was. It made sense in the heat of the moment. Now, he just had no idea.

Duncan was busy proving that he had no aptitude for this game.

Amaretto was just staring around the club. Her mind was spinning with all she had witnessed tonight. She could not fathom any of it.

"You're putting off the inevitable." A voice called out from behind Keith, catching his ear. "It's only a matter of time, now. You get that, right? There's no magical escape from this."

Turning, Keith saw Vic now sat on a stool at the end of the bar, sporting a wide grin. He motioned for Keith to take a seat next to him.

Cautiously, as he had no idea what else he could do, Keith stepped toward the bar. Out of the corner of his eye, as he took a seat, he could feel Katrina's still burning stare on him.

He wondered where the police had gotten to, and if it was possible that they would return to check up on them, to make sure they left the city.

"It's only a kid," Officer Jackson said. "We can't just leave her on the streets."

Inside their squad car he and Officer Lorenzo looked out of the windscreen, out to the little girl cradling a homemade doll in her arms. She looked sad and lost as she sat on the curb outside an empty burned out building.

"Let's call child services and get out of here," Lorenzo complained. "I got only a few weeks left and I'm not gonna waste it on this scum and their problems."

Jackson *should* have listened to his partner.

Jackson *should* have called it in, then left, ignoring the face look of innocence on the child.

Jackson *should* have ended his shift right then and gone home.

If he did any of those, then he and Lorenzo would have survived the night. Instead of ending up as a food platter for the little girl to demolish in the most painful ways imaginable.

"You don't think you're all gonna get away with this, do you?" Keith said, not convinced of his own words, as he sat at the bar next to Vic.

Matter of factly and with no malice in his voice, Vic nodded. "Of course we will. You know how many people disappear in this city every year? Not hundred—*thousands*. You're, and I'm sorry to say, just another sad statistic, kid. And when I say I'm sorry about that. I truly am."

"We'll be missed," Keith protested. "They'll come looking for us."

"They?" Vic laughed heartily. "Who's they? *All* those people you told you that were coming to a strip club on the bad side of town? You talking about *them*?"

Keith didn't answer. His bluff had failed.

Vic continued. "Who knows you're here then? Nobody, that's who. Because nobody tells anyone they're going to a place like this."

"Then why us? Why d'you pick on us? Why not anyone else in here? There's plenty of other people here who, more deserving, right?" Keith dreaded the answer to this question.

Moving in his seat uncomfortably, Vic shrugged, "More deserving? That's mighty elitist of you. What, you and your friends're too rich? Too middle class? The people here to see some tits and ass make them lower down the rungs than you?"

"No I didn't mean—"

"Your friend was a simple *mistake*. You could call it a bureaucratic error. A simple communication problem. One that I am trying to ensure never happens again. You see, we usually vet the food. But the system broke on this one. One weak link and it all goes to shit. And for that I do sincerely apologize to you. If I could take it back I certainly would, but unfortunately we find ourselves right here. Right where we are now. And there's no changing what's transpired. No matter how regrettable it is. Think of it like a car spinning out of a cliff, when it starts, nothing you can do can stop it, no matter what you try."

Turning to the stage, Vic then glanced at Katrina now well into her second song. The audience, still hypnotized as she bared every inch of her body to them.

Keith couldn't believe the banality of Vic's answer. "You're so incompetent that you screwed up, so because of that, we became a statistic?"

"Hey, *I* didn't screw up," Vic reacted defensively. "It was someone else that screwed up, and they've been dealt with in the most severe way you can imagine. This wasn't just a slap on the wrist, ya know. We take this shit seriously," he paused for a beat. "You see, I try to run a reasonable business in a reasonable way; and it does us more than reasonably well. Everyone's happy when it all runs smoothly. And everything's been fine for longer than anyone could've hoped for, but inevitably, regrettably, there was bound to be a small error at some point. Nothing runs perfect forever. Just a little unavoidable mistake."

Keith kept an eye on Amaretto, who stood blankly watching the embarrassing game that Duncan was now stuck in.

Vic shook his head, "Ya see, I run an essential service here. Like a kind of waste disposal!"

Keith turned shocked at this man's callousness.

"That's right," Vic continued. "The lost, the sick, the dangerous, the forgotten, the absolute *dregs* of this society. They inevitably wind up here and we *take care* of them. Do you miss 'em? Does anyone? You people out there would be up to your asses in derelicts, pimps, hookers, criminals and insurance salesmen if it weren't for us! We clean up your towns. And it costs you nothing but looking the other way."

"And you took my best friend, and now want to kill me?" Keith protested.

Defensively Vic hit his hand onto the bar. "Hey! Nobody's perfect. I do the best I can with what I got, okay? Okay fine, you are not our target demographic, but that's a moot point now, isn't it?"

"Why are you even telling me all this?"

Vic shrugged, still slightly annoyed at Keith's accusation of incompetence. "Honestly? I can't talk to anyone else here. And frankly I thought you deserved answers before you died. It's only the right thing to do. I mean, you *shouldn't* be here. But fate is fate and we can't get off that rail."

As Keith took in all that was being said, Katrina's act ended and she exited the stage.

The house lights then brightened, and over the mic the DJ called for the last orders of the night.

With a collective sigh, the audience all resigned themselves to having to go home. The end of their perverse revelry now come to an end for yet another night.

Then over the speakers, the smooth tones of Frank Sinatra played out at a low volume. As Vic heard this, he closed his eyes, swaying his head side to side for a moment.

Unseen to any of the staff, Keith caught sight of a hidden doorway at the back of the bar. He watched as a barmaid walked through it and into the bar, holding a mop and bucket in her hands.

Vic then slowly opened his eyes, smiling and began to talk. Nostalgically reminiscing, reminded by the song being played. "I used to own this place, you know?" Vic wasn't actually having a conversation anymore, nor waiting for Keith to respond, he was just unloading his problems now.

"That's right, I owned it!" he continued. "And it was gonna be a class act nightclub. Buddy Greco was gonna play here. Louis Prima. Even Phil Harris! The best of the best. We were even gonna open a second club when we got big enough. We were gonna go to Vegas, get Frankie, Sammy and Deano... You ever been to Vegas? I know, its just down the road... I always wanted to go there. I can't though. She'll never allow it... It's so classy, see? I wanted this place to be like it would be there. This place was gonna be... Classy. But... But then *she* came..."

For a moment, Vic glanced sadly downward, imagining how it may have once been.

Keith, meanwhile, was formulating his plan on what to do next. He sat silently, letting the Maître D vent his frustrations. Conscious that as each second passed, it was another second closer to sunrise as well as his potential demise.

"Now," Vic said. "Now my partner lies in a heap downstairs, and all we had, is now *hers*; *Theirs*. The place, the money, me, Squeak. Vlad... We... We just exist at her... at her sadistic pleasure. And there's fuck all any of us can do about it." He reached forward and patted his large hand upon Keith's knee. "So, I am sorry. But don't expect me to feel sorry for you. Not when I got all this going on."

Keith had hardly listened to what the man said. He was busy looking behind the bar. His eyes having now fallen upon the line of liquor bottles along a shelf on the wall, then to the lit candles positioned at intervals along the edge of the bar top. Each letting off their warm welcoming glows.

"I see what you are doin'," Vic smiled, noticing Keith's concentration.

Snapping out of his plotting, Keith's blood suddenly ran cold. "Excuse me? What I'm doing?"

"Just accept it. You shouldn't waste your time thinkin' of escaping," Vic explained, "*We* in here are not the only ones you'd have to run from, see? It's not just fangers, though there are more and more each day out there. You got those protecting us to deal with. Security if you will. Like our disposal guy, who ya met already out back. Transportation. Shipping. Hell, d'ya think people like us could run clubs all over the world, feeding on millions of the lowest that society has, without those in power not only knowing about us, but actively encouraging and protecting us?"

Keith now paid attention to Vic. *Of course* others helped them, but he had not considered the scope of what he was in the middle of.

"They all allow club's like ours to feed, and really that makes it impossible for you to truly escape. If you *do* get out, if you killed us all? They would come *after* you. Simple. It's why Squeak and I had no choice. We *had* to follow. It's a wide—so fucking wide network. Even if the Emperor of goddamn Russia couldn't stop her, someone from the sticks of bumfuck nowhere ain't gonna have a chance. You get me?"

The club was rapidly starting to thin out, as customers began to leave and return to their own lives. Keith glanced over to the pool game that was nearly finished. To his surprise, Duncan, though terrible, had somehow made it last longer than Keith thought possible.

Back to Vic, Keith forced a smile. He knew that the chances were slim, he knew he was exhausted and his body ached—but he had to try. He *had* to. "How about a last drink for me and my friends?" he asked. "A kind of last request if you will."

Vic looked unconvinced.

"It's the *classy* thing to do? Right?" Keith said. "What would Frankie, Sammy and Deano do?"

Keith had hit a home-run with that choice of words. His

random callback into the conversation, now blindly paid off in spades.

With that, Vic knew he could not deny this request. "Sure. Just like Frankie, Sammy and Deano." He smiled. "All the way, baby!" As he called over the barmaid, Vic pointed at Keith. "Whatever this kid wants, okay?"

The barmaid looked unimpressed and made no attempt to hide her fangs from either of them.

"Three whiskeys?" Keith said as he looked at Vic. "Any suggestions?"

Vic smiled and said to the barmaid. "Three Glenfiddich. The good one, okay?" He then dismissively shooed her away with his hand.

Keith called out after her, "Make it doubles—no, wait. Triples, hell make it the whole bottle!"

"Hittin' it hard, eh?" Vic smiled in amusement.

"Well, we're not driving home are we?" Keith laughed, trying with all his might to not break, to not show the fear within him.

Vic nodded. "I guess you won't be, no," he replied as he caught a glimpse of Katrina now walking across the club floor, over to a booth. Sitting in its shadows, her eyes glowed a dull red as she stared back at him.

As the barmaid returned with a bottle and three glasses, she growled as she placed them on the bar. Annoyed that the familiar was allowing their food any preferential treatment.

"Have fun kid," Vic said to Keith. "I hope you get some happiness before... Well, y'know..."

With a nod of fake appreciation, Keith filled up the three whiskey glasses to their rims, then carried them—as well as the bottle—across the room to the pool table. With each step he took, a large splash of whisky splashed out the clumsily held glasses, onto the carpeted floor below.

Vic watched with amusement for a moment, then shook his head and turned back to the bar. Back to his old memories.

Amaretto and Duncan now stood at the table, $450 worse off, the bikers having left the club victoriously. Keith quickly sidled up to them with the glasses of whisky. Still spilling them with each step. He handed one to each.

Katrina watched as she looked at Keith whisper to Duncan, then walk with Amaretto back toward the bar, casually dribbling whiskey from his glass and bottle along the way.

The Queen regarded him like a scientist would watch an ant. Impressed at their actions, no matter how banal they may seem. She had seen empires rise and crumble, she had seen the powerful become the weak and vice versa. She had seen everything this earth had to offer. Now she took joy in watching these ants. Watching them scurry in a panic. Watching their plans fail to come to fruition. She allowed them to exist as she considered how and when to trample upon them.

As Keith got to the bar, he accidentally (on purpose) bumped into Vic who still sat on his stool. As they collided, Vic was ripped away from his nostalgic what-if daydreams, whisky spilling over him.

Keith looked on apologetically, mouthing the words '*I'm sorry*'.

Amaretto stood silent. Looking more and more nervous.

Vic grimaced as he saw the alcohol now soaking into his clothes, and without a word, he stood up, stepped back from the bar and began to wipe himself off.

Keith and Amaretto then carried on down the length of the bar, casually spilling as they went, more whiskey from the bottle onto the carpet, and more from the glass onto the bar.

Now in the club, only a half a dozen customers remained, frantically drinking the last of their drinks, trying to elongate their revelry for as long as possible.

Now halfway down the bar, at the end of the whisky bottle, having spilled its contents all the way here on all surfaces, Keith placed the bottle and his glass, onto the glass top.

Turning, he smiled at Amaretto then nodded. He grabbed one of the lit candles from the bar, turned the flame downward to the spilled whiskey, and ignited it.

With a sudden *whoosh,* the flames hurtled all the way along the bar's surface, retracing his and Amaretto's path here. The fire creeped down off of the bar and onto the carpet as it went.

"Duncan!" Keith called out. "Now!"

As the waitresses and barmaids saw the flames building, they all hissed in anger, their fangs and claws exposed as they began advancing on Keith.

Giving no time to his fear, Keith casually dropped the still-lit candle into his quarter full glass. The remnants of the whisky inside ignited immediately.

Before anyone could stop him, he quickly turned then threw the fiery glass with all of his might, straight at the liquor bottles that ran along the shelf at the back of the bar.

Duncan meanwhile, stumbled across the club toward them, picking up lit candles along the way, just as Keith had asked him to do.

As one barmaid jumped back from the billowing flames in front of her, and dropped the bottle in her hand. It smashed against the floor and burst into an almighty billowing flame, consuming her within seconds. Her wails screeched throughout the club, over the music, and the whole place descended into mass panic and fury.

As the few remaining customers raced for the exit, the staff tried to advance Keith and Amaretto, but the flames held them back at the far end of the bar.

The conflagration blossomed up from the carpet, running back to where Vic stood, now wide-eyed and furious.

Duncan arrived at the bar, out of breath and still

staggering from his drunken stupor. He placed three lit candles in front of Keith. "Good enough?" he slurred.

Amaretto handed Keith her nearly full glass of whisky. With a wink, he lit it with one of Duncan's candles, then threw the glass between them and a few approaching waitresses that had emerged from the table area. The glass exploded into a wall of flame between them, ensuring that they were surrounded and protected from any immediate attack.

"Quick!" Keith shouted as he motioned his friends toward the basement door on the other side of the bar, now blocked off on either side by burning alcohol.

The fire made a clear path for them.

As they hopped over the glass bar top. Keith kicked the last of the candles down onto the carpet behind them. The liquor-soaked floor they had stood on then burst into a burning mountain.

The last thing that Keith could see through the flames was Vic standing at the far end of the bar, looking unsure of what to do as the glowing eyes of Katrina, still unmoving from her booth, watched the ants fight back.

As they approached the open door to the basement, Duncan quickly hesitated as he winced in pain. Without having any time to ask if he was okay, Keith grabbed him and pulled him down the staircase.

Amaretto followed, slamming the door behind her.

CHAPTER 14
ASH AND BLOOD

The three of them came sprinting down the wooden staircase and into the club's basement. The fire that still burned on the level above them roared loudly as it consumed everything in its wake, hisses and screams of the vampires could be heard amongst the burning cacophony.

Looking around the basement, Keith fumbled with a lightswitch, but when he flicked it, nothing happened except a small click that echoed in the large room.

"I can't see that much," Amaretto said, as she tried to focus through the pitch black.

"I don't feel so good," Duncan said in a whimper.

The screams overhead continued.

"There!" Amaretto pointed to an old liquor elevator that sat at the far end of the room slightly illuminated from within the shadows. A sliver of light from a streetlamp above fell down from the ceiling, shining off the elevator's metal platform as if pointing them there.

A wooden cracking sound suddenly cut through the noise of the fire, from the top of the stairs behind them.

"They're at the door," Keith shouted urgently as he motioned them to the elevator.

They all hurried over to the platform. As Keith ran, he could have sworn he had heard something. Something down there with them. Something amongst the sounds of fire and screams. A moaning.

Amaretto searched frantically for the switch to turn on the elevator, and raise them upwards.

Duncan trembled as his eyes closed, his whole body sweating uncomfortably. He coughed as he held his stomach that twisted as it contracted.

Keith still tried to listen closely to the strange noise down there, but before he could discern what it was, light and smoke streamed in from the top of the stairs, as the wooden door smashed inward.

The remaining vampires screamed in a fury as they scrambled down the staircase, almost tumbling over each other trying to get their revenge.

Pushing away an empty box on the elevator, Amaretto spotted what she had frantically searched for, the activation switch!

Flicking the switch hard, the elevator quickly sprang to life as red warning lights flickered on, signaling the imminent movement of the platform.

Out on the curb side, two metal doors sprung open as the club's elevator appeared, rising up from within the club's basement.

As Keith, Amaretto and Duncan staggered off the platform, smoke billowed up from around its metal edges.

In the basement below, the fire had followed the vampires downward, blocking their escape back to the bar. Now with the underside of the platform raised, they clawed at the metal as they frantically tried to escape.

The blaze soon caught up with them and coursed through their cursed bodies. Indiscriminately ripping apart their eternal life in its embrace, burning it asunder with a merciless fury.

One by one, in quick succession these trapped vampires exploded to ash and bone as they violently thrashed and clambered helplessly.

And with each of these deaths, upstairs Katrina felt a sting in the pit of her dead heart.

In the burning club, as the flames ate all the surfaces around her —slowly crawling their way nearer—The Queen calmly rose out from the shadows of the booth. Before this inferno could pose any real threat to her, she had made her escape at a casual pace.

Absconding without another thought for those left here, she did not really care about this turn of events. The pangs of her vampire coven loss may have hurt, but it was not a pain she dwelled on.

Running around the front of the After Dark Club, Duncan, Keith and Amaretto joined in the rush of scattering customers who now escaped in a panic from the inferno.

"C'mon!" Keith yelled as he reached into his trouser pocket. Suddenly he realized that he hadn't checked for the Cadillac keys since AJ had handed them to him. He prayed he hadn't dropped them in the club or in the dumpster or the sewer. As his hand found then grasped the plastic and metal of the keys, he smiled with relief.

Quickly approaching the Cadillac, Keith hurriedly unlocked the doors and slid into the driver's seat, behind the wheel.

Duncan, half-awake, trembled clutching his stomach as he

fell with a thud through the open door into the backseat. Amaretto afterwards took the passenger side seat with a terrified expression plastered over her face.

Turning on the ignition, Keith took no time to put the car into gear, ready to get them out of here, when suddenly Amaretto let out a piercing, bloodcurdling scream.

Before he could even register what was going on, a dumpster truck emerged from nowhere and rammed into the broadside of their car, sending it and them hurtling against the far building's wall.

Thrown like rag dolls, all three struggled to regain any sense of place as the truck hit reverse, then pulled back across the street, ready to ram them again.

As its loud engine roared for round two, it's teeth-like grille straightened up and zeroed in as the driver sped up on his collision course.

Still dazed, Keith blindly hit the accelerator, projecting the Cadillac forward along the sidewalk, as it used all of its horsepower.

The dumpster truck, narrowly missing them, course corrected speedily, turning after them on the street.

With a row of parked cars standing between them, the truck ran parallel to the now sidewalk mounted Caddy.

This race was not equal though, as the truck sped along *much* faster, and *much more* powerfully. It comfortably beat them to the end of the block by a few hundred feet, where it turned around. It pulled up onto the sidewalk, facing them, blocking their exit.

"Shit," Keith shouted as he slammed on the brakes, as the Cadillac screeched to a sudden and jerking stop.

With no noise from the backseat, Keith, though worried about Duncan, had no time to check up on him.

The truck faced them now, its headlights shining blindingly as it revved its huge engine. Without a second thought, Keith threw the Caddy into reverse and hit his foot down on the accelerator pedal.

Before they could make any significant progress backwards, Keith had to slam on the brakes a second time, as he stared into the rearview behind them, a look of shock on his face.

"What're you stopping for?" Amaretto cried in a panic, "Go!" As she turned to see what was behind them, she fell silent as she too saw the problem.

At the other end of the sidewalk far behind them, another truck pulled up. This time, it was the tow truck that Keith had seen outside the hotel.

These two vehicles effectively trapped them on this sidewalk, the line of parked cars acting like an impassable wall.

Keith turned frantically in both directions. He saw no way to go.

Duncan, meanwhile, shook uncontrollably and silently in the backseat. He gritted his teeth as nausea hit him in increasing waves.

Keith's mind spun trying to figure out what to do, when he finally spotted one of the club's customers, getting into his parked car just a few feet away from where they were trapped.

Bleary eyed, the man didn't even notice the trucks or the Cadillac in a standoff. He just sat in the driver's seat trying to regain his drunken focus, enough to put his key into the ignition.

"There!" Keith victoriously pointed to the man's car.

A loud rumble quickly roared towards them as the tow truck at the rear suddenly lurched forward, speeding up from behind. Its tow bar now craned forward, pointing out like a huge metal joust, ready to pierce through them upon impact.

In front of them, the dumpster truck followed suit by

revving louder and louder, until it too sped its way toward them with ferocious speed.

The dumpster's two pronged metal forks, like the tow-truck's tow bar, aimed threateningly at them.

Meanwhile, the man from the club struggled at first to turn his car on. Then after he succeeded, he proceeded to drunkenly inch the vehicle back and forth, trying to maneuver out of the space, over and over.

Both advancing trucks were now halfway to the Cadillac, each gaining speed rapidly.

Amaretto closed her eyes. Willing the man from the club to move faster. "Come on.... Come on… Pleeaaaasse."

Barreling down on them. The trucks got closer.

Sweat dripped off Keith's face as he sat waiting for the man from the club to move. A man who was still oblivious to their predicament.

"Get a move on, you asshole!" Amaretto finally screamed at the top of her voice.

Though this man didn't hear, but as if on her command, he suddenly managed to maneuver his car out of the parking space.

Without a second to spare, Keith hit the gas.

The Cadillac peeled out and burst through the now vacated parking space, onto the street. The man from the club —none the wiser—drove away drunkenly.

A split second later, with the two trucks caught off guard, they had no other choice but to collide—head first into one another. The set of forks and tow bar joust decimated through each of the driver's cabs. The front of both vehicles collapsed in on each other in a din of deafening proportions, as metal on metal collided with insurmountable force, twisting around each other violently.

Wiping the sweat from his brow, Keith sped down the street, not wanting to stay and watch the devastation.

"Which way can we go?" he asked Amaretto urgently.

"Hang a right!"

Keith immediately screeched the car around the corner, following her order.

In the burning room, Vlad still obediently stood by the club's exit.

He had watched as Katrina walked away from the fire. As he saw her stand up from the booth, she glanced over in his direction. But, she left without a thought—without any order for him to join her. As a wall of flames shot between their paths, Katrina disappeared backstage, into the safety of the darkness.

So, without any order from her, he stood in the place he was told to stand.

"Vlad, come on!" Vics creamed from the other side of the raging inferno.

Vlad heard this call, but this was not the order from his Queen, and he was only ever supposed to obey Vic during club hours. After closing, such as this, he was to *only* obey the Queen. That was the way it had always been, and the way it was now.

Grand Duke Vladimir Alexandrovich did not feel it when the fire eviscerated his body. He did not feel the flame turn each ancient morsel of his decrepit guts into nothing but ash. He did not even know that he was in pain. He felt nothing. He just stood patiently by the exit, waiting for his next order. Waiting, as the fire consumed the rest of his damned life.

As the flames stole his final remnants, so too did it take the rest of the main room of the After Dark Club.

The Cadillac cruised along a darkened street. The hum of its motor provided the only soundtrack to the emptiness around them. It's engine's bassy hum reverberated down this long run of brick and glass. Echoing along the buildings, asphalt and concrete ground.

From the passenger seat, Amaretto had searched for a familiar landmark, something—*anything* that she could recall.

Tonight, though, this ramshackle part of this city seemed an impassable maze of intertwining streets. Each looking the same as the last.

In the back seat, Duncan was still no help to anyone. He lay unconscious. His skin was clammy with sweat as he breathed the shallow breaths of sleep.

Meanwhile, Keith had wished he paid more attention to their journey from their dorm. Maybe then they would have been on their way home by now, instead, he found himself turning down every street hoping for a signpost out of there.

"I'm starting to think that this wasn't the street I was thinking of," Amaretto muttered as she turned to Keith. "I've only been in town a few days, I'm sorry."

"It's not your fault," Keith replied, still visibly shaken from the two-truck escapade, not to mention the rest of the night.

Before she had time to turn around again, to continue her search for familiarity, a loud smash from above sent her cowering down into her seat.

Keith swerved with shock as the soft-top roof was torn open, and a smoking clawed hand cut its way through the night air toward them.

As a thin, charred arm groped through the torn roof for any victim, Keith slammed on the brakes as hard as he could.

The tires screeched and slid as the car grinded to a juttering stop. Its sudden move flipped the creature from off of the roof, hurtling them through the air to land onto the street in front of the Caddy.

It was Alina. The elder performer from the club. Her clothes had been completely burned away by the fire. Her flesh, scorched and mostly burned away to her bones.

Clambering slowly to her clawed feet, she stood facing the car and wailed angrily. Over half of her body had been destroyed, leaving only exposed bone, charred flesh and an insurmountable vampire's rage. She was a picture of extreme grotesquery.

Before she could mount a second attack, Keith had already floored the pedal, sending the Cadillac barreling toward her. Giving her no time to even raise a defiant claw.

The car plowed into her with such force, it broke apart the rest of her body, sending its many parts flying over them, as each part burst into flame and broke apart into nothing but ash.

Vic had woken up in front of the bar to the screams from the basement. A large panel of ceiling plaster had fallen down on him, protecting him from the first onslaught of the fire, but knocking him out in the process.

Getting to his feet, he surveyed the damage, then witnessed Katrina calmly exiting through the backstage curtains—abandoning them all to a fiery doom.

With the flames still raging around the room, Vic noticed Vlad by the exit. Stood to no one's attention. The fire was eating through this bouncer's flesh and bone without any quarrel or fight.

Vic tried to call over, but Vlad did not answer, nor even turn in his direction. He just stood quietly and waited as the blaze stole him away.

With the screams down in the basement now subsided, Vic rushed down there. He *had* to, despite the fire still burning strong. He could not abandon his one, true friend. Not again.

Skirting the lapping flames at the bar, Vic descended down the smoldering staircase into the basement, the fire having moved further in.

The lower level room was now awash with flames that

licked up the far walls. The remaining vampires still alive still tried to claw upwards to freedom, but it was fruitless. The fire soon caught up, and they wailed in a futile attempt to scare away the death that approached them.

"Help us!" one of the waitresses screamed to Vic through the fire.

For a split second, he tried to remember where he had placed the extinguisher in this room, blindly accepting the call to save his trapped masters. But, as he recollected where it was, he also remembered why he was down here—why he came down to the basement. It was not for them.

Turning to his left, he saw that the fire had not yet reached on the cell where the remains of Mark 'Squeak' Coombs lay.

Without another thought, Vic stepped around the fire and toward the cell.

He could feel the heat licking at him, as the flames got closer, raising up and eating into the structure above him.

Around him, the whole building creaked and groaned as the fire ate at its very core.

Walking into the cell, with the approaching fire filling it with its orangey glow, Vic saw the trembling remnants of Squeak, huddled into the corner of this once pitch black room.

"Hello old friend," Vic smiled as he got down to his knees in front of him.

Through the open doorway smoke began to make its path inward, as the fire curled over the threshold, slowly eating across the cell's ceiling.

Vic moved next to the pile of living carrion called Squeak, and lifted the mutilated body onto his lap. He placed one hand on what was once Squeak's face and felt something he thought he would never feel again. Happiness. "I'm sorry, Mark," he said. His voice cracking.

After decades of assisting murderous creatures—albeit

without a choice—Vic had become numb to happiness, to love, to anything that was not quiet grief and annoyance.

Now though, what was left of his soul allowed him a parting gift, as tears fell down his face, he smiled a truly happy smile. He was gonna leave with Squeak. With his friend.

Squeak howled in the pain of being held. His exposed nerves burned as Vic's arms wrapped around him.

"Shhhh," Vic said as the tears fell more and more. "We're gonna be free soon, my friend."

Squeak's eye stared up at Vic, as the howls faded, and his mouth grotesquely gargled, "Aaaaannnnnnnkkk ooooooooooo."

Sniffing, Vic chuckled softly. "You shouldn't thank me. I should've helped you before they did this. I should have been there for you."

"Eyyyyy ooovvvvv oooooo" Squeak said, his voice barely audible though the gurgling.

"I love you too, Mark…"

Squeak's voice became softer and weaker with each syllable. "Eeeyyyyuusss?" he managed to gargle.

Vic looked down lovingly into his friend's monstrous eye. "Yeah, Vegas. We're gonna go to Vegas now."

The sound of the fire pushing its way toward them stole Vic's attention upward. The fire chewed its way overhead, and down the walls toward them.

For a second he wondered if Katrina's will would pull him away from this course of action, but he felt nothing from her. No pull. No silent command.

He finally was allowed to feel at peace.

"We *will* open the club," Vic said, feeding the comforting lie they now shared. "We will have a big velvet club right on the strip. We'll call it *Vic and Squeaks,* and *everyone* will wanna be there."

The fire crawled closer and closer, as Vic held Squeak tighter and tighter.

"I'm so fucking sorry," Vic spluttered as he tried to hold it together. "It *will* happen. We *will* get to Vegas. Okay?"

Squeak's mouth smiled as much as it could.

"Frankie, Sammy and Deano... They'll be there on opening night."

The last words either of them said in this life was spoken in unison, as the fire saved them both from the Queen's eternal damnation.

"All the way baby."

As they slowly drove through the streets, looking for a way out of this hellish night, Duncan lay, still unconscious in the back seat.

Keith looked at Amaretto, "What're we gonna do?" he asked, worried that they may never escape.

Amaretto didn't answer. She was busy scanning the outside. At every shadow that lay in wait. Her eyes darted across every part of the streets around them.

Despite Keith's best efforts to remain positive, the events of the night had caused palpable fear to consume him. *If one vampire made it out of the club alive, then others must have too,* was his logical train of thought.

Suddenly pulling himself out of his own negativity, he took a gulp and said to himself—answering his own doubt, more than to Amaretto—"We're gonna make it. We're definitely gonna make it."

A moan emitted from the back seat.

Amaretto glanced back and saw Duncan coming out of his slumber. His moan sounded pained.

"He doesn't look too good," Amaretto said, turning to Keith. "How much did he drink?"

"Too much," Keith replied as he adjusted the rearview mirror into the backseat. He watched as Duncan slowly slid his way up into a seated position. His face was pale, and he looked as if he was still fighting back a mountain of vomit from being expelled.

"Duncan? You okay, buddy?" Keith asked, half looking to the back, half on the street in front. "You want to stop? You need to chuck up?"

"I... I'm hungry." Duncan mumbled.

Amaretto smiled as Keith laughed

"You're okay, buddy. We'll be home soon, okay?"

"No." Duncan replied. His voice was now different and sounded stronger. "I mean I'm *starvin'*, guys."

Keith looked worriedly into the rearview and saw Duncan grip his stomach tightly as he gritted his teeth.

Keith forced a laugh as he remembered AJ doing exactly the same earlier, "Okay, first burger joint we see... once we're out of here."

Duncan glanced up into the rearview, his eyes bloodshot, a pained expression consuming his face.

"You okay with burgers and—" Keith's words tailed off as he looked in the rearview again.

The back seat was empty.

Duncan nowhere to be seen.

"What the—?" Keith turned around and was immediately confronted by Duncan in mid-vampiric transformation, his body no longer showing any reflection.

Duncan's bloodshot eyes began to luminize as his cheeks sunk inward. In his mouth, large fangs sprouted from in front of his human teeth, and his skin began to turn translucent, exposing the veins and muscles beneath.

Immediately, Keith stepped on the brake then slammed on the gas as he skidded around the corner, into an empty parking lot.

Speeding along, he turned the steering wheel back and forth, keeping Duncan off-balance by turning left then right, left then right. This jolting movement sent the new vampire flying around the backseat, unable to get any purchase.

The Caddy zig-zagged across the parking lot as it headed for the car park's exit opposite.

Amaretto gasped loudly as she hung onto her door handle for dear life.

Up ahead at the exit, a sign warned *'Severe Tire Damage—Entrance Only'*.

Duncan roared from the back seat as his transformation took a tighter hold of him.

The Cadillac ran over a set of traffic spikes at speed. The tires shredded apart on impact. A quadruple bursting noise caused both Keith and Amaretto to scream.

Their cries of fright mixed in with Duncan's monstrous roar, as Keith spun the wheel as hard as he could. The now-tireless car haplessly skidded across the intersection in front of them, sparking over the ground, then heavily slammed into a street light—stopping their escape dead in its tracks.

The cacophony of this impact was dwarfed in comparison to the sound of the engine rupturing, then igniting. White hot flames then erupted from underneath the hood, licking up over the bonnets paintwork.

As Duncan thrashed in the back seat, Keith tried to open the driver's side door, but it was blocked by the street light that was now twisted over the car's roof, blocking any escape through the driver's door as well as the tears made by Alina.

Amaretto, dazed but slowly getting her bearings, tried her door too, but it was stuck firm. The frame around it now was too bent out of shape, no longer flush to its fittings.

Keith reached his leg across her, and kicked her stuck door as hard as he could. After a couple of attempts it flew open with a cracking sound.

"Quick!" he urged.

Amaretto moved to exit, but as she did, Duncan's claw-like hand shot out and grabbed her by the shoulder.

In one swift movement, Keith knocked the vampire backwards with a single punch to his nose, sending him reeling back.

The flames now crawled out from the engine and over the roof of the Cadillac.

Keith and Amaretto tumbled out of this burning wreck, slamming the passenger door shut behind them. It's twisted metal only half-closing, Keith kicked it harder from the outside, cracking it back into place—effectively trapping Duncan inside the vehicle.

In the back seat, Duncan had been fully transformed. He thrashed angrily as he clawed at the windows and roof, trying to escape as the flames got larger and larger around him. His wolfen-like cries of torment pierced the night.

"I'm sorry, buddy," Keith said weakly, as he stared at this monster now screaming with fright in his car, "Sorry I got you into this."

As the car began to emit a hissing sound from its engine, it snatched away Amaretto's attention. "Back!" was all she managed to shout as she dragged Keith away from the fire with a yank.

The underside of the car then sparked and clicked loudly before an explosion broke throughout the vehicle. Its flames engulfed everything within, breaking through its insides and consuming Duncan in an undead heartbeat.

The fire burst outward so far that Keith and Amaretto could still feel its heat emitting from laying on the other side of the street. The force of the exploding gas tank having knocked them to their knees.

Around, flaming pieces of the car scattered down, luckily missing both of them.

Quickly scrambling to her feet, Amaretto turned to helped Keith up.

"I'm sorry about him, Keith," she said with a tremor in her voice. "He seemed nice... But... I...." She searched her mind for the right words. "How were they... I mean... Vampires? *How*? How does no one know this? Shouldn't everyone know they exist? Shouldn't I have *known* when I got the job? Were they gonna kill me? Turn me?"

Keith, though, could not listen. His eyes were transfixed on a storefront behind them.

Dud's Pawn'n'Go was Dudley Garland's pride and joy. A place he loved more than he did his wife and child. A wife who hated him back, and a child so obnoxious, that Dudley could not stand to be around them. A child that took after his mother one hundred and fifty percent.

The *Pawn'n'Go* was intended to be a thrift store. A place where you could find treasures buried within its dusty aisles. The kind he used to frequent as a young boy, growing up across the country in the town of Folkstone Bay, Maine. It was a town that was the living embodiment of how Dudley saw himself; proud, weather beaten, and almost forgotten by the rest of humanity.

When it had originally opened, the store had been called *Dud's Hidey-Hole*. The contents of which were items that he had bought from swap meets all over the county. A mix of trinkets and doodads, that no one really needed, but some may pay a few bucks for. Dudley was never looking to make a fortune, he only looked to make rent, buy some more stock, and keep him in American Spirits. He essentially craved the simple life, and this store was his attempt to get that.

But, as with everything on this side of town, nothing was immune to the deterioration and rot that had infected it. As the other businesses gradually closed around him, Dudley quickly realised that the people that lived here had gotten more and more desperate by the day. They didn't want to buy needless things, they wanted to pay the bills and live safely. And it was in this fact that Dudley saw a real opportunity.

Getting his pawnbrokers license was the easy part, so too was changing the name of the store. The desperation of the people made them flock to the *Pawn'N'Go*, to offload their more expensive items in order to help them buy their necessities. Of course, they had all hoped (and promised to) Dudley that they would return to reclaim their items by the end of the month, but no one ever did.

Over the years, the *Pawn'N'Go's* clientele also changed. Gone were the desperate families looking only to put food on their tables. In their place came the junkies and criminals looking to offload items they had 'acquired' by unlawful means. But in regard to this, Dudley had a saying, *'No serial number, no problem'.*

The type of items he sold also changed with the clientele. Gone were the antiques and heirlooms handed over in desperation for food money, instead were home entertainment items that could be carried out of a broken window, as well as items that could be mugged from random passers by.

The money, of course, did not pour in as the customers got poorer. Dudley had come close to having to close his doors permanently on multiple occasions. After all, there were only so many VCRs that one business could sell. Not like he could resell anything to junkies after all. It was only the stolen jewelry that kept him afloat. Items he could take to dealers in other cities. Jewels he could sell for much more than he paid, but mostly for way less than what they were worth. Any amount more than he paid to unload them.

The streets quickly became more dangerous and more desperate. As more people went missing, as more gangs roamed the street, as more dead bodies piled up—Dudley realized that he could cater equally to *both* the criminal and non-criminal element with the same service. Not to mention the ability to make a much bigger profit.

The non-criminal element that still lived here had a desperate need for protection as much as they did food, and the criminal element had a need for items to enable their work—Weapons.

So, Dudley acquired his Federal Firearms License, and soon began using his limited savings to buy in everything from hunting supplies to handguns. He barely had time to care that his wife and child had left him, as his business was his main love and his main focus.

This supply of weapons soon began to take over the public's need for his pawning service, but even so, he kept it, as well as the store's name.

Dudley was not stupid, though. He knew about the infestation of monsters that had gripped these streets. At first they had kept their presence well hidden, relegated to the After Dark Club, but for the people who lived and worked here, the creature's presence became more and more known with each passing year. And everyone knew that nothing could be done about it. Yet everyone still needed a weapon, So it was Dudley's shop that they went to, and he was more than happy to oblige.

Keith stared through the iron lattice work that protected the pawn shop. He stared at the weapons that could be seen within the darkness of this closed premises—The rifles on racks, the pistols adorning the walls, the body armor on the mannequins.

As he glanced at the protective shutters, he tried to see a way to break in. Amaretto, meanwhile, hid within the shadows of the shop's doorway.

Keith then grabbed the shutters and shook them. Hoping for a break and for them to come apart in his grip. The shutters, of course, didn't. He instead just created a loud clanking of metal.

"What are you doing?" Amaretto whispered harshly. "Keep it down!"

Keith knew she was right, that the noise *had* to be kept to a minimum, at the same time he knew that they *had* to get in there. "I think it's gonna have to get louder if we wanna protect ourselves."

He then quickly noticed a padlock on the bottom of the shutters.

Bingo, he thought.

Grabbing a metal litter bin placed on the sidewalk, Keith used all of his strength to carry it over to the shop. Lifting it up, he hurled it down onto the shutter's lock.

The metal lattice around the lock buckled, and behind it, the plate glass window cracked; immediately sounding the store's wailing alarm.

Picking up the litter bin again—intent on finally breaking the lock—Keith suddenly stopped in mid-swing. He stared wide-eyed into the store.

He stared at the figure within.

Amaretto, waving back at him.

Stunned, he moved toward the shop door. The iron grillwork had been bent out of shape and the glass of the door smashed inward.He looked suspiciously from this warped iron to the now grinning Amaretto.

"Looks like we're not the first midnight shoppers." she said. "It was already open!"

Slowly, Keith put down the bin and walked through the new opening into the shop. His eyes did not leave Amaretto's.

He didn't buy what she said. The alarm only just sounded. *This forced entrance had to have been made by her.* But, there were more important things at hand. He *needed* a weapon in case Snow or more vampires came, and if his current fear was right, he would need a weapon against Amaretto herself.

Racing past her, he got to the gun case. Taking no time, he slammed his elbow into the glass. Shattering it upon impact.

"Bullets!" Keith called aloud as the siren blared in the background. "We need bullets!"

Amaretto nodded as she began to rifle through nearby drawers, but there were no bullets there. Then she turns to scan the contents of the large metal shelves along the wall. Still nothing.

Keith meanwhile searched the rest of the store. HE didn't trust her at this moment, so looked in places she had already looked.

Stopping in his tracks, his mouth gaped wide at what hung on the wall in front of him; A sports bow and a quiver of arrows.

"I can't find any bullets." Amaretto called out as she searched more places unsuccessfully, but Keith didn't respond. His thoughts of guns were gone. He was too busy taking the archery weapon from off of the wall with a big grin across his face.

Then a loud crash sounded behind him.

In one swift and perfect motion, Keith wheeled around, grabbed an arrow from the quiver, and had it drawn back in the bow within a few seconds.

He aimed toward Amaretto, who now stood next to a fallen shelving unit.

She looked at Keith apologetically with a shrug, "There's no bullets."

After a few uncomfortable moments, she took a step forward, Keith keeping the arrow aimed in her direction. The bow now drawn back fully.

"Get back," he warned. "I'm very good with this, believe me."

Amaretto stopped, staring at him, then the arrow that now pointed at her head.

"What are you doing?" she said nervously, "You're scaring me."

"Likewise. Now get back."

Disheveled, streaked by dirt and makeup, with eyes reflecting the firelight from the other side of the street, Amaretto looked somewhat terrifying.

Suddenly, she opened her mouth and pointed at her teeth. Her very human teeth. "Look, no fangs, alright?" Her expression flickered with annoyance. "C'mon, Keith, you've known me since—"

"I *don't* know you! *Who are you?*" His aim stayed steady and true at the target. "I know you escaped with me. But were you in real danger? Just when I think you are in it with me, you do something weird."

"I... uh," Amaretto frantically searched for words, as a palpable fear tickled up her spine. "I... I met you on holiday once... and, uh..."

"Your name," Keith barked. His voice got louder by the syllable. "Tell me your Goddamn real name *right* now!!! Or I swear to God..."

"Look, you don't know my face, what difference will my name make? Anyway you used to get beaten up by Waylon Whatshisname right? And.. uh... I... I..."

Immediately Keith released the arrow. Amaretto had no time to scream as she saw it hurtling toward her.

As it hummed past her cheek, the arrow violently skewered through the chest of an attacking person from the club, the DJ, now in full vampiric mode. As this projectile split through their heart, their body fell to the floor, screaming and cursing and they burst into ash.

Amaretto ran over to Keith, forgetting what was said, and awkwardly embraced him. He hurriedly fit another arrow to the bow, then stared at her. Still thinking that she could be a threat.

"I thought you killed me!" she said, almost in tears.

Keith had no time to react as she leant into his face, mouth first, closing her eyes. He expected the fangs to come next, but instead, she just kissed him on the lips.

"Believe me... I am not one of those. I just know that you don't remember me... And I remember you... So telling you now... Makes what I once felt for you seem stupid... I thought you'd know me as soon as you saw me... Like we were meant to be together... I just don't want to hear that you have no clue who I am if I tell you my name... Does that make any sense? And this shop was already open. I *swear*!"

He did not know what to think.

"What the hell is this?" A loud voice boomed from the doorway.

Keith and Amaretto froze as they turned to see a man walk in. A man carrying a large shotgun.

Immediately, Keith drew an arrow toward this man. "Get back!" he shouted, hoping the man would just leave them alone.

"Back?" the man shouted, "This is *my* goddamn place!"

Stepping forward, the man glanced around at the fallen shelves, smashed glass and dissolved the vampire on the floor in front of him.

"The name's Dudley, and you guys look like you've had one of those nights."

In reflex, Amaretto replied, "Pleased to meet you, Dudley."

Keith kept the bow drawn, tracking the man as he surveyed his destroyed shop.

"You better get going, " Dudley said, looking at the mess. "There'll be more, so I gotta get this place secure quickly. Or at least hide the guns til sun up."

"You're not gonna call the police?" Keith asked.

Dudley laughed in response. "Police? Here? C'mon, get going. I don't want any more bodies to clean up." He looked up at them with a kind smile. "This isn't the first time this has happened, and it won't be the last... Part of the joys of livin' in vamp country I guess."

As he looked closer at Keith, he noticed the silver watch on his wrist, as well as the shiny earrings on Amaretto. His pawnbroker skills, finely honed, even in this half light.

"I would let you stay here, but I can't afford to be associated. Looks like you have all hell in yer wake."

Keith could not disagree.

"Before you go though," Dudley corrected, "I'll let you take the bow, if ya leave your watch and those earrings. I could sell those for a nice sum."

"They're glass," Amaretto said weakly.

Dudley shrugged. "If it looks nice. It's gonna sell. And that bow... It's been up on that wall close to ten years now, makin' me nothing but dust."

Keith didn't need any more convincing. Lowering his aim, he then removed his watch.

CHAPTER 15
ROOFTOPS AND SEWERS

As they left the demolished pawn shop, minus one watch and a pair of earrings, Keith caught a glimpse of his reflection in the mirror by the door. On instinct, he quickly tried to catch sight of Amaretto's as well—still not fully convinced that she was all she said she was—but he just missed it.

Walking down a lightless side street, he paced a few steps behind her. Bow in hand, with arrow in position, ready to be aimed in an instant. The quiver was now strapped firmly over his back, and offered up more ammunition should he need them.

"We're not getting anywhere," Amaretto complained. "It's just another dark street."

"We gotta keep moving," Keith replied as he glanced further ahead, as well as up to the tops of the buildings.

"Where can we go? For all we know we're heading right for more of those 'things' to jump out at us at any moment. Anyway… Where am I gonna go? Back to the hotel?" She turned to him and asked hopefully "Back with you?"

Still looking upward, Keith didn't answer. He instead

smirked as he noticed a fire escape ladder leading down from one building that was currently under construction.

"We need a better view. Up there..."

Inside his shop, Dudley had been busily nailing a large wooden board over the hole in his front door.

Working as fast as he could, he hammered one nail in after another, through the boards and into the wooden door frame.

The mess within the store could wait until sun up. But he had to try to—

His thoughts were quickly stolen away as he felt something. A presence just on the other side of the door.

Peering between a gap above one of the boards he had just nailed up, he caught a glimpse of a figure, shrouded within the darkness, silhouetted by the glowing flames from the crashed car across the street.

"I didn't help them," Dudley garbled in a panic. "I did just as we've agreed. I'd never break that."

The figure didn't move or reply.

Nervously Dudley continued. "They stole a weapon from me, though."

Still no reply.

"They headed toward Tully Street, that's all I know."

On any other night, Dudley would have been left alone, having done as was expected; Leaving the vampires to their feeding without any intervention. They lived in a coexistence of unspoken terms between him and the nest inside the club.

Tonight, though, was different.

There was no more nest.

There was no more club.

And soon, there would be no more boards put on the door, as there would be no more Dudley.

. . .

Climbing a ladder after having been through hell and back was bad enough, but for Keith, it was having to do so in front of someone you didn't know or trust, which made it all the more difficult. He *wanted* to trust her. He *wanted* her to be all that she seemed. He just knew his luck was not that good. Sure, people act differently in bad situations. But something rubbed him the wrong way.

'I'll go first,' he had said without thinking, purely out of some misguided chivalry. Despite the fact that she had shown herself more than capable of handling danger, even more so than he probably could.

If someone had held an arrow at him? He would have probably buckled to the floor and burst out crying like a baby. She, on the other hand, then ran up and *kissed* him. If she wasn't a vampire, he thought, she sure was crazy.

Still, despite his misgivings, he couldn't help but still feel an undeniable attraction to her.

Now at the top of the building, Keith and Amaretto looked out toward the downtown area of the city—Its neon glow shone brightly. A stark contrast to the ruined and dark streets they were now lost in.

Glancing at Amaretto, Keith wanted to kiss her, even though he doubted her sincerity, her humanity even. She had worked for the club, the club where they were all vampires. Therefore she *must* be a vampire. *Right*? His mind flitted between thinking that, and thinking that they could become an item. She may be a vampire, but *dammit* he couldn't shake the fact that she kissed him, albeit only fleetingly.

"It's beautiful isn't it?" she said softly, as she stared at the distant lights.

"Yeah." Keith couldn't help but agree, however he wasn't talking about downtown but the view next to him.

This whole evening had been a rollercoaster of emotions, and it almost seemed like a dream. None of it seemed real. All the death, all the monsters, poor Duncan... and... AJ.

A wash of grief returned over him. He had forgotten about it for a while. But AJ was *gone*. Forever. Made a demon, then killed by his own hand. Self defense or not—whether his friend forced the stake into his own heart or not—he had killed him. AJ had been a part of him, and now that he was gone, it left a huge gaping hole in his world.

Amaretto turned to the now forlorn looking Keith, realizing that his thoughts were veering far away from the hopeful ones she now had.

"It'll be okay. You know that right?" she reassured. "None of this was any of our fault." She smiled as he looked up and feebly smiled back.

Stealing his focus away from the past, Amaretto then dragged him back into the present with a question as she pointed to downtown. "So, which way should we take?"

Keith swallowed as he looked at the snaking streets that lay in front of them. He did not notice Amaretto suddenly looking out, fearful toward the building across the alley.

"We should take that street there," Keith pointed. "Looks like it runs straight downtown. And looks well lit. Don't you think so?"

Glancing back, Keith's expression matched Amaretto's as he too noticed what she stared at in horror.

Standing on the building's edge opposite them was Candi, Dominique and two waitresses. All with contorted vampiric faces, claws and glowing red eyes. Each charred to varying degrees from the club's fire, though that didn't seem to slow any of them down.

"Fuck," Amaretto muttered under her breath, as she felt Keith hand on her arm, pulling her backward a few steps. "What do we do?"

Keith realized that if she was indeed one of them, vampire or familiar, then he would probably find out right about now.

Removing his bow from being slung over his shoulder,

Keith readied the weapon with an arrow, all while keeping a keen eye on the vampires on the opposite roof.

Each vampire breathed open mouthed, staring at their intended prey like hyenas waiting to attack.

Soon an eerie silence settled in, as the two groups stared at each other. Keith and Amaretto waited for the vampires to make their move, but they didn't move. The vampires instead, stood motionless, basking in the stench of fear coming off of their intended victims, lovingly elongating the standoff out of perverse glee and their need for vengeance.

Keith could feel his heartbeat drumming loudly in his ears, as he tried to steady his breathing to still his grip on the arrow.

In an instant, Candi then leapt across the space between the two buildings. Claws forward, mouth open, fangs bared.

Keith couldn't help but smirk at this oncoming easy target. Releasing an arrow, it flew straight for Candi at incredible speed. The tip pierced her heaving chest, splitting her dead heart in two. She careening off from her intended target, and screamed as her body missed the edge and she slammed into the side of the building. Candi ignited from within as her bones tumbled down to the alleyway far below, ending her undeath before she even landed.

Like frogs in succession, and before Keith could react, Dominique and the two waitresses leapt the incredible distance between the two roofs with ease.

As their feet landed, the three vampires scrambled to surround Keith and Amaretto. Dominique intentionally positioned herself to block their path to the ladder, which led down to the alley.

With hardly any time to get on the defensive, Keith hurriedly reloaded his bow with another arrow, as the three monsters closed in fast.

One waitress lunged for Amaretto, but before their claws could slice her skin, Keith loosed another arrow. It brushed past Amaretto's arm, as the sharp tip cut through the waitresses taloned hand, dragging it back into her own chest —through her heart. As the vampire wailed then collapsed dead to the floor, Keith reached into his quiver.

He only had one arrow left.

Glancing at the fallen waitress, Keith exhaled in frustration as he witnessed the arrow in her chest start to burn away as she erupted into flames.

Dominique and the other waitress quickly advanced, pushing the two closer toward the edge of the roof.

"How did they find us?" Amaretto asked in a frightened whisper.

Keith raised his bow defensively. Trying to keep the approaching monsters at bay, alternating his aim between them.

Both of the vampires growled and snarled as they stepped closer.

Keith and Amaretto were now backed up against the ledge of the building. Amaretto's foot nudged by a broken cinder block beside her. Quickly, she bent down, picked it up, then held it up ready to use as a weapon against the attackers.

That's when she noticed their one chance; a construction chute lay a few feet away along the edge of the roof. A collection of circular plastic bins tied together, that led down to a skip at the bottom of the alley.

The vampires still inched closer.

"When I say three," Amaretto whispered, "follow and jump with me, okay?"

"What?" was all Keith managed to say before he felt Amaretto yank him along the edge with her.

"Three!" she yelled as she scrambled a few steps then blindly jumped down into the chute.

Keith paused as he turned back to the vampires, who now roared louder, and began to hurtle toward him.

Without a second thought, Keith followed down into the dark chute, holding the bow and arrow close to his chest.

On the stock room floor of his coffee shop, Hayim lay in the dark, covered only by a thin blanket.

On any normal night where he missed his window to get home, he would have slept like a baby. In this stock room adorned with crucifixes and with garlic hanging from the walls, not to mention a three deadbolt door with no other way in, he was in no danger from gangs or even worse.

But tonight it was not the danger to himself that caused him anxiety. It was the screams.

Those terrible screams.

He was used to hearing the occasional poor soul begging for mercy, and as terrible as that was, tonight the screams were too much.

The sounds of both human and inhuman cries reverberated down the hollow streets and crawled in through the vents of his stock room. Explosions and crashes too. Noises that made it seem like a war was raging outside. A war that Hayim hoped he would never live to be in the middle of.

But it was the last scream that he heard, that was the final straw for him. The one that forced him into a panic and convinced him that it was indeed time to flee this town and move somewhere else.

"Please!" the familiar voice cried in the distance. "I didn't do anything wrong."

Despite Hayim not liking Dudley too much, he didn't wish him ill. He hated that Dudley sold weapons in a town that needed peace, but that was a professional not personal quibble. Hearing his fellow store owner getting eaten alive in the next street was just too much to endure. He could accept the other screams as they were people he would never meet. People who he would never have occasion to know, but Dudley? Dudley was as much a staple of these streets as he was. And if Dudley was so easily murdered, then no unspoken pact of mutually assured existence would apply to him any more.

As he cried to himself, hunched in a ball by a shelf of cleaning products, Hayim prayed for daylight. Prayed for the morning. Prayed for an end to the madness he had been a silent part of for so long.

He would move. Maybe to Las Vegas...

Like human bobsleds, Keith and Amaretto slid down the winding chute; bouncing off the sides as they descended at high speed.

Mere seconds after they made the leap from the roof, they had crashed into the large construction bin beneath, where a mix of masonite boards and cardboard boxes had broken their fall.

Without a moment to spare, Amaretto had hit first, scurrying out of the way of Keith falling directly behind her.

Clamoring over the side of the bin, she turned and thankfully saw Keith following her lead.

As they both sped off down the street, neither of them had any inclination to look back. Not wanting to see if Dominique and the waitress were in close pursuit.

The blood pounded in Keith's ears and he felt his energy depleting fast. He was never an athlete. He was too scrawny for any contact sport, and too lazy to try out for any track teams. That was why he stuck with archery. It was something he could do while standing still, and tonight was the first time he had felt proud of that choice. If it had been any other way, then he would have had no chance of escaping these vamps, and would have most likely met his end in the pawn shop.

"Bus!" Amaretto shouted as she turned a corner of an

intersection, spotting a large bright silver transit bus, out on its regular late night journey, driving down the street toward them. Downtown lay just over a mile away, and this bus's journey proudly stated that destination in bright orange lights across the top of its large windscreen.

"Oh thank Christ!" Keith exclaimed as they both ran out into the center of the street, blocking the bus's path and flagging it down.

As they both waved and jumped screaming *'stop!'*, both Keith and Amaretto both felt a euphoria they never thought they would feel tonight.

The bus quickly slowed, then turned to the side of the street. A glimmer of hope that they could escape.

As the bus's doors hissed and swung open, Keith's smile was quickly smashed away as the driver turned and bared his large fangs toward them.

"I found you!" he hissed. "This is your last stop!"

Pulling Amaretto away, Keith whirled around in a panic and they both rushed across the intersection, away from the now cackling bus driver.

"There's no escape, meat bags" the driver yelled from his vehicle. "We're all out to get you!"

And he was correct; many more creatures crawled out of the dark streets, blocking their path.

The remaining waitresses and barmaids from the Club, Dominique and a few other performers, the Hotel Desk Clerk, the old bellboy, the Bum with his gnawed rat, the little girl, and even Dudley—having freshly been turned—now faced them.

Keith held his bow tight. Though now, in *this* fight, one arrow was useless.

As Amaretto and Keith backed up under a street lamp, she muttered softly. "I'm sorry. "

Keith readied his final arrow.

"Not like you did this." he said with a maudlin smile. "Unless you did?"

He took aim and pulled the bow string to his cheek.

"I'm sorry I never told you who I am."

"Well," Keith said as he scanned his aim across the approaching monsters. "We got a few seconds left to live. You could tell me now."

Before she could reply, a bright light burst out of one of the streets, and a car engine was revving loudly.

The Dragons had returned.

As they skidded across the streets, the vampires dispersed into the shadows out of fear of what may be coming.

"Friends of yours?" Amaretto asked as the car came to a halt less than ten feet from them.

"Not exactly," Keith said in a panic. As the attention on them was temporarily diverted, he took her arm then pulled her with him down the nearest alleyway.

"*Get them!*"

As they ran the length of the alley, Keith heard Snow's yell clearly, followed by the sound of car doors opening then quickly slamming shut.

Hitting the next street over, Keith's eyes widened as he recognized these surroundings from earlier.

Behind them, the battle cries of the Dragon's could be heard running down the alleyway.

"Your turn to trust me!" Keith said as he sprinted over to where a manhole cover still lay half open.

"Quick!" he shouted, noticing the many vampires spilling over the buildings around them, not to mention the bloodthirsty gang barreling out of the alley their way. Snow leading the Dragon's charge, a long serrated blade held firmly in his hand. His screams at them were guttural and pained.

Snow was closely followed by Clay and Dade, the mustached and tattooed twins, whom both held matching crowbars. Then came Maven, with her eyes raging with the same fury, gripping two switchblades, holding them in front of her like two small jousts. Lastly came Dolly, who suddenly became more aware of her surroundings than her comrades. Her expression turned terrified as she noticed the vampires crawling down the buildings, descending around them.

As Keith turned to move the manhole cover, he saw Amaretto blocking his way.

"Keith, it's time..." She said meekly. "It's now or never."

"Huh?!" Keith screamed pointing to the manhole cover. "Move it!"

"My name... I'm Allison. Allison Hicks."

Keith glanced from the encroaching vampires to the gang —all closing in fast. He then stared back incredulously at Amaretto.

"Summer vacation, 6th grade? Sue Leonard's basement. We played spin the bottle, I spun, it landed on you and you wouldn't kiss me. Remember? I had such a crush on you then, and always have. Please say you remember me and feel the same. I don't want to die like this."

A look of recognition suddenly sparked across Keith's face. He even smiled for a second. But there was no time now. No time at all.

Moving in, Keith suddenly kissed her as he picked her up, and moved her to the side.

He then let go, turned and struggled with lifting the manhole—His strength had been depleted from the events of the night. "Fuck!" he exclaimed.

Bending down to help Amaretto easily lifted her side of the iron cover.

Keith's stomach dropped seeing her show of strength.

But there was no time to dwell.

With the violence nearly upon them from both human and vampire, Keith and Amaretto rushed down the ladder without another word.

As they reached to the bottom, and speedily stepped onto

the sewer floor, the sound of the Dragons and vampires colliding, echoed down the manhole from above.

"They're *mine*!" Snow yelled to Dominique as they got to the open manhole.

Dominique could only show a drooling, fang-filled grin back at him.

The red mist that clouded Snow's better judgement started to disappear as he noticed the amount of vampires that now surrounded them.

Clay and Dade held their crowbars aloft at the ready. Waiting for their master's command.

Maven, too, held steady, waiting for Snow to begin his attack. But unlike the twins, a cold fear now crept over her as she saw the many sets of fangs and glowing eyes that leered eagerly at them.

A tear rolled down Dolly's cheek as she knew what was about to happen.

"I love pale meat," Dominique gleefully sneered, her eyes glared at Snow's neck hungrily.

The battle that ensued only left one of them standing.

In the next sixty seconds, the vampires and the gang would nearly be extinguished.

The sounds of the war on the street above didn't stop Keith and Amaretto hurrying further into the sewer tunnels. Nor did it stop Keith remembering Amaretto's strength with the manhole. All he could think was if she *was* one of them, she *was* helping him. There was no other way about it. Could she be a good vampire?

As they moved along the water lined concrete, trying to keep the echoes from their steps as minimal as possible, Keith then remembered more about Allison Hicks.

A year after they had met, Keith and AJ had to say goodbye for the summer as Keith's parents took him on their annual vacation to his cousin's house in Seaside Heights, New Jersey.

Each year growing up, this had been the best part of the summer vacation for Keith. He got to spend time with his cousin, Ellie, who, though two years older, included him in all that she got up to. And hanging out with her was a *lot* of fun. She was always the most popular girl in school, and the popular girl in town. *Everyone* knew her and *everyone* loved her, and by association, they loved Keith too.

That year, it was Ellie's best friend Sue's birthday party. A party he had been invited to every year. A party that he always got nervous to go to, but still happy to be invited. And he was especially nervous this year as he would get to see Allison Hicks again. A girl his age whom he had met a few days earlier at the town's summer festival, and who was also a friend of Ellie's. A girl whom he spoke to for a whole day and night about everything and anything. He told her about his past, he told her about AJ—who even at a young age, girls called Mr. Dynamite—he told her about everything he had ever experienced. And she did the same in return. She made his stomach feel like it was full of worms.

This party would only be the third time he had ever seen Allison, and would be the one he would kick himself for, for years to come.

As the bottle spun and landed on him, Keith looked up terrified to Allison, who smiled victoriously back.

"You lucky dog," Ellie whispered while nudging him. "She likes you as much as you like her."

"Shut up Ellie!" Allison complained as she crawled over the circle of people, toward Keith.

Breaking out in a cold sweat, he then did the unthinkable.

"I... I'm sorry," he stuttered as he stood up. "I can't"

The look of dejection on her face stayed with Keith for a long time. But that night was also the last time he would go to Seaside Heights.

Ellie's parents split a few months later, and she was taken across the country to live in San Diego. Far from New Jersey, and far from Allison.

Keith always regretted that night, regretted not being braver. When he got back home and told AJ of what happened, his friend smiled and said, *'That's such a Keith thing to do!'* He had really wanted to kiss her, but his nerves ruined everything.

From that day forward, anytime either of them lucked out with women for doing something stupid, it was referred to by AJ as *'doing a Keith.'*

The memory of that mistake stuck with Keith for a long time, but the memory of her face slipped away over the years, blurred with the rest of those memories. And soon he had forgotten she even existed.

What Keith never saw though, was what his actions that day of Sue's party had done.

As he got up and ran away from the on-coming kiss, Allison was left, in the circle of laughing friends, sobbing.

It had only been earlier that day that Allison had confided in Ellie that she like Keith. *Really* liked him. She didn't know why. She had never felt anything like it before. She had seen lots of boys before she thought were good looking. All appealing in their own way But that moment she first saw Keith, she felt a sting in her stomach, as if she had been pulled downward on a frantic rollercoaster. She could not quantify it. But she knew that he was special.

And unlike Keith, she would remember everything about that night. About him.

In the sewers, quietly walking along and hoping that none of the Dragons or vampires had followed them underground, Keith now wondered if they were even going in the right direction.

"So, you do remember me? Right?" Allison asked.

Keith smiled at her and nodded. He didn't want her to know that he had forgotten her face.

"You finally kissed me," she continued.

Before Keith could reply, the faint echo of other footsteps drifted through the stench filled air toward them. Catching them both off guard, the sound froze them to the spot.

Allison spoke so quietly Keith could barely hear her. "I thought you said it was safe down here?"

"It's probably just an old wino or something?"

Keith had no idea but didn't want to scare her more, despite him being utterly terrified himself.

"A wino," she mused. "In high heels."

Quickly, Keith motioned for them to carry on, creeping along the tunnel.

Their pace though was too slow to escape the oncoming footsteps, as the heels clicked and clacked, louder and louder, nearer and nearer.

Turning a corner, Keith and Amaretto came to an immediate halt as they were faced with a shadowed wall ending the path they were on.

"Shit!" Keith exclaimed.

The footsteps got nearer, the pace quickened.

Almost instinctively, Keith and Allison backed up against the wall, hiding in the shadows that coated it.

With these footsteps almost upon them, Keith didn't know what else to do. So, with his free hand he reached through the darkness to hold Allison's.

As he moved his arm along the wall toward her, he suddenly touched something. Something metal. Something solid.

Flinching, he turned into the dark, and pulled his hand away.

"What is it?" Allison asked quietly.

Reaching toward it again, he quickly realized what it was. He grabbed hold of the metal again and twisted.

The hinges creaked loudly as he pushed the door open wide, conscious that the footsteps were seconds away.

Pulling Allison through the doorway into the dark chamber, Keith quickly and quietly shut the door behind them.

"I can't see a thing," Allison whispered. "Where are you?"

Reaching toward her for the second time in as many minutes, Keith managed to eventually find Allison's hand through the pitch black. He gripped it, but she gripped back even more firmly, both of them scared of their surroundings.

At the end of the chamber, a dull sliver of light dropped in from the ceiling, giving Keith a target to walk toward.

"Let's go," Keith whispered as he took a step forward. But as he did, his foot trod on something. A crunching sound emanated from beneath his shoe. Allison followed suit, and the same crunching sound came from underneath her step.

"What the hell are we standing on?" she asked hesitantly.

But instead of guessing, Keith didn't want to know. He just wanted out of here. "Let's just keep going, " he said with a fake reassurance.

They both took more tentative steps forward, and the crunching underneath their feet continued.

As they tried to be as quiet as possible, a slow creaking noise sounded.

A creaking from somewhere in this chamber.

A creaking that was not from the door behind them.

They both stopped in their tracks.

"Wait," Keith said, as he let go of her hand, "I forgot… I got some matches." He then blindly searched his pockets.

His fingers found the complimentary pack of matches that he had absentmindedly picked up from the club.

Quickly he swung the bow over his shoulder, flicked the pack open, tore off a match, then struck it alight.

As the small flame blazed into life, its radiance spread across the chamber, illuminated all brightly for a few moments before dulling to a low yellow glow.

Allison shrieked loudly.

The match cast its flickering light over two rows of coffins, running along the edge of the chamber, in addition to dozens upon dozens of both human and animal remains that had been scattered across the concrete floor. Remains that they had unknowingly crunched under foot.

"Oh shit," Keith said helplessly, as he felt his stomach churn for the hundredth time that night. He looked at Allison with palpable dread.

Seeing the coffins and remains, they both knew where they were…. standing in a vampire's lair.

"Why, there you are," came a sickening voice from behind them, as the door creaked open behind them.

Dominique stood in the half-light that spilled in from behind her. The whole of her charred front was caked in blood and gore, remnants of her battle from up on the street. Down here in the darkness, her eyes glowed brightly at them, no longer a dull hue.

Together, Keith and Allison stumbled backward, further into the chamber.

"The coffins!" Allison yelped as she realized what the other creaking sound had been.

From a casket of rotten wood, the lid opened fully as a

female vampire started to rise, dressed in a Club's waitress outfit.

As she hissed at the interlopers, Keith's match burned itself out, casting them into a momentary darkness that neither of them wanted to be in.

"Get back," Keith hissed urgently to Allison.

Fumbling, he lit a second match and without a pause, threw it at the female vampire, who was crawling halfway out of her coffin to them.

With a scream, the vampire wailed as the match hit her dry clothes and ignited its flammable material. This ignition filled the chamber with a brighter light than the match could, showing Keith and Amaretto a better look around.

At the open doorway, Dominique screeched in fury.

As she did, the other coffins started to creak open in unison. Dominique had sounded a battle cry to her slumbering brethren, those that had the night off from the club. Those who had no idea what had befallen the coven tonight.

Within seconds, the undead here were all rising. Each of them now shrieked the same as Dominique, sharing her cries.

Noticing some old clothing amongst the remains at their feet, Keith quickly bent down and snatched it up. It was an old shirt, covered with dry bloodstains.

Thrusting the matches into Allison's hands, he couldn't help but shout his command in his panic, "Keep throwing the matches!"

At speed, he ran over to the burning vampire, convulsing in her death throes, as the other vampires clambered out of their coffins towards them. He reached the shirt into the flames over her, causing the material in his hand to catch fire.

"You called me Allison," she replied as she urgently fumbled with the matches.

"The matches," he shouted incredulously at her, *"Just light them!!"*

"I'm trying!"

Keith then threw the lit shirt toward the nearest raising vampire, one whose clothes also quickly caught alight. The flames spiralling over them in an instant.

The shrieking of these creatures became deafening in this stone room. As they slowly crawled out of their dazed slumber, the fire began to catch from coffin to coffin.

Allison meanwhile was furiously lighting matches and tossing them where she could, only half of them hitting their target, and only half of those landing still lit.

Smoke began to quickly fill the room as bedlam erupted. The vampires became more focussed on their own survival and less concerned about Keith and Allison. Even Dominique ignored them as she ran over to her own empty coffin, frantically trying to save it from the fire that had now caught onto it.

All these vampires squealed as they too threw themselves atop their blazing shelters, trying to save their own sanctuaries, ignoring the fact that their own bodies were combustible to this flame. Their screams of fury soon turned to hideous screams of pain in a matter of moments. They were like woodland animals running into a forest fire to save their winter stores of food. Not using their brains, instead running solely on blind instinct.

On the opposite side of the chamber, Keith could barely see through the blossoming smoke. He could only hear the cries of pain from within this inferno that had spread between them and the vampires.

With a glance, he soon realized that Allison was no longer by his side. He turned back towards the fire in a panic. "Allison?" he called out. The screams around him almost drowned him out.

"Get to the door!" He frantically called, hoping she could hear him.

Coughing, he stumbled around the fire and through the

vampire carnage. The smoke now stopped him from clearly seeing anything, or them being able to see him. All that could be seen was the ghastly silhouettes the fire cast up onto the walls. The dark shadows of the vampires flailing around in agony, like some grim shadow play. Soon he saw these shadows bursting into clouds of ash, one by one.

Getting to the open door, Keith turned back. Allison was not here either.

Squinting, he tried to look back through the smoke.

"Allison?" he called out again.

Nothing could be heard but screams of the dying monsters.

His lungs strained under the heaviness of the chamber's smoke, causing him to cough uncontrollably.

It was too much to stand in here much longer.

"Allison?" Keith tried to call out again, spluttering and wheezing as he did so.

The air itself was growing more and more noxious, not only from the smoke, but from the stench of the burning undead mixed with rotting wood.

Having no option, he stumbled back into the tunnel, coughing harder and harder as the smoke swirled around him, licking at his feet and curling up his legs.

Suddenly, a blood curdling scream pierced over the roar of the fire, deep in the chamber in front of him. Overshadowing the cries of the vampires from within.

"Keeeeiiiittthh!" came Allison's tormented voice.

Chills ran down his spine as his name echoed off the tunnel walls and spun around him.

Keith took a large breath in, gritted his teeth, then with a steely determination reentered the smokey furnace.

Swinging his bow off his shoulder, he held an arrow loaded. Pointing forward. *It's your last one,* Keith had to remind himself. He would make it count.

As he stepped through, he scanned his aim left and right.

But there was not one target here to shoot at. The fire had burned the last of its fuel, feeding on the remnants of the coffins. The vampires themselves, now disintegrated.

"Keeeeiiiittthh Heeeelllllllp!" Allison's scream rang out again.

Speeding his step, Keith kept the bow aimed, and hurried deeper in the room. Squinting from the smoke, holding his breath as best as he could.

Further along the wall, a stream of orange light broke out from one of the walls. A doorway he has not seen before. One masked by smoke and commotion.

"Keeeeiiiittthh!"

Without a second thought, he rushed ahead and pushed open the small wooden door—bow first, at the ready—into the small, candlelit antechamber.

This room held a single ornate coffin. Not one like the small wooden makeshift one that had been in the last room. This one had antique gold fixings, and the wood itself seemed to shimmer in this low light.

Scattered around the floor lay an indescribable amount of human remains. Much more than in the previous room. There were newer bones and rotting flesh that caused a stench worse than any sewer could.

"Keith!" came the cry from the end of the room, from behind the ornate coffin itself.

Stepping out into the candlelight, Katrina, naked and in her full vampiric glory howled at him. She held Allison's hand behind her back with a taloned claw. Her other gripping Allison's hair, pulling it backward, exposing her pulsing neck to her waiting fangs.

Katrinas eyes glowed brilliantly, as she alternated a furious and hungry stare between Keith and Allison.

Pulling his bow tauter—his final arrow readied—Keith sighted his aim directly at Katrina. But, there was no good aim to be had. Allison was being held in front of where Katrina's heart was.

A forked tongue lolled out of the Queen's serrated maw as she turned, running its thick and blackened fleshiness up Allison's neck.

"Get off of her!" Keith screamed in desperation, to which Katrina reeled her eyes toward him, still licking her prisoner's neck. A smile broke out over her ancient, grotesque face, as she enjoyed their torment like a fine wine.

Slowly, Katrina retracted her tongue, then lowered her fangs to within a fraction of an inch from Allison's jugular. All the while staring at Keith intently. Playing with them both, with sadistic, perverse glee.

Keith tensed as he tried to keep his composure. As he tried to keep the bow steady. The string of which started to dig into his fingers.

His mind flickered back to his training, to his time with Old Man Miller. *He must hold fast... there must be a target.*

Keith could clearly see the fear in Allison's eyes. The pain from Katrina's grip was evident as this Queen smiled wider and wider, almost seeming orgasmic at the tortures he was causing. Low groans emanated from her, as if this was foreplay.

Slowly, realizing that no clear shot would be forthcoming, Keith slowly began to lower his bow, the string still taught.

"No! Shoot her, please!" Allison screamed in a panic as she saw Keith's aim moving. "Shoot her *through* me! I don't matter!"

Keith gripped his bow tighter, but he found it impossible to even consider her request.

"Don't let her turn me," Allison sobbed as Katrina pulled her head back further, her fangs getting nearer, teasingly resting upon her skin.

Keith could hear his own heartbeat loud and clear again, thumping in his eardrums like a drum beat leading his way into battle. His lungs hurt from the smoke inhalation. His bow fingers throbbed as the string cut in his skin. His back hurt. His whole being just ached, as if he had been through a meat grinder.

The heat and stench in this antechamber didn't make matters any better, as he struggled to catch his breath, and had to force his focus to remain steady with all his might.

As sweat dripped down his forehead, it smeared the soot that had been caked onto him from the fire. Ash and tears dripped into his eyes, stinging on their impact.

"Please," Allison croaked again.

With a forced renewed vigor, Keith knew he had little choice. He finally screamed in frustration as he raised the bow, aiming directly at Allison's heart, and in turn directly at Katrina's heart. He held the string so tightly that it cut deeper into the flesh on his fingers, sending droplets of blood down it.

Holding his ground firmly, Keith continued to stare at his target. Blinking the soot and sweat from his eyes. Trying to restore total focus. Ignoring the pain. As his target now closed her eyes, Katrina screamed a loud cackle. Enjoying the stand-off between her and these ants… her intended food.

As blood continued to drip slowly from his fingers, drop by drop it worked its way down the string, pooling on the bottom of the bow, then falling off the edge— straight down and splattering onto his white sneaker.

Catching this scent of this fallen blood, Katrina's attention fell toward Keith, then down to his sneaker. The red of the blood starkly contrasted against the white of his shoe.

Like a cat, the Queen hissed toward him, with her mouth open wide, her fangs on full display. Her hunger for him was palpable and her eyes glowed stronger. Brighter.

In a moment, Keith's aim dropped to the floor as he sighed, causing Katrina to loosen her grip for a moment, causing Allison to buckle slightly to the floor. Then just as quickly, Keith raised his aim again, speedily finding a different target.

He fired his last arrow.

Whooshing through the air, the projectile flew above, and slammed directly into Katrina's gaping maw. Slicing through the back of her throat and throwing her whole body backward. As the Queen's talons lost their grip on her prisoner, as the arrow forced her off her feet, it pinned her to the stone wall behind. The arrowhead, embedded deep.

Allison, now scrambling on the floor, turned to see the Queen, who now struggled to get free, convulsing, pulling at the arrow in her mouth weakly.

Allison quickly grabbed a broken bone from the many that had been strewn across the floor. With a battle cry she ran up to the struggling Katrina, and plunged the shattered bone deep into Katrina's throat, spilling black blood outwards and down her monstrous twitching body.

She yanked the bone out, and again, stabbed into the Queen's throat.

"The heart!" Keith yelled. "In her heart!"

Jerking violently, Katrina wailed louder and more grotesquely than before. She pushed Allison away, then pushed her body forward uneasily. Trying to rip her head off the shaft of the arrow.

Before the Queen could remove herself fully, Allison advanced again—bone in hand—and she rammed the makeshift weapon though Katrina's breastplate, into her heart.

For a moment the screams from the Queen stopped, as the only sounds in the room became the burning of the coffins outside.

Her undead, furious eyes stared wide at his attacker, as a high pitched whine began to escape the open wound in her throat.

Allison turned to Keith, but before she could speak, the

vampire Queen burst into flames, as her body combusted from the inside out.

Simultaneously, her skin and flesh aged and charred. Her flesh shriveled off her body as her bones collapsed into nothing but a corpse dust.

CHAPTER 16
ESCAPE

Standing outside of the Antechamber, Allison and Keith embraced tightly.

"You could have killed me..." she whispered softly into his ear. "You've fired three arrows at me now, you stupid ass!"

Keith couldn't help but smile. She *wasn't* a vampire, she was just a teensy bit crazy, and somehow he loved every part of it. He may have forgotten her face but he remembered the feelings that he felt for her, back during that summer. And now, that feeling had returned, but unlike then, he was no longer a child and no longer too scared.

Looking into his eyes, Allison returned his smile. "You know, that bitch never paid me for tonight."

"You wanna go check her pockets?" Keith joked. "We can, if you want to?"

Allison's face fell deadpan. "Yes. Lets."

"You're not normal," Keith chuckled. "you know that right?"

"I am a fearless vampire killer!" She joked playfully in reply. "Watch your tongue!"

"No shit. You saved the day!"

As Allison smiled again, she planted a large kiss on Keith's lips. One that was long, long overdue. Not a peck, not a polite kiss, not one out of charity, but a passionate one. A deeply passionate one.

Making their way through the sewer, they stepped past the ruined remains of the chamber, past the mix of human bones and piles of ash. Past the small fires that still burned their final cries, as their smoke became weaker and weaker with each passing moment.

Neither of them realized it at first, but they walked away from this hand in hand. Half from affection, half from a fear that it may not be over.

"See what happens when you don't clean up after you eat?" Keith had joked on their way past the remains on the floor.

"You say something like that," Allison retorted. "And *I'm* the one who's not normal?"

As they walked on out into the main tunnel system, they didn't talk much more. They just walked quietly. Happy for this moment of peace they now found themselves in.

Keith briefly mused about what happened up on the street. Did the vampires win the battle? Were the Dragon's now all dead? Could they be waiting for them up there?

As the manhole cover lifted up on the desolate street, Keith peered out cautiously, half expecting Snow to be there, waiting with revenge in his eyes.

Smiling, Keith turned down the ladder toward Allison, who was at the bottom looking up. "Get up here," he said. "You gotta see this."

"It better not be any more goddamn vampires," she mumbled as she began climbing.

"No..." He said looking back out onto the street. "It's clear."

Noticing her climbing nearer, Keith pushed the cover further upwards with his shoulder, letting in the beams of early morning sunlight. Glaring brightly downwards, straight into Allison's wide curious eyes.

With a scream she suddenly turned her head.

As her voice reverberated around the manhole, Keith's mind was thrown into the recurring possibility of her being a vampire—But only for a fleeting moment.

"What was that for?" she said pained as she blinked the brightness from her eyes. Adjusting to this new light as fast as she could. "Was that supposed to be funny?"

"No... I..." Unable to answer her, Keith quickly pushed the manhole cover up, and scrambled out of the manhole and onto the street.

Turning, he reached his hand down to her. To help her out, but had no time to react as she was suddenly yanked downwards. Pulled at incredible speed into the hole, disappearing back into the dark shadows below.

"Keeeeeeeeith!" Her scream faded as she disappeared from his sight.

Without considering his own life, he immediately clambered down after her. Keeping his eyes on the darkness below with each frantic step he took down the rungs.

As his feet hit the dirty sewer floor, he tried to focus his eyes in the darkness. He raised his hands defensively to anything that may be there.

"Allison?" he said weakly.

As his eyes adjusted, he saw Allison in the grips of one of them.

Dominique.

She had not died in the chamber.

Almost all burned with many bones exposed, half her face was now gone. She was a vision of pure, abject horror. Simply the most terrifying sight either of them had ever seen. A walking, psychotic massacre on legs. Burned, mutilated legs.

Her sharp claws were now wrapped around Allison's throat, lifting her off the floor with incredible ease. As the charred vampire growled, she glared at Keith hatefully .

"You killed my queen... you killed my coven... you destroyed my home..."

Keith looked down at his hands. He had no bow. No matches. No weapons. Balling his fists was all he could do.

As the vampire began to squeeze tighter around Allison's neck, she spoke with a sickening grin, "I will eat her slowly... and will I make you watch... Then I will eat your flesh as you scream for mercy, from your groin to your gullet. "

Then, seemingly from out of nowhere, a jagged wooden stake suddenly exploded through Dominique's back, through her heart, bursting out of her chest. Immediately this vampire wailed as a fire broke out from under her skin, and spread across her body. Spewing out of all orifices simultaneously.

As Dominique's body fell to ash and bone, Keith ran over to Allison, who had been dropped to the floor, clutching her now sore neck, coughing painfully.

"Are you ok?" he asked in a panic, as he knelt down beside her. Not even thinking to look at where the stake had come from.

"If only vampires could stop taking me hostage," she spluttered. "That'd be so great."

Then, hearing a footstep, Keith looked up to the figure that had saved them. A tall dark presence whose features were masked in the darkness of the shadows.

"Thank you," Keith said cautiously. "Who are you?"

Stepping out of the dark with a confident strut, AJ stood. Smiling. He was still pale, still had sunken eyes, but also still had *that* smile.

Allison leapt back toward Keith in fear. "Jesus Christ," she shouted, as she gripped him tightly.

Pulling her up to her feet, Keith stepped backwards toward the ladder leading to the street, not letting his eyes slip from off of AJ.

"Hey," AJ smirked. "Don't thank me or anything, you asshole. I do this, and what? You treat me like I'm a bad guy?"

Keith gulped. "I killed you—I mean, *you* killed you. You got staked right through the goddamn heart."

AJ nodded and pointed to the weapon he used on Dominique, the one that now lay on the floor amongst the smoldering ash. "That thing? Well, call me a dumb guido, but I always thought the heart was on the right side of your chest." He motioned to his shirt, where the rip in his shirt exposed a half healed wound, on the opposite side to his heart. "So I was down for a bit, cos trust me, that shit still *hurts*. But then I came to. All of that club was burning down around me. So I came down here, and thank all the Gods and monsters that I did. Oh also, I don't hear them any more... the voices... Nothing. She's gone, right? I'm free."

AJ's glance then moved to Allison—her arm firmly around Keith. He smiled at her, then back to his Keith. "Anyway fuck my problems. Look at you, you dawg," he laughed as he spoke. "You find time to hook up during all this mayhem?"

"It's Allison," Keith said meekly. "Alison Hicks?"

AJ suddenly looked genuinely shocked. "What? No. *The* Allison Hicks? As in the girl you did *such a Keith* thing with?

"Such a Keith thing?" Allison asked Keith.

"Yeah," AJ replied. "As in didn't kiss 'cos he pussied out? A *Keith* thing." He then regarded Allison again. Impressed. "Wow. Well, pleasure to finally make your acquaintance. Been a while huh? I hope that schlub finally kissed you like he should have done back then."

Allison smiled and nodded embarrassed. Forgetting he was a vampire for a moment. "You remember my name?"

AJ laughed. "With how much this ass talked about you? Who couldn't?"

Keith, not knowing what to do, still backed his way up to the ladder with Allison by his side, then motioned for her to go up first.

AJ looked a bit hurt by this. "Relax, will ya? Queen bitch is dead. She got no hold over me. We'll work something out I promise!"

Keith felt a pang of guilt as he climbed the ladder below Allison, who was already standing up on street level having gone before him.

"These tunnels go everywhere, you know." AJ's voice echoed. "So, you're not gonna ditch me that fast, buddy. I'll tell you that much. Besides, we got finals soon. Ya think I can take them at night?"

"You're a vampire," Keith retorted.

"And so? You're a prick, we're not all perfect!" AJ laughed. "It's all just one long journeypath we're on!"

"You and your fucking journeypath…" Keith muttered as he climbed the ladder. Not taking his eyes off AJ until the last minute. "I'm sorry" was the last thing he said before he climbed out onto the street.

After fully closing the manhole, Keith and Allison began their long, pained walk toward downtown. Their bones and muscles ached with each step.

They were, though, not alone. At each sewer grating the walked by, Keith glanced down, only to see AJ there, smiling and making a different quip;

"I can work the graveyard shift, somewhere?"

"Ya think vampires can still get a dentist?"

"And really... How the hell are vampire's clothes invisible in reflections? That literally makes zero fucking sense!"

"Don't make me say journeypath again!"

"More importantly... more than all the death and mayhem... I really need a new shirt..."

Same old AJ.

He hadn't changed.

Even in his undeath.

He was just a little paler now.

Keith and Allison couldn't help but laugh along with him.

"That's such a Keith thing to do," AJ said with a laugh as he patted Keith on the back.

As they sat on the bridge overlooking the river, dangling their legs over the side, these boys happily spoke of the missed events from each other's summer vacations.

Having just returned from Seaside Heights, AJ had been told all Allison Hicks and the missed kiss.

"Well, okay you didn't kiss her, but that's not the end of the world, is it?" AJ shrugged. "End of the day, I hope at least you told her about me."

"Of course I did, what else would we talk about," Keith replied with a smile.

As the evening closed in, it became almost time for them to go home. AJ got to his feet and said at Keith "If there is one thing life has taught me in my few short years on this rock," he said. "Is that if it's meant to be, it's meant to be. Que Sera Sera and all that."

Keith nodded. "I guess so."

"No guessing about it. If there's someone up there looking out for you, and if this Allison girl *is* the one? Then you'll meet her again someday. Maybe tomorrow? Maybe years. May be after the sky has fallen—"

"Sky has fallen?" Keith chuckled.

"Or nuclear war, I dunno. Point is. Fate will make sure it happens, if it's *meant* to happen. Everything else is... dust in the wind. So don't you worry your pretty little head about it."

As they walked home, AJ wrapped his arm around Keith's shoulder, as he was did often.

"And don't you worry," he said." I'll be *right* there with you. Every step of the way."

MEMORIES OF VAMP

DONALD P. BORCHERS
Producer/Writer

What inspired you to come up with the idea for Vamp?

The word play of the word *Vamp*. It had a double entendre meaning. Sexy girl and lethal monster. At the time, Richard Wenk and I were trying to work together on something. We took a run at an original treatment by Barry Blaustein, Richard Wenk and Judy Simon entitled, *It Came… All Night!* We couldn't get enough interest to go to script. Because Richard had made a short entitled, *Dracula Bites the Big Apple*, a feature length horror/comedy vampire movie seemed like a natural progression. And it was. We got it made.

CHRISTIAN FRANCIS

How did you come to cast Grace Jones?

Distributers very much like it if you have people who are famous in your movie—Movie stars, I mean. Since DW Griffith made *Birth of a Nation* people want movie stars.

The director and I were totally excited when we found out that we could get Jerry Lewis in the film as *Vic*. We were shocked when the head of foreign sales told us that he was a 'negative box-office element'. We're looking at Martin Scorsese doing *King of Comedy* and everybody knows he's big in France and we're making our lame argument… But you got to go with sales, so we cast that part down and cast the vampire part up.

Grace Jones had two feature credits at that time, *A View to a Kill* and *Conan*. So, from a salesman's point of view, that's going to immediately position *Vamp*—starring Grace Jones—to earn the kind of money that they did. We only had a three-million dollar budget, they were like twenty-million dollar pictures. So for sales, Vamp should get the same sales numbers because of Grace.

So, we put Grace in, and the director immediately realizes that he's challenged by directing her to actually *perform an act* because she doesn't have a lot of range. She has a lot of *presence*—I mean she is a movie star, so if you can cast her right you're doing very well for yourself. Because of this he simply removed all the lines and just had her perform by simply… having her perform.

. . .

VAMP

Now, getting Grace was no small achievement, because I didn't want to contact her and have her say I just did *A View to a Kill* and *Conan,* why do I want to do a low-budget movie for New World Pictures. So, I called up the people who were within my sphere of getting, as I wanted to assemble the top team possible in order to attract her to the project.

I got:

- Alan Roderick-Jones as the production designer.
- Elliot Davis—I gave him his first shot as a DP. (Sadly during that time Elliot had to take one week out of our five week shoot as his father passed, so he calls his friend Steve Barnum up who then comes in shoots for a week on our show—Now we have the top DP in the world shooting our picture!)
- Dar Robinson was doing our stunts
- Greg Cannon, who had just won the Academy Award for *Cocoon,* was doing our special makeup FX.

So, I put this fabulous team together before I call up Grace, and really talked her into doing the movie.

How did Keith Haring end up painting Grace Jones for Vamp?

The reason Keith Haring worked on *Vamp* is because of the way he met Grace the year before, at one her shows in an underground club in Manhattan.

The concert was going to start at 10pm. Everybody who bought tickets was there waiting at 10pm... the concert eventually started somewhere around two in the morning... and nobody had left. Around three in the morning, Keith Haring made his way to the stage and handcuffed his wrists to Grace's ankle. He then took his art kit, and proceeded to paint on her, what we now know to be her look in *Vamp*.

We got him to recreate that look for the film, and it just was something that he came up with in that Manhattan club on that night.

As I understand the history, that's the day that made Keith Haring, Keith Haring.

What was the most memorable part of making the movie, and why?

Two things. The first was the schedule. It was the most challenging movie to schedule I have ever produced. The first problem was the rain. It rained so much we had to use every one of our interior sets for rain cover, and that was not enough. One night we got rained out so badly that we had to do an unscheduled company move in the middle of the night to our stage and then shoot our scheduled driving shots form later in the schedule, as so-called "poor man's" process shots. The second problem was the construction contract. In going with the lowest bid, I encountered a start-up company with virtually no business acumen. They used their first instalment payment from me to purchase fixed assets and had no money left for the construction materials. It was a nightmare. We had to re-schedule the sewer sequence because the set was not ready.

. . .

And then there was Grace Jones. Her fame for being late for a performance was on full display as she reported for her call time as much as 8 hours late on any given day. I knew this would be a problem when makeup artist Greg Cannom called me during preproduction and said Grace was a no-show for her facial prosthetic fittings. I called her manager in New York, Bob Caviano, who said he would have Grace call me. She did. From Paris. Azzedine Alaïa had asked her to do a runway show, so she hopped on a plane. In consolation Azzedine Alaïa asked how he could make it up to me, I said to send her back with triples of the gown we use at the end for her death. He did. After that I had a Production Assistant, with a pager, assigned to Grace 24/7.

The other thing had nothing to do with the movie, but it happened while we were filming. On January 28, 1986, the Space Shuttle Challenger broke apart 73 seconds into its flight, killing all seven crew members aboard. On that day we were downtown filming the sequence where the car spins. In order to film that I paid for an L.A. City filming permit that required me to hire 8 off-duty police officers; 2 stationed at each compass point of the intersection, for safety and traffic control. Well, after our third take, we, apparently, gridlocked all of downtown Los Angeles. L.A. Police Chief Daryl Gates was stuck in traffic and made his way over. He told me he was going to revoke my filming permit for having gridlocked the city. I told him I was going to sue him and the city for providing and requiring the supervision of 8 off-duty policemen that actually were responsible. He grumbled and walked away. We finished our work in the intersection within an hour and traffic was back to normal… after a couple hours.

If this were the last time you ever spoke of the movie Vamp, of being a part of it, what it meant to you, and its legacy, what would you say?

Go figure.

FIND OUT MORE

Wikipedia @ Donald_P._Borchers
YouTube @DonaldPBorchersOG

DEDEE PFEIFFER
Amaretto/Allison Hicks

What were your initial thoughts when you read the script, then when you got the role of Amaretto?

Well... considering that at that time, that role could possibly be my first starring role, my initial thoughts were, "PLEASE PLEASE PLEASE hire meeeeeee!!!! I LOVE this role and I AM Amaretto!!!"

My thoughts when I got the role were, "OMGGGGG! What? I REALLY got it? Wait! Are you sure they meant to hire ME???" Then called my family and friends on the phone (yes, hard wired into the wall kind of phone. Ya know the ones with the rotary dial?) to tell them that I finally got a leading role in a great film!!! :)))

What was the most memorable part of making the movie, and why?

Oh my! Where do I begin? There are SO many lol! I would say all the times when Richie (the director), Chris, and I would be making fun of all the absurdity around us on a nightly (all night shoots) basis to keep us sane because if we didn't laugh…. We would have been crying! LOL!!! We laughed A LOT! Richie and I, to this day, are still laughing at all that happened with the making of our little love film named, *Vamp*.

If this were the last time you ever spoke of the movie Vamp, of being a part of it, what it meant to you, and its legacy, what would you say?

Vamp was a passion project and to see so many still following (and appreciating) it warms my heart to no end! It was my baby before I had a baby!

Playing Amaretto and being a part of *Vamp* was a dream come true and I will forever be grateful to Richie for giving me that amazing opportunity which absolutely helped jumpstart my career. Here's a big CHEERS (w/coke… I'm sober lol) to being in one of the coolest cult classics of my time!!!

What do you think happened to Allison/Amaretto after the film ended. What would you like her story to be?

I think Amaretto went on to save all the animals in the world! Ya know why? Because she can!

FIND OUT MORE

A single mother of two young men, Dedee has been hard at work during her recent time away from Hollywood earning a bachelor's degree in psychology at Pierce College, Valley College and California State University Northridge. It was at UCLA where she earned a Master of Social Work. Her area of concentration includes mental illness, substance abuse and homelessness.

Television fans will know this talented actress from her series regular roles on *For Your Love* with Holly Robinson Peete, Tamala Jones and James Lesure; and from the award-winning comedy series *Cybill*, opposite Cybill Shepherd and Christine Baranski, which won a SAG Award for Outstanding Ensemble Series. Other notable small screen guest roles include *Ellen, Seinfeld, CSI, CSI: New York, Wanted, Friends* and *ER*.

No stranger to the big screen, Dedee also had impressive roles in the films *Red Surf*, opposite George Clooney, *Falling Down* with Michael Douglas, *Tune in Tomorrow* with Keanu Reeves and *Into The Night* with Jeff Goldblum, not to mention, of course, *Vamp* with the legendary music icon Grace Jones. In addition, she has dozens of other studio and independent films to her credits including producing the indie award-winning film *Loredo*. The short film *The Tub,* in which she starred and produced, won multiple awards including a festival Best Actress Award.

Follow Dedee on Instagram @dedeepfeifferofficial

ALAN RODERICK-JONES
Production Designer

What were your initial thoughts when you read the script? Were there any aspects that you thought may be particularly challenging in your role as production designer/art director?

Don Borchers approached me after working with him in Mexico on *Triumphs Of A Man Called Horse*. He wondered if I would be free to work in Los Angeles on a new vampire film as the Production Designer. So, I agreed to meet up with him and the director. They both expounded on the prospects of the film, having hopefully signed Grace Jones—But on reading the script, I had my reservations… I was concerned about whether they had enough construction monies to build the various sets, especially the underground sewer system. Well, Don put me at my ease and we then began to consider various locations, as well as what we could shoot on a sound stage. I then pulled my team together, who without their backup and no matter how or what I designed, the work on *Vamp* would have not been accomplished without them.

What is your fondest memory about making the movie?

My fondest memory was really working along side Grace and with her friend Keith Haring (who production brought to LA to paint Grace's body make up). I had found that great armchair that he also applied his black and white visual language onto too (I have always wondered where it disappeared to have production was completed). Grace, Keith and I would often sit together in Grace's trailer and have our lunch. And often there would be a knock at the door, and standing there standing would be *another* Grace... make up and all... There were so many drag queens in LA who adored her.

If this were the last time you ever spoke of the movie Vamp, of being a part of it, what it meant to you, and its legacy, what would you say?

The legacy of *Vamp* for me, if there is one, would be that it is one of the many productions that I have worked on in my long career that started in 1961, and continues today in various areas of film design. All of these productions I worked on have accumulated into a wealth of wonderful memories. More personally than professionally, though, *Vamp* to me is Grace and Don. We all had an inspirational few months and Don and I have continued to be dear friends.

FIND OUT MORE

The Empty Stage - A Memoir by Alan Roderick-Jones

Alan Roderick-Jones is one of those rare entertainment industry hyphenates whose illustrious career has never been told before. A London and Hollywood production designer, art director, artist, director and producer Alan's career spans over five decades.

His contributions include such film classics as The Lion in Winter, Nicholas and Alexandra and Papillon. One of the unsung heroes of the design team for Star Wars - A New Hope, Alan's professional intersections include film industry icons such as Peter O'Toole, Richard Burton, Richard Harris, Katherine Hepburn, Sophia Loren, Marlon Brando and producer Sam Spiegel…as well as the legendary Charles Chaplin.

More than just a fascinating professional saga, Alan's memoir, The Empty Stage is also a warm personal story and a spiritual journey filled with humor, warmth, humanity and visionary perspectives of a world as it can be. Already a hit with "the inner circle" The Empty Stage is a book that will delight (but not surprise) all those who know Alan well.

GEDDE WATANABE
Duncan

Vamp was something of an anomaly when I look back at it. Duncan was perhaps my first colorblind role. Meeting Keith Haring when he was painting Grace Jones in the makeup trailer was something I will never forget. The shoot was bound with all kinds of difficulties almost closing down. Bad behavior was rampant... How Richard Wenk and Donald Borchers kept it together was a miracle in itself. Would I do it again?... You betcha!

PHOTO GALLERY

SMALL & SEDUCTIVE
LOOKING FOR AC
SEX ADS BY PHONE
161 W Trilby Rd
Phone 462-1212
Opens Nightly
After Dark
The After Dark Club
Hottest Acts Anywhere
Ask about our
SINGLE MAN'S SPECIAL
CALL ME N
(213) OR (
976-
3)976-6969
SAN DEIGO (619) 976-6969

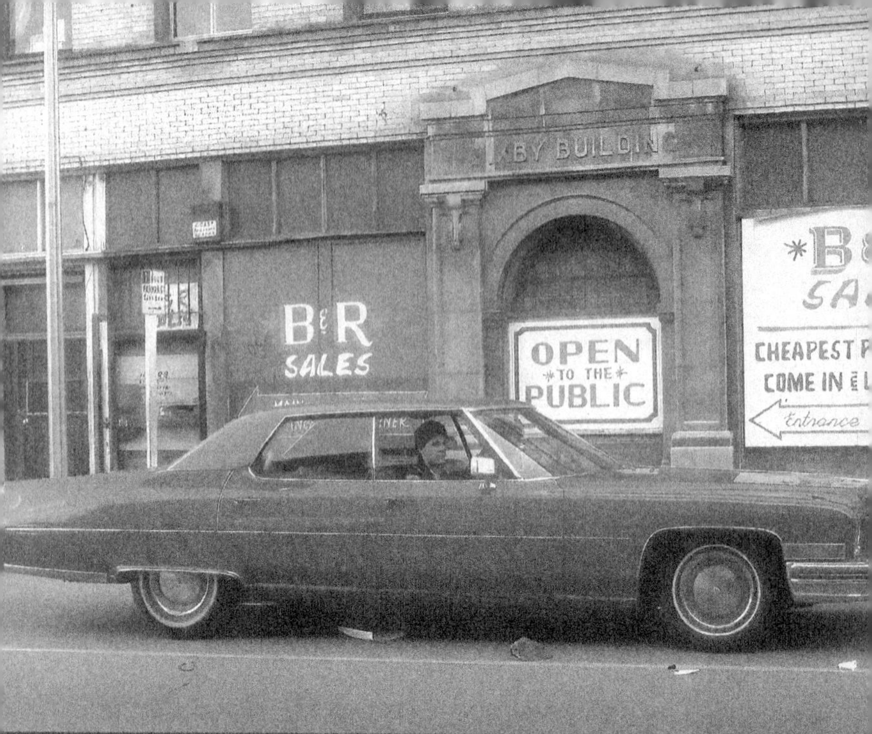
B&R
SALES
OPEN
TO THE
PUBLIC

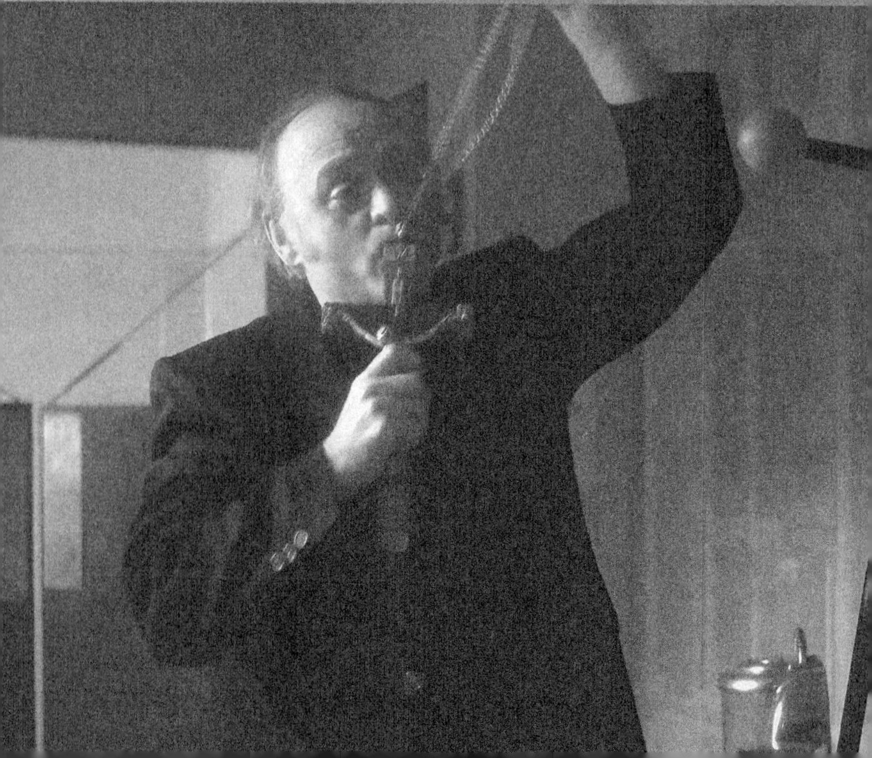

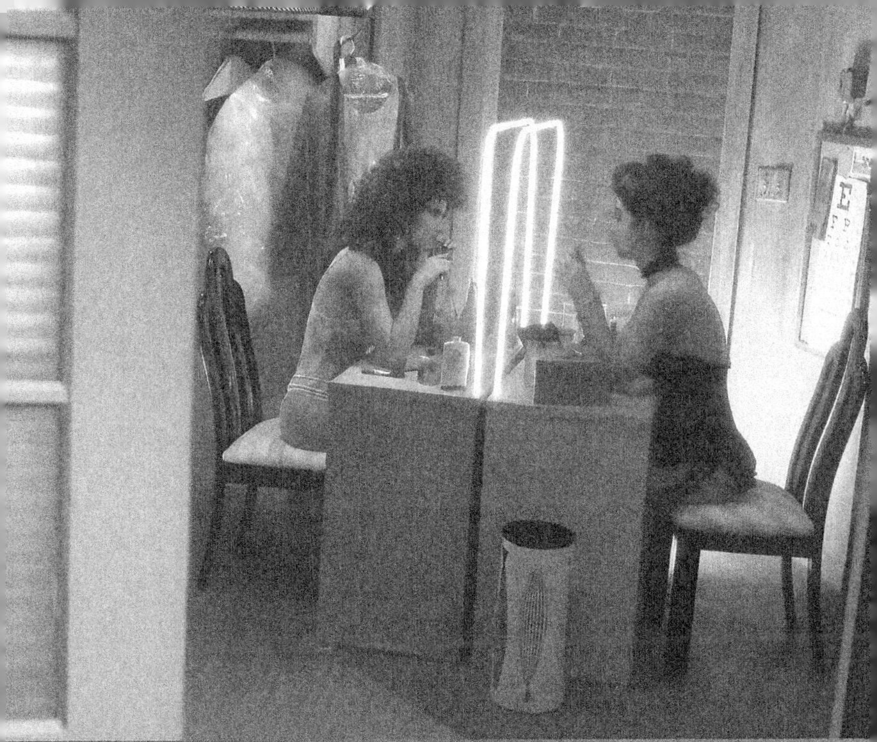

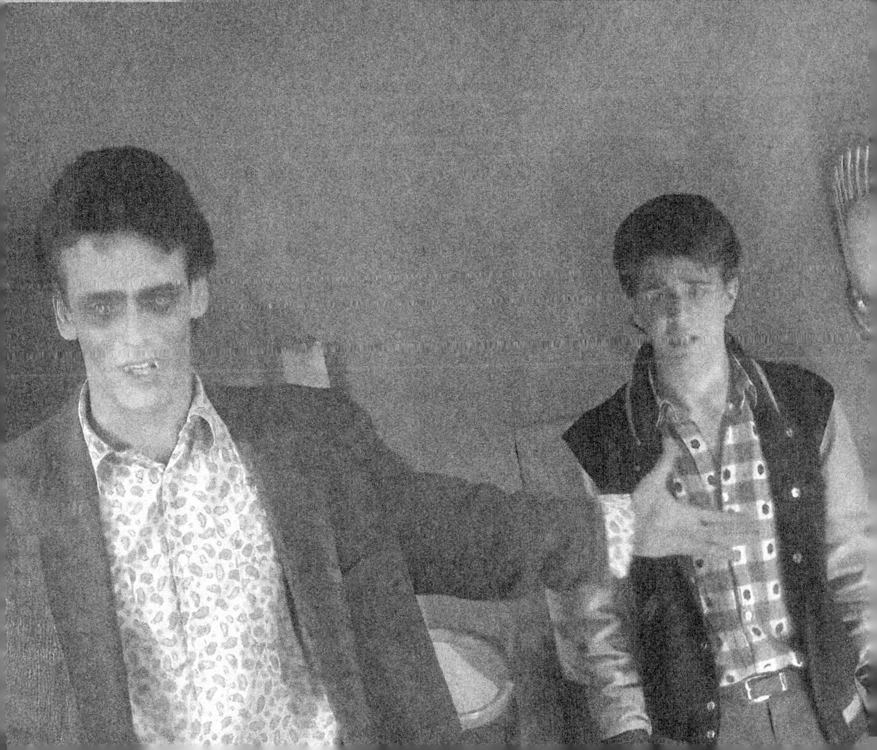

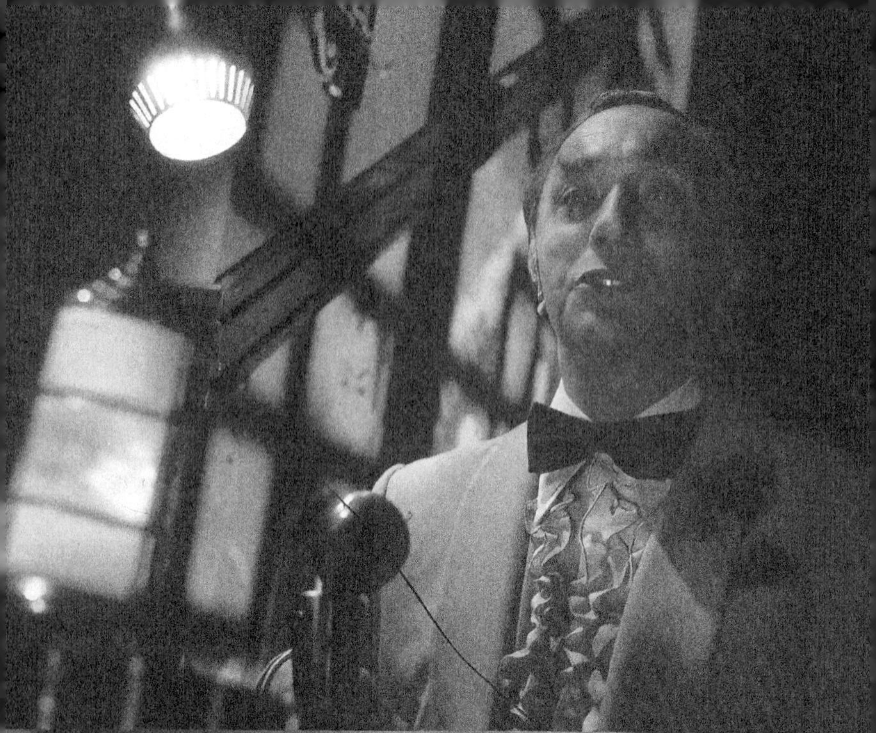

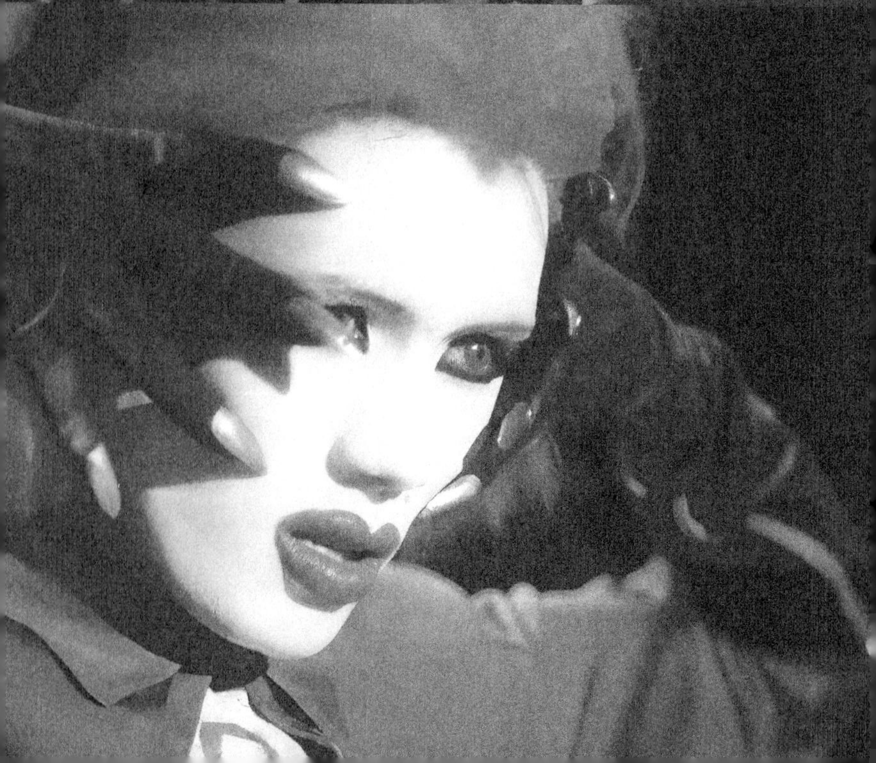

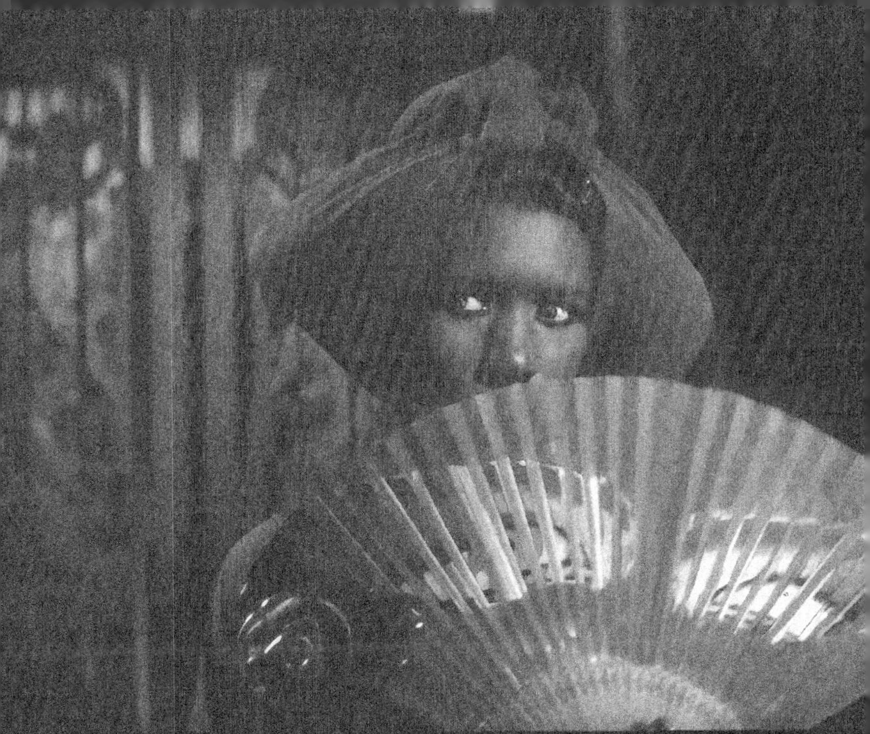

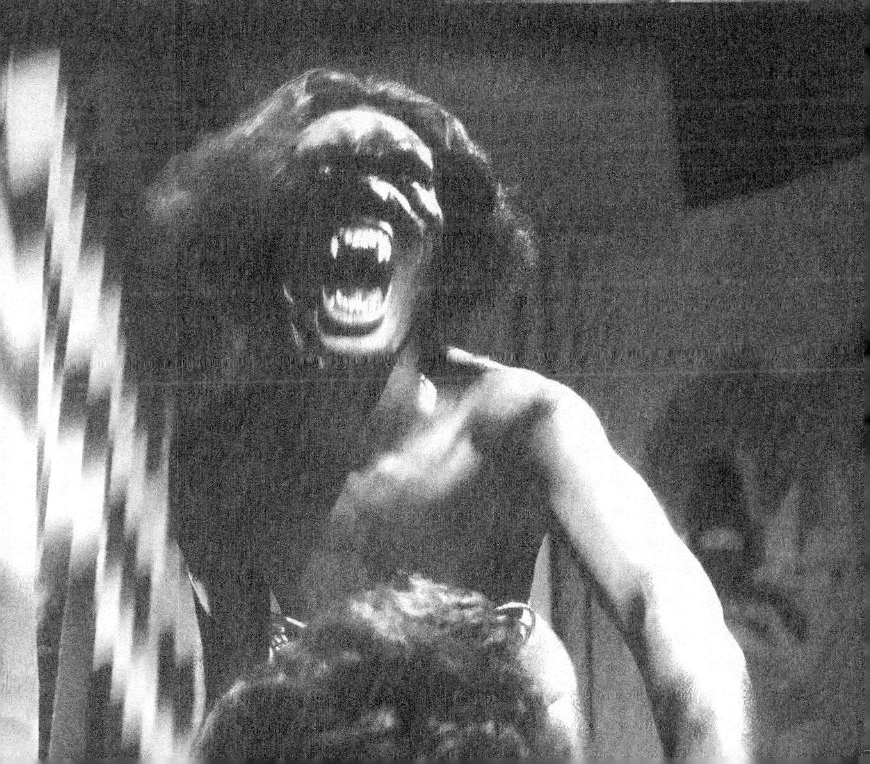

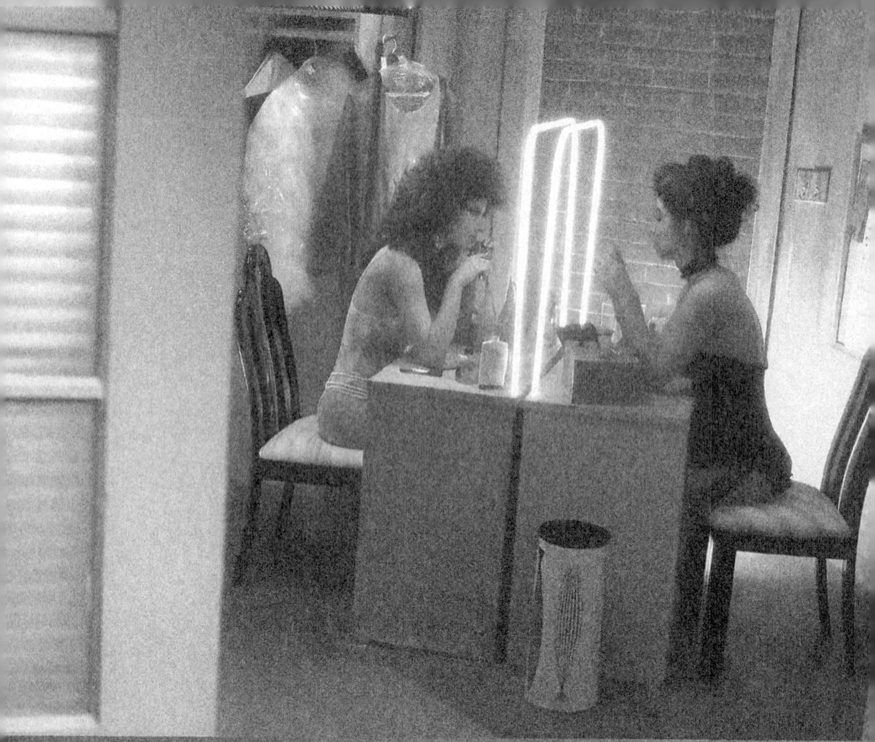

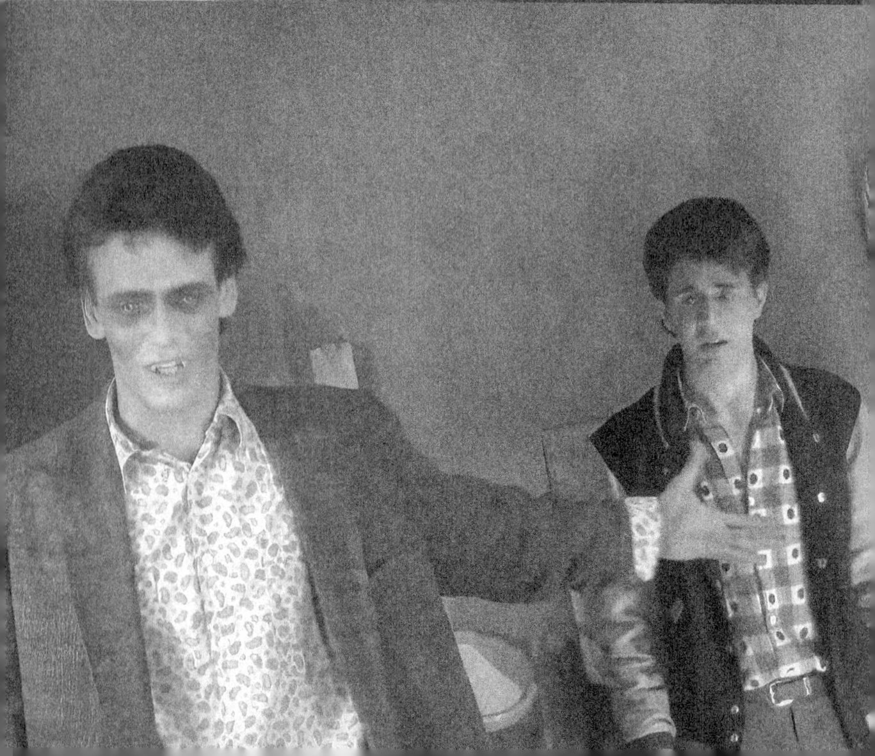

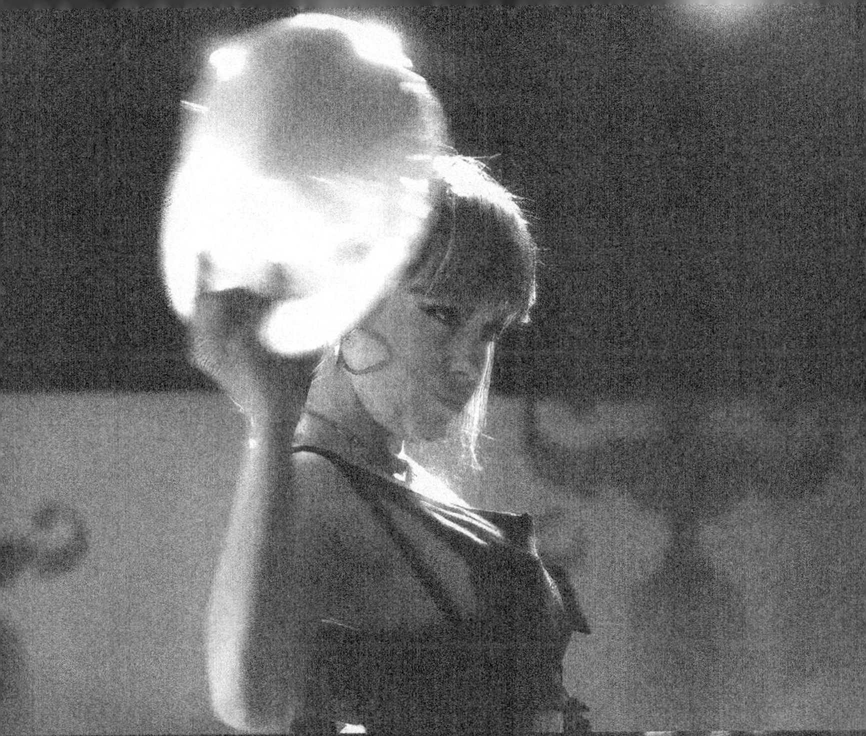

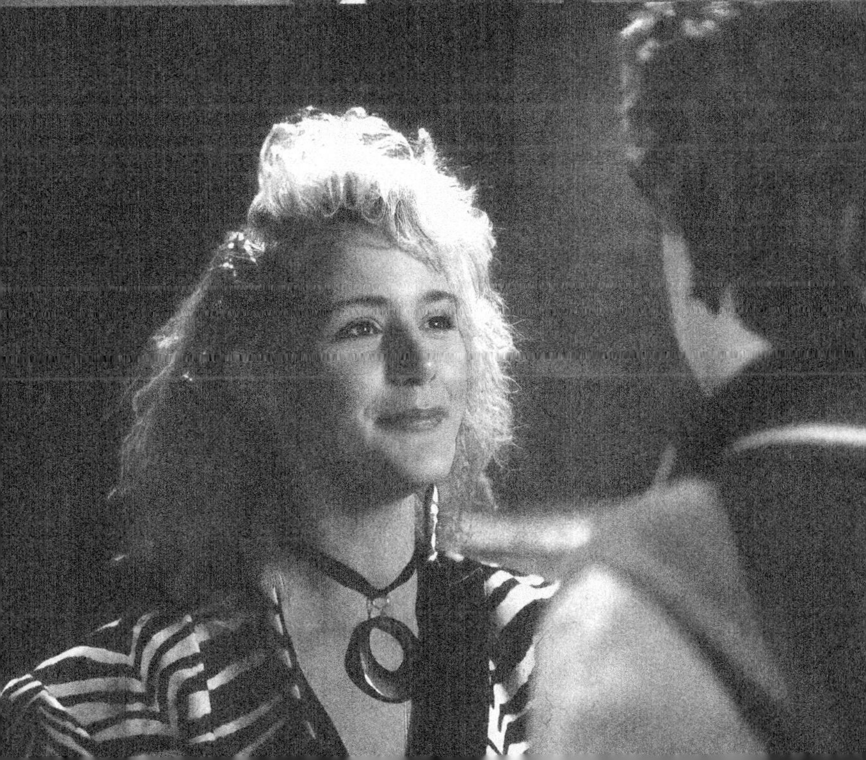

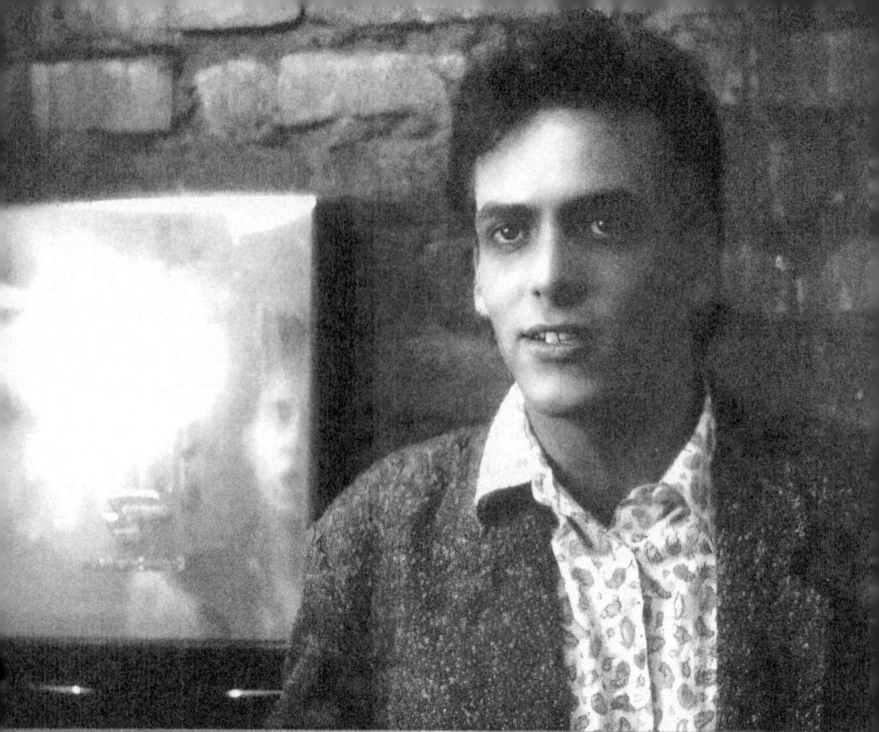

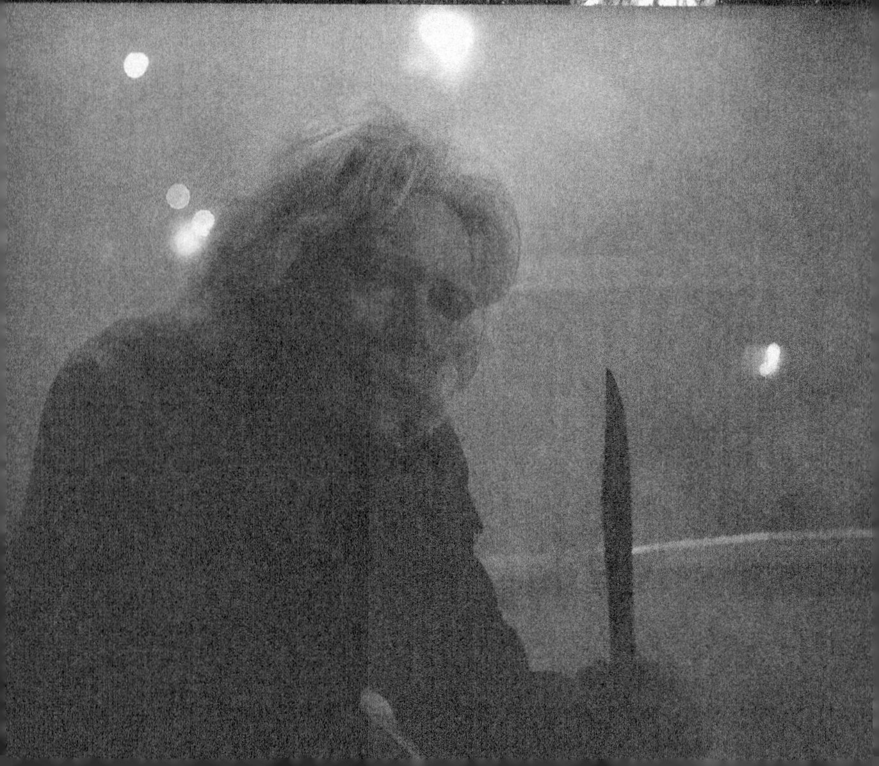

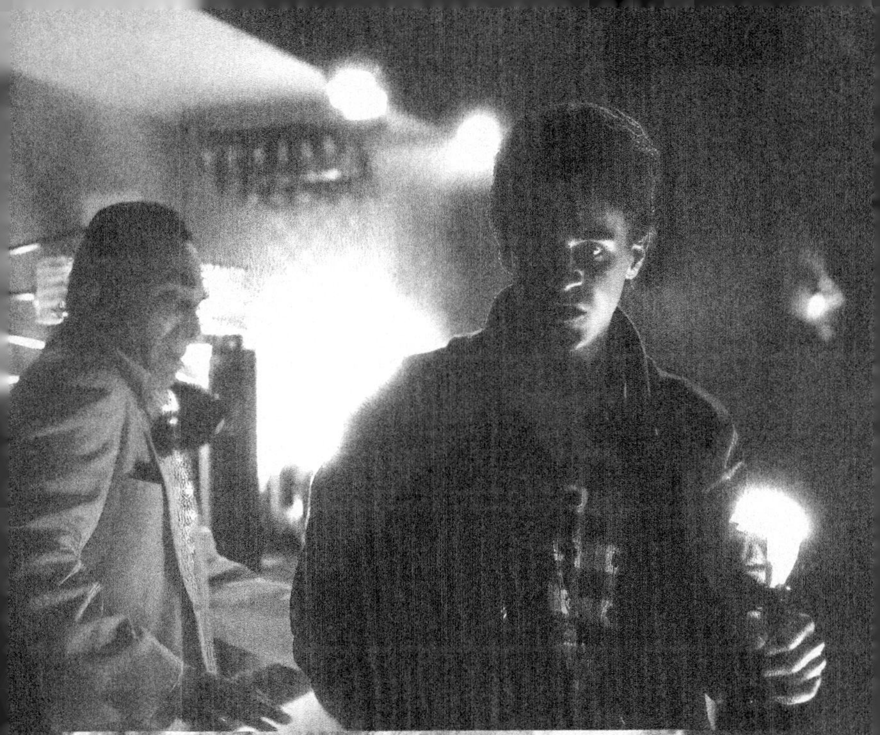

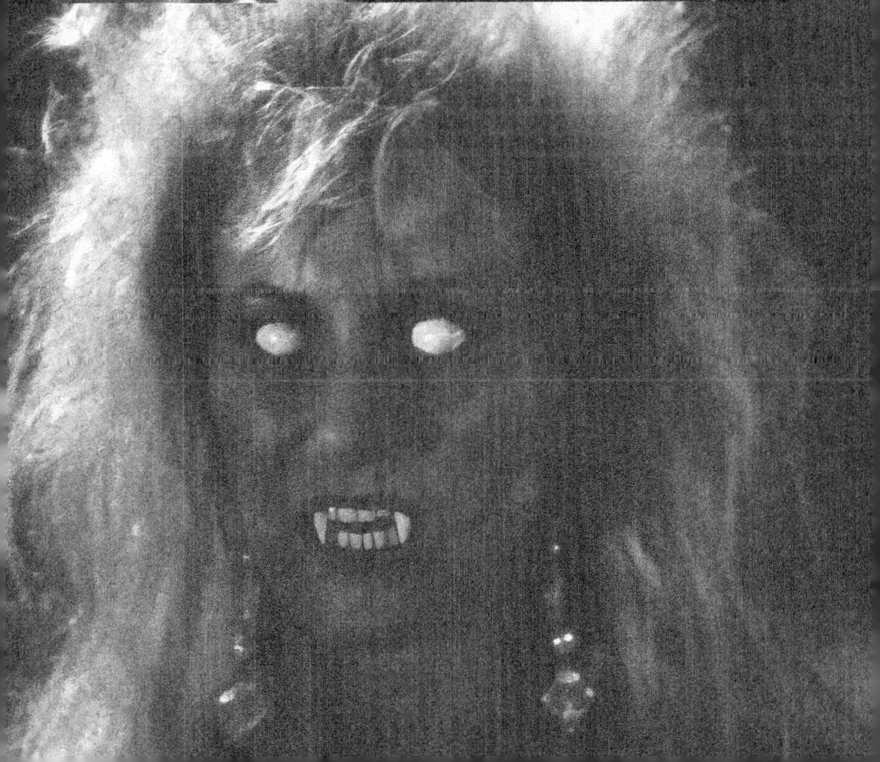

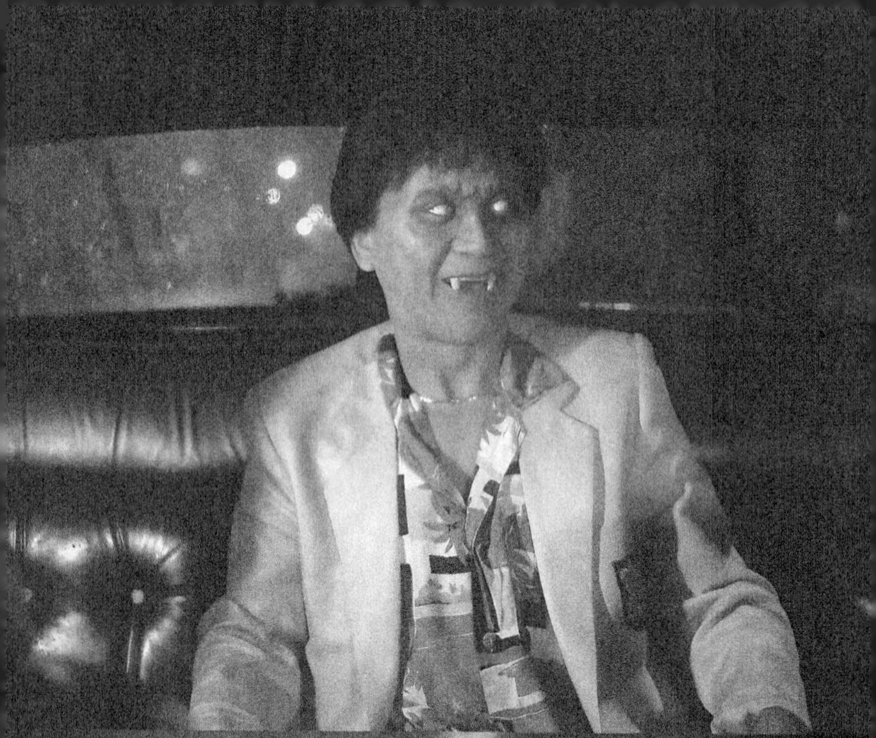

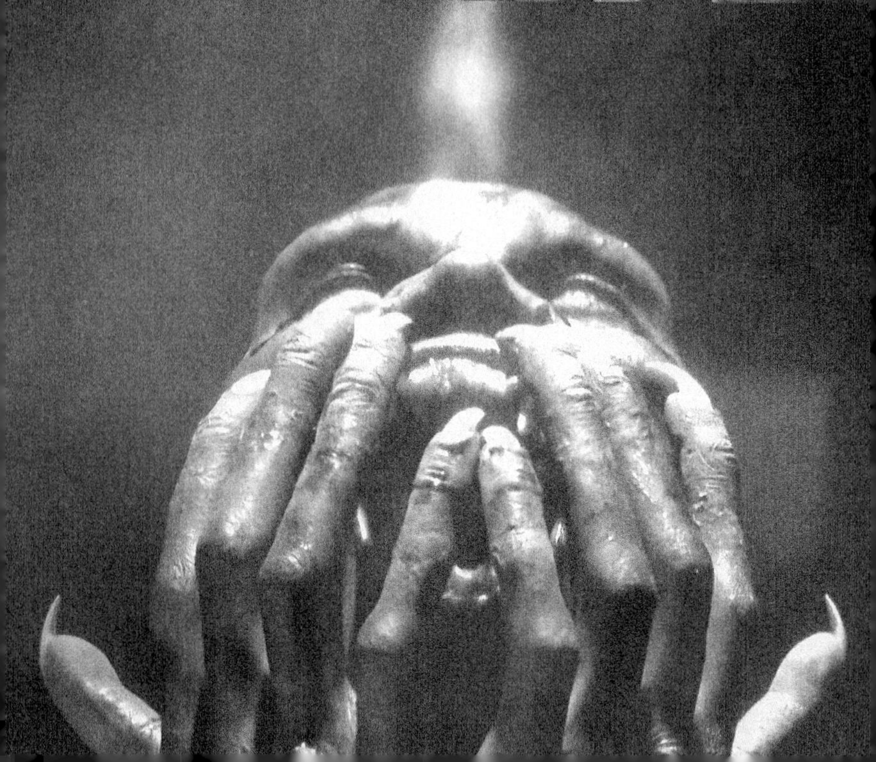

VAMP

THE ORIGINAL SCREENPLAY

[Third Draft]

by Richard Wenk
Story by Donald P. Borchers and Richard Wenk

A BLACK SCREEN

The SOUND OMINOUS MUSIC fades in as the TITLES begin. MUSIC continues, building in intensity. Then, a thunderous, reverberating NOISE is heard. A brilliant flash of blue light slices across the screen, only to go black again. This sequence repeats several times until TITLES end.

The camera begins to track backwards out of the blackness. Suddenly, a large iron hammer flies past the lens. The slice of blue light appears again. Now it's clear. WE'VE BEEN INSIDE A GIANT BELL- the blue flashes become the early morning sky

The CAMERA CONTINUES to PULL OUT until we arrive at:

EXT. BELL TOWER - MORNING

The huge bell swings back and forth. A bat flies from the belfry; a full moon still visible. The OMINOUS MUSIC continues.

The CAMERA CRANES down the exterior of the old tower to a huge wooden door. The double doors creak open and are held there by TWO FIGURES dressed in white robes and hoods. Each holds an ivory candle.

Now up the steps walks the LEADER wearing a crimson robe adorned with an ornate gold medallion. He is followed by more SHROUDED FIGURES who drag TWO struggling YOUNG MEN with them

The candle-bearing procession moves into the Tower.

INT. CHAMBER

A dark, sparsely decorated room. Everything is draped with sheets except for a long table that is littered with chalices, burning candles and ancient scrolls. The robed figures take their places about the room as the two young men are placed atop wooden stools.

ANGLE - THE CAPTIVES: Their bands are bound behind them, as masked Executioners move into place beside each stool. MUSIC loudens.

ANOTHER ANGLE: Hangman's nooses are lowered from the ceiling. The Executioners place the nooses around the prisoner's necks.

ANGLE - KEITH: A good-looking, all-American guy, KEITH stands atop the second stool trying desperately to keep his composure. Straining his neck, he shoots a glance to his left.

Three YOUNG MEN dangle at the end of ropes. Their blue bodies slowly swing back and forth. Turned over stools beneath their feet. Keith quickly turns to his fellow prisoner.

ANGLE A.J.: Bigger and stronger than Keith, A.J. is a tough-looking kid. He is weathered and handsome with a killer smile.

A.J. calmly looks from the bodies to Keith and winks.

THE CHAMBER: The Leader steps forward. The OMINOUS MUSIC continues to build...

> LEADER
> (evilly)
> Welcome... To your own worst
> nightmare.

CLOSE ON A.J.'S HANDS: Twisting his wrists, A.J. begins to loosen the ropes.

ANGLE - THE CLAN: Illuminated only by candlelight, they move forward, MUSIC building. Keith looks to A.J. Hls hands almost free.

The leader raises his arms. The Executioners take their positions next to the stools.

                    LEADER
          You are about to make the
          ultimate sacrifice. Many have
          done so, few have survived...
               (dramatic pause)
          The supreme test of
          immortality... The Rope!!!

He lifts his hood to reveal a hideous rope burn.
The MUSIC builds to a deafening crescendo. Tre
LEADER drops his arms. The Executioners begin to
pull the stools. And then:

The MUSIC begins to skip.

ANOTHER ANGLE: Everyone freezes. A robed LACKEY
rushes over to record player and removes the needle
from a warped record. Keith looks to A.J. who grins.
The Leader tries to regain the atmosphere.

                    LEADER
          Uh... The supreme sacrifice and
          uh, the ultimate test wlll
          take place and...

                    A.J.
          Jeez, I'd rather hang than
          listen to this again.

A.J. leaps from the stool. The rope slides harmlessly
from the beam above.

THE ROOM: The clan is startled... Keith gives A.J.
a grin.

                    A.J.
          This isn't a Frat House.
          It's a half-way house for
          morons. Spooky costumes? Phony
          hangings? Gimme a break...

                    LEADER
          Silence pledge! The EMMA DIPSA
          PHI initiation has only begun.

                    A.J.
          Yeah, get it. You're trying to
          bore us to death.

We NOW SEE that A.J. and Keith are clad only in
jockey shorts. The Executioner's masks are women's
underpants. The robes and hoods Just bedsheets.

A.J. gathers up his and Keith's clothes and tosses
Keith his things. A.J. holds up a balled-up
'designer' shirt. No one moves.

                    A.J.
          I told you to be careful with
          my clothes. Who wrinkled my
          shirt?

Intimidated, the Fraternity brothers remove their
hoods, shrug their shoulders and look to one another
like children caught red- handed. A.J. turns to the
'bodies' dangling beside him who open their eyes
and mumble 'not me's'.

                    LEADER
          It looks like we've misjudged
          you two. You're obviously not
          DIPSA PHI material.

                    A.J.
          Actually, it's Keith and I who
          seem to be mistaken.
              (to Keith)
          Am I right?

                    KEITH
          Fooled completely.

Keith and A.J. exchange tell-tale glances.

                    A.J.
          We were under the impression
          that this was the house on
          campus. But if you're the kind
          of organization that takes in
          any dickhead that'll jump off

                    a stool with a noose around
                    his neck, well... obviously
                    you people don't see the
                    advantages of your position.

Blank looks from the fraternity.

                         A.J.
                    Is it me?

                         KEITH
                    Try talking louder.

As if on cue, Keith and A.J. turn their backs and
slowly begin to gather up the remainder of their
belongings.

The Frat brothers whisper to each other.

                         LEADER
                    What advantages?

Both Keith and A.J. smile.

                         KEITH
                         (under his breath)
                    Gotcha.

A.J. quickly spins around and flashes that killer
smile.

                         A.J.
                    Well, gentlemen... and I can
                    see that you are gentlemen
                    -let's start with the basic
                    situation: You have something
                    we want: plush accommodations,
                    cable TV, adult movies...
                    now instead of making us
                    go through these stupid,
                    immature... uh, what's the
                    word I'm looking for?

                         KEITH
                    Asinine.

> A.J.
> ... Asinine "tests" which, by the way, we find incredibly boring.

Keith yawns.

> A.J.
> Wouldn't it be smarter to use this situation to get something for yourselves?

The Frat brothers are intrigued.

> A.J.
> Look, you're having a big party tonight, right? Now you gotta need something for it. What? Beer, music, entertainment? Keith and I provide it - you name it, <u>anything</u> you want -and we're in. Simple, right?

The Leader confers with some other Frat members.

Keith pulls A.J. aside.

> KEITH
> That was good, except for the 'anything' part. Couldn't you have said <u>a</u> thing? Or <u>some</u>thing?

> A.J.
> Relax, will ya? These guys are operating on empty.
>   (over Keith's
>   shoulder)
> Whatta ya say, guys? Deal?

> LEADER
>   (a gleam in his eye)
> <u>Any</u>thing?

                    KEITH
          A.J.

A.J. and the Leader stare hard at each other. Then
A.J. smiles that killer smile.

                    A.J.
          Anything. Anything at all.

EXT. BELL TOWER DAY

The door flies open and out come Keith and A.J.

On the stone wall behind them is a sign: KEAN
COLLEGE - MISSION TOWER.

                    KEITH
          A stripper! And by tonight!
          That's nice... I can't wait to
          see how you're gonna get us
          out of this one.

                    A.J.
          After all these years, you
          don't trust me?

Keith shoots A.J. a look.

INT. DORM HALLWAY - DAY

CLOSE ON A.J.: He's talking on a pay phone, one
finger in his ear to block out surrounding NOISE.

                    A.J.
               (laying on the charm)
          Just one number, that's it.
          Now I know you're a dancer,
          professionally trained and
          all, but I was thinking how
          interesting it would be if you
          did it without your clothes
          on...

CLICK! A.J. hangs up and crosses out that number from a list in front of him. A dozen are already crossed off.

He begins to dial again. The NOISE LEVEL increases. We PULL BACK to reveal the entire hallway. GENERAL CHAOS: students rush about spraying water hoses and fire extinguishers. A slice of pizza splatters and sticks to the wall next to the phone. A.J. hangs up in disgust. Unable to operate here, A.J. calmly rips the pay phone from the wall and pulls the wire along the ceiling until he reaches his room.

INT. DORM ROOM -DAY

A.J. enters with phone. Keith sits on his bed adjusting the sight of his high-tech competition BOW.

The room is tiny. Keith's side is sloppy. Two archery trophies sit atop his dresser. A practice target hangs over his bed; a lone hole dead center. A.J.'s half is done in "Early Adult Motel"; mirrored ceiling, wine cooler, velvet bedspread, etc.

      A.J.
    (falling onto his
    bed)
  We gotta get out of here. The
  place is a zoo.

A.J. reaches into a small refrigerator next to his bed, removes an apple and momentarily sets it on top. He dials another phone number. Suddenly a blur flashes past the screen. A.J. reaches for the apple only to find it sliced in two. Keith's arrow still vibrating in the wall. A.J. tosses half the apple to Keith as he continues to use the phone.

      A.J.
  Hey. I'd do it for you, Sandi.

CLICK! Undaunted, A.J. gets another idea. He pulls out a newspaper from under his bed.

                    A.J.
          Field trip. We'll hire
          ourselves a pro.

                    KEITH
          Call me when you get back.

                    A.J.
          How much money you got?

                    KEITH
          They're not worth it, A.J.

                    A.J.
          They? I could care less about
          those guys. It's their Frat
          House. What a place to operate
          from! You see those rooms?

                    KEITH
          C'mon... You're giving me a
          headache. We're two hundred
          miles from civilization, with
          no money and no way to get
          there. Tell me the DIPSA PHI
          house is worth that kind of
          aggravation...

A.J. opens the door to the hallway. NOISE pours in.
A.J. shuts the door.

                    KEITH
          I got 82 bucks.

                    A.J.
              (collecting it,
              counting)
          Right. We total 168. That and
          a little charm should get us
          a stripper and one deadly
          number... Now all we need are
          some wheels.

Both faces drop. This is a problem. Suddenly there
is the sound of a THWACK! And a crowd CHEERING

coming from up above. Keith and A.J. look to the
ceiling and then to each other.

                    KEITH/A.J.
          Duncan.

EXT. DUNCAN'S ROOM

A.J. and Keith stand in front of Duncan's "door".
Video surveillance cameras scan the area. A porch
light is mounted on the wall along with a private
mailbox.

                    KEITH
          What're you gonna say?

                    A.J.
          Relax, I can handle this. No
          problem.

Keith rings the bell and DINNER CHIMES sound. The
door is answered by a goofy-looking KID of 17.

                    A.J.
          Hey, Duncan...

                    KID
          I'm not Duncan.
              (pointing with contempt)
          That's Duncan.

                    KEITH
          Good start.

INT. DUNCAN'S ROOM

The room is four times the size of other dorm
rooms and has a walk-in kitchen, wet bar and the
latest in audio-visual technology. Across the room
a group of nerdy-looking STUDENTS work diligently
at computer terminals.

DUNCAN himself stands on a patch of Astroturf and is driving golf balls into a giant net. He wears brightly colored pants, shirt, and golf cap. Next to him, another STUDENT stands holding Duncan's golf bag and talking into a "Mr. Microphone" imitating Pat Summerall. Duncan coils and whacks the ball into the net.

                    STUDENT
               (incredibly bored)
          Duncan Spriggs unleashes a
          monstrous drive right down the
          center of the fairway. It's a
          beauty.

The Student then flips on a tape recorder and the SOUND of a crowd cheering fills the room. Duncan smiles. He then turns to see Keith and A.J. standing there. Panic spreads over his face.

                    DUNCAN
          Whatever I did, I'm sorry. I
          wasn't thinking.

                    A.J.
               (puzzled)
          You have a car, right?

                    DUNCAN
          I'll pay for the damages. I
          shouldn't have had it parked
          there, I know that what car
          was it, anyway?

Keith and A.J. exchange looks.

                    KEITH
          No, we need a car.

                    A.J.
          Have to make a little trip.
          We'd like to work out a deal
          for some transportation.

Just then a BUZZER SOUNDS. There is a collective

sigh of relief. The students at the computers shut them down and put away their work. The student holding the golf bag drops it and everyone heads for the door.

>   DUNCAN
> Hey, where ya goin'? I was
> gonna order some pizza. Stick
> around, fellas. C'mon, I'm
> buying.

They don't. On the way out one student stops to hand Duncan some papers and then holds out his palm.

>   STUDENT #2
> Your Russian Lit essay.

Duncan peels off a fifty and hands it to the kid.

>   DUNCAN
> Great... And listen, leave
> your number on the service. I
> can use you during mid-terms.

The kid shoots Keith and A.J. a look on the way out. Duncan turns to the two with a big grin.

>   DUNCAN
> It'll be a pleasure to help
> you guys out - can I call you
> "guys"? Great. Ya know, I
> mostly get your basic dorks
> hangin' around here. They just
> seem to gravitate towards me.
> I don't know why.
>   (looks around the
>   empty room)
> Yeah, this place is usually
> swingin'. You ought to pop up
> some time. So! You're takin' a
> little trip. Need a rod, huh?

Duncan checks a row of key hooks and folder slots. All are empty except one.

                    DUNCAN
          You're in luck. One left. Now,
          normally I charge your average
          schmo-

                    A.J.
          We're not talking money here,
          are we?

                    DUNCAN
          No. right. Of course we're
          not.
               (pause)
          What are we talking about?

                    KEITH
          We were thinking of something
          along the lines of a favor. To
          be returned, of course.

                    DUNCAN
          I see... hey, that's a great
          idea! One hand washes the
          other, right!

                    A.J.
          Right... if there's anything
          we can do for you. any

Keith clasps his hand over A.J.'s mouth and gives
him a dirty look.

                    KEITH
          If there's something we can do
          for you

Duncan hands Keith the keys.

                    DUNCAN
          I already know. Be my friends.
          Take me with you.

                    KEITH
               (gives back the keys)
          Uh...

                    A.J.
          No way.

                    DUNCAN
          Okay, okay... for a week. Take
          me with you and be my friends
          for a week.

A.J. and Keith stare at Duncan.

                    DUNCAN
          Alright... take me with you
          and just pretend to be my
          friends for a week.

Keith and A.J. look to each other.

                    DUNCAN
          Please?

Keith looks to A.J.

A.J. thinks for a moment and then nods to Keith. Keith reaches out and takes the keys.

                    DUNCAN
          This is fantastic!

Duncan runs into the next room and comes racing out tucking in a Hawaiian shirt and wearing a yachting jacket. Keith and A.J. can only look on helplessly.

                    DUNCAN
          Hey, pals! I'm psyched! Let's
          party!
               (finally it dawns on
               him)
          Where we going?

                                        CUT TO:

INT./EXT. CAR/HIGHWAY - DAY

The incessant traffic reflected in the mirrored lenses of a fashionable pair of sunglasses. A.J. is behind them. Keith rides shotgun. Duncan is scrunched in the back seat. The NOISE of CLATTERING VALVES and a CHATTERING TRANSMISSION.

PULL BACK to reveal: An extremely large-sized, late model Cadillac convertible. In yellow. Cars are zooming past this monstrosity left and right.

> A.J.
> When's the last time you had this boat tuned?

> DUNCAN
> I don't know. When I ordered it, I guess. I don't drive 'em. The broads'll dig it, you wait and see.

INT. CAR - LATER

Keith reads the map. Duncan pages through "Jism" magazine ads, reading them aloud...

> DUNCAN
> How about "Tallywackers"? "The G Spot"? Here's one: "Boob-O-Rama"...

A.J. motions to keep going.

> DUNCAN
> "Strip Search" "The Meat Rack" "Lido Lounge"

A.J. grabs the paper from Duncan and it while he drives. Finally, he smiles

> A.J.
> This one.
>   (hands paper to Keith)
> Yeah... I can feel it.

Duncan cranes his neck over Keith's shoulder.

               KEITH
          (reading)
     "The After Dark Club" -
     Hottest Acts Anywhere!
     Sounds classy. Think we need
     reservations?

Duncan whips out his wallet that is about to burst at the seams, and shows it to A.J. and Keith.

               DUNCAN
     I'm ready.

Duncan opens his wallet and an accordion-like display of credit cards tumble out.

There must be a dozen or more.

A.J. examines the wallet, shakes his head and hands it back to Duncan.

               A.J.
     Looks like you got a full deck
     here, kid. Not a bright idea
     to bring these with you. I
     mean you're in a car with guys
     you two hardly know, going
     somewhere you've never been.

               DUNCAN
     Hey, you're my buddies!
          (A.J. and Keith turn)
     For a week... Just a week...

               A.J.
     Look, Dunc... I just don't
     want you walking around down
     there looking Like a meal
     ticket...

Then A.J. smiles that smile.

               KEITH

                    (looking at A.J.)
                Yeah, some people find
                it hard to resist.
                Give it back.

A.J. grins and holds up one of Duncan's credit cards. Duncan goes to take it. A.J. fans it out like a poker hand, revealing three cards behind it. Duncan takes them sheepishly.

EXT. CAR

The Caddy putters down the highway and off an exit ramp.

EXT. CAR - DOWNTOWN

The Caddy rolls down what looks to be a main drag. The normal hustle and bustle. Hotels, department stores, taxis, etc. Typical looking of any major city downtown.

INT. CAR

Keith is struggling with the map. He looks at the passing street I signs and then tries to locate them on the map.

                    KEITH
                We're lost.

ANOTHER STREET

As the car coughs and wheezes along, the "look" of downtown begins to change. Very few people walk the street. Shops are already closing - store owners are pulling down heavy iron gates.

People push and shove to get into the already crowded buses. A bag lady pounds frantically on the door to a Salvation Army.

                    KEITH
          Some swingin' place.

                    A.J.
          Patience. When the sun goes
          down, this place'll probably
          wake the dead.

ANOTHER INTERSECTION

The car pulls up to a red light. A HOOKER leans against a telephone pole. She bends down to see inside the car.

                    HOOKER
          Getting dark, boys...
               (thrusting her
               pelvis)
          Wanna go bump in the night?

As she leans down WE SEE three or four "Missing Persons" posters tacked to the pole. Light changes and the car pulls away.

INT. CAR

Duncan's mouth is open. Turns excitedly to A.J.

                    DUNCAN
          Wait! Maybe I'm interested!

                    A.J.
               (mumbling to himself)
        Meal ticket...

                    KEITH
          Dunc... that was a guy.

Duncan peers out the window to take another look.

INT./EXT. CAR - FURTHER DOWN

The car swings onto another block. Keith glances from map to street and back again.

                    KEITH
          How am I supposed to know
          where the hell we are when
          there aren't any street signs?

It's beginning to get darker now. Except for an occasional wino, junkie, or bag lady, the streets are deserted.

The car cruises past a Coffee Shop that appears open but mostly everything else seems closed for the evening.

SUDDENLY, out of nowhere, a bizarre-looking BUM throws himself in front or the car. A.J. hits the brakes hard. The Bum presses his race to the driver's side window screaming:

                    BUM
          They got 'em! They got my
          friend! Please... They got my
          friend!

A.J. steps on the gas and the Bum falls away.

                    KEITH
          What the hell was that?

                    A.J.
          A guy looking for his friend.
          I thought he made himself
          clear.

INT./EXT. CAR -SIDE STREET

The car makes a left onto a deserted block. Up ahead sits the "After Dark Club". The car pulls over and all three get out or the car.

EXT. AFTER DARK CLUB

The club is nothing but a plain, windowless, red-bricked building with a half-lit neon sign blinking the club's name. Next to the door is a glass display case containing faded pictures of the girls working there. The place doesn't appear to be open.

                    KEITH
          What do you think?

                    A.J.
          I think we're years too late
          ... Let's check it out.

ANGLE - FRONT DOOR: Keith walks up and knocks. He looks to A.J. and Duncan who approach. Suddenly the door opens a crack, stopped by a thick chain. A strange looking face peers out. Sunglasses covering the eyes, he stares at the visitors suspiciously, but says nothing.

                    KEITH
          You open?

The face shakes its head "no".

                    KEITH
          You gonna open?

The face looks at the three and then responds eerily:

                    VLAD
          After dark.

The door slams shut. Keith, A.J., and Duncan look at each other and then look skyward. Duncan looks troubled.

                    DUNCAN
          I gotta drain my main vein.

                                        CUT TO:

INT. COFFEE SHOP -DUSK

The place is empty. A.J. and Keith sit at a table near the front window of the shop drinking coffee out of plastic containers. In the background, the elderly PROPRIETOR cleans up. A.J. cranes his neck to check the sky.

>   A.J.
>   I mean it's dark...
>
>   KEITH
>   But is it <u>after</u> dark?
>
>   A.J.
>   No, but. I think it's
>   definitely dark, now.
>
>   KEITH
>   But it could have <u>just</u> turned
>   dark. The guy clearly said
>   after dark.
>
>   A.J.
>   How are you supposed to know
>   the <u>exact moment</u> it's dark? If
>   we knew that, then we could
>   wait a few seconds and it'd be
>   <u>after</u> dark.
>
>   KEITH
>   So when is that?
>
>   A.J.
>   (taking a sip of
>   coffee)
>   How should I know?

The PROPRIETOR finishes wiping the counter and looks at the clock on the wall. It reads 7:24. He places his apron on a hook, then puts on a plastic "priest's collar", his coat, and finally dons a large gold cross. The Proprietor starts for the front door. He appears nervous.

                    PROPRIETOR
          Hurry it up. Closing time.

                    A.J.
               (shouting at door
               marked 'Men's Room)
          Duncan! Let's go!

                    DUNCAN (O.S.)
          I'm going as fast as I can!

The Proprietor flips open the door sign to 'Closed'.
Suddenly the door is forced open, knocking him
backwards. In steps an eerie, evil-looking Albino
male. This is SNOW. Behind him follow two stunning-
looking BLACK GIRLS. They all wear gang jackets
with "Dragons" embroidered on the back.

                    PROPRIETOR
          I just closed.

                    SNOW
          You just opened again.

He pushes the Proprietor back to the counter.

                    SNOW
          Coffees. Six. To go.

At table, A.J. continues to sip his coffee; his
back to Snow. One of the girls catches Keith's
attention. This is MAVEN. She smiles at Keith.
Keith smiles back.

                    A.J.
          Don't be stupid...

Maven's eyes bore into Keith. She winks at him.
Keith winks back; first one eye then the other.

                    A.J.
          I'm not kidding...

Maven seductively puts on lip gloss, running her
tongue over her pouting lips. Keith grins, loving

it. NOW Maven smiles a big smile - showing her teeth. Or rather what's left of the three remaining ones... a few pieces and those mostly silver.

Keith is stunned and spits coffee out of his mouth and quickly looks away.

THE COUNTER: Maven is visibly shaken and turns to Snow.

                    MAVEN
          Snow...

Snow turns, looks at Keith and heads for the table.

THE TABLE: Keith freezes. A.J. calmly sips his coffee.

                    SNOW
          You see something funny?

Keith Looks to A.J. who pretends that nothing is happening.

                    KEITH
          A.J., this isn't funny.

A.J. calmly looks out of the window. Keith stares at A.J., pissed.

                    KEITH
          I live, you die.

Snow grabs Keith by the chin and twists his head around. In a flash, Snow and Co. whip out blades.

                    SNOW
          I'm going to let Maven cut off
          your balls...

Just then the Men's Room door creaks open. Everyone turns.

ANGLE - DUNCAN: Duncan steps into the room, quickly

surveys the situation then takes a half step back. His mind grasping.

> DUNCAN
> Uh... Plummer.
> (to Proprietor)
> Louie, it looks like I'll be another hour or so on those toilets. These pipes are tough. So, if you'll excuse me, I'll get back to work.

And Duncan disappears back into the bathroom.

> A.J.
> (to Keith)
> I'm not sure, but I think the yachting jacket gave him away.

A beat. Then, from inside the Men's Room:

> DUNCAN (O.S.)
> (a little too loudly)
> I wish you SWAT TEAM members would go outside and clean those automatic WEAPONS! I'm trying to work in here. Go in the other room and do that!

Two beats. The door opens a crack. Duncan peers into the room, spots Snow and Co. still there and pulls back inside.

THE ROOM: Maven slides next to Keith, takes her blade and slices off the top button of his shirt. She then runs the steel over Keith's neck. Snow leers. A.J. takes one last look out the window.

> A.J.
> (out window)
> Yeah, it's after dark now...
> (turns, very friendly)
> Snow, C'mon. All this over three lousy teeth?

SNOW
                  (furious)
              Who spoke to you!

Snow slaps Keith's coffee cup across the table.
Coffee splashes onto A.J.'s shirt.

                    KEITH
              Uh oh...

A.J. looks at Snow and gives him that smile.

In a flash: A.J. throws his coffee into Maven's face.
Snow lunges for A.J., his blade headed for A.J.'s
heart. But it stops inches away from it. Fear
spreads across Snow's face. CAMERA reveals that
A.J. has Snow by the balls... literally.

                    A.J.
              Drop the blade, Snowflake.
              C'mon! Her too... or you'll be
              picking these up off the floor.

The blades are dropped. Maven claws at her burning
eyes. Keith picks up the blades as A.J. backs Snow
against the counter.

                    A.J.
              Duncan! If you're finished with
              those toilets...

Duncan meekly exits the bathroom, catches on to
what's happened and suddenly begins to strut.

                    DUNCAN
              Lucky they didn't try the
              bathroom. I was ready in
              there. What I would have done
              to them.
                  (shudders)

Keith grabs Duncan and pulls him out the door and
into the street. A.J. smiles once more at Snow and
then gives him a hard squeeze that sends him to the
ground. A.J. pays the tab, dips a napkin in some

water, and as he wipes the stain from his shirt, strolls out the door.

EXT. COFFEE SHOP - NIGHT

Keith tosses the blades into the sewer. A.J. walks past Keith and Duncan, still wiping the stain from his shirt. Keith catches up to mumble a "sorry" while Duncan stands peering through the shop window.

> DUNCAN
> Messing with my buddies! Wham!
> Right in the tchotchkes...
> One guy takes on the three
> of us... Hey, let's wait and
> see if he wants to go another
> round... A.J.
>   (back to Duncan)
> Dunc... He ordered six coffees.

Duncan looks around then breaks into a run.

EXT. AFTER DARK CLUB

The boys approach the club from across the street. It's now open; a lone man is seen entering.

> DUNCAN
>   (singing at the top
>   of his lungs)
> I'm in the mood for love...
> Simply because they're naked!
> Guys, I'm on a roll tonight,
> and I attract women like flies.

A.J. glances at Keith who nods back in acknowledgement.

> A.J.
>   (crossing the street)
> I'll see ya in a few.

Keith leads Duncan down the block as A.J. disappears

into the club.

                    DUNCAN
               (confused)
          Hey, where we going?

                    KEITH
          To the car. We got to be
          getting back soon. A.J.'s
          gonna take care of everything.

                    DUNCAN
               (pulling away)
          Wait a minute. That's not
          fair. I come all this way and
          don't even get to watch? I
          think I should have a say in
          the selection.

                    KEITH
          You can interview her in the
          car.

                    DUNCAN
          Uh uh. One for all and all
          inside. I'm going in.

                    KEITH
          Don't do it...

Duncan heads back toward the club. Halfway there he turns and calls for Keith:

                    DUNCAN
          Six coffees.

Keith takes a beat, trying to act cool, then spins and races up to Duncan.

INT. AFTER DARK CLUB

The boys enter through the open door, turn right and head down a short, narrow hallway to a set of' black velvet ropes and red nylon curtains.

Suddenly: the curtain parts and standing over them is a tall man of fifty. This is VIC, the club maître d' He eyeballs Keith and Duncan.

>   VIC
>   Good evening... Got some I.D.,
>   boys?

Both fumble with their wallets. Vic is impatient and grabs Duncan's from him. His eyes immediately focus on a Gold American Express card.

>   VIC
>   (giving it back)
>   Good enough.

Duncan takes back his wallet and immediately goes through it. Vic unhooks the rope and ushers them inside, past a huge bouncer named VLAD who sits motionless by the door.

INT. CLUB - MAIN ROOM

The look is that of a decaying 1950s nightclub; one that's been suspended in time. To the left, nestled in the corner, is a large, curved bar staffed by TWO scantily clad BARTENDERESSES. There is a stage in the center of the room against the back wall. Tables of various sizes surround it. Lining the front wall, engulfed in shadows, are private booths. A tattered pool table adds the finishing touch.

>   VIC
>   Bar or table?

Keith spots A.J. at the bar.

>   KEITH
>   Table.

>   DUNCAN
>   (holds out a ten)
>   <u>Ringside</u>.

Vic snatches the bill and leads Duncan away. Keith remains, trying to get A.J.'s attention.

THE STAGE: A stripper steps off, gathering up tips. This is Amaretto, around 20 and adorable. She spots Keith and her eyes light up. A CUSTOMER stuffs a dollar bill into her waistband. Amaretto looks at it (her hands are filled with fives and tens) and hands it back.

                    AMARETTO
          You keep it. Send your kid to
          college.

KEITH gets A.J.'s attention, points to Duncan and shrugs helplessly. A.J. winces. Keith turns back to see where Duncan is headed and when he turns back to A.J. his view is blocked by Amaretto, who half-waves at Keith, then pauses, unsure.

Uneasy, Keith turns to catch up with Duncan. Amaretto grabs her tray and runs a parallel course, trying to get a better look at Keith.

TABLE AREA: Vic sits Duncan and Keith at a stage-side table while delivering his standard rap. Keith notices Amaretto's scrutiny, as she moves toward him, and grows even more settled.

                    VIC
          There's a basic six drink
          minimum and fifteen dollar
          entertainment charge. Per
          person.
               (continues)
          Tipping is _more_ than just a
          courtesy; it's expected. Our
          ladies get _very_ enthusiastic
          about tippers, know what I
          mean?

THE STAGE: A stripper wearing only a hard hat and a tool belt is performing. She winks at Keith and Duncan. Duncan blows her a big kiss and waves a bill for her to see.

TABLE AREA: Keith, doing his best to become invisible, looks away to see Amaretto coming right for him. But just before she gets to him, Amaretto is stopped by a loud, rowdy GROUP at the next table. A SHORT GUY begins to pester her.

                    SHORTY
          It's a bet, see? He says
          "thirty-four" but I know
          thirty-six's when I see 'em.
          So?... Whatta ya say. It's
          thirty-six, right?

                    AMARETTO
          If we're talking about your
          I.Q., I would say yes.

Amaretto spins away. The group breaks into loud, derisive laughter. Shorty burns.

Amaretto turns and bends down to stare directly into Keith's face.

                    AMARETTO
          You don't remember me, do you?

Keith is startled. Duncan is impressed.

                    AMARETTO
          It has been a long time...
              (laughing)
          But I remember you.

Amaretto puts her tray down, and puts on a pair of glasses that hang around her neck. Unseen, from behind, Shorty has reached out for the knot that holds up Amaretto's halter top.

                    AMARETTO
              (modeling glasses)
          Maybe these'll jog your
          memory...

Shorty pulls open the knot and the top starts to fall. But Keith sees it coming. In a flash he tosses his jacket over Amaretto before she's 'exposed'. Amaretto wheels to deliver a blow to Shorty, when out of nowhere VLAD APPEARS. He blocks Amaretto's fist, knocking her into Keith's lap. Vlad picks up Shorty, who in the struggle spills his drink all over Vlad. Vlad hoists him high in the air.

> DUNCAN
> (on his feet)
> Alright, Frankenstein! Go on, rip his arms off! Pulverize him!

Vlad turns and gives Duncan a frightening stare. Duncan quickly sits down. Keith and Amaretto stare at each other. She smiles as she re-ties her top from under the jacket.

> AMARETTO
> You always were the gallant type.

She winks.

> KEITH
> I think you got the wrong guy. I...

Vic's outraged arrival ends further discussion. From the bar, A.J. watches in disbelief.

> VIC
> What the hell you think this is? Madison Square Garden? Let's restrain ourselves, okay?
> (oozes over to Shorty's table)
> Her first night, guys. Haven't broken her in yet. You understand. Next round's on me, Okay?

Vic turns to Amaretto who hands Keith his jacket back.

                    VIC
              (to Amaretto)
         You - ya want your first night
         to be your last? Don't compete
         with the stage show. It's hard
         enough up there. You hurt?
         Something broken? No? Then why
         aren't you moving?

                   KEITH
         Wait a minute. Those guys
         grabbed her and -

Vic drapes an arm over Keith's shoulder and steers
him away from Shorty's table.

                    VIC
         By "those guys" you mean my
         paying customers, right?
         And by "her", you mean that
         helpless, innocent maiden in
         the skimpy top and bikini
         bottoms, right? They took
         advantage of her. Sit down
         and cool off or I'll have Vlad
         explain it to you... outside.
              (to all concerned)
         We'll have no more
         difficulties, am I right?
         Right.

Shorty waits for Vic and Vlad to leave, then flips
"the finger" at Keith and Duncan.

                   DUNCAN
         Oh, very mature.

Keith and Amaretto have been eyeing each other
hypnotically; both snap out of it. Amaretto, aware
of Vic's gaze, acts business-like.

                  AMARETTO
         I'm Amaretto...
              (whispers to Keith)
         Not really...

> (louder, for Vic)
> And I'll be your waitress.
> What can I get for you?

> DUNCAN
> I'd like a 'slow, comfortable
> screw'...

Keith gives Duncan a cold stare.

> DUNCAN
> Uh, and a beer. And one for my
> buddy.

Amaretto looks to Keith who stares fixated at her as she continually fixes her strap that keeps falling.

> AMARETTO
> I know. I've got to get it
> fixed. Drives me crazy.

Amaretto gives Keith a mischievous glance and leaves.

> DUNCAN
> (to himself)
> Drives you crazy...
> (to Keith)
> You don't remember _that_? I'm
> going to remember that the
> rest of my life!

THE STAGE: Hard Hat finishes her routine by doing a pas-de-deux with a jackhammer. Smattered APPLAUSE and a few WOLF CALLS.

> VIC (O.S.)
> A builder of major
> erections... Our construction
> engineer, Hard Hatted Hannah!

TABLE AREA: Duncan football kicks a five onto the stage then turns and gives A.J. a big wave at the bar. A.J. quickly loses himself in the crowd. Amaretto returns with _the beers. She plops a

bottle in front of Duncan but a glass in front of
Keith. She then lovingly fills Keith's glass with
beer, smiling at him the whole time, enjoying his
confusion. Duncan watches in awe.

>   DUNCAN
>   You have any friends that want
>   to remember me? Nah, I didn't
>   think so.

Amaretto finishes pouring the beer.

>   AMARETTO
>   You figure it out yet?

Keith fumbles for an answer. With great pleasure,
Amaretto lays the empty bottle on her tray and
gives it a spin. She looks at Keith, as if to say
"get it?" Keith then breaks into a big grin.

>   KEITH
>   You're not Tina Ryan's little
>   sister!?

Amaretto's Jaw drops, but with a gleam in her eye.

>   AMARETTO
>   That slut? Miss Upholstery
>   Dressing? Moi? You pig!

Amaretto exits. Keith turns to Duncan.

>   KEITH
>   Our waitress called me a
>   pig... This is a strange
>   night.

Suddenly the lights dim.

>   VIC (O.S.)
>   Gentlemen... For your viewing
>   pleasure. Katrina

THE STAGE: She does not walk on. She is simply
there. On a chair center stage, her back to us. The

eerie strains of "Welcome to my Nightmare" begin. Slowly she stands. Her movements dreamlike. She wears a long, white, satin nightgown. Her hair is platinum blonde, her skin milky white.

Now the tempo of the music changes. Her movements become <u>fierce</u>. She rips off the blonde wig to reveal jet black hair. The virgin? like gown is shed to expose black lace and leather. A stunning creature. She straddles the chair, the movements slow and sensual. Pure eroticism. The audience is at her mercy. <u>This</u> is Katrina.

ANGLE A.J.: He looks on, mesmerized. His eyes tell us <u>this</u> is the one.

KEITH AND DUNCAN: Their eyes fixated on Katrina. Their jaws hang open.

THE STAGE: Katrina completes her act. The lights come up, but she's vanished. Money showers the stage. A child-like Oriental girl, SEKO, collects Katrina's tips.

TABLE AREA: Keith and Duncan exchange "did you see what I saw?" looks. Both look at A.J.

Their POV: A.J. talking to Seko. He begins his pitch and we SEE <u>that</u> smile.

<u>During this</u>, Hard Hat has CROSSED FRAME and seated herself at the table between Keith and Duncan and A.J.

<u>As</u> we WATCH A.J. and SEKO, we HEAR the stripper rapping with her lonely customer. It almost seems as if the O.S. questions could be coming from Seko.

                HARD HAT (O.S.)
    All alone?

A.J. glances at the table: Duncan gives him the "thumbs up" sign. A.J. looks back to Seko and shakes his head "yes".

                    HARD HAT (O.S.)
               From around here?

A.J. shaking his head "no".

                    HARD HAT (O.S.)
               You married? Got kids?

A.J. laughing and giving a "who, me?" shrug.

                    HARD HAT (O.S.)
               So, you looking for some
               company?

A.J. smiles that smile and moves with Seko toward the backstage curtain.

                    HARD HAT (O.S.)
                 (seductively)
               I seem to have you all to
               myself. Why don't we go
               someplace more private.

A.J., with a sly smile toward the table, disappears through the curtain.

                    DUNCAN
                 (fist in the air)
               Yes!!! He scores!

Keith smiles, then turns in time to see Hard Hat escort her customer into one of the back booths.

BACKSTAGE HALLWAY

A.J. follows Seko down a narrow corridor; half naked girls come and go. As they pass the cramped dressing room of the strippers, A.J. backs and peers inside.

                    A.J.
               Loved the show, girls.

INT. STRIPPER'S DRESSING ROOM

The room is small, cramped and messy. Clothes racks, make-up cases, etc. Down the center is a row of make-up tables. Only there are no mirrors; just the lighted frames.

A.J. looks puzzled. One GIRL sits across from another GIRL, each making the other one up -using themselves as mirrors. And up close, they look different. The make-up is caked on extra thick. The eyeliner and lipstick are just a little off.

Seko pulls A.J. away from the door and down the hall.

>   A.J. (O.S.)
> You know, I never knew how
> important lighting could be.

EXT. KATRINA'S DRESSING ROOM

Seko unlocks the door and motions A.J. inside.

>   SEKO
> Katrina will be with you
> shortly...

A.J. steps inside and Seko shuts the door.

TABLE AREA

A new STRIPPER begins her act.

>   VIC
> She melts in your mouth and in
> your hand... Here's Candi!

Keith watches Amaretto flit about the room, still trying to place her. She catches him and feigns indignation. Keith checks the backstage curtain, then his watch. He gets up.

                    KEITH
          I'm gonna go to the bathroom
          before we leave.

Keith slips through the tables toward the Men's
Room. As he passes a back booth, he sees. Hard Hat
and her customer entangled in the shadows.

INT. BATHROOM

It is small, with three stalls on one side and two
urinals on the other. Keith stands at one of the
urinals and is about to go when he hears the sound
of running water.

Keith turns to find Vlad standing by the sink,
washing out the stain on his shirt. Keith stares at
his exposed torso. It is <u>covered</u> with tiny puncture
marks. Thousands of them. Like a human pin cushion.
Vlad stares back at Keith; an eerie smile crosses
his lips. Keith tries to hurry it up and now can't
go at all. He zips it up and heads out of there.

BOOTH AREA

Keith exits the bathroom and moves past Hard Hat's
booth. Vic is dragging the apparently passed out
Customer from the booth. Hard Hat is nowhere in
sight.

                    VIC
          I'm <u>trying</u> to run a
          respectable joint here.
          Anybody want to claim this
          lush? No? Going once...
          twice...
              (over Keith's
              shoulder)
          He's alone. Clean this mess
          up.

Suddenly the hulking figure of Vlad steps by Keith
from behind. He scoops up the limp body like a

suitcase and carries it across the club and out the door. Keith looks at his watch again.

> KEITH
>
> C'mon A.J.

INT. KATRINA'S DRESSING ROOM

A.J. wanders the room. It is sparsely decorated with a few functional antiques; and a large fish tank with exotic fish. The only thing that seems out of place is a clothes rack on which hangs 6 or 7 plastic garment-like bags.

A.J. is staring into the fish tank, using the reflection to fix his hair. He turns and is startled to find Katrina standing there. She wears a blood red dressing gown.

> A.J.
>
> Katrina. Nice name... I'm A.J.

Katrina stands by the couch, her eyes never leaving A.J.

> A.J.
>
> Caught your act out there.
> Some show. But then this
> audience seemed very easy to
> please. I was wonderin' if
> you'd be interested in taking
> on some real men... Sort of
> an encore performance, later
> tonight.

Katrina smiles and now begins to circle A.J.

> A.J.
>
> I'm willing to pay you top
> dollar, 'cause I like you.

Katrina maneuvers A.J. on to the couch. She slides off his jacket and begins to unbutton his shirt.

A.J.
          And, I can see you like me,
          too.

Katrina lies A.J. back on the couch and straddles him.

She slips the dressing gown off and begins to lick, nibble and kiss A.J.'s chest, slowly moving towards his neck. A.J. lays back and smiles.

Katrina has pinned A.J.'s hands behind his head. NOW a small bead of sweat begins to drip down, Katrina's cheek. Her make-up begins to run and underneath translucent skin is revealed. Veins can be seen pulsating. A.J. tries to rise but can't. Katrina raises her head. The make-up is completely gone. Her mouth distorts and razor sharp FANGS snap into place like switchblades. Katrina hisses. A.J. is horrified. With animalistic ferocity, Katrina drives her teeth into A.J.'s neck. Her fangs rip open a gaping hole. A.J. attempts to yell but all he can do is emit a pathetic gurgle, as his life spills into Katrina's mouth.

FRONT DOOR AREA

Keith strolls over near the entrance then glances at the backstage curtain. Vic stands at the podium popping what look to be pieces of licorice into his mouth.

                    VIC
          She's not much upstairs,
          but what a staircase... The
          glorious Dominique!

A WAITRESS walks by. Vic stops her to put those little umbrellas in the drinks. Pissed, Vic heads for the bar.

Keith is getting impatient. Unconsciously, he reaches into the mint bowl behind the podium and pops a piece of licorice in his mouth. Only it's not licorice. Tiny legs struggle against his closed lips. It's a live cockroach. Keith spits it out horrified. He looks in the bowl to find it is filled only with cockroaches.

> KEITH
> (spitting)
> That's it, that's it... We're outta here.

THE BAR

Keith rushes over, grabs a bar napkin and wipes his mouth. He spots Seko strolling by and stops her.

> KEITH
> Excuse me. Would you go tell my friend that his buddy is waiting. That it's time to go?

> SEKO
> Friend? I not see any friend.

> KEITH
> Yeah, he's the guy you took backstage, you remember. Tall guy, leather jacket...

CAMERA DOLLY'S IN CLOSE on Seko's face as fear spreads across it. She is suddenly terror stricken.

> SEKO
> I take no one back...

Amaretto cuts between Keith and Seko, a tray in both hands.

> AMARETTO
> Aren't we fickle...

Amaretto's strap falls but both her hands are occupied. Keith reaches over and slides it back on her shoulder. Amaretto smiles. Seko uses the opportunity to disappear through the backstage curtain before Keith can stop her. He turns back to Amaretto.

                    KEITH
          Ever have one of those nights?

BACKSTAGE HALLWAY

CLOSE on a pair of high heels as they rush down the hallway to Katrina's door. The door is thrown open.

THROUGH the pair of legs we see a chair spin around to reveal Katrina. Her lips smeared with blood. Her eyes red. She licks her bloodied hands like a cat.

On the floor, A.J.'s body is being wrapped into a black garment bag by Vlad.

                    SEKO
          There is a problem. He was not
          alone.

Katrina tenses, snapping out of her drug-like state. The door closes.

BAR AREA

We come in on the tail end of the conversation.

                    KEITH
          ... That's it. One number to
          get into a Frat. Except now I
          don't care. I just want to get
          A.J. and go...

                    AMARETTO
          A.J.? You're kidding. Not
          Mr. Dynamite. You guys still
          hangin' out?
              (Keith nods)
          Come on. I bet _he_ remembers
          me.

Amaretto pulls Keith through the curtain.

BACKSTAGE HALLWAY

The corridor is busy. STRIPPERS come and go. The eerie hall lighting makes their faces look Fellini-esque. This hasn't escaped Amaretto.

                   AMARETTO
        (to Keith)
    Welcome to bow-wow city.
        (to girls)
    Hey, any of you see a guy back
    here? Tall, good looking.

The girls shake their beads and mumble "no". There is an uncomfortable pause. Amaretto checks the dressing room. Nothing.

                   KEITH
        (to Amaretto)
    Well he came back here. I saw
    him. He was <u>brought</u> back here.
        (looks around)
    By her!

Seko calmly approaches.

                   SEKO
    You. Very sorry, I remember
    now. Your friend wanted to see
    Katrina. I tell him no one
    sees Katrina.

                   AMARETTO
        (into Keith's ear)
    He didn't have much of a
    chance with <u>her</u>. She <u>owns</u> this
    dive, sweetheart.

                   SEKO
  After that...

Seko shrugs. Everyone looks at Keith. Amaretto goes

back to look in the dressing room.

                    KEITH
          A guy doesn't just
          disappear...

                AMARETTO
            (rushing back)
          Wait Where's Candy!

                  SEKO
          She's half-shift tonight.

Amaretto grabs Keith and pulls him to the curtain.

                AMARETTO
          I'm afraid A.J.'s decided to
          hold auditions.

                  KEITH
          He wouldn't just leave.

                AMARETTO
          Not even with a girl that'll
          'melt in your mouth <u>and</u> in
          your hands?'

Keith looks miffed, but concerned.

                  KEITH
          I'm going to kick his...

                AMARETTO
          But what a coincidence! It's
          time for my break and I just
          got to go pick up a change
          of tops at the hotel. Some
          of the girls stay there. I
          bet we could catch A.J. if we
          hurry... Meet me at the side
          entrance in <u>two</u> minutes.

Amaretto pushes Keith through the curtain.

THE CLUB

Using hand signals, Keith tries to communicate to Duncan what's going on. Duncan waves him off, happy where he is. As Keith heads for the front door he becomes aware of a sudden cooling in the club's atmosphere. The "help" seem to be eyeing him all at once. The ENTIRE LOOK OF THE CLUB SEEMS DIFFERENT. From a booth near the door, KATRINA glares at Keith, her pupils glowing in the murky candlelight.

FRONT DOOR

Keith saunters up to Vic who is on the phone.

> KEITH
> I got to run out for a minute.
> Do I need my hand stamped or
> anything? To get back in...

> VIC
> Uh... that won't be necessary.

Keith leaves. Vic goes back on the phone. He's tense. Terse.

> VIC
> He's on his way.... Whatever
> you want, as long as it's an
> accident. With a capital A!
> Those are the orders I got, so
> don't screw up... right.

Vic hangs up the phone and looks into the booth next to his station. Katrina glares at him.

> VIC
> I told 'em like you said.
> Everything should be okay...

From one of the booths a hand raises up out of the shadows to signal Vic. A STRIPPER emerges and slinks across the room. Wearily Vic, with Vlad in tow, strides over to the booth.

                    VIC
          Alright... who owns this lush?
          Anybody want to claim him?
          Going once...

EXT. AFTER DARK CLUB - SIDE ALLEY

Keith stands waiting. It is extremely quiet. Then:
the SOUND of rolling wheels. From behind the club
appears Vlad, pushing a trash bin; large bags
overflow from the top.

Keith watches as he disappears behind the alley
wall then reappears moments later with an empty
bin. Half-way back Vlad is met by a TOW TRUCK
DRIVER. Vlad hands him several wallets and then
continues back to the club. The TOW TRUCK DRIVER
checks a wallet then backs his truck up to a car
in the lqt.

BANG! The side door of the club flies open. Keith
jumps! It's Amaretto.

                    AMARETTO
          Aren't we jumpy tonight?

EXT. HEWITT ST. -NIGHT

It's dark and deserted. Only an occasional streetlamp
or traffic signal light on the way.

                    AMARETTO
          God, this is weird. It's like
          a reunion or something.

                    KEITH
          Yeah... I just wish I knew
          with who.

                    AMARETTO
            (playfully)
          When the time is right, I
          promise, I'll tell you.

They turn the corner.

LINDLEY AVENUE

As Keith and Amaretto walk, WE sense that there is movement in the shadows surrounding them. Too fast for humans, too large for animals.

They pass a dilapidated housing project. Outside on the stoop, a precious LITTLE GIRL of 6 plays. She is thin and tired looking. Amaretto stops and watches.

>   AMARETTO
> That's so sad... Parents like
> that should be shot.
>   (to child)
> Little girl? Where's your
> mommy?

Frightened, the Little Girl runs into the building.

Amaretto is lost in thought. Keith looks at her warmly. She catches him staring.

>   AMARETTO
> You're dying to ask me.

>   KEITH
> What?

>   AMARETTO
> Why I strip.

>   KEITH
> No, I'm...

>   AMARETTO
> Yes you are. It's okay...

>   KEITH
> But I'm not...

                    AMARETTO
            Why not?

                     KEITH
            Because it's none of...

                    AMARETTO
              (interrupting)
            It's nothing to be ashamed of.
            It's natural curiosity. The
            club's not a permanent stop
            or anything, if that's what
            you think. I mean, the job's
            easy to get. I do what I want,
            it's loose, I get to express
            myself. And _that's_ important.
            Because I'm still looking for
            my purpose in life. God knows
            I've looked. Tried the acting
            thing for a while. Was on
            the Dating Game. Got picked,
            too... CUT TO:

INT. KATRINA'S DRESSING ROOM

Vic paces back and forth. A KNOCK on the door. Vic opens it, lets Seko in, then closes the door. Seko stands timidly. Prom behind, Vic leans over her shoulder.

                      VIC
                (sneering)
            You screwed up. You're _sushi_,
            baby.

Katrina sits facing Seko on the couch. She is not happy. Seko tenses like a child waiting to be scolded. But Katrina just stares at her. The silence is chilling.

                      SEKO
            H-He was so beautiful. I was
            sure you would like him.

                    VIC
          You knew the...
               (to Katrina)
          She knows the rules. Only the
          ones that can't be traced. The
          transients, the loners, the
          strays.

                    SEKO
               (pleading)
          He said he was alone. That he
          was passing through. He fit the
          profile.

                    VIC
          Ha!

                    SEKO
               (next to tears)
          ... He was a gift...

                    VIC
               (sarcastic)
          Nice gift.
               (to Katrina)
          We'll have to kill the others.
          That's two of 'em. I'm taking
          care of that...

Katrina looks at Vic with disdain. Vic continues to suck up to her.

                    VIC
          Now if I had some control,
          this would never ha--

Katrina cuts Vic off with only a look and then waves him away in disgust. Vic can't believe it.

                    VIC
          You're not going to punish
          her? Nothing? If it was me,
          I'd---

Katrina hisses; eyes on fire. Vic, suddenly meek,

flinches.

                    VIC
          I'm going. I'm going...
               (on way out)
          But this wouldn't have
          happened if we were in Vegas.

Vic leaves. Katrina motions for Seko to sit next to her. Katrina begins to stroke Seko's hair; caress her. Katrina smiles.

                    SEKO
          Thank you. I am loyal to you
          forever. I will be more care--

Katrina hisses and plunges her talon-like hand into Seko's still-beating heart.

EXT. LOCKHEART BLVD.

Keith and Amaretto approach the blinking sign of the Trilby Hotel. Amaretto can't stop talking.

                    AMARETTO
          ... So for a while I was a
          limo driver but I kept getting
          tickets. After that I did the
          receptionist thing; 'Hello,
          may I help you'... 'Hello, may
          I help you'... really boring.

Up ahead a car has stopped at a red light. A WOMAN slides up to the passenger side and she gets in. Keith watches this out of the corner of his eye.

                    AMARETTO
          I don't know what it is, but
          I just can't seem to stay
          interested in anything.

                    KEITH
          I'm in school...

                    AMARETTO
          So am I. In a way. Actually
          it's a correspondence course.
          For "Training Seeing Eye
          Dogs". Isn't that great?

Keith has no idea how to react.

                    AMARETTO
          There's a demand for trainers,
          you know. I mean, have you
          ever met someone who trained
          seeing-eye dogs?

                    KEITH
          Uh... Not really...

                    AMARETTO
          See?
              (looking up)
          Here we are.

EXT. TRILBY HOTEL

14 stories tall, it's a residential type that is
very old and looks it. As they walk inside, Keith
looks back at the car sitting at the light. The
WOMAN exits and heads down the street. The light
turns green but the car does not go. The driver
Just sits behind the wheel, motion? less. Motor
running. Keith catches up to Amaretto.

INT. HOTEL LOBBY

As seedy as they come. The paint is puke green,
furniture old and full of mildew.

FRONT DESK

The DESK CLERK is a plump woman in her '70's with
wild, bright red hair. She is reading "Police
Stories".

                    DESK CLERK
               Twenty bucks a half hour.

                    AMARETTO
               I'm from the Club. Checked in
               this afternoon? I'd like the
               key to room 1311.

A look of recognition spreads across the woman's
face. She hands her the key. Keith steps up behind
Amaretto.

                    AMARETTO
               And would you please ring
               Candi? The redhead.

The desk clerk smiles, goes to the switchboard and
tries it.

                    DESK CLERK
                  (turning back)
               It's busy. But you can go on
               up. Room 1309.

Keith and Amaretto head for the elevator. The desk
clerk watches Keith and suppresses a strange grin.

EXT. ELEVATOR

The door is open. Keith and Amaretto start to step
in. They are startled by a very old, decrepit
ELEVATOR OPERATOR. He steps aside to let them enter.

INT. ELEVATOR

It's a push button elevator. The operator must be
close to 90. Thin as a rail, eyes hollow, cheeks
drawn. His uniform jacket fits as if there were
still a hanger in it.

On his head is a solid black toupee that sits there
crookedly. Keith and Amaretto exchange looks.

                              AMARETTO
                        Thirteen please.

The door slams shut, as the operator pushes the
button marked "13".

INT. MOVING ELEVATOR

The car jerks and starts upward. The numbers
above the door lighting up as the car passes each
corresponding floor. It moves slowly.

Hunched over, the old man stands facing the
elevator panel. Keith and Amaretto dart looks in
his direction

5... 6... 7... the SOUND of a bump. Keith and
Amaretto look over at the old man. His head is
propped up against the button panel; his toupee
hanging off his head. Keith and Amaretto start to
laugh. They look away from each other, trying to
contain it.

TIGHT ON KEITH AND AMARETTO: Laughter escapes from
Amaretto. Keith nudges her to keep quiet, but can't
stop laughing <u>him</u>self

9... 10... 11... Both are ready to burst. Holding
it in. Then: the elevator door opens.

Keith is out first.

ANGLE   AMARETTO: She stops. Something's wrong.
She looks up to see that number "12" is lit. Wrong
floor.

                              AMARETTO
                        (laughing)
                  Wait.

The door starts to close. Keith lunges for it. Too
late. The door slams shut.

11TH FLOOR HALLWAY

Keith stops laughing. He looks left and right. Nothing but rows of doorways. He pushes the elevator button and waits.

Keith begins to pace. No elevator. He pushes the button again. Nervously tapping his foot. Hums. Nothing.

Keith walks down the hallway and stops in front of a "Fire Exit".

ANGLE - STAIRWELL DOOR: Keith opens the stairwell door and peers inside. Pitch black. Keith can hardly make out the stairs.

Keith looks back to the elevator, then back into the darkness or the stairwell.

INT. STAIRWELL

Looking from the darkness out. Keith. The light from the hallway silhouettes his figure. He starts to enter. He stops.

>   KEITH
> Yeah, right.

He walks away and the door closes.

We are now in complete blackness. Then: We see the whites of an eyeball and... the glimmer of a fang.

HALLWAY

The SOUND of the elevator door opening.

Keith races down the hallway then slows as he reaches the elevator. He stands in front of it, peering inside. No elevator operator.

KEITH'S POV: Everything seems normal. The light inside is working. The motor hums without a glitch.

ANOTHER ANGLE - ELEVATOR: Keith starts to step inside. With the speed of a freight train, the elevator door smashes into Keith, knocking him backwards and pinning him to the door jam, half-in and half-out. The door crushes against his shoulder. He can't move. Using his outside hand, Keith tries to push the door back. It doesn't budge.

ANGLE - KEITH: Inside. His arm flails about... it reaches for the "Door Open" button. Straining. Almost there. Keith's face: red with pain.

The hand finds the emergency switch. Hits at it. Misses.

ANOTHER ANGLE - KEITH AND ELEVATOR: Suddenly the elevator starts to move downward. In seconds Keith will be cut in two. His hand stabs at the moving button panel. It hits something. Glass. The encasement for the small fire extinguisher! Using all his strength, Keith smashes open the glass with his fist. The extinguisher starts to fall. He grabs it.

The ceiling is almost upon him. Keith slides down sideways into the elevator, momentarily avoiding the oncoming beam.

Without a second to spare, Keith wedges the fire extinguisher next to his head. The ceiling beam bangs into it... and holds there, inches from his skull.

Keith slowly begins to squeeze himself out. His head, arm, and now his leg. Almost there. At the last second, Keith's foot hits the fire extinguisher. The elevator starts down.

Quickly Keith pulls his foot out as the door slams shut and elevator disappears downward.

INT. 11TH FLOOR HALLWAY

Keith is sprawled out on carpet, shaken and trying to catch his breath.

                    KEITH
          This is not happening.

A noise. It jars Keith to his senses. He stands up, holding his shoulder, and looks around, down the hallway.

A window. He rushes up to it. A fire escape. Keith pushes the window open and climbs out.

EXT. HOTEL - FIRE ESCAPE

Rusted and rickety. He steadies himself and begins to climb down the ladders.

Each platform shakes as Keith steps on it.

2ND FLOOR FIRE ESCAPE

Keith lands on the second floor platform and looks over the edge. No ladder. Keith looks skyward. Now Keith notices that a second floor window is partially open.

INT. 2ND FLOOR APARTMENT

Keith squeezes through the window and into the apartment. He stands still, letting his eyes adjust to the dark. Light filters in from the next room. A television is on. The theme from "Green Acres" is heard.

Keith tiptoes across the room towards the front door. As he moves closer to the door, WE SEE that the wall behind him is covered with crucifixes, mirrors and wreathes of garlic. <u>Hundreds of them</u>.

Keith: almost to the door... then... a gnarled human hand grabs across the face; another wraps itself around his neck.

Keith's eyes bulge: in front of him is another shadowy figure. And it's coming at him with a stake!

>   OSCAR (O.S.)
>   (heavy Hungarian
>   accent)
>   Get him, Eva! Now!

Keith breaks free and stumbles over the coffee table. The figures continue towards him, now moaning.

>   OSCAR (O.S.)
>   Nosferatu! Nosferatu! Back...
>   back...

Keith keeps moving backwards, just out of reach of the dark figures. His back slides against the wall and hits a light switch.

The apartment lights up and there, shuffling toward him are TWO withered, old HUNGARIANS.

The man holds up a giant cross; the woman now splashes Holy water onto Keith's face while shrieking Latin:

>   EVA
>   Ego te Absolvo in nomine
>   Patris, et Filii, et Spiritus
>   Sancti...

Keith shields his eyes from the water and fights his way out into the hallway. The Hungarians stop in the doorway.

INT. HALLWAY

Keith stumbles halfway down the hall, then turns. He looks incredulously at Oscar, holding the giant cross and Eva, with the bottle of Holy water.

                    EVA
          Go to Christ, Prince of
          Darkness! Die! You dead
          bastard!

Eva spits. Keith can only look wide-eyed, as he backs into the stairwell door and down the stairs.

HOTEL LOBBY

Keith rushes in out of breath, about to blow his top. But there is no one there. No desk clerk, no elevator operator. No one. Keith stalks out.

EXT. LOCKHEART BOULEVARD

Keith starts down the street past the same car at the light. Only now it is being hooked up to the tow truck.

He spots Amaretto walking up ahead and takes off after her. Behind Keith the tow truck driver watches him closely.

                    KEITH
          Hey!

KEITH - AMARETTO: Amaretto looks surprised to see Keith.

                    AMARETTO
          What happened? They told me
          you left.

                    KEITH
              (out of breath)
          Did you find him? A.J.

                    AMARETTO
          No... God, you look awful.
          What hap--

KEITH
(cutting her off)
The girl. What did the girl
say?

AMARETTO
Well, it's weird. I went to
her room and there wasn't
anything in it. Empty. Like no
one ever stayed there... What
are you so testy about?

KEITH
That's great... just great.
You wanna know why I'm testy?
I'll tell you why. Today I
was nearly hung, got into a
fight with a psychotic albino,
met a human pin cushion in a
bathroom, ate a cockroach, my
best friend disappears and now
I'm almost assassinated by a
runaway elevator. Look... I
just want to find A.J. and get
back to school. Is that too
much to ask?

AMARETTO
No... but I don't see what the
big hurry is. He'll—

KEITH
For your information, there
are six coffees running around
here looking for us.

AMARETTO
I don't remember you being
this excitable.

KEITH
(takes a breath)
Listen... where else do you
think a girl like... Candi
would take A.J.

                    AMARETTO
               (suddenly hurt)
          You mean a girl like me, don't
          you? Why don't you just say
          it. Look, I was only trying to
          help. I just thought we might
          spend some time... Maybe...
          Screw off!

Amaretto strides across the street; Keith walks along on the opposite side; They shout at each other across the boulevard, neither noticing the car that runs parallel to them on the next block over.

                    AMARETTO
          If you knew me any better...

                    KEITH
          I don't know you at all!

                    AMARETTO
               (stopping)
          And that's another thing...
          How come I remember you so
          well and you... obviously our
          moment together wasn't as
          important to you as it was to
          me.

                    KEITH
          Look.

                    AMARETTO
          Look yourself.

                    KEITH
               (exasperated)
          Just how does a girl like you
          get to be a girl like you...?

                    AMARETTO
          Breeding!

She huffs off and out of sight. Keith stands in the

empty street dumbfounded.

INT. APTER DARK CLUB

Duncan wanders the room, begging for action. A STRIPPER passes him.

                    DUNCAN
          I love you...
              (another passes)
          No, I love you...

Duncan stops a third waitress as she walks by.

                    DUNCAN
          Hey babe, what time you get
          off?

                    WAITRESS
          Two-thirty.

                    DUNCAN
          Can I watch?

Without a word, the Waitress walks off.

                    DUNCAN
          She'll be back.

INT. VIC'S OFFICE

It's a small closet of a room, just off the hall to the bathroom.

It is decorated with mementos. Faded pictures of celebrities adorn the wall: Sandler and Young, Pat Cooper, Phil Harris, Vic Damone. All with Vic's image missing from the photograph.

Vic paces nervously. Vlad dusts an etching of Katrina.

                    VIC
          I don't like this... we should
          have heard something by now.
          And if it went wrong... the
          queen bitch'll chew my ass
          out.

Vlad continues to stare lovingly at the etching.
Vic shakes his head.

                    VIC
          Forget it Vlad... she don't
          dig you anymore. You're
          nothing but a quick fix now...

Vlad spins and growls. Vic backs off.

                    VIC
          Hey, but what do I know.

Vic goes back to watching Duncan.

INT. CLUB

Duncan walks up behind a WAITRESS who is cleaning
off a table.

                    DUNCAN
          Excuse me. I couldn't help
          noticing that incredible
          perfume you're wearing... it's
          so sensual. What's it called?

                    WAITRESS
          Perspiration.

Duncan sees another STRIPPER take a customer into a
back booth. As they slide into the shadows we HEAR:

                    STRIPPER
          So it looks like I have you
          all to myself. Hmmm...

They begin to fondle one another. Duncan's eyes are

like saucers.

INT. CLUB BOOTH AREA

> DUNCAN
> If the mountain won't come to
> Mohammed...

Duncan strides past the occupied booth, catching a glimpse of the Stripper nibbling on the man's neck. He seats himself one booth over and lights the tabletop candle as a signal to the other Strippers. The CAMERA follows the candle's smoke as it billows into the next booth. Now the Customer sits motionless; a shadow from the chest up. A blood-stained napkin is placed on the table. The Stripper departs.

The CAMERA slowly tracks back into the room. The FACES of the customers; their eyes glazed over watching the act on the stage. Oblivious...

Vic and Vlad begin their clean-up tactics. Duncan, illuminated by candlelight, sits and waits his turn.

EXT. HEWITT STREET

Keith walks down the street. Coming towards him, out of the shadows, is the hotel desk clerk. Behind Keith the tow truck keeps pace. No one sees, in the center of the block, a car sitting motionless; it's motor running.

Keith is ten yards from the car when SUDDENLY: The headlights flash on and the doors fly open. FOUR MEN and TWO WOMEN leap out. It's SNOW and the Dragons.

> SNOW
> We be lookin' for ya...

Keith stops dead in his tracks.

                    KEITH
          Hey, Snow Ball... how they
          hangin'?

Now the Dragon's leader steps out of the car. He, too, is Albino. A 7-foot, 250 LB. one.

                    KEITH
          Shit.

Keith spins and tears off. The gang members split up. Two head after Keith. Another slips down a side alley. The others jump in a car and screech off.

A DOWNTOWN STREET

Keith racing for his life. His heart pounding. The gang member close behind.

INTERSECTION

Keith runs into the middle of the street and stops. The SOUND of foot?steps, VOICES, the car's engine, ECHO From all over. Closing in. But from which direction? Keith looks around.

MERCHANT STREET

Gang members appear from out of the shadows. They begin to close in from all angles.

The car rolls slowly down the street.

No sign of Keith. They begin to search doorways, behind garbage cans. Any hiding place.

GANG MEMBER Walks up to a worksite and looks down in an open manhole. His POV: nothing but blackness. He stalks away.

INT. MANHOLE

Keith clings to the iron ladder, pressing himself into the shadows.

Keith freezes. Then slowly a shadow falls across him. Keith looks up; the LEADER'S PACE INCHES PROM HIS!

                    LEADER
          Gotcha.

Keith retreats down the ladder. Then: the SOUND of heavy metal sliding over the pavement.

EXT. MANHOLE

SNOW and company push the manhole cover over the opening.

INT. SEWER

Keith stands helplessly as blackness slowly engulfs him. Muffled LAUGHTER from above.

                    KEITH
          This is really not happening.

Keith spots a small sewer pipe, and peering through it, sees that it widens a few feet away. He squeezes through.

INT. MAIN SEWER PIPE

At eight feet high and almost six feet wide, it's more like a tunnel. Keith slides through and stands. A small current of water runs down its center. Moonlight streams down into the pipe from the street corner grating.

As Keith walks, he notices rats. Dead ones. Skeletal

remains and dehydrated bodies. Occasionally, a live rat darts by.

Keith quickens his pace as he HEARS shouts from the gang overhead. SNOW'S VOICE echoes through the pipes.

>   SNOW (O.S.)
>   You're going to rot down
>   there...

ANOTHER TUNNEL

Keith finds a street corner grating and peers out of it. The street: Empty and desolate. Then out of nowhere the LITTLE GIRL of 6 appears, wandering about aimlessly. She sits herself down on the curb across from Keith and begins playing with her toy.

>   KEITH
>   Psssst. Hey... Pssssst.

Suddenly: a boot steps down onto Keith's grating. The Leader. He moves across the street for the Little Girl. The Girl looks up and smiles.

Panic in Keith's eyes. He watches helplessly. The Gang Member picks up the Girl and starts tossing her around.

>   LEADER
>   Where's your momma, little
>   girl?

Suddenly: the Girl bares a set of tiny FANGS and chomps into the gang Member's wrist! He screams and tries to shake her off, but she hangs on like a terrier. She flops about like a rag doll but her mouth remains clamped on tight.

The Gang Member lifts her into the air. The Girl then dives onto his neck, attaching herself with ferocity.

They struggle over top of Keith's grating and then out of sight. Keith can only HEAR the struggle for a moment, and then: Silence. Keith stares upward. Nothing but street.

SUDDENLY: from above, the head of the Gang Leader falls across the grating; inches from Keith's face.

THE TUNNEL

Horrified, Keith backs away from the grating. He only gets a few feet when out of nowhere a HULKING HUMAN FIGURE looms before him. Keith tries to run but bis legs slide out from under him, landing him on his back.

KEITH'S POV: It's the bum that threw himself against the car earlier. He looks curiously down at Keith. A rat struggles in his hand. Keith gets up slowly and backs away.

> KEITH
> (nervously)
> Cute little fellow... what's his name?

Keith continues to back down the tunnel. The bum remains silent.

THE BUM watches Keith disappear. Then he seems to remember something.

> BUM
> Hey... I found my friend!

He then looks at the rat, bares a set of FANGS and bites into it.

INT. AFTER DARK CLUB

Amaretto glides through the backstage curtain (wearing a new top). She grabs her tray and strides past the booths. CAMERA HOLDS as she passes DUNCAN;

bending the ear of an unseen person, and obviously very drunk.

Two untouched drinks sit in front of him.

> DUNCAN
> ...See the problem with me is _money_. I have too much of it! Always have... and for what? All I ever wanted is to belong... but nooo. Since I was little, whatever Little Duncan wanted was 'bought' for him... a new bike, a horse, a sports franchise... so naturally I grew up believing you could 'buy' anything. So I 'bought' my friends. I 'bought' my Varsity letter. I 'bought' my first sexual experience... actually my first fifteen sexual experiences... and now here I am again, willing to pay big cash for the pleasure of talking to and hopefully getting fondled by a beautiful woman... and you know something? I'm getting used to it.

Duncan cracks up. Amaretto walks by and he stops her.

> DUNCAN
> Am-a-ret-to! What's happenin'? You see my buds around?

> AMARETTO
> No. Hey, you don't look too good...

And he doesn't.

In fact he looks like he's going to be sick.

                    DUNCAN
               (sliding out of
               booth)
          Excuse me...

Duncan heads for the bathroom. The girl in the
booth now turns to face Amaretto. It's Katrina.
Amaretto smiles.

                    AMARETTO
               (smiles nervously)
          Sorry to interrupt. I know,
          I was told "never interrupt
          booth activity" but I wanted
          to say what a nice club you
          have here... it's my first
          night. I'm Amaretto. We were
          supposed to meet later. I
          thought I'd say 'hi' now...
          Well, anyway, see ya later...

Katrina stares at Amaretto as she walks away.

INT. SEWER TUNNEL

Keith walking. Searching. He notices some crumbling
cement along a portion of the sewer wall. He pulls
some pieces away and peers inside: <u>Another tunnel</u>.
Keith pulls away more loose sections and climbs
through.

                    KEITH (O.S.)
          All this for a fucking
          fraternity...

INT. ABANDONED SEWER TUNNEL

Standing, Keith notices that the ground is dry. He
starts down the tunnel. Faintly at first and growing
in volume, the sound of music can be heard. He
walks along, his eyes watching the ceiling.

Now the bass sound of the music reverberates through

the tunnel. Keith is right under the club.

Keith scans the area for a way out. Above him, the rotted tiles show through to the location above. Keith Gan only make out a few stenciled letters; UM BAC.

TUNNEL - FARTHER DOWN

Keith's eyes scan above him. Then; he sees it. A manhole cover.

Keith climbs the ladder and notices a small latch next to him. He flips it. He puts his shoulder to the cover and pushes. It pops open easily.

EXT. 4TH PLACE

Keith emerges from the sewer and drops the manhole cover into place. The SOUND echoes down the street.

KEITH'S POV

The gang - poking their faces into the grating, looking for Keith. Others stand over the body of the Leader.

                    SNOW
          There he is! Kill him!

EXT. ALLEY

Keith tears down the alley. Then down another. It's a dead end.

Keith tries the fire exit into a building. Locked. He races further down the alley.

He stops and listens. The gang is coming fast. Keith spots a garbage dumpster. He leaps over its edge and buries himself in the trash.

INT. GARBAGE DUMPSTER

Only Keith's eyes show. The SOUND of the gang converging in alley. They move about. SHOUTS to each other. The sounds get fainter, then finally no shouts at all. Keith removes the garbage from around his head.

Keith is about to get up when the sound of an engine is heard. He ducks back down.

EXT. ALLEY

Headlights coming right at us. It's an industrial garbage truck, and its forks are heading right for the dumpster.

INT. DUMPSTER

Suddenly the dumpster jerks harshly. Keith's eyes open. "What the..." The dumpster jerks again as it is lifted off the ground. Garbage shifts inside the dumpster. Something starts to fall at Keith. But it's not garbage.

It's A.J. His face white, lifeless. The eyes rolled upward. Keith SCREAMS and pushes the body off him.

ANOTHER ANGLE: Keith is in shock. He frantically tries to climb out of the moving dumpster. His feet slip on some garbage.

As garbage is pushed aside we see that also buried in here is Seko, her face barely visible amongst the trash.

Keith gets a hold of the top and pulls himself up. He swings one leg over. Then the other.

ANGLE - THE DUMPSTER: Keith holds on for dear life. The dumpster is 20 feet in the air. Keith screams at the driver.

                    KEITH
          Hey! Help! Heeeey!!!

Suddenly the movement stops. The dumpster swings precariously in mid-air.

Keith continues to scream.

The winch on the truck starts to jerk the heavy metal container up and then down.

Keith's grip is loosening. One arm lets go. His fingers slipping.

Keith falls from the dumpster, crashing against the hood of the truck and then rolling off that and hitting the pavement. He lies there, dazed.

The garbage truck tips the dumpster and the garbage and bodies fall into its hull.

Then the truck operator dangles the green container directly over the helpless Keith.

KEITH'S POV: The large green dumpster is falling right at him.

Without a second to spare, Keith rolls out of the way. The dumpster crashes to the pavement, just missing Keith.

THE ALLEY

Keith struggles to his feet. He turns just in time to see the forks of the truck as they SMASH into the cinder block wall. He ducks under the forks and rushes to the mouth of the alley.

The garbage truck turns and the headlights REVEAL

VLAD standing in the shadows, holding two more
garment bags. He watches Keith disappear and then
turns to the DRIVER.

RIDGE STREET

Keith races to the center of the street and
frantically searches for a phone. He spots one a
half-a-block away and heads for it.

PHONE BOOTH

Keith throws open the door, steps inside only to
find that the receiver has been torn off. NOW through
the glass, Keith spots the Dragon's car heading
towards him down the street. Keith slides open the
booth's door, putting out the light, then sinks
down into the shadows as the car cruises by...

INT. KATRINA'S DRESSING ROOM

Vic nervously paces back and forth. Katrina sits on
her throne? like chair, staring at him, her eyes
hard and cold. Vlad stands behind her, against the
wall.

                    VIC
          You know I'd do anything you
          say. But not that... not that.

Katrina's stare intensifies. Vic starts to sweat.

                    VIC
          Look, I can take care of the
          police. I'll explain it just
          like I always do. They never
          follow up on these things,
          anyway. Not down here.

Katrina moves for her bag. Vic flinches as she
removes a silver razor blade and begins to slide it
over her wrist, back and forth...

                         VIC
                  (changing the
                  subject)
            You give any more thoughts to
            my idea? A club in Vegas? We'd
            do nicely there. New blood...
            and everybody's a tourist!
            I hear it's quite a place.
            Nightclubs are big in Vegas...
            just like in the old days...

Vic, his face sweating, stands trance-like in front
of Katrina, watching the razor blade and licking
his lips. He is a beaten man.

                         VIC
            Alright, alright... I'll work
            something out.
                  (to Vlad)
            Have the trash brought back
            here.

Vlad leaves; Vic slides up next to Katrina. She
makes a tiny incision in her wrist and black blood
begins to seep out. She then offers the gurgling
vein to Vic.

                         VIC
            This is a nasty habit...
            nasty.

Vic begins to suck on her wrist like a baby as
Katrina pets his head.

EXT. LINDLEY AVE./HEWITT STREET

Keith running. Searching, He gets to the intersection,
stops, looks around and then spots the blinking
neon of the "After Dark Club". He races to it.

INT. CLUB

Vic is cueing up music and making a light change as

Keith stumbles in nearly in shock.

                    VIC
          Whoa... what's going on he-

                    KEITH
          The phone... I gotta call the
          police! They got my friend!

Vic steps aside and lets Keith use the phone. Shaking, he dials "911". He holds one hand over his ear to block out the blaring MUSIC. A CLICK.

                    VOICE
          You have reached the 911
          emergency service. All lines
          are busy at this time...

Keith slumps into Vic's stool wishing the operator on the line. He gazes about the room; a stark contrast to what's happening; Duncan at the pool table losing money; Vic schmoozing with CUSTOMERS, Amaretto on stage half-waves at Keith. Another CLICK!

                    VOICE
          Emergency 108...

                    KEITH
          I'm at the "After Dark Club".
          My friend was killed. By a
          gang... they were albino...
          He's in a dumpster. Please
          send someone.
               (breaking)
          The "After Dark Club".

VIC - HIS POV: Looks up from his customers and eyes Keith. Keith exhaustedly hangs up, then doubles over like he is going to be sick. He then heads for the bathroom.

Vic looks over to Vlad and nods.

INT. BATHROOM

Keith enters, makes his way to the sink, and splashes water on his face. He reaches for paper towels but there aren't any. Keith walks over to the last stall toilet and walks in.

INT. STALL

Keith dries his hands and face with toilet paper. Now he closes the door and sits on the toilet... suddenly the SOUND of the men's room door opening... footsteps.

Keith stops moving. He listens. The footsteps ECHO through the room. Keith hears the first stall door open, then shut again. Keith pulls up his pants but stops when the sound of the footsteps move to the second stall. Again the door opens and closes. Keith sits frozen. The footsteps now move right outside his stall.

                    KEITH
          It's occupied...

Silence. The door begins to rattle again.

                    KEITH
          Someone's in here.

The door is being pulled harder now. Keith looks around for a weapon. The rattling gets LOUDER. Suddenly the door is ripped open.

It's A.J.

Alive.

                    A.J.
          Hey, relax, it was just a
          joke.

Keith is speechless, looking at the disheveled A.J.

He steps from the stall

BATHROOM

Keith walks up and touches A.J.'s arm as if to make sure he's really there.

                    A.J.
              I look that bad, huh?

                    KEITH
                 (fumbling)
              What the... I thought...

Keith suddenly grabs A.J., fuming.

                    KEITH
                 (shaking him)
              You stupid idiot! You scared
              the shit out of me, you know
              that? Huh?

                    A.J.
              Relax, will ya...

                    KEITH
              Relax?! Twenty minutes ago
              you were dead in a dumpster
              somewhere, I thought Snow
              White got you, you son-of-a...

                    A.J.
              I was rolled. Hey, anyone can
              have an off night.

                    KEITH
              Off night! We're getting out of
              here now.

                    VIC (O.S.)
              You.

Keith turns to see Vic standing near the bathroom door. Keith gestures to A.J.

                    KEITH
          I found my friend...

                    VIC
          Yeah? Well, some uniformed
          gentlemen to see you... in the
          back.

INT. STRIPPER'S DRESSING ROOM

TWO POLICEMEN question Keith as A.J. plays footsie
with a STRIPPER. Duncan is there along with Vic who
listens intently.

                    KEITH
          He looked dead. I mean...

                    OFFICER #1
          He looks real dead to me...

                    KEITH
          But in the...

                    OFFICER #2
          Your friend here apparently
          likes to flash his money
          around. In this neighborhood
          that makes him a meal ticket.

                    DUNCAN
          Hey, tell me about it... I
          am a meal ticket. I should
          know...

A.J. smiles a hollow smile.

                    KEITH
          Look...

                    OFFICER #1
          No, you look... my stomach
          is all upset now, thanks to
          you and your dead buddy over
          there. This is not a nice area

                    and I don't like coming to
                    it. So before I lock you up,
                    I want all three of you outta
                    here. Go home.

                              KEITH
                    I've been trying to do that
                    for the past three...

                              OFFICER #1
                    Now!

The Officers put away their note books. Vic smiles.

                              VIC
                    I'll walk you guys out. I
                    gotta cue up the music for the
                    last act anyhow...

Duncan's eyes light up.

                              DUNCAN
                    Hey guys... if you don't mind,
                    I think I'll catch one last
                    act before we split...

                              A.J.
                        (laughing)
                    Go ahead, buddy. We'll be out
                    in a minute.
                        (to the cops as they
                         leave)
                    And I promise, you'll never
                    see us again...

Vic smiles at Keith as he closes the door behind him.

INT. DRESSING ROOM

The Stripper is massaging his shoulders.

Keith shakes his head and smiles. Only A.J.

                    A.J.
          They treat you real good here.
          Real good.

                    KEITH
          I'm pissed at you...

                    A.J.
          So you were in the garbage
          with me.
               (laughing)
          That's a friend for ya...

Keith moves closer. A.J. seems different. His stare is blank. Dark circles rim his eyes.

                    KEITH
          It looks like no fraternity
          for us, so let's go.

                    A.J.
          What's the rush? I think I've
          found a home right here.

A.J. looks at the stripper and winks.

                    A.J.
               (to Stripper)
          Why don't you clean up my
          friend here. He can't go
          looking like that.

Keith looks a bit uncomfortable.

                    KEITH
          I'm fine. I think we should get
          going... NOW.

But the stripper continues to advance, circling Keith.

She takes a big wet rag and rubs it over Keith's body and face; her dreamy eyes boring into Keith's. Her hands soothe his body Keith starts to relax. She moves behind him, pressing her body against his back. He is helpless. Then: overwhelming heat.

Keith starts to rise. He doesn't make it. He is stopped by the Stripper's powerful grip. Keith lets out a cry of pain. He turns to see her face.

FANGS bared. Skin white. Veins show as the makeup drips from her body. Her eyes on fire. The Stripper tosses Keith across the room like a feather. Keith SMASHES against the wall.

Keith looks to A.J. for help. But A.J. stands in the corner motionless, torn and weak.

                    KEITH
     A.J.!

Keith gets to his feet and grabs a chair. HISSING, the vampire lunges. Keith smashes the chair over her. It breaks into fragments but doesn't faze the creature.

                    KEITH
          A.J.! Help me!

A.J. doesn't move. There is confusion in his eyes. The vampire swings her head. It knocks Keith down.

ANGLE - KEITH: Dazed, Keith looks up to see the vampire ready to leap on him. He GRABS something just as the vampire falls.

The vampire lands on Keith, her fangs inches from his neck. But she doesn't strike. Her eyes fill with blood. Her face contorts.

Keith pushes the body off his chest. A spiked heel is stuck into the vampire's heart.

Keith struggles to his feet.

Keith turns to A.J.

A.J., a little surprised, steps forward staring at the vampire's body.

> A.J.
> I didn't think you had it in
> you.

Keith just stares at his friend. All of it is slowly sinking in.

> A.J.
> Yeah... looks like you
> discovered the only way out of
> here, pal...

Keith just looks into A.J.'s soulless eyes.

> A.J.
> You see, this is my new home.

A.J. moves toward Keith. Keith backs up.

> KEITH
> What the hell are you
> saying...?

> A.J.
> You don't know by now? The
> Club. Everybody here. They're
> <u>vampires</u>.

A.J. opens his mouth and FANGS snap into place; his eyes begin to glow a bright red...

> A.J.
> (visibly torn)
> I can't let you leave.

Keith is backing up.

He quickly bends down and picks up a jagged piece from the broken chair.

The two friends begin to circle each other.

> A.J.
> (shuddering)
> We got a problem here.

                    KEITH
              (frightened-reaching)
         Yeah. ? Well let's go home.
         We'll find a doctor or
         something. Let's just go. You
         and me...

A.J.'s body is wracked by spasms and shivers, like
an addict going 'cold turkey'.

Katrina's wounds of death break out all over A.J.'s
body.

                    A.J.
         You don't get it, do you?
         Home's a million miles away
         from me now... home's another
         planet. I'm a fucking zombie
         now. Can't ya tell?

Keith's eyes are wet. He looks hard at A.J., trying
to find out if anything is left.

Suddenly, A.J. starts for him! Keith scrambles back
away.

                    A.J.
         Watch out, man.
              (shivers)
         Wanna know how bad things are?
         You're all I care about in the
         world. You're all there is. I
         love you. But all I see right
         now is food... you're carrying
         my next meal around in your
         veins. And I'm starving! They
         got me... They got me good...

                    KEITH
         A.J., don't! We'll figure a way
         out of this. We've gotten out
         of jams before...

                    A.J.
         This is different...

                    KEITH
              (holds out his arm)
         Here... take what you need for
         now... to get you through.

                    A.J.
              (laughing, then
              spasms)
         You're too much. That's sooo
         nice...
              (mean)
         Do I look like a mosquito? No,
         you'd have to put a muzzle on
         me... keep me on a leash. I
         can't be trusted, buddy...

A.J. looks torn. Like someone whose insides are
being torn apart. He looks down at himself.

                    A.J.
         Awwww, will you look at these
         clothes. Ruined!
              (looks up at Keith)
         How do I look? Do I look real
         bad? You know it's just like
         the movies. No reflection.
         Can't see yourself. Weird...
              (pounces)

                    KEITH
              (dodges)
         You're really gonna do it,
         aren't you? You're gonna kill
         me? Or am I gonna come back
         like you...?

                    A.J.
              (stalking)
         Sorry pal. Only the chicks
         can do that. See, it's their
         blood. They have the gift. You
         drink some of their juice and
         you're talkin' forever. We
         guys can only feed... and just
         blood. No more beer if you can

believe that.
(bitter)
They tell me it's like a
beehive here and we're the
drones. But I've got plans to
change that around...

Keith has backed himself against the door. He tries the doorknob. No luck. A.J. has him trapped. Inches apart. A.J. places a hand on either wall, boxing Keith in. Tears in Keith's eyes as he looks at his friend. For a moment A.J.'s face appears serene...

KEITH

Do me a favor...

A.J.
(grinning)
For old time's sake? Sure,
buddy, anything. Anything at
all.

KEITH

Make sure I don't come back
like you.

A.J.
(offended)
Hey, you think I like this? Or
them? They're boring creeps.
They don't call 'em the
walking dead for nothing. Try
talking to one of them.

KEITH

I did...

Keith lifts his arm and half-heartedly puts the broken chair leg to A.J.'s chest. He holds it there a beat... and then starts to lower it.

KEITH

Shit.

A.J. grabs it, positioning it back at his heart.

                    A.J.
          Can't, can you? Even though
          you know... it works... it
          does... wooden stakes. Fire
          and sunlight, too. I got a
          list here somewhere.

A.J. pats his pockets.

                    A.J.
          Yeah, just like the movies.
          They're strong as bulls. And
          they can jump like giant
          frogs...
               (pause)
          Go figure it... but they can't
          fly. No bats.

He looks off into space; smiling... a sudden spasm: he recovers and stares at Keith.

                    A.J.
          You're ready to die for me,
          aren't you? You would... you
          can't believe I'm not me
          anymore... that maybe there's
          something left, huh? Jesus.
               (thinking)
          Maybe there is...

A.J. looms over Keith, leaning towards him; his mouth opens -the fangs appear. But it's only for a cry of pain. There is a RIPPING SOUND.

ANOTHER ANGLE: A.J. has hugged Keith; forcing the stake into his own heart. Keith struggles to hold on to A.J. as he slumps to his knees, fighting back the tears.

                    A.J.
          Now get lost fast.
               (then grabbing Keith)
          Remember... you can burn 'em,
          or keep 'em from their coffins
          past sunrise... and...

                    (looking at his own
                    chest)
               Well, you know the other.

A.J. sinks to the floor. His body quickly stiffens; the wound on his neck reappearing. Keith stands over his friend. Then the SOUND OF THE DOORKNOB RATTLING.

Keith picks up another chair leg as a weapon and moves behind the door.

The doorknob turns. Keith readies his stake. The door opens. It's Amaretto. She sees the carnage and starts to scream. Keith puts his hand over her mouth and closes the door.

CLUB - MAIN ROOM

Vic stands at the podium, nervously tapping his fingers. An act is ending on stage. Vic eyes the backstage curtain.

BAR AREA: Duncan stands with an untouched drink in his hand. He, too, is staring at the curtain. He is about to walk towards it when:

BACKSTAGE CURTAIN: Amaretto walks through. All eyes follow her as she walks to the service area of the bar, picks up her tray and heads for the tables.

She passes by Duncan and gives him a look. Duncan slinks back into the crowd at the bar.

STAGE AREA: MUSIC COMES UP. Katrina appears on stage. The closing act begins.

TABLE AREA: Amaretto glides through the tables looking for anyone who needs a refill. She is tense but tries not to show it.

FRONT DOOR: Vic watches Amaretto intently. His gaze shifts from her to the backstage curtain, and then back again.

THE BAR: Duncan watches Amaretto, then shoots a look toward Vic.

TABLE AREA: Amaretto finishes taking another drink order from one table. She turns and stops at another. It's the table of men that hassled her earlier. Shorty gives her the finger.

She starts past the table, then stops and spins around.

                    AMARETTO
          What did you call me, you
          little bastard?

She doesn't wait for an answer. She tips the table of drinks onto the guy, then whacks him across the face with her tin tray.

Shorty reels over backwards, hitting the floor.

THE ROOM - WIDE: General commotion. Customers look to see what's going on. Other waitresses rush over to break it up.

Katrina watches from the stage. Vic moves in to restore things.

THE BAR: The crowd at the bar cheering Amaretto on. Duncan steps forward to get a better look. Suddenly a hand reaches out from the crowd and grabs him.

Duncan turns to see Keith standing there.

                    KEITH
               (whispering)
          We're out of here... now.

TABLE AREA: Vic has broken up the fight. He pushes Amaretto away. The crowd going back to their seats. Vic looks to the backstage curtain.

BAR AREA: Keith and Duncan reach the end of the bar. Almost there. The front door unattended.

THE STAGE: Katrina doing her act. But her eyes scan every inch of the room.

FRONT DOOR AREA: Keith and Duncan break from the crowd. They get to the opening. About to turn the corner. SUDDENLY: Vlad steps into view. His massive arms block the exit.

From behind: Up steps Vic. He grabs Keith and spins him around. Their eyes bore into each other. He pulls Keith back into the room.

>   VIC
>   (loudly)
> Gentlemen... there seems to be
> a problem with your bill. If
> you don't mind, let us proceed
> to the back to straighten this
> untidy matter out.

Keith searches for a way out: the hall to the men's room, the backstage curtain... all blocked. No way out. Surrounded.

TABLE AREA: Keith pulls Amaretto away from the other waitresses and all three move to the center of the room. From all angles, the Vampires close in.

Keith, Duncan and Amaretto weave their way through the tables as Katrina dances onstage.

>   CUSTOMERS
> Hey! Down in front!

>   KEITH
> These people are VAMPIRES!
> Real Vampires!

>   MAN
> Yeah, I saw my bill. They
> sucked my pay envelope dry!

Laughter and more shouts of 'move', etc. The Vampires are close now. But the customers pay no attention. All eyes are on stage. On Katrina.

KEITH: He spots a MAN and his BUDDIES playing pool by the bar. Suddenly Keith grabs Duncan's wallet from his back pocket.

                    KEITH
          Come on.

CLOSE ON POOL TABLE: A pool ball heading right for the pocket. Suddenly a hand reaches out and picks up the moving ball. Keith.

                    KEITH
          I hear you cheat at pool, you
          pencil-neck geek.

The man's face turns red. His buddies slide off the bar stools and surround Keith and company.

                    MAN
          What... did... you... say...?

Keith looks around. The Vampires have stopped for the moment.

                    KEITH
              (holding up wallet,
               rifling it)
          I got... $400 to your $40 that
          says you can't beat this guy.
          In front of me.

The man grabs Keith by the collar and sneers down at him.

                    MAN
          Rack 'em up, boys...

Keith, Duncan, Amaretto and the men move to the pool table. The Vampires hold their ground. Kept at bay for the time being.

Katrina watches from the stage.

POOL TABLE: A crowd gathers.

                    AMARETTO
               What are you doing?

                     KEITH
               Buying time.

                    AMARETTO
               For what?

                     KEITH
               I don ' t know...

Keith moves next to Duncan, who is trembling.

                     KEITH
               Just keep the game going...

                    DUNCAN
               For how long?

                     KEITH
               Till the sun rises...

                    DUNCAN
               Great.

After all sorts of gestures, Duncan knocks the cue ball clear off the table.

Keith begins to sweat and looks for a way out.

The vampires go about their business, but keep a watchful eye on the pool table.

BAR AREA: Vic slips onto a stool directly behind Keith. He smiles wickedly at him, then leans towards him.

                     VIC
               You're putting off the
               inevitable. It's just a matter
               of time, now.

THE BAR: As pool game continues, Keith moves to the bar where Vic is still perched. He speaks to him over the NOISE and MUSIC:

				KEITH
			(not looking at him)
		You don't think you're gonna
		get away with this, do you?

				VIC
			(matter of fact)
		Of course...
			(turns to Keith)
		You know how many people
		disappear every year? Not
		thousands -tens of thousands.
		You're a statistic, kid.

				KEITH
		We'll be missed... they'll
		come looking for us.

				VIC
			(laughing)
		Who will? Who knows you're
		here? Nobody, that's who.
		<u>Because nobody tells anyone
		they're going to a place like
		this</u>... what a racket, huh?

				KEITH
		<u>Why us?</u> Why did you pick on
		us?

				VIC
			(uncomfortable,
			awkward)
		Your friend was a <u>mistake</u>.
		Call it a bureaucratic error.
		A communication problem.
		Sorry.

				KEITH
			(sarcastic)
		That's nice. Sorry. You

screwed up so we become a
statistic...

> VIC
> Hey, I didn't screw up,
> someone else screwed up! I try
> to run a reasonable business
> in a reasonable way; it does
> more than reasonably well.
> Everyone's happy. Everything
> is fine for longer than anyone
> could've hoped, and one little
> mistake - not even my mistake,
> mind you -and suddenly I'm
> incompetent! I'm the one who
> gets chewed up or out, if I'm
> not careful.

KEITH'S POV: The game is coming to an end. Keith winces. Amaretto is nestled safely between two truck drivers.

BAR: Vic is starting to look forlorn.

Keith still searches for an escape route.

> VIC
> Ya see, I run an essential
> service here. <u>Waste Disposal</u>!
> That's right. The lost, the
> sickies, the dangerous, the
> forgotten. The <u>dregs</u>. They
> wind up here and we take care
> of them. You miss 'em? Does
> anyone? You people out there
> would be up to your asses in
> derelicts, pimps, hookers,
> criminals and insurance
> salesmen if it weren't for us!
> We clean up <u>your</u> act. And it
> costs you nothing.

> KEITH
> Just my best friend.

                    VIC
               (defensive)
          Hey. Nobody's perfect. I do
          the best I can with what I
          got, okay?

Just then: Katrina's act ends: "last call" is announced. People at the tables start to leave. A SONG BEGINS PLAYING OVER THE P.A. Keith reacts strangely to it. He's heard it before.

                    VIC
          Your self pity makes me sick,
          ya know that? Let me tell you
          something... I used to own
          this place. That's right! And
          it was a class act nightclub.
          Buddy Greco played here. Louis
          Prima. Phil Harris! The best.
          Now... now it's all hers;
          theirs... the place, the
          money... me. I just work here
          now.
               (pause)
          So don't expect me to feel
          sorry for you.

Keith is hardly listening. He is looking behind the bar. His eyes fall upon a case of liquor stenciled "RUM BACARDI". Keith looks closer. CAMERA TRACKS IN TIGHTER UNTIL we see only the letters, UM BAC.

Keith shifts his eyes; next to the case is the trapdoor to the cellar. The SONG PLAYING is what he heard in the sewer... Vic sees Keith searching...

                    VIC
          Don't waste your time. "We"
          in here are not the only ones
          you'd have to run from...

Keith looks surprised.

                    VIC
          That's right. There are more

>   of "us" out there. See, we
>   have everything a small
>   community needs: security,
>   disposal - you've already had
>   the pleasure, transportation.
>   We even offer home delivery
>   services. There's just enough
>   of us to keep things running
>   smoothly. So you see; you
>   don't have to get out of
>   here... you have to get out of
>   "here"... Hey, ever been to
>   Vegas?

Keith shakes his head. The pool game is almost over. The place is thinning out.

THE BAR: Vic is still brooding. Keith turns to him.

>   KEITH
>   How about buying me and my
>   friends one last round? A
>   last request, like they do in
>   Vegas.

>   VIC
>   (thinking)
>   That would be classy, wouldn't
>   it? Sure. Why not?

Vic calls over a bartendress. She stares at Keith.

>   KEITH
>   Let's see... brandy... three.
>   Make 'em doubles, no -triples.
>   Hell, leave the bottle. We're
>   not driving anywhere.

THE CLUB: Katrina has taken her place in her private booth. Ready for the kill.

THE BAR: The Bartendress returns with the bottle and three glasses of brandy. Keith takes them and moves toward the pool table. He takes all three - making sure to spill just enough along the way.

POOL TABLE: Keith hands Amaretto and Duncan their drinks. He whispers something to Duncan and pulls Amaretto back towards the bar with him.

On the way back, Keith dribbles liquor from the bottle. The floor is now soaked.

THE BAR: Vic looks oddly at Keith and Amaretto. Keith spills his drink on the bar and partly on Vic.

                    KEITH
     Oh, hey sorry...

Vic steps away from the bar to wipe himself off.

KEITH'S POV - The club: only a few scattered customers remain.

Down the far end of the bar: both bartenderesses pour their final drinks.

The pool table: the Man sinks the 8 ball.

THE BAR: Keith turns and slides one of the bar candles down the bar. It hits the glass of liquor and explodes into flames! The startled bartendress jumps back, dropping the bottle. It SMASHES against the floor and bursts into flames.

THE CLUB: Mass confusion. Customers race for the exits.

A ring of fire now separates the bartenders from the trapdoor. Keith grabs Amaretto.

                    KEITH
     Quick!

Keith helps her over the bar. Then he takes another candle and smashes it to the floor. The liquor-soaked floor bursts into flames.

                    KEITH
     Duncan! Let's go!

Duncan hesitates. Keith grabs him and sends him flying over the bar. The room fills with smoke.

                    KEITH
          The trapdoor!

Now Keith notices Vic start for him. He grabs another candle and holds it up. Vic stops dead in his tracks.

Keith starts over the bar. Suddenly a hand grabs him and pulls him back. It's the pool player.

                    MAN
          You owe me money...

ANOTHER ANGLE: Keith struggles but the Man is too strong. The vampires close in. With his free hand, he reaches down and squeezes the man's balls.

                    KEITH
          Let go or you'll be picking
          these off the floor.

Keith squeezes and the Man drops.

                    KEITH
          Hey, it works!

BEHIND BAR: Fire everywhere. Keith makes it to the hatch. Amaretto and Duncan start down. The last thing Keith sees through the flames are Katrina's eyes.

INT. CLUB CELLAR

The three come tumbling down the wooden stairs. The room is dark and musty. Crates of liquor everywhere.

But no way out. No windows. Nothing. COMMOTION and SHOUTS are heard above.

Keith spots an old liquor elevator. It goes up to

the street. Amaretto, Keith and Duncan jump on.

They can't find the switch. Amaretto and Keith search frantically. Duncan trembles against the back wall.

ANGLE - THE CEILING: Light and smoke stream into the cellar. The trapdoor is open. Vampires head down the stairs.

ELEVATOR: Amaretto pushes away some empty cartons. The switch! She pushes the button and the elevator heads upward.

EXT. CLUB - SIDE STREET

The metal doors in the sidewalk fly open. The elevator appears. The three jump off and race into the street. People scatter. Cars drive away. They head for the car.

EXT. CAR

Keith races up, 'Unlocks the door and slides behind the wheel. Duncan falls into the back seat. Amaretto gets in next to Keith.

INT. CAR

Keith turns the ignition and the car starts up. He begins to pull out when all of a sudden: Amaretto screams!

AMARETTO'S POV: Heading right for the car is the speeding tow truck! It rams into the car broadside.

INT. CAR

Everyone is thrown about like rag dolls. The truck backs up for another run. It's teeth-like grille zeros in.

EXT. CAR

Keith steps on the gas and drives the car up onto the sidewalk. Keith races the car down the sidewalk using the parked cars as shields.

EXT. THE STREET

The tow truck races down the street parallel with the car. The parked cars are between them. The truck is faster and more powerful. It beats the Caddy to the end of the block.

It pulls up onto the sidewalk, blocking Keith's way out. The head? lights shine into the car.

INT-. CAR

Keith slams on the brakes.

                    KEITH
        Shit...

INT. CAR

Keith throws the car into reverse and heads backwards as fast as he can. Suddenly Keith slams on the brakes.

                    AMARETTO
        What are you stopping for? Go
        on!

Then she sees it. On the back window the garbage truck can be seen pulling up onto the sidewalk at the other end. Trapped. Keith looks both ways. No way to go... Duncan shivers and trembles in the back seat.

Keith. His mind at work. Then, a few yards away, he spots one of the club's customers getting into his parked car.

INT./EXT. CAR STREET

A RUMBLING SOUND. Behind the Caddy the garbage truck heads for the car.

Its forks raising into place, ready to plunge through the car's roof. In front of them, the tow truck starts for them.

The ENGINE of the parked car TURNS OVER. Now the driver has to squeeze out of the tight space.

ANGLE - THE TRUCKS: Halfway to the Caddy and gaining speed.

THE PARKED CAR: Inching back and forth. Trying to get out.

CLOSE ON AMARETTO Wishing the car to move faster.

           AMARETTO
        (mumbling)
    ... Come on... come on...
        (then: screaming out
        window)
    Move it, you asshole!

THE TRUCKS: Barreling down on the Caddy. Closer and closer.

THE PARKED CAR: Almost out.

THE TRUCKS: Almost on top of the Caddy.

KEITH: Sweat dripping off his face. But he doesn't flinch.

THE PARKED CAR: Pulls out from its space.

THE CADDY: Keith floors the accelerator. The car peels out and bursts through the vacated space onto the street.

ANGLE - THE TRUCKS: They are caught off guard.

They CRASH headfirst into each other. The forks from the garbage truck impaling the janitor through the heart. The garbage truck driver flies through the windshield.

INT. CAR - ATWELL ROAD

Keith wipes the sweat from his brow. Amaretto just stares at the road. Duncan appears more calm.

              KEITH
   Which way?

            AMARETTO
   Hang a right here!

Keith SCREECHES the car around a corner.

VIC'S OFFICE

Vic sits alone as fire sweeps through the club. He stares at the wall above him where the faded photographs hang. In his hand: a travel brochure of Las Vegas.

Vlad appears with a tray containing two drinks. He slides across from Vic and hands him one of the glasses of scotch. Vic holds it up and stares at it lovingly.

            VIC
   My first drink in 75 years...
     (clinks glasses with
     Vlad)
   I would have liked to have
   seen Vegas, though... to the
   good old days.

Vic turns, salutes the pictures on the wall and then gulps down the drink as the fire now reaches them, the flames dancing in his glass.

EXT. ROSELLE STREET

Silent. Dark. The Caddy cruises along. The HUM of its MOTOR the only sound.

INT. CAR

Amaretto is searching for a familiar landmark.

> AMARETTO
> Maybe this isn't the street I was thinking of...

SUDDENLY: A LOUD THUD! A Vampire lands on top of the car. Its hand tears through the convertible roof! The deformed hand gropes for a victim.

Amaretto takes a knife from her purse and slices the sinewy arm.

Keith floors the accelerator and the Security Guard falls from the car.

> AMARETTO
> No... this wasn't the street...

Keith looks at her and gulps. Duncan still has his eyes closed.

INT CAR. 12TH STREET

Keith clutches the wheel, his eyes searching every shadow. Pear pervades the car.

> KEITH
> We'll make it.

A moan from the back seat.

                    KEITH
          Duncan? You okay?

Duncan rises, looking ill.

                    DUNCAN
          I'm hungry...

Keith and Amaretto laugh.

                    KEITH
          You're okay.

                    DUNCAN
          No. I mean I'm starvin'...
          guys?

Duncan sounds different. Keith looks over his shoulder to the back seat. Duncan is holding his stomach. He stares right back at Keith. Eyes bloodshot.

Keith returns his eyes to the road. Worried.

                    KEITH
              (forced laughter)
          Okay, the first burger joint I
          see. Once we're out of here.

Keith looks in the rear view mirror.

                    KEITH
          If that's all right you y-

KEITH'S POV - REARVIEW MIRROR: The back seat. It's empty.

ANOTHER ANGLE: Amaretto's smile drops, Keith spins around:

Duncan is in mid-transformation. Eyes luminizing; cheeks hollowing, fangs sprouting, skin turning translucent. HE'S ONE OF THEM.

Keith steps on the brakes and then slams on the gas.

EXT. CAR

The car skids across the street and into an empty parking lot.

INT. CAR

Keith swings the car back and forth to keep Duncan off balance.

The car cuts across the parking lot and heads for the other side. A sign warning of "Severe Tire Damage" looms ahead.

EXT CAR

The car runs over the razor-sharp hooks. ALL FOUR TIRES BLOW. The Dodge skids across the intersection and slams into a pole.

The front end bursts into flames.

INT. CAR

Keith kicks open Amaretto's door.

Amaretto squeezing out. Suddenly Duncan's claw-like hand grabs her shoulder.

In one swift movement, Keith pushes Duncan back and pins him down with the seat belt.

EXT. CAR

Keith and Amaretto run from the burning wreck. Duncan, now fully transformed, tries squeezing out the back window. But he is stuck.

ANOTHER ANGLE - THE CAR: Keith and Amaretto watch horrified and Duncan's WOLF-LIKE CRIES pierce the night.

SUDDENLY the underside of the car EXPLODES and Duncan, caught half-in and half-out, is consumed by the fire. He becomes a ball of' flames.

EXT. STREET CORNER

Keith stumbles away from the flaming wreck, pulling Amaretto with him. Both are knocked to their knees by the force of the EXPLODING GAS TANK. Flaming pieces of the car scatter about the street.

      AMARETTO
    (rising)
  Him... My God. And I was
  getting to like him... how?

Keith doesn't hear. He stares across the street at a storefront illuminated by the flames. A pawnshop. He pulls Amaretto towards it.

EXT. PAWNSHOP

Keith peers through the iron latticework that protects the shop's window as Amaretto hides in the shadow of the doorway. He sees what he'd hoped for: a case of handguns and a rifle rack.

Keith grabs a wire mesh litter barrel and slams it against the ironwork. It buckles. Another slam. The plate glass shatters; the ALARM SOUNDS. Keith rears back for another blow but stops in mid-swing; there, inside the shop, is Amaretto. She half-waves to Keith.

Stunned, Keith moves to the Pawnshop door. The iron grillwork is bent back and the glass smashed.

INT. PAWNSHOP

Keith looks suspiciously from the warped iron to the grinning Amaretto. AMARETTO Looks like we're not the first midnight shoppers. It was already bent...

Keith doesn't seem to buy that. He races to the gun case and shatters it with his elbow. He grabs a pistol.

> KEITH
> Bullets! Find some bullets!

Both begin to ransack the shop. Keith rifles through drawers, overturns cases and clears off shelves. Pushing aside a garment rack, Keith suddenly stops and gapes at what hangs on the wall: <u>a couple of bows and quivers of arrows</u>.

Keith grabs a bow and a handful of arrows. Suddenly there is a crash behind him.

ANOTHER ANGLE: In one swift motion, Keith wheels and has an arrow knocked and drawn back to his cheek.

Amaretto rises from a pile of debris.

> AMARETTO
> Will this help?

She holds up a bazooka.

> KEITH
> You got ammo with that?

> AMARETTO
> You mean bullets? No... hey, where'd you get that?

She takes a step forward, then stops as Keith raises the arrow toward her.

> KEITH

> Get back. I'm very good with this, believe me.

AMARETTO
> Stop kidding, okay? You're scaring me.

KEITH
> Likewise. Now get back.

Disheveled, streaked by dirt and makeup and eyes reflecting the firelight, Amaretto *does* look scary. Suddenly she throws her mouth open.

AMARETTO
> (pointing)
> Look, no fangs, alright? C'mon, Keith, you've known me since -

KEITH
> I don't know you! Who are you?

AMARETTO
> (frantic)
> I... uh... I... I lived down the block from you and, uh...

KEITH
> Your name. Tell me your real name I now!!! Or...

AMARETTO
> (hyperventilating)
> You used to beat up Randy Whatshisname and. uh. I. I. this isn't the time I had in mind, ya know...

Keith releases the arrow. It hums past Amaretto's cheek and skewers an attacking Vampire in mid-leap as it appears behind her. It was the already bloodied Garbage Truck Driver.

Amaretto runs to Keith and awkwardly embraces him

as Keith fits another arrow to the bow.

                    AMARETTO
          Oh, my God... I thought you
          killed me!

Amaretto starts to kiss Keith; her open mouth plunges toward him. Keith freezes, waiting for any sign of fangs. There are none. They kiss.

                    AMARETTO
          Thanks... I needed to do that.
          Did you really think I could
          be one of those?

                    KEITH
          You? Never.

They start out of the Pawnshop, Keith notices his fire-lit reflection in a blacked-out storefront. He tries to catch a glimpse of Amaretto's, but just misses.

EXT. STREETS

Keith and Amaretto run out of the firelight and down a dark street, to another street. Amaretto stops mid-block.

                    AMARETTO
          We're not getting anywhere.

                    KEITH
          Just keep moving...

                    AMARETTO
          To where? For all we know
          we're heading right for those
          'things'.
              (folding her arms)
          I'm not going any further
          until you find out which way to
          go!

EXT. BUILDING ROOFTOP

A building undergoing renovation. Keith pulls himself up from the top rung of an iron ladder and then turns to help Amaretto onto the roof. J They tiptoe to the edge of the five-story building and look out. THEIR POV: Only a mile away are the lighted buildings of a busy downtown section.

> KEITH
> Come on... we can make it.
> We'll take that road straight
> into town!

THE ROOF

Amaretto and Keith turn and are frozen in their tracks. Across the alley, on the next roof, stand Candi, Milkman, the two Bartenderesses and two other girls from the Club, their fangs bared. Keith and Amaretto back up.

Keith readies his bow. Candi leaps across the space between the buildings. Keith lets fly with an arrow. A Bull's eye! Right into the heart. She hits the side of the building and falls to the alley floor below.

Like frogs the others leap the incredible distance and land on the roof containing Keith and Amaretto. Surrounded. The ladder down is blocked. The Milkman lunges for Amaretto! Keith puts him away with an arrow through the chest. But now K<u>eith has only one arrow left.</u>

KEITH AND AMARETTO: Trapped, they begin to back up.

> AMARETTO
> Jesus... where'd they all come
> from?

The Vampires begin to move in. Keith tries to keep them at bay with his bow but there are too many. They back up against the front ledge of the building.

Amaretto picks up a broken cinder block, ready to hurl it. That's when she spots it. A construction chute a few feet away.

                    AMARETTO
               (under her breath)
          When I say three... jump.

                    KEITH
          Jump where?

                    AMARETTO
          Three!!

Amaretto grabs Keith by the arm and pulls him with her into the wooden chute.

THE CHUTE

Like human bobsleds, they slide down the winding chute; both bouncing off the sides.

Then: the chute <u>ends at the second floor</u>.

EXT. BUILDING

Keith and Amaretto fly through the air and crash land into a construction bin, their fall broken by masonite boards and cardboard boxes.

EXT. STREET

The two scramble over the side of the bin and race off down the street.

EXT. SPRING STREET

Keith and Amaretto running as fast as they can.

Keeping to the center of the avenue, they race out

into the intersection and look down the street.

A mass transit bus headed right for them!

                    AMARETTO
          We're saved!

ANOTHER ANGLE: Amaretto stands in the center of the street and waves the bus down. The DRIVER pulls the bus over to the curb.

THE BUS: Keith races up to it. The Driver swings open the door. Keith's POV: The Driver smiles and bares a hideous pair of fangs.

                    DRIVER
          Last stop.

EXT. STREET

Keith pulls Amaretto away from the bus. He whirls around.

This time there doesn't seem to be any place to run.

As Keith and Amaretto walk slowly up the center of the street, "They" begin to appear. Out of the shadows; on all four street corners: Girls from the Club, the Security Guard, the Milkman, the Hotel Desk Clerk, the Bum, the Little Girl. One arrow seems useless now.

ANOTHER ANGLE - THE STREET: The Vampires moving in for the kill.

Keith and Amaretto stand under the streetlamp. Keith readies his final arrow.

Keith takes aim.

Then: a bright light. The SOUND OF AN ENGINE FOLLOWS.

It's "The Dragons". And their car is rumbling right at Keith and Amaretto.

It SKIDS within 10 feet of Keith and Amaretto. The Vampires disappearing into the shadows...

                    KEITH
            Talk about timing...

                    AMARETTO
            Oh... are these friends of
            yours?

                    KEITH
                (taking her arm)
            They are now... let's go!

Attention diverted, Keith pulls Amaretto down a narrow alleyway. Snow and "The Dragons" take off after them.

MARKETPLACE

Keith and Amaretto hit the street on a dead run. As they run, Keith is looking around. The surrounding's familiar.

4TH PLACE

They round the corner, their feet pounding the pavement. Keith sensing something.

A HOLLOW CLUNK! Keith stops. He looks behind them at the pavement.

<u>It's the manhole cover to the abandoned sewer tunnel.</u>

KEITH'S POV: Coming toward them, Keith can make out the forms of the Vampires leaping about. From behind, the Dragons bear down.

THE STREET

Keith bends to lift the manhole cover but Amaretto is standing on it.

                    AMARETTO
          Keith, it's time. It's now or
          never.

                    KEITH
          Huh? Come on, help me!

                    AMARETTO
          My name... I'm Allison.
          Allison Hicks.

Keith looks from the Vampires to the gang: closing in. He then stares incredulously at Amaretto. She's still talking.

                    AMARETTO
          Seaside Heights? Summer
          vacation, 6th grade? Sue
          Leonard's basement. We played
          spin the bottle, I spun, it
          landed on you and you wouldn't
          kiss me. Remember? I had such
          a crush on you.

A look of recognition crosses Keith's face. He even smiles. Then the SOUND of approaching bodies. He stands, grabs her shoulders, kisses her, picks her up and places her off the manhole cover.

                    KEITH
          You have incredible timing.

                    AMARETTO
          Thanks.

Keith struggles with his side of the manhole. Amaretto easily lifts hers.

Keith looks at her strangely.

                    KEITH
          Go on, get in.

                    AMARETTO
          In there? You've got to be
          kidding. It's dark enough out
          here.

Keith gives her a stern look. Amaretto climbs down.

INT. MANHOLE

Keith follows her down and latches the cover from the inside.

                    KEITH
          We're safe down here. It's an
          abandoned system. We'll take
          this to the main pipe and from
          there to the city.

                    AMARETTO
          Great...

EXT. 4TH PLACE

Snow and the rest of the gang have reached the manhole cover and are trying to lift it.

It doesn't budge.

As Snow stands up the CAMERA reveals that the gang is surrounded by Vampires. The gang readies for a fight.

                    SNOW
               (staring)
          What gang is this?

The Vampires attack.

INT. ABANDONED SEWER TUNNEL

Keith and Amaretto make their way along the tunnel wall. Amaretto holding on to Keith's arm.

TUNNEL - FARTHER ALONG

Keith and Amaretto walk quietly. Their FOOTSTEPS ECHO down the tunnel. Then Amaretto stops to take off her heels.

Suddenly the FAINT ECHO OF OTHER FOOTSTEPS are heard. Keith and Amaretto freeze.

                    AMARETTO
          I thought you said it was
          safe?

                    KEITH
              (trying to think)
          It's probably an old wino or
          something.

                    AMARETTO
          In high heels?

Quickly the two of them start back down the tunnel.

TUNNEL

The FOOTSTEPS are LOUDER now. Keith and Amaretto continue back. Then suddenly, it ends.

Keith and Amaretto slide against the wall. FOOTSTEPS ALMOST UPON them.

KEITH'S HAND: It runs along the wall. Then touches something. A handle. They're leaning against a doorway!

KEITH AND AMARETTO: Keith turns the handle. The DOOR CREAKS open. Keith signals Amaretto to follow.

INT. TUNNEL CHAMBER

Keith pulls Amaretto into a dark chamber and shuts the door. Pitch black. We can barely make out their figures. As they walk, a CRUNCHING NOISE is heard.

CLOSE ON AMARETTO AND KEITH: They don't move an inch. Frozen with fear.

ANOTHER CREAKING SOUND is heard but it is not from the doorway. It's something else.

Keith and Amaretto stay silent. No sound. Nothing at all. They reach into Amaretto's purse, Keith pulls out a book of matches.

Keith lights the match. Amaretto shrieks!

KEITH/AMARETTO'S POV: The match illuminates the chamber. Scattered about the floor are <u>rows of coffins</u>. And they are surrounded by layers of human skeletons.

The Vampire's lair.

WIDE - THE CHAMBER: Another <u>figure</u> stands at the doorway. It is Dominique - barely recognizable without makeup.

Keith and Amaretto stumble further back into the room. Suddenly from behind - one of the coffins start to open. A waitress starts to rise.

Keith is startled and drops the match. Momentary darkness.

                    KEITH
Get back against the wall!!

Then: without warning the chamber becomes illuminated again.

ANOTHER ANGLE - THE CHAMBER: The match has landed on the dried-out shirt of one of the skeletons and has caught fire.

Dominique screeches. The fire. Other coffins start
to open. The Vampires are rising. Others enter
shrieking.

Keith quickly grabs the rag on fire and tosses it at
another coffin. It begins to burn.

>   KEITH
>   Allison!! The matches! Throw
>   them!

Amaretto looks at Keith.

>   AMARETTO
>   You called me Allison...

>   KEITH
>   (incredulous)
>   The matches!

Amaretto snaps out of it. She begins tossing matches
toward the oncoming Vampires.

THE VAMPIRES: The fire spreads quickly over the
rotten bones and tattered clothes. The Vampires
begin to panic.

Smoke fills the room. There is bedlam. The Vampires
have forgotten about Keith and Amaretto, solely
bent now on protecting their coffins.

ANOTHER ANGLE: Too late. The Vampires throw
themselves atop the blazing coffins and begin to
burn themselves.

HIDEOUS SCREAMS fill the chamber.

The Vampires melt and shrivel. Their bones falling
to the floor to mingle with their victims. One by
one they meet their death.

KEITH AND AMARETTO: They are on opposite sides of
the chamber. Keith can barely see her through the
smoke.

                    KEITH
               (screaming)
          Get to the door! To the
          tunnel!

AMARETTO: She can make out Keith's form through the smoke.

KEITH: He stumbles through the carnage, finally making it to the door. He waits for Amaretto. And waits...

THE TUNNEL

Keith stumbles out into the tunnel. The smoke from the chamber swirls about. No Amaretto.

Suddenly: A BLOODCURDLING SCREAM.

                    AMARETTO (O.S)
          Keeeeiiiittthh!!!!!!!!

Chills run down Keith's spine. The CRY ECHOES off the tunnel walls, bouncing about.

Keith spins about; no idea which way to go. He turns and re-enters the chamber.

THE CHAMBER

The Vampires have perished. Themselves and their coffins only ashes.

Keith spots a small orange light coming from a crack in the wall.

A hidden doorway.

Keith readies his bow, pushes open the stone door, and steps inside.

INT. ANTECHAMBER

Keith sees her right away. Katrina. And in front of her she holds a struggling Amaretto. Her hands behind her back, head pulled to one side exposing her neck. Katrina's fangs are bared...

KEITH: He pulls the bow taut. The final arrow readied. He sights his target. But there is no target to shoot at.

Amaretto blocks Katrina's heart.

KATRINA: Her eyes bore into Keith. A deadly smile on her lips.

She lowers her fangs to within a fraction of an inch from Amaretto's jugular.

ANOTHER ANGLE: Keith tenses. He struggles to keep the bow taut. Fear in Amaretto's eyes.

Keith starts to lower the bow.

>   AMARETTO
> No! Shoot her! Shoot through
> me!

Tears well up in Amaretto's eyes. They both look at each other.

KEITH: Struggling to hold back the bow. The gut cutting into his fingers. Blood seeps onto the bowstring...

AMARETTO: She looks at Keith. Tears now streaming down her face.

>   AMARETTO
>   (gently sobbing)
>   Don't let her touch me.
>   Please...

KEITH: Sweat dripping down his face, falling into his eyes. With one last push of strength Keith pulls taut the bow. The arrow aimed at Amaretto's heart. Droplets of blood running down the bowstring; welling up at the bottom.

ANGLE - THE BOWSTRING: The blood continues to ooze from Keith's fingers. Drop by drop. Then: A drop falls from the bow, splattering onto Keith's white sneaker.

KATRINA: She smells the blood. Her eyes fall to the sneaker. Like a cat Katrina hisses - her mouth wide.

KEITH: In one swift motion he aims and fires the arrow.

ANOTHER ANGLE: The arrow whooshes through the air; past Amaretto -and hitting Katrina through the mouth. The force of the arrow throwing her back and pinning her to the wall.

Amaretto pulls free, falling to the floor.

KATRINA: Struggling to get free. Pulling at the arrow in her throat.

ANOTHER SHOT: Amaretto reaches down and takes hold of a broken skeleton arm. Standing, she plunges it into Katrina's heart.

Katrina jerks violently. Her hands go limp, letting go of the arrow. The hand of one of her victims protruding from her chest. But Katrina continues forward! Keith reaches down, picks up a fragment of burning cloth and tosses on to her.

Katrina bursts into flames, her body aging, shriveling to nothing but dust. Amaretto and Keith run to each other and embrace. Amaretto holding tight.

                  AMARETTO
              (pulling back)
       You stupid bastard! You could
       have killed me...!

Keith gives her that "You're nuts" look again.

ANTECHAMBER

Keith and Amaretto start out of the room

> AMARETTO
> The bitch owed me money.

> KEITH
> You wanna check her pockets?

> AMARETTO
> You're sick.

CHAMBER

Keith and Amaretto move through the rubble. Ashes from coffins, Vampires and skeletal remains.

> KEITH
> (on way out the door)
> See what happens when you don't clean up after you eat?

> AMARETTO (O.S.)
> (disappearing around door)
> Sick...

INT. TUNNEL

Keith and Amaretto walk arm in arm through the sewer. Both too tired to talk. Finally Amaretto looks down at the bow Keith is carrying and spots the blood on Keith's hand.

> AMARETTO
> (picking up his hand)
> You're bleeding... are you all right?

                    KEITH
              It's nothing... the gut just
              --

Keith's face turns ashen as Amaretto brings his hand to her mouth and begins sucking at the wound.

                    AMARETTO
                 (motherly)
              It could get infected. We'll
              have to have this checked.

She puts the hand down. Keith relaxes. He kisses her.

                    AMARETTO
              What was that for?

                    KEITH
              I just felt like it...

ANOTHER SHOT: Keith comes upon a manhole outlet. He climbs the ladder and props open the cover. Daylight streams in. Keith shields his eyes.

Keith turns to call for Amaretto but hesitates. He looks up at the sky and then back into the sewer. He steps back down the ladder partway, closing the cover.

                    KEITH
                 (calling down)
              Hon. Come here for a second. I
              want to show you something.

MANHOLE LADDER

Amaretto scurries up the rungs next to Keith.

                    AMARETTO
         What?

                    KEITH
         Look...

Keith throws open the manhole cover. Sunlight streams down into Amaretto's face. She pulls back, her eyes hurt by the light. Keith watches her closely.

Amaretto's eyes quickly adjust to the harsh light. She glares at an embarrassed Keith.

                    AMARETTO
          What was that for? Was that
          supposed to be funny?

                    KEITH
          No... I...

Keith quickly scrambles out of the manhole.

EXT. STREET - MORNING

Keith bends to help Amaretto. She is half-way out. SUDDENLY: Amaretto is jerked down with a sudden force. Keith loses his grip and she disappears back into the dark sewer.

                    AMARETTO (O.S.)
          Keith!!!

Keith scrambles down after her.

INT. TUNNEL

Keith's eyes adjust to the light. In front of him stands the hulking presence of Vlad. His giant fingers are wrapped around Amaretto's throat.

                    VLAD
          You killed my Katrina. You...
          she. must die too...

Vlad begins to squeeze. Amaretto's face turns blue. Keith starts for him. Then: OUT OF NOWHERE -a jagged wooden stake explodes from Vlad's chest piercing his heart. Amaretto struggles to Keith. Now Vlad falls and reveals a very live A.J. standing there. A.J. looks from Vlad's carcass to Keith and Amaretto. They stand speechless.

> A.J.
> Don't thank me or anything.

Keith steps forward to get a better look at his friend.

> KEITH
> (pointing to his heart)
> But.

A.J. pulls the broken chair leg he used to impale himself with from his back pocket.

> A.J.
> Formica. Hey, a guy's gotta cover all the bases... hi Allison.

Amaretto waves back. They all exchange looks. Keith backs up, unsure, and helps Amaretto up the ladder. Then he begins to climb.

> A.J.
> (calling out)
> Relax, will ya? We'll work something out...

EXT. STREET

Keith climbs out and drops the manhole cover back into place. In the distance the SOUND of Fire Engines and Police Sirens.

> A.J. (O.S.)
> After all these years... you don't trust me?

Keith glances into the sewer grating, then takes Amaretto's hand and they begin to walk down a street into the sunrise. TITLES BEGIN TO ROLL.

As Keith and Amaretto get to a street corner, we HEAR from the corner grating:

>   A.J. (O.S.)
>   Hey, there's always night
>   school...

And as they walk off, every time they pass a sewer grating, TITLES STOP as we hear A.J. pleading to his best friend.

>   A.J. (O.S.)
>   I can work the graveyard
>   shift...

Etc. Etc. MUSIC UP and it's...

THE END.